Jar of Pennies

BY JOHN YEARWOOD

Other Books by John Yearwood

In the Icarus series:
    The Icarus Jump
    The City and the Gate
    The Gender of Fire

Forthcoming novels:
    The Lie Detector App
    Detritus of the Sun
    The Golden Pine

This is a work of fiction. Names, characters, places, and incidents are the product of the author's imagination or are used fictitiously, and any resemblance to actual persons, living or dead, businesses, companies, events, or locales is entirely coincidental.

Printed by Kindle Direct Publishing, Seattle, WA
Available from Amazon.com and other online stores.
Available on Kindle and other devices

Library of Congress Control Number: 2019917036
CreateSpace Independent Publishing Platform, North Charleston, SC
Copyright © 2022 The John and Stephenie Yearwood Management Trust
All rights reserved.
ISBN-13: 979-8-9852957-0-2
Design by Bill Carson Design

Darryl and Mary Stewart lived on Hill Street, the only busy street in Whitmire, Texas, because it was the highway leading out of town. One morning Darryl stormed out of the house carrying his tool belt when Mary came out behind him wearing only a nightgown. "Darryl, Darryl," she called, lifting the gown over her head to show her bare body, "You can have it all if you'll just apologize."

Darryl dropped his tool belt on the hood of his pickup and went back inside. The belt was still there at 4 p.m. It's Whitmire. Nobody wants somebody else's tools.

CHAPTER ONE

Beaufort Sebastian Maclean shivered in his thin coat as a cascade of ice needles shattered down on his bare head from overhead pines. It was almost Christmas, 1979.

Nobody called him Beaufort Sebastian Maclean. Even his mother had called him "Beau."

His friends, his very few friends, none of whom were female, called him "BoMac." Everyone else in this little lumbering village in East Texas called him "that BS who edits the *Standard*." At 24, he got plenty of grief from those who thought themselves older and wiser, some of it far less innocent. The town's only newspaper reporter, he was both popular and unpopular. He was popular with those who wanted their names in the weekly paper he produced. He was alternately unpopular when his stories were unflattering. Some weeks he could be best-friend popular with some and then despicable-enemy unpopular with the same people. One county commissioner, George Brown, was candid with him, and BoMac appreciated him for it. "I hug everybody," Commissioner Brown had said, "because I'm hugging a vote." Then he hugged BoMac. Even after the *Standard* ran a carefully researched article showing how the commissioner had skimmed money out of the 1978 budget for the county's new jail, a "consulting fee" the audit called it, the commissioner hugged him the next time they met.

"You're a son of a bitch," he'd whispered to BoMac as he hugged him, the wintergreen smell of tobacco snuff heavy on his breath. "But everybody who hates you loves me now. Ain't no such thing as bad publicity for a politician."

"I wish the sheriff felt that way," BoMac replied.

"Some people are good people, but they've got small minds," the commissioner said, slapping him affectionately on the shoulder and grinning at him with tobacco-stained teeth as the crowd gathered for the monthly commissioners' meeting.

"I'd like to see more good," BoMac replied, but it was too late. The meeting was about to start, and Brown had already turned away.

BoMac dug his hands into his jacket pockets, remembering. That commissioners' court meeting happened right over there on the first floor of the courthouse now sitting dark and silent in the late December night. The three-story Victorian brick edifice with its tall arched windows and strangely gothic corners could have been the setting for a horror movie, he thought, more terrifying than anything Hollywood could dream. The banality of the first floor, with its clerks and minor officials, contrasted starkly with the district courtroom on the second floor, a scene where men and their marriages met death and fate.

The first man executed in the newfangled electric chair at the state prison in Huntsville, Charles Reynolds, had received his death sentence for rape in that district courtroom. BoMac learned that Reynolds wailed incessantly that he didn't do it. It was 1923. They could not shut him up. They tried opium, barbiturates, getting him drunk. That didn't shut him up. Even in an opium daze he muttered and cried, "I ain't done it! I ain't done it!" While waiting for the carpenter to finish constructing the chair out of the wood formerly used for the gallows, his jailers, no doubt prodded by the incessant wailing, took to testing their homemade corn whiskey on him. The day of the execution, they gave him an extra pint to hush him up, and then guided him reeling to the chair.

Some of the folks in this little town of Whitmire, Texas, had complained about the expense of electrocution.

"If hanging was good enough for my daddy," one man complained, "it's good enough for that sumbitch." BoMac assumed everyone agreed with the old coot, and he didn't doubt that part of the story. All it took to hang someone was a rope and a stool. None of that newfangled technology.

BoMac had less faith in the rest of the story, though many took it for gospel truth. He was told Reynolds roused when his head was belted back against the chair with the electrode. His eyes popped wide, they said, and he began his wail again, "I ain't done it! I ain't done it!" All the guards looked at one another with that look of failure and shook their heads. The executioner put his hand on the knife switch, staring at the clock. When the minute hand ticked to midnight on February 8, he pulled the switch, and lights all over Huntsville dimmed. The lights went out completely in the execution chamber, but not before the guards saw Reynolds's eyes bulging wide, his mouth dropping open as though screaming. Then the room went dark, and a long tongue of blue flame erupted from Reynolds's mouth, lighting up his wild face. The moonshine had caught fire, and the executioner, startled, jerked the knife switch to off.

While jailers retched and vomited in the room from the smell of burning flesh and the terror of the blue flame, Reynolds began moaning. "I ain't done," he moaned, jerking around on the chair.

"He ain't dead!" yelled the jailers. "Hit him again, Joe," they yelled at the executioner as the lights flickered back on in the room.

The executioner pulled the knife switch again and this time he left it on. When they finally turned it off and the lights came back on, they found that the electrodes had burned away Reynolds's flesh all the way to the bone.

They electrocuted four more men that night, all, like Reynolds, Black. One of them was named George Washington. BoMac had looked it up.

That part really happened.

Beats crucifixion, though, BoMac thought, glancing in the direction of the white cross on the top of the First Fundamentalist Church, gleaming like a white icon of execution and redemption in the dark mist half a block from the haunted courthouse.

In his three years listening to the people of Whitmire, he heard many stories, most of them partly if not completely fiction. But the murder trial that concluded today was not fiction. BoMac had a minor role to play in the case brought Jesse Grinder into that courtroom, adding him to the end of a long, grim parade of condemned heading to obscurity and extinction. The trial had been horrifying in its details, but all you could do was shake your head at the stupidity of it all. Grinder had no reason to kill that young mother and her three-year-old daughter. And now the haunted house of justice sat dark and silent in the winter night, all the judges and clerks and bailiffs and jurors gone and Jesse already incarcerated for what little remained of his life. The lights were off in the building. Only he himself was moving on the square. No other sound but his careful shuffle on the icy sidewalk and the sighing wind in the frozen pines overhead could be heard.

Another puff of air coming down from the north dislodged more ice from the dark pines, showering it down on him.

The way the ice scattered over the sidewalk brought to mind his western civ class at the University of Virginia, stirring thoughts of Kristallnacht, the night of broken glass. That was the night when Hitler's Nazi thugs prowled the dark streets of Germany breaking Jewish storefronts and burning books in what became a reign of terror, murder, and war, scattering broken glass over the streets.

He smirked at himself for the thought. That had happened long before he was born. History repeats, his professor had said. Well, no it doesn't, he had come to realize in his three years on the *Standard*. It's not history that repeats, but people. People are always the same. Just their methods change. We move from crucifixion to electric chairs to death needles. Same stuff, different methods.

At least this was ice and not glass, he thought, digging his hands deeper into his coat pockets, watching his labored breath fuming ahead of him. Such dark thoughts.

Hill Street, creatively named "hill" because it went up a steep hill from the creek where the train once ran, was becoming treacherous in the icy night. He reminded himself to keep the police scanner on so he could go out with his camera to cover the wrecks that would surely happen on such a night. His old pickup, the only inheritance he received from his father's bankrupt Virginia alfalfa farm, could probably get him just about anywhere. He'd need to take it easy, but the dirt roads would be safer. They would not get as slick as the paved ones. This was a temporary freeze, after all. Though ice had caught in the trees, the ground would not freeze, remaining muddy and potholed under its thin white skin.

Several times a week he went to fatal accidents somewhere in the county. He had seen a baby's brains wiped across the pavement, decapitated bodies, wrecks so bad it took days to know how many people had been in the car. He spent one Saturday morning helping the county coroner—actually, the local undertaker with a side job as the coroner—hunting through roadside weeds for an eyeball missing from a wreck victim the night before. It was against state law to leave human remains on the side of the road, and they searched for an hour before giving up.

"Probably some animal," John Quick, the mortician, had said. "Unless that eyeball was sucked into his carburetor when he went through the engine compartment."

"Yeah," BoMac said. "Maybe an animal. I bet that engine wasn't running by the time he went through the windshield. He smacked into that tree going pretty fast."

"Heh heh," Quick chuckled. "Maybe not. But he left the top half of his skull in there. I got that already. Scooped his brain out like an acorn squash. Just missing one of the eyes."

"He was on his way to get married, wasn't he?" BoMac asked.

"That's what I heard. Works hard all day, gets his best boots on, and heads out to drive ninety-some miles to get married. Guess he went to sleep. I ain't smelled no alcohol on him."

"Yeah," BoMac said. "Yeah. Lousy breaks."

"We ain't gonna find that boy's eyeball," Quick finally said, pushing aside more weeds. He was sweating through his black suit. "I'm gonna say it was taken by an animal."

"Okay," BoMac had said. "Okay."

And now it was dark December. So many more senseless deaths since that poor bridegroom.

He took another long look at the dark courthouse, looming in the freezing mist. Somewhere in the back, down below where the furnace was, one remaining human was in the Gothic pile. Davey Jones was sleeping in his old wooden chair, pretending to keep the furnace going. Once it had been a coal-fired furnace, and the county created a position for coal stoker. Davey had been the official coal stoker for fifty years. Even though the county had switched to electric heat decades ago, the commissioners never got around to abolishing the job of coal stoker. Besides, Davey was a harmless old Black man who needed the job. So, there he was, faithfully watching the electric furnace in the dark December midnight and collecting his pitiful salary.

And, BoMac knew, somewhere not far from Davey's nodding head, back in the dark recesses under the courthouse, beyond the damp cellars and out under the floors where the pipes ran, was Old Coil, a slumbering rattlesnake, fattened on mice and rats, and just waiting for the breeding imperative of spring. Everybody knew Old Coil was there. He'd been spotted once or twice over the years, unless there was more than one snake. The most reliable reports said he was six or seven feet long, but others put his size at fourteen feet and one at sixteen. He was said to carry a hundred rattles on his tail, which would make him about a hundred years old. Same age, give or take a decade or two, as the courthouse. If you didn't believe in ghosts, you could certainly believe in a courthouse haunted by a deadly snake.

"Sleep tight, Davey," BoMac thought. "Try not to smell like a rat tonight."

"Betty Lou, tell Henry I'm ready," said Mrs. Jane Elkins to her maid, shrugging into her mink coat. When she saw the powder-blue 1963 Cadillac pull into the portico, she went and stood by the kitchen door, waiting for Henry to open it for her. A lady never opened her own door. Moments later she was driven at no more than 10 mph down to her row of clapboard shacks on Railroad Avenue to collect weekly rents, drumming her gloved fingers on her black purse. This week she would evict John Coleman. He was just too uppity as a tenant.

CHAPTER

TWO

His garage apartment was uninsulated and cold, the electric space heater buzzing its dangerous glow over piles of paper stacked on every surface. He settled into his chair thinking over the trial, from time to time glancing at his reflection in the frosty window, tracking the dropping temperature by the splinters of frost creeping from the sash. It had all been so stupid! So unnecessary! Over the weekend, he would write up the report for next week's paper, not that anyone didn't know the outcome. No, they didn't read the paper to learn new information. They read it to confirm what they already knew. Or, as one old woman had chuckled at him, who had got caught at it. But tonight, he would begin on his first book, a book about the murders, his mind unwinding and stretching through night shadows of cold and fear. The trial had reawakened the terror of the preceding summer, and he knew this was it. This was the start, the first step of his next career, and it would be about unnecessary tragedy.

He nodded to himself as he rolled a fresh sheet of paper into his antique Underwood typewriter, his mind poring over the short, brutish life of Jesse Grinder. In the chill outside, if you had passed by the rickety garage apartment, you would have heard the irregular tapping of his keys tattooing, on and on. Here, oh passerby, is the story you heard forming in the dark primeval forest where life balances so precariously, and people struggle to survive.

11

At the end of the fall semester of his sophomore year, Jesse Grinder dropped out of high school. He was sixteen. He didn't see any use in it, since he wasn't learning anything and didn't want to. To celebrate, he drove his pickup down to the county line, where there was a liquor store, and bought a bottle of wine. It was his first time to drink, and he'd heard from friends that wine was the liquor of choice.

He didn't care much for it, but by the time he got back to Whitmire, he was pretty well plastered.

Jesse was a big boy. He was 6'2" or 6'3" and easily 245 pounds. He might have been more than that. His mother made him breakfast the next morning, which consisted of two pork chops, half a dozen eggs, a pan of cornbread, some buttermilk to dip the cornbread in, and a quart of coffee. He ate it all. Then he went out in the backyard and threw up. He had a bell ringer of a hangover.

Then his father came out and beat hell out of him with a belt and told him he was going to work in the woods, hangover or not. So Jesse meekly followed his father out to the pickup and went to the woods. From dawn to sunset, he cut timber into eight-foot lengths and stacked it sideways on a log truck, lifting the logs by hand. Some of the logs weighed more than four hundred pounds, but he worked at it and learned how to handle the weight with the least effort. By noon, he'd sweated out the hangover and drunk three gallons of water. It was not easy work, but it was cool weather. He worked like that the rest of the afternoon, his father on one side of the truck and him on the other, throwing pulp wood logs up onto the racks of the log truck. When the truck was full, the driver who had been sleeping in a blanket in the cab woke up and drove off, and another truck pulled in to take his place.

That kind of work went on day after day, five days a week. They didn't work seven days because the mills were closed on Sunday, and they went to church on Saturday. Otherwise, they would have. They needed the money. But they spent the one day off a week trying to grow vegetables in their garden and maybe doing a little hunting to put protein on the table. They were never much good at fishing, which required patience and a boat. And church took up all of Saturday.

Most White men found other, easier work, but the Grinders were not the kind who would do that. They were born poor, scrimped and saved, went to the Jehovah's Witness church, and washed their few clothes in a nearby creek. The Witnesses were a good church for them, because the harder you worked, the more likely you would be one of the 144,000 chosen by God to go to heaven, according to the Book of Revelation. Also, it didn't have any Black members in the congregation. They were close-knit, even cultish in their fervor, and the Grinders found acceptance and validation for their earnest hard work with the Witnesses.

Jesse had a younger brother, Joey, who was even bigger than he was, and by the time Joey was fifteen and Jesse was nineteen, Joey could whip his ass. Jesse's father could whip his ass, too, though he didn't. Hell, even Jesse's mother could whip his ass, because she was a large, blunt, and powerful woman. The four Grinders would have tipped the truck scales down at the feed depot at almost twelve hundred pounds. They were large people, and Jesse was the runt. He was the tallest, but he didn't have the physical strength or sheer mass of his father and brother.

A life of really hard work could make a man out of some people. It sure seemed to make men out of Jesse's father and brother. But Jesse had a little spending money now. He had an old beat-up pickup truck he could drive around in, and he got to burning up the highway to the county line on Friday nights. After his first experience with wine, he discovered that cheap vodka could mix into a Coca-Cola just fine, or a Big Red, which he preferred. Then he'd go looking around for a woman. Women were not that hard to find, if you didn't set your sights too high, and he soon learned that he could have a good time with any of several older fat girls at the bars if he would just buy them something to drink.

By the time he was twenty-two, he had moved out and found other work. He worked in a warehouse, sweeping floors, and he got another job over at the patio furniture manufacturer stamping aluminum sheets. But that was seasonal work. They always shut down in the summer, because they'd moved all their stock out and wouldn't need to start making any more until the following fall. So in the summer, he collected shopping carts in the parking lot at Walmart, and mopped floors at the Dairy Queen, and carried out the garbage at the Pizza Hut. He also would get fired from those jobs from time to time and go back to throwing pulpwood up onto log trucks. And he made a few friends, but really he figured he would just rather spend his time and money on those girls down at the county line, who were easy and less demanding.

He drifted away from his family, who missed his income but not his appetite, and that was that. He also stopped going to church. Obeying a higher power was not a big item on his agenda of things to do. He had a higher power. And her names were Sue, Peggy, and Margie at beer joints along the county line.

He finally decided to get away from Whitmire altogether and drove off one day heading east until he came to a little city named Piney Creek and saw the Camelot Mobile Home Park with a "for rent" sign tilted out on the highway. That sign had been there a long time, he figured, the way it was almost fallen over, so he drove into the park to look around. These were his kind of people. They hung their wash out on lines beside their trailers, their dirty little kids scampered around outside barefoot, the only men were cadaverous looking smokers arced over like flood-bent reeds and hacking at their cigarettes, and they were all White. But the manager said he didn't want someone like Jesse living there, money or no money. Jesse had to have a job, and he had to be gone all day. Those were the rules. Job, and gone. Jesse just stood there, kind of looking at his toes, trying to think of something that might change the man's opinion, and then the door to the man's trailer opened and a bosomy, youngish woman came in.

"I'm here to pay on the rent," she said to the manager.

"Son, what's your name?" the manager asked Jesse.

"Jesse Grinder."

"Well, Jesse, just wait outside for me for a few minutes."

"Okay," Jesse said.

As he left, he heard the manager say to the woman, "Honey, just lock that door and come over here. Take off your top."

Jesse stood around outside in the shade of a corrugated metal carport attached to the manager's trailer. He just looked around. If he'd had an idea, it would have drowned in his brain.

About twenty minutes later, the woman came out of the trailer and caught Jesse's eye. She spat.

"Be glad you ain't born a woman," she said at him, and then went away.

Jesse didn't much like the manager. He was an older man, balding, and his eyelids were sewn up to his eyebrows with catgut, some kind of medical thing to keep the lids from drooping. Jesse wasn't disgusted. Just confused.

He stood around outside waiting for another thirty minutes. Eventually the man showed and acted surprised.

"You still here?" he asked Jesse.

"Guess so," Jesse said.

"You must be hard up."

"Nope. I just like it around here. What's that girl's name?"

"Oh her?" the manager replied. "Her name is Annabeth. She's married to a guy who works offshore named Shorty. They have a baby daughter."

"Uh huh," Jesse said. He just stood there waiting.

"Well, okay," the manager said, "if you've got $200, I can show you a place I've got not far from here and you can have that. The rent is $105 a month and you pay utilities. We are on a water well out here, so there's no charge for the water. Your rent keeps the pump going. The way things are these days, I've got to keep a place open for Blacks if they want to rent out here or I get in trouble with the gummint. So this is the place I keep. It's not much, but it's private and it's away from these other folks.

You don't mind that, I'm sure," he said, sizing up Jesse, taking in the cheap Walmart clothes and the boots just about worn completely out.

"Well, okay," Jesse said.

They drove out in the manager's pickup and looked at it. It was a single-wide trailer with two bedrooms, one end jacked up five feet off the ground because of the slope.

"We ain't got sewer out here," the manager said. "The toilet just empties out underneath the house. That shouldn't be much of a problem, less you have dogs or kids."

"Don't it stink?" Jesse asked.

"That's what the air conditioning is for," the manager replied, pointing to the two window units hanging at steep angles out of the sides of the trailer. "Besides, it all runs downhill, and if you go down there, you'll find the nicest batch of tomatoes growing wild you ever seen."

"Guess I'll take it," Jesse said, pulling out the last of his money. He'd drive to the next town and get some kind of job. It would mean skipping Margie and Peggy for a few weeks, but hell, those girls were not going anywhere. Sue, though. He really didn't want to skip Sue. Jesse didn't know much more than what his father and the Witnesses had beat into him, and that was that money was work and work was salvation. He didn't mind work if that was the only way to get money. And that big girl Sue, with her big boobs. Why, maybe she'd move in with him. If he had the money. And the booze.

And there was Annabeth.

Photos this week: burning bus, upside-down Crown Vic in the creek (no body visible), candlelight service at First Fundamentalist Church. That would be a nice photo, with six hundred people holding up candles and filing out singing "Silent Night," that big Christmas tree in the front all lit up. What were those symbols they hung on the tree? Chrismons? Was that right? Check spelling for cutline. Girl Scouts in front of Walmart, with Salvation Army Santa. One of the Christmas tour mansions garlanded and festooned. Maybe with Ms. Needle posed in front. The other house fire? Did he have that?

CHAPTER

THREE

Grinder got a job over in Piney Creek making a little money, and one night he drove down to see Sue. She was at the bar, like always, and they sat together in a booth giggling. She liked being touched, and when he put his hand on her thigh, she rested her hand on his. When he moved up a little further, she slid her hand over to the inside of his thigh.

Then they were in the front seat of his pickup, which was okay for a blow job but not much good for really getting at her, when he asked if she could go with him somewhere.

"Come back to my place," she sighed. "Richard is there, but he won't mind."

"Who's Richard?" Jesse thought to ask.

"He's the guy I married. Used to work on radio towers. Went up to service a tower one day and the guys on the ground thought it'd be funny if they turned it on while he was up there. Zapped him pretty good. He can't get it up no more and gave up trying. He won't mind."

"You sure?"

"Yeah. It ain't like I never done it before."

"I'm pretty tired."

"You don't feel tired," she said, stroking him. "Gimme some money and I'll go back inside and get us some beer, then we can go over."

"Okay," he said, digging his wallet out of his unzipped pants. He gave her a twenty-dollar bill.

"Be right back," she said happily, like a girl.

They drove over to her house, about a mile from the bar. It was dark, a small bungalow with a concrete stoop. A plastic garbage can full of empty cans sat next to the door. The door wasn't locked, and she walked in, leading him by the hand.

"Just a minute," she said, flipping a light switch and heading through a dark interior door.

"Richard? Hey Richard, wake up. I need the bed," he heard her say. "Come on, wake up. Go sleep on the sofa."

He heard a male voice, indistinct.

"Come on. I'll help you sit up."

A minute later a man in a tee shirt and boxer shorts leaned against the doorframe, his skeletal frame shaking. He stared at Jesse for a minute with bloodshot eyes, then staggered over to the sofa. He was asleep again by the time he hit the cushions.

"I'll just turn on the TV," Sue said. "He'll sleep right through everything like you was never here," and she took Jesse by the hand to lead him into the bedroom, holding the six-pack in her other hand.

Much later, on his way back to the Piney Creek mobile home park, Jesse rolled his truck in a ditch and was in a coma for three days. When he woke up in the hospital, he saw his mother sitting there, watching him. "You gonna kill me, boy," she said when she saw his eyes open. "You gonna kill me with all this. You remember what happened?"

He couldn't shake his head for the neck brace.

"Naw," he mumbled. "Where am I?"

"You're in the hospital in Lufkin," she said. "Cops found you in a ditch and they brought you here. You been asleep for three days and your leg's broke. They's worried about your head. I've been sitting here the whole time."

"What about Pop?" he asked.

She looked at him like he was crazy. "What do you think? He's working extra to help you get through this. Him and Joey both. Joey's going to the woods during daylight and working at a call center all night."

"Yeah. Okay then." He closed his eyes.

News budget for the week between Christmas and New Year's: Girl Scout cookie sale proceeds, Lions Club chili dinner at the firehouse, fatal wreck when Essie Wainwright, eighty-two, slid her car backward off an icy bridge into Toby Creek, three home burglaries mostly of Christmas presents (already wrapped) but including one television, six DWIs (ignore peccadillos at Christmas?), proceeds from the Ladies Book Club home tour benefiting their $500 scholarship fund, three obits including Ms. Wainwright, two house fires including one of a school bus occupied by a seventeen-year-old pregnant girl and her year-old tot. No school or county news.

Ellen Etheridge took a final look around her cozy little house, checked the thermostat, added an extra cup of water to each of her thirty houseplants, and urged the grumpy cat into its cardboard carrier. "It will only be a little while," she chirped, "then we'll be at Momma's." She lifted the satchel of term papers in one hand, the cat carrier in the other, and went out to get in her Honda Civic for the drive to Sugar Land and Christmas. The wrapped Christmas presents were already in the trunk, along with her gym clothes. "At last," she breathed.

CHAPTER

FOUR

Jesse Grinder was out of the hospital in a month and back at work with his neck still in a brace, sending his mother half his pay to cover the $69,000 hospital bill his family had paid. It would take him eight years and leave him about $400 a month to pay rent and buy groceries. He qualified for food stamps but was too proud to apply and Witnesses didn't take charity. Besides, he was taught to work, not beg. His job was sweeping up at a welding shop, and then doing the same at a service station next door. Both places closed by 8 p.m., and he walked down the highway to hitch a ride back to his trailer. Sometimes a trucker would pick him up. Sometimes he walked the whole seven miles in the dark. He didn't mind. Wasn't much to do back at the trailer anyway, because he didn't have television, so he'd just open a can of beans and eat them cold, then go to bed. He'd throw the empty can in the unused bedroom. He figured by the time that room got too full of empty cans to get any more in there, he'd have found himself another place to live and be making more money. It's not like, he thought to himself, the place was the Taj Ma-fucking Hall.

But something was certainly wrong with his brain. He knew that. He'd stopped laughing after the wreck. Everything was dark even during the day. He saw things in the shadows as he walked home, but he didn't care. They might be about to eat him, he thought, and he didn't care. Let them come on. He'd ball up his fists hoping for the chance to hit something. He wasn't scared of anything. He didn't like anything. He didn't want anything.

One day as he was walking into town on his way to work, it started to rain. He was early. They didn't expect him to be there until 9, so he was in no hurry. But he didn't like the cold rain and was looking for a place to get out of it. He was walking along a sorry Piney Creek street in what passed for a business district when one of his spells hit him and he just stood there, the rain dripping off his nose and ears, his mouth half open. That happened a lot. He wasn't aware of it, because Jesse Grinder was gone. Just his body was standing there. He never knew how long he had spells like that, but this one in the rain was arousing some concern from the few folks driving down the gray street.

He was standing on the sidewalk in front of Hall's Locksmith Shop and was still standing there when the shop owner came to work. What would have been Jesse, if Jesse had been there, was just about blocking the door, so the locksmith, under an umbrella, asked him to step away so he could open the door. When Jesse didn't respond, the locksmith, a man everybody called Will, gently put a hand on him and urged him sideways a little. He got the key in the door, realized that Jesse was not only not all there but not there at all, and tugged on the young man's sleeve to get him off the sidewalk and inside out of the rain.

Jesse seemed to wake up and shuffled in, then went away again, and Will went back to his little coffee pot and started brewing coffee. Pretty soon the aroma of coffee overwhelmed the finer acrid smells of oil and metal filings, and Jesse let out a sigh, kind of moving his head around a little.

"You want a cup of coffee?" Will asked.

Jesse looked at him like a sleepwalker just coming to.

"Coffee?" Will asked again.

"Uh, yeah," Jesse said, wiping a meaty hand over his face. "Yeah. I guess so. My head ain't so right since my wreck."

"Your neck got busted up too, looks like," said Will.

"Yeah. It hurts some. I ought to go back to the doctor to see about this brace, but ain't got the money."

He wandered over to a stool at the shop's counter, staring through the dusty glass at rows of padlocks and types of keys. Will set the coffee on the counter.

"Ain't got milk or sugar," Will said. "I drink it black."

"I like my women black," said Jesse, with a grin. "At least the interesting parts of them."

He and Will chuckled.

"When was your wreck?" Will asked. "Tell me about it."

"Don't remember much. Totaled my pickup. That's why I walk everywhere. Woke up in the hospital. They said I was out for three days."

"Bad luck," Will said. "What kind of work you do?"

They visited for a while and the rain let up. It was about time for Jesse to go on up the street to his job, and they parted.

It was the nicest Jesse had ever been treated by anybody in his whole life. Maybe, he thought, Will would teach him how to work on locks.

Stopping by Will's shop became Jesse's new ritual. He stopped on his way to work, and on his way home. Most times Will was gone by the time Jesse got off work, so he'd just loaf in the doorway catching his breath. Nothing to hurry for anyway. No pickup, no going down to the county line to visit with the girls. That Annabeth out at the mobile home park was still there but wouldn't speak to him. "Be glad you weren't born a woman," are the last words she spoke to him, and she acted like she didn't recognize him on the few occasions when their paths crossed. So Jesse just idled. Once in a while a police cruiser would drift down the street, but he had become invisible again. He didn't see them. They didn't see him. He might have been lounging in the doorway at 9 p.m., but nobody cared.

Sometimes Will came back to the shop after a long workday, and then he and Jesse would sit on the stools in front of the glass counter and drink the last of the coffee. Will liked his warmed up, and had a small microwave for that, but Jesse didn't care. And eventually Will started showing Jesse how locks worked, and what to do about them.

A few months of this camaraderie, and Will helped Jesse open the simple lock of a pair of handcuffs. And a few more months, and Jesse could open a deadbolt lock, if it was simple.

One evening in the spring, Will came in late with tears in his eyes just as Jesse was about to set out for the trailer park.

"Jesse," he sighed, "she's gone. We did the best we could, but she's gone."

"Who?" asked Jesse.

"My wife. We've been married forty years, but the cancer got her. She's been in hospice for about two years."

Jesse didn't know what to say, so he didn't say anything. Instead, he just sat at the stool and stayed quiet.

Eventually Will started telling him the whole story. The one surviving child, a drug addict in Houston. The family dog. The long illness. How much it cost. How unfair it all was. How he could never pay the bills, which is why he thought she'd been murdered instead of died. That the doctors just killed her to cut their losses for the money they were owed. Will was angry and devastated. His chest heaved.

Jesse just sat there. He wondered at Will, but nothing stirred in his own breast. He could care less about the guy's sick wife or his bad kid. Hell, life was no fun anyway. Not his life.

Eventually Will managed to collect himself and stared around at the shop, illuminated by the glaring fluorescent overheads.

"Thanks for listening," Will finally choked out. "C'mon, I'll give you a ride home."

"If you don't mind," Jesse said.

Ads: Happy New Year ads from Ketchum's Tires, Citizens National, Dairy Queen (open all night Dec. 31), Smith Truck Stop, Farmers Insurance, Dewberry Legal Services, NAPA Auto Parts, Tattersall Quick Loan, the EF Hutton place, Sonic, Woolworth's, Susie's Fabrics, True Value, Candace Tea Room and Fashions. Clearance ads from Walmart, Worthy Dept. Store, JCPenney, Bealls. Two-page grocery ads from the grocery stores trying to compete with Walmart: Crooks Bros. and Piggly Wiggly. Why did they bother if they weren't going to keep Walmart's hours? Classified free to subscribers. Most ads were already built. Rejected: "White Christmas" ad from local KKK.

CHAPTER
FIVE

O ne hot spring day while Jesse Grinder was sweeping out the repair shop and the used car dealership, his boss came back to ask him a favor.

"Jesse," he said, "I need to run over to Leesville. Gonna take me about two and a half hours before I get back. I need someone to make a delivery for me."

"I ain't got a car," Jesse said.

"Can you drive? You got a license?"

"Yes, sir. I got a license. Lost my truck when I was run off the road by a logging truck."

"Okay, I'll loan you a car. If you like it, we'll figure out how you can pay for it."

"I'd rather have a truck," Jesse said.

"I've got a beat-up pickup over there. But where I need you to go, that pickup will look way out of place. I'll put you in that Accord out there for the afternoon. Just to make this delivery."

"I guess so," said Jesse.

Bob McKinney, owner of Jeff's Used Autos, wrote down the address and then showed Jesse where the place was located on the big map in his office.

"Think you can find it?" McKinney asked.

"I think so. It's a ways, ain't it."

"Too far to walk. You go up 91 to 362, turn left. Look for a big ranch with fence posts made out of drill stems and drilling bits. Go past that and turn in the next driveway on the right. Big red-brick entrance with tall iron gates. Couple of big live oak trees down near where the road turns off. Pull up slow to the gates and in a little bit they'll open. Go over the cattle guard but go slow so the security cameras can see you, then pull around to the back of the house. It's about half a mile to the house from the gate. She'll come out to the car. Don't get out."

"Who's coming out to the car?" Jesse asked.

"House belongs to that congressman, Rip Johnson. His wife is the one coming out."

"Well, okay," Jesse said.

McKinney handed him a small box wrapped in brown paper and sealed.

"Don't open anything. Don't open the gate, don't open the car door, don't open that package. Just hand it to the lady comes out. She's skinny and blonde. If she gives you something, just bring it back here and don't open it either. I should be back from Leesville about the time you get back from this chore."

"Okay, then."

"Do you need me to send someone with you?"

"No, I got it."

"Run that Accord through the car wash before you go. We want to wash off all that pine pollen. I'll get a temporary for it and have it ready when you get back from the wash."

Jesse did as he was told.

He hadn't told Bob McKinney about his spells, but he thought maybe he could just pull off on the side of the road if he felt one coming on. Thing was, he didn't always feel them coming on. Still, it was a break from sweeping the shop out again. The other workers, three of them, were all busy getting those cars running. "Can't sell a car don't run," Bob McKinney was always yelling at them. "All it's got to do is drive off the lot. It doesn't need to make a round trip to fucking Las Vegas."

Jesse drove up 91 through town, enjoying the air blowing in the window. For a few miles, the houses all huddled up close to the road and had chain link fences or discarded kid toys in the yards. Nobody seemed to be at home. After a time, though, he got to 362 and turned off into a different world. Huge places with the houses sitting back from the road a quarter mile or more. He'd never seen such big houses before. Some off in the distance were three or four stories tall with big columns on all sides. Lots of them had long drives through live oak trees and between pastures. He wondered what kind of rich people lived in them, and he figured he was about to meet one. Maybe she'd have boobs. It'd been a while since he saw a nice set of boobs. If you was rich, didn't your women have boobs? Why else would you get rich? Go to the trouble? For Jesse the world was pretty simple.

About thirty minutes after pulling away from the car lot, Jesse spotted the long row of fence posts made out of drill stems and bits. It went on for a mile along the highway, and then he came to two gates. The one on the left punctuated the row of drill stems and was standing open. The one on the right was red brick and sure enough, two enormous live oak trees huddled up behind it. The black iron gates were closed, but he pulled in. On top of the gate was a security camera. Jesse watched the opening mechanism come to life and slowly the gates began to roll apart. A post just inside the gates had a red light glowing on it. When the gates stopped, the light turned green. Jesse figured that was his signal, so he drove slowly down the majestic driveway.

Man who lives here got a lot of money, Jesse thought.

The house at the end of the long drive was multistory and all dark red brick, except for eight enormous white columns on the long porch. The driveway turned into brick when he neared the house and split into a set of curves to go around the front of the house. He stayed right and saw a small white sign with an arrow that said "deliveries." He followed the drive that way and found himself in a brick courtyard at the back of the house with a six-car garage off to one side.

Waiting for him was a skinny blonde woman of about fifty with large boobs. She was wearing a sunhat and a bikini, and she was tan all over, like all she had to do was lie around in the sun. Through a bricked walkway covered in some kind of vines, Jesse saw a swimming pool and a few more women.

She walked over, peering at him from under the hat.

"You from Bob?" she asked.

"Yes'm," he said. He didn't move.

She bent down to get eye level with him and showed the deep cleavage of her breasts. Jesse gasped.

"Well?" she asked.

"They's beautiful," he said.

She held her hand out under his nose.

"Give me the package, you fool," she hissed, but Jesse was having a heart attack. Those tan boobs were the only thing in the universe, and he was dying.

She raised her voice to penetrate his fog. "Now!" she commanded.

"Uh, uh"—Jesse tried to find words to express his admiration—"uh. What? Oh, yeah. Okay. Here." He handed her the wrapped parcel off the car seat.

She snatched it out of his hand and inspected it, making sure it had not been opened.

"Wait here," she said, and she turned and walked back toward the big house on her high heels. Jesse observed absolutely everything about her hips and her butt crack and the way her back dimpled. She was too skinny for his tastes, but any woman was better than no woman. And this one was almost ready for him. Pull that one bow loose from her hip and he'd be able to screw her in any dark place he wanted to.

Two or three minutes passed, during which Jesse finally remembered to close his mouth to keep from drooling down his shirtfront, and then a small, wasplike Black woman dressed in a black uniform with a starched white collar came out of the house scowling. She thrust a sealed package wrapped up in pink ribbon at him.

"Here," she snapped. "Get out. Wait for the gates to open and give this to your boss when he gets back."

She turned on her heels and jerked back into the house, every movement telegraphing warning.

Jesse got through the gates before the spell hit him. He drifted off to the side of the road and into the open gate of the big house with the drill stem fence posts. Fortunately, his foot was off the accelerator, because he just slowed to a stop off the driveway in an azalea bush. He had no idea how long he was there.

He woke up dreaming about that butt crack and smelling something sweet, and a Black man with a shotgun tapping on the roof of the car. "This ain't your place," the Black man said. "Boss says to tell you to get out of his azalea bush and off his property."

Jesse felt like he could take the man on and whip his ass, if it was just the two of them. A Black man doesn't speak to Jesse Grinder like that. But the shotgun made three of them, and he calmed down.

"Yeah. Okay," he said instead, swallowing his rage. He held the little package wrapped with pink ribbon in his hand, stoking it with his thumb. "Okay. I ain't been right since my wreck. I think I passed out."

"What's in the package?" the Black man asked, lowering the gun to hold it in two hands.

"Don't know. Lady over there give it to me to take to my boss."

"Her old man, he's in the house yonder with my employer. Maybe you need to come see him before you go back."

"No, thanks, I think I'll just go on back."

The car was still running, so he put it in gear to back out, but the Black man lowered the shotgun.

"Nope," he said, "you get out of that car and march up to the house or I blow your head off for trespassing. Either way, my boss and her husband gonna see what you carrying."

Jesse stomped on the accelerator, backing out of the driveway onto the deserted highway just as the shotgun went off, blowing out a side window of the car. He ducked down below the window level where his head wasn't exposed and roared off down the highway, not seeing where he was going, popping up only long enough to make sure he was still on the pavement until he was out of range of the shotgun.

"I'll be a sonofabitch," he said through clenched teeth. "That boy gonna learn a lesson from me."

McKinney was not pleased at all the extra work he was going to need to do on the Accord to get it ready for the lot, and a little anxious that he'd get a phone call from the sheriff. But the sheriff didn't call, and a can of Bondo and some paint fixed up the damage to the body where shot had punctured the skin of the car. It was easy enough to scavenge a different window out of another Accord. There were lots of Accords in the world, and they all had exactly the same rear windows.

For the millionth time he asked Jesse, "What were you doing in that judge's yard?" The drill stem fence line belonged to a US District Judge in Tyler named George Hornsby, appointed by John F. Kennedy and approved by the US Senate. He and the congressman were lifelong friends and partners, as they say, in crime. Everybody in East Texas tried to stay on their avaricious good side, which meant providing them a variety of incomes from various untraceable sources, almost all of them illegal. Bob McKinney was perfectly aware of this arrangement. He provided methamphetamine to the congressman's wife to help her with her weight control, she paid him three times the going rate on the street, and he got about half of that back to the congressman through a variety of contacts. The circular nature of this trade had not yet emerged into Congressman Rip Johnson's consciousness, mostly because it was such a small amount compared with his other avenues of graft. And McKinney dreaded the day he found out. My God, he thought, what if this fool floor sweeper blew the whole thing? A Black man with a shotgun on the Judge's gate duty? A Black man? Black? With a shotgun? Holy shit, what next?

It was scary enough being the drug runner for all the rich bitches on the west side of Piney Creek who needed speed to keep their fat off. All of them were in a race with fate: to stay skinny enough to keep their wealthy husbands until the men drank or ate themselves to death, leaving them wealthy and independent. Corpulent White men on booze. What a culture, thought McKinney.

"What were you doing in the judge's yard?" he asked again.

"Don't know," said Jesse. "Went through the gate like I was supposed to and just kinda blacked out."

"You blacked out? That's a good one. You damn near GOT blacked out, by a Black guy with a shotgun," McKinney leered. "Ha. Ha. Ha. Funny story," he said without cracking a smile. "Do you black out often?"

"No, except sometimes since my wreck," Jesse said.

"Oh, you were in a wreck?" McKinney asked. "You didn't tell me you were in a wreck. Do you think I would have asked you to go on this errand if I'd known you were in a wreck? Do you?"

"No sir," said Jesse. He'd heard that tone of voice before. He always heard it just before he got fired.

"Well, it's been a week and so far, nothing's happened. Everyone had a little fun. Look at me. I'm enjoying the shit out of this. I get to use up a can of Bondo and replace a window in an Accord. I'm glad you didn't shit yourself when that Black man shot at you. Getting shit off the seat of a Honda Accord is a lot harder than ladling on some Bondo and cheap paint."

"No sir. Ain't had much to eat that day."

McKinney looked at him like he couldn't' believe what he was hearing.

"Not much to eat," McKinney replied.

"No sir. Not much. Nothing that day. Can of beans the night before."

"If my bitches could stick to that diet, they wouldn't need me," muttered McKinney.

"Okay, then," he said to Jesse. "I guess we'll let it go. I might even use you again. But I might not send you out to Mrs. Johnson again."

"She was purty," Jesse said. "Nice tan titties."

"Let me give you a word of advice, Jesse," McKinney said. "When you are talking about a woman as wealthy and powerful as Mrs. Johnson, you don't see anything about her body. Got that? She could be standing there completely nude, and you wouldn't notice. For you, she does not exist. She is so far above you in the scale of things, she ain't got titties, even if they are tan and full and unclothed. And if you make the mistake of noticing them, you could get yourself seriously beat up and killed. That Black man with the shotgun across the highway? She's got security guys too. Did you happen to see the big catfish pond when you drove in? That sucker is forty feet deep and it's got catfish in it weigh a hundred pounds. All they'll find of your body, if anybody cares enough to look, is the bones of one foot wearing a concrete boot where you were dropped overboard in the dead of the night. Don't mess with some people. Don't cross them. Don't get in their way. If you can make their miserable lives a little easier, you might get something for it, and you might not. Even if you don't get something, you thank them and do it again. That's the kind of people they are. Understand?"

"No sir, all I know is she had some fine titties."

Bob McKinney spit on the floor of the shop.

"Clean that up," he said to Jesse, and marched back to his office.

CHAPTER SIX

Michael Campbell Elkins was a young oil and gas attorney in Houston at the period when the petroleum industry was just beginning to replace railroads and shipping as the most lucrative in the world. Born in Whitmire to a long line of attorneys and judges, he inherited a fortune from his family when they died fairly young. Already successful in Houston, Michael's new wealth added cachet to his bachelorhood and expanded his connections throughout the legal and political spectrums of Texas.

He was in his thirties when he found Jane at a Petroleum Club Ball in Houston. She was nineteen, from a rich oil family, and enrolled in Rice University. Like all young women of her generation, Jane's sole imperative in life was to find a suitable husband. By nineteen, she knew how. They married six months later and then their twin fortunes really took off. Her connections through her father added further to Michael's stature, and he became fabulously, insanely wealthy. At age sixty, Michael retired from law and moved back to Whitmire, ostensibly to watch his longhorn cattle growing fat in his thousand-acre pastures and to entertain himself in a few business interests: a newspaper, a bank, a feed store, a lumber mill, a tractor dealership, and in a few richly endowed, nontaxable cultural icons: a major Houston museum, an educational foundation, and hospitals. His charitable work mostly protected some of the interest on his income, which continued unabated after his retirement. His bank proved useful to his friends, including a congressman and a federal judge in a neighboring county, but too much beef and whisky bought him an early grave, and Jane buried him when he was sixty-seven. The funeral procession stretched ten miles.

Jane was fifty-one when she was widowed. She left his half-empty crystal whiskey glass and his wooden rocker sitting on their back porch overlooking the nearest pasture, where it gradually disappeared under years of pine pollen and spiderwebs. Unencumbered by marriage at last, she decided right then she did not really enjoy any of her Houston friendships. Charles had been right. It was better to be a queen in a small place than someone else's duchess in a large one; better to forego the constant backbiting and rivalry with all those rich bitches and their private aerobics lessons, and to live a life where no one dared question your superiority. Jane liked being the queen. She liked everyone bowing to her. Well, bowing in a figurative sense. These people were too ignorant to know how to bow properly, but they would if they knew how.

Jane Elkins had a small mouth, thin lips, and a sharp nose. Her eyebrows thinly overshadowed her narrow-set eyes, and at seventy-four, without her youthful glow and smooth skin, her appearance resembled her personality. She was a hatchet. Certainly, none of the charm she must have displayed at the Petroleum Club Ball in her youth survived her marriage to Michael.

She and Michael never had children, but her late brother in Galveston had an unemployed forty-five-year-old daughter named Sarah, whom Jane hired as receptionist and spy at her newspaper, the *Whitmire Standard*. She had her hands full with Michael's other properties, anyway, making mineral leases, planning timber income, overseeing proceeds from the tractor dealership and the feed store, investing in stocks, participating in cattle auctions, supervising the charitable foundations, and keeping the cash flow of the bank properly managed. Michael's longhorns were famous for, well, long horns. She viewed this as a kind of delicious irony, since in her experience nothing implied by horns had applied to Michael once he started drinking.

She considered Michael's "midlife crisis" desire to own a newspaper as just a millstone around her own neck, not understanding how control of the local press permitted much more freedom to Michael and his friends in moving and legitimizing their money. All she knew is that he had invested heavily in the paper, which they could afford, and she did not want to sell it if she couldn't recover that investment. Also, the market for country newspapers was not robust, so she considered herself stuck with it. At least through Sarah she knew everything that was going on in town and some things that weren't. She knew about that slut Betty Parris down at the bank who was pregnant, probably with the preacher's bastard, and which women in town had been fitted for bras at La Chipita's. She didn't care, but it was nice to know about people she might need to deal with. Social standing was about having dirt on other people, and she had always been the queen of dirt. She thought of the newspaper's losses as a kind of tax she had to pay to stay on top of the low hill of Whitmire society.

Henry drove her down to Railroad Ave. to collect the rents and honked his horn at the first one-room shack. An elderly Black woman came to the door, wrapped in a quilt, and a broad grin on her winkled old face. She waved at Mrs. Elkins and then spoke sharply back into the house. A moment later, a little barefoot boy about five came running out the door and vaulted off the steps onto the dirt path. He dashed up to the car and held up his hand with the fourteen dollars in weekly rent. He was wearing a dusty pair of loose-fitting trousers and a man's cotton shirt cross-buttoned. The window eased down with a small squeak, and he placed the rent gingerly into Mrs. Elkins's white glove.

"Merry Christmas, Miz Elkins," called the old woman waving, and the boy piped in his high voice, "Merry Christmas, Miz."

"Next," she said to Henry, raising the power window without a glance at the shack.

The Whitmire city council's contest to name the new sewage treatment facility was a huge success. The leaders for the "honor" were announced in the Standard, *and then donations in support of each candidate were collected. Local attorney Ira Burdick won by a landslide. Burdick suspected his fellow members of the local bar, with collusion from certain court officials, and for good reason.*

Given a week to mull over his retort, Burdick was gracious. "I've been cleaning up your messes for nearly thirty years," he said, "and can't imagine anything more appropriate."

"Neither can we," retorted someone in the laughing crowd.

BoMac wondered why a woman easily worth a billion dollars collected rents herself. He also wondered if she ever spoke to her tenants but decided probably not. She didn't speak to him, either, except during their monthly meetings, never pleasant. He was the help, like Betty Lou and Henry. Once a month he would be summoned into her dim parlor, where she would read over the accountant's report on the newspaper's losses while he stood. Eventually she would look up at him, remove her glasses from her pointy nose, and tell him he was not making enough money. Then dismiss him.

Only once did she comment on the news content of her paper.

33

"That article about that fool commissioner," she had said, "it was stupid. People don't care. Everybody knows he'll steal. He's just like they are, so it's no surprise. Got it?"

She waited for him to nod his reply.

"No more of your sophomoric so-called investigative journalism. These stupid people need happy news. You can't teach them, and you can't make them think. And now they've got a reason to be angry at the newspaper, so you'll sell even fewer ads."

"Yes'm," he replied. But he wondered who had complained to her, and why.

These were predictable events. He had endured almost thirty of them, but after this rebuff over the commissioner, he decided that he needed to look into Mrs. Elkins herself. It was dangerous, snooping around in the county clerk's office looking at old deed records and contracts, because nothing he did went unreported to someone. He knew that. And besides, he knew that Sarah was her spy, and probably went through his desk when he was out. Still, from time to time, he would drift over to the ground-floor office of the county clerk and just read up on papers being filed: deeds, marriage licenses, loans, judgments. It was part of the job, like looking through the sheriff's record of arrests. Paying attention, he said to himself, it was just paying attention, but secretly he hoped he'd find something on her. It would be nice to have dirt on the old bitch. Secretly watching her visiting her rent houses from down the street, he realized that she would drive directly to the grocery store, and he knew in his heart of hearts that she was not reporting the income from those rents. Tax evasion? It had to be. And how long had it gone on? Decades? Forever? Since before the Civil War? Did the Elkins family have a plantation around here and build those shacks as slave quarters? He would look back into the county records next time the courthouse opened.

"Blow the horn again, Henry," Mrs. Elkins said.

Henry gave three long toots. Up and down the street, people peeked out at the billion-dollar woman in her Cadillac.

Finally, the door opened, and a broad-shouldered man of about forty stepped out. Despite the cold, he was not wearing a coat.

"I ain't got it, Miz Elkins," he said when he got close to the imperious gloved hand extended through the window. "The boss can't pay until Monday, and I can't get to my money until the bank reopens tomorrow."

"Get out, Coleman," she said. "Get out tonight. I'll rent it tomorrow to someone who will pay. Henry, drive on."

CHAPTER
SEVEN

It was Saturday, Dec. 23. Monday would be Christmas Day, and a holiday. The paper went to press at 10 p.m. every Tuesday, ready or not, unless Tuesday was a holiday. On holidays, it went to press a day early.

BoMac had too much to do to take any time off. He had the after-Christmas ads to build, the Happy New Year's ads and specials to write up, and the curious story about an image of Jesus spotted in a screen door on a house in Port Neches, Texas. It was the kind of story his readers would like to see as they celebrated the holiday. The miraculous image of Jesus in a screen door. At Easter he had run a story with a photo of a cypress knee that miraculously resembled the Virgin Mary. So sure, why not a screen door Jesus story. Light reading. Keep the reader interest up so they could absorb the harder news.

He went down to the office on Saturday to work up the Jesus story while listening with one ear to the police scanner. Around midnight, he walked back to his little uninsulated garage apartment, literally the size of a two-car garage, up a rickety set of wooden steps. He knew Mrs. Elkins would have gladly let him climb a ladder to his room rather than keep the stairs repaired, but so far they were still holding. He just had to remind himself to avoid the third step, which was busted through.

By about 3 p.m. on Sunday, he got so bored with what passed for football on his small TV that he just gave up and went back to the office. Why wait? He could write up his notes from last week's commissioners court meeting and summarize the records from the jail. There had been two fatal wrecks on the icy roads, four burglaries of Christmas presents, and three fires. All of them warranted stories. The schools—the single largest employer in the county of 15,000—were closed, so no news there. The library was closed. The police were talking about raiding a place selling illegal alcohol over on Railroad Ave., in the "quarters," that exclusively Black neighborhood of laborers where Mrs. Elkins had her rent houses. But they were waiting, for some reason. Maybe they were looking for a particular suspect, or maybe they were lazy, or maybe they were waiting for permission from Mrs. Elkins. Or maybe, with the inscrutable reasoning of police, they were waiting until Christmas Eve to break up the holiday spirits. At any rate, it was not a story yet. He'd think about what the cops were waiting on after he got to the silent office and sat drinking old office coffee at his keyboard.

He liked the smell of his Dodge pickup, the fourteen-year-old model he inherited from his bankrupt father. It ran smoothly, it was broken in, and he knew every rattle and squeak like an old friend. Also, it reminded him of his father.

His father. Well, okay, why not think about his father as he eased the mile down to the newspaper office on that drab Christmas Eve afternoon. The roads were still slick from the previous night's freezing mist, but the truck didn't mind, and he'd go slow. He sat in the cab waiting for the engine to warm up and the heat to blow, thinking about his father. How his father had finally sold off all the horses on his Virginia piedmont farm and converted the pastures into alfalfa. And then, how the alfalfa hadn't covered costs and his father had let the help go. How his mother, who had never cooked a meal or washed a dish in her life, found herself trying to figure out the logic of a vacuum cleaner as more and more of the farm fell into disrepair and his father began selling off fields he couldn't tend by himself.

Sitting in the truck, the engine purring, he daydreamed about his father on that yellow Cub Cadet riding lawn mower, waving a bottle of scotch at him with a big grin as he set out to mow the long driveway down to the county road. He loved the old red-headed aristocrat in his tattered long-sleeve shirts, his sweat-stained straw hat keeping the sun off. The alfalfa was tall in what used to be horse pastures, but nobody would come to help them bale it. Well, who could blame them? His father always forgot to pay, and never sold enough. What was it with the old man? Was he already senile? Had he left the planet on his own interstellar voyage to the great unknown, and not told anyone? BoMac's sophomore year at the University of Virginia had been interrupted with a rude wake-up call when the bursar's office called him about an urgent matter. That's when he discovered that his father's tuition checks had bounced. He owed the University of Virginia $33,512.13 in unpaid tuition and fees that his father had reneged on, and they would collect interest at double the prime rate. He was nineteen. He had taken three courses in journalism as electives and liked them, so he began looking for jobs in journalism. Anything. He got a paper delivery route, which included two hours a day sweeping out the mailroom. After shuffling burgers and waiting tables for almost two years in Charlottesville to supplement the now unsteady drip of his allowance and his piss-poor manual-labor income, he finally landed a reporting job in a podunk lumbering town in East Texas. Whitmire, Texas, pop. 1873, which corresponded to the year the town was incorporated.

The newspaper publisher was Mrs. Jane Elkins. Her husband had died and left her the paper, which she hated. When he responded to her ad in Editor and Publisher, she offered him a job and the garage apartment for a wage that might have shamed a hobo. Still, it was a job. It was a first job, more to the point, and now he'd been doing it for almost three years and getting by—if he was very, very careful with his money. He knew everyone in the community, he ran photos of their kids playing football and baseball, and of their livestock in the county fair, and of their weddings. He sampled their chili, their cakes, their cookies, and their pies, and reviewed them all in glowing reports. He rewrote obituaries from the funeral home. He updated his elaborate genealogy of county families, because you never knew whose feud might segue into violence again. He attended their ribbon-cuttings and the spring mayhaw festival, and he relished collecting all the stories he could not publish.

Maybe someday he would write a novel. Maybe, if he dug in enough, he'd be the Faulkner of East Texas. The gothic shadows of life were deep in East Texas. If you didn't live here, you wouldn't believe it.

I wonder what Ellen Etheridge's doing for Christmas, BoMac asked himself, unlocking the door to the dark office. The smell of stale cigarettes and burned coffee wafted through the open door into the clean December air. Sarah Bibber, the newspaper's only other full-time employee and its receptionist, insisted on her "Constitutional right to smoke." Since no one else ever came into the office, BoMac just tolerated it. Whitmire, Texas, was not exactly catching up with the rest of the world at any record pace anyway, and smoking inside public places there would last a lot longer.

Story idea: lung cancer.

Christmas comes and goes in Whitmire. At midnight on Dec. 24, the silent streets suddenly begin filling with pickup trucks, cruising out of town in a slow and easy parade. They head off in all directions and reappear about an hour later laden with swing sets, new televisions, boxes carefully ribboned and bowed. The men of the town have been hiding their Christmas gifts out in their hunting camps. By the time the children are old enough to go hunting, they're too old to believe in Santa Claus. So, the tradition goes on year after year, quietly, gently. Like snow.

CHAPTER EIGHT

B asketball and band are the only two sources of entertainment after football season ends. Band is a yearlong sport, of course, but the transition from marching band to concert band is no less compulsive or time-consuming for the students and for their parents, or for the facilities at the school. But for the community, after Christmas is the long snooze. Nothing happens in Whitmire in January. Some people drive out to West Texas to do some quail hunting, others to the coast for the ducks and geese. But deer season is over, and the freezers are stocked. Venison and fish will get them through another year, with the more easily obtained but costly protein from the Crooks Bros. grocery store.

Until the end of January, when the Miss Sweetgum County pageant gets underway, nothing happens but an occasional basketball game and a whole lot of band. As they say, BoMac reflected, "publishers eat snow in January." All the Christmas shopping was over, and all the Christmas advertising. Nationwide, seventy percent of all ad revenue occurs between Thanksgiving and Christmas. He knew that. But the January drought that shrank the paper to eight pages and squeezed the obituaries onto the opinion page for lack of room was ironic syncopation to the constant rain and cold wind misting through the dark green pines.

Thank God for the Crooks Bros. and Piggly Wiggly two-page ads every week. That and a few small ads from the car dealers were all he had as income to pay for the printing and postage. And at least once during January, Crooks Bros. would cut their ad in half to one page. They wanted to hit the first and last days of the month, when the Social Security and pension checks came in, and the second week was when people who were paid biweekly would get their salaries. But that third week was a squeaker. Nobody wanted to buy or sell anything.

If he'd been making a decent income himself, he would have just closed up shop the third week of January and flown off to some place with a view and a beach. It helped his state of mind to be able to look off more than a quarter mile without the pine curtain drawn across the horizon. But he did not have the income, and his employer did not care about his financial strait. She was perpetually unhappy with the paper and its poor financial prospects anyway, and BoMac knew all he had to do was complain about anything and she would just close it. Then Sweetgum County and the town of Whitmire would not have any way to let people know about community events and obituaries. Or the grocery store specials, which were, no pun intended, the meat and potatoes of the business.

At least there was basketball, so something was happening that could be reported. BoMac went to every sporting event in Whitmire, looking for news. He carried his camera, he took pictures of athletes and their parents, of the cheerleaders and their boyfriends, of the coaches and the referees. He made copious notes. He interviewed players, coaches, and parents on both sides of the gym. He invaded locker rooms. Thankfully at least some action occurred at a basketball game to provide interesting photos, unlike band practice. The band director screaming red-faced at the trumpet section once again would be an award-winning photo, but the director was too wary to be caught on film. Instead, when he saw a camera he would simply make the kids play the same four measures of music over and over, forever, until the photographer gave up and went away. So, covering the band practice was not really newsworthy, whereas at the basketball game at least the kids were trying and having fun, and sometimes doing daring and heroic things. Action shots were good for the paper, even in January.

Toward the end of the month, however, BoMac knew that the Miss Sweetgum County beauty contest would begin. This long-awaited and eagerly anticipated event, the first step toward the culminating Miss America contest, was fiercely fought over by many of the local mothers and their daughters. It was a newspaper feature begging for coverage, despite its utter and total vapidity.

Moreover, it was an alternative to the much more cherished title of Queen of the Mayhaws, a long-running spring festival when one senior girl from the five spread-out high schools in the county was crowned as the symbol of fertility. The town was unaware that it was a fertility ritual. Well, of course they were unaware of it. They thought they were Christians, not pagans, and they would have become furious at the mere suggestion that one of their seventeen- or eighteen-year-old daughters could be chosen for such a role. Nevertheless, the county had been holding the ritual every single year for more than sixty years, even during World War II. BoMac found their stubborn innocence about human fertility rather charming, but then he was from the horse country of piedmont Virginia, where fertility was an important and accepted aspect of life. The uptight churchgoers of Whitmire with their corseted Puritanism would not entertain the notion. However, they had no problem with thinking her the symbol of the mayhaw, which in the grand scheme of things was probably insulting.

The same puritanical attitude did not apply to the Miss Sweetgum County contest. Here, girls from ages four to eighteen were expected to be explicitly sexual and alluring. They were expected to show off their bodies and their skill at applying makeup and dressing their hair. They were expected to provoke lewd thoughts and possibly more in the minds of the audience. They were to exhibit the power of the female body to sway and persuade males and their wives. And it was a fierce, almost deadly contest. BoMac attended the dress rehearsals and went backstage to take candids of the contestants but was so drawn to the feral, febrile expressions on the faces of the mothers that he ended up shooting camera roll after camera roll of dumpy older jealous women.

"BoMac," said one mother rushing up to him during the actual contest. She was breathless, urgent, disturbed. "BoMac!"

He was seldom called BoMac, in fact he was seldom addressed at all, so she got his attention.

"Do you have any duct tape? Quick! It's important."

"Duct tape? That sticky silver tape?"

"Yes. That. Do you have any?"

"Maybe at the office."

"It's after closing. The hardware store is shut, and we need some duct tape like right now."

"What for?" He started putting his camera away. He knew he would go looking at the office for it.

"Never mind that. Do you think you have some? We need it right now." She tried to give him a nice smile to persuade him, but she was obviously so agitated that she failed. It came out as a grimace.

"Okay, I'll go look." He snapped his camera bag shut, and headed for the door, the woman tagging along.

"Don't tell anyone," she whispered. "It's important, but we don't need to spread it around."

BoMac was mystified, but it was a short distance from the school auditorium to the dark newspaper office, and he wouldn't miss anything. The five-hour show was about to go to intermission, and the judges wouldn't announce the winners until nearly midnight. He'd only publish one, maybe two, photos of the hundred or so he took, and most of the story would be lists of winners in different categories. "Miss Congeniality," ages five through seventeen. "Miss Talent," ages five through seventeen. And so on.

He parked his pickup in front of the office and unlocked the door, stepping into the darkness and fumbling his way toward the light switch off to the side. The staggered lines of fluorescent lights blazed on, though most of them were dark and needed to be replaced, and he went ambling off toward the back where the coffee pot and the darkroom were. He rummaged around for a while under the layout tables, pushing aside old copies of the paper and notebooks full of negatives, and finally found a set of tools and, sure enough, a roll of duct tape. He stuck his hand through the hole in the tape spool and went back to the auditorium.

"Thank you thank you thank you," breathed the mother when he got back. The intermission was still on, but the atmosphere backstage had become tense. "Julie is not the only girl who needs it. Two of the other girls in her age and three of the seniors also need it. You're the hero of the night, BoMac."

"Don't know what I did," he said. "What do you need duct tape for?"

"You don't know? Ha ha," she laughed, "well, you're a boy so why would you." She was hurrying away, and he was trotting to keep up with her.

"It's the pushup bras," she said back to him over her shoulder. "Several of the girls forgot to bring them, or they don't fit the costume."

"What about the pushup bras?" he asked, digging his camera out of the bag as he trotted.

"We use the duct tape to hold their boobs up. Can't have a fourteen-year-old with droopy boobs, can we?" she laughed.

BoMac stopped dead in his tracks. The image of these young girls putting duct tape on their tender breasts hit him like a hard slap. How would they get that tape off? It was going to hurt. And yet at least five girls were standing around backstage trying to shape their young breasts with industrial grade adhesive. One of them, he knew for a fact, was in the fifth grade.

"Oh my," he breathed to himself, deflated. "Oh my God. What the hell?"

He put his camera back in the bag and went back out to the pickup, sitting in the front seat for a long time trying to drive away the image of those young women torturing themselves for a few minutes of, what? What would you call it? Showing off? Sexual contest? What were they doing it for?

Then he drove slowly down to the courthouse and parked, staring at the dark edifice outlined against a starry sky. The white cross atop the First Fundamentalist Church across the street glowed in the streetlights, silent and stark as usual.

"I'm not sure I can keep doing this," he said aloud in the empty truck. "I'm just not sure."

In late January, redbud trees blossom, heralding spring with bursting crimson flowers, even under a sheath of ice like rubies in crystal. Native Americans once gathered the flowers for food, and the seeds in late summer for roasting. Today, the spindly redbud just grows senescent and becomes hollow, providing sanctuary in winter for long, winged roaches.

When the old redbud in Jack Post's front yard on Redbud Street fell over, he sawed the logs and tossed them in the fireplace. As they warmed, thousands of roaches buzzed out, swarming the house and driving out his wife, screaming. "Well dang," said Jack.

45

CHAPTER

NINE

One March after the rain washed pine pollen into golden mud along the streets and gutters, a puddle formed at the corner of Hill and Beech Streets, next to Darryl and Mary Stewart's long front yard. The puddle stayed there through April, the pollen thick on it like a crust, and then through May. All summer, it never dried up. Darryl sometimes looked at the muddy pool from his kitchen window, still holding water months after that first rain, and wondered if a spring had opened up under the street. Perhaps it never dried up because they'd had steady downpours. Still, after six weeks of summer drought, with the sod in the front yard cracking and the grass turning brown, the pool was still there.

He had other things to do than worry about some mud puddle, though, so he went and did them. But it nagged at him, kind of like Mary did, in the back of his mind. He'd tune it out for a while, just like he did her, but then it'd sort of scratch its way back to consciousness.

For the first year or two that the puddle was there, city residents going down Beech Street just drove their cars right through it, acting surprised by the sudden splash of water under their wheels and the great sheets of water that cascaded onto the sidewalk and washed up into Darryl's yard. On weekends when he wasn't fishing and stayed home, Darryl would hear cars hitting that puddle all day. Once a pickup loaded with Mexican workers on their way to the woods struck that puddle going too fast and splashed water all over the truck. "Ai yi yi," yelled three or four of them at once. Darryl heard them over the cartoons he and Mary pretended to watch on Saturday mornings. Actually, they were just waiting for a Roadrunner cartoon, because that's when they always made love. Something about the Roadrunner cartoons got Mary all hot. The rest of the time, she talked at him. So, he wondered, did the Mexicans drive into the

47

water BETWEEN Roadrunner cartoons, and that's why he heard them, or did they drive into the water DURING a Roadrunner cartoon and he heard them because Mary had shut up? He couldn't figure that out.

By the third summer, that puddle began to piss him off. He liked that corner, and the way his house sat and how it looked from the street, and the puddle was a detraction. He thought it was hurting his property value and said so to Mary, who just nodded and brought him another beer. He'd take the beer and go out to the yard to stare at it for a while.

It was growing wider and was now really a pool. Greenery was springing up around it, and it flooded the sidewalk on Beech Street. Some kind of marshy-looking plant was growing where the curb was supposed to be. His yard was filling up with crawfish chimneys, which clattered in the lawnmower when he ran over them. Overall, the puddle was becoming a nuisance, so Darryl decided to take action. That pool, almost a pond, had to go. He started going to the monthly meetings of the city council, held in the old bankrupt bank building that served as city hall. He complained about the pool, sometimes calling it a swamp, sometimes calling it a bay gall. He pronounced "bay gall" as "bay-gaw," which was what people in that part of East Texas called such places. And every month, the board members would smile at him and nod at him and agree that something should be done, but what? They didn't have the budget to completely tear up Beech Street, and Hill Street was actually a federal highway, so it was "gummint's" problem, not Whitmire's. Their teeth were all glittery with their gold crowns and their cheeks wagged at him in their good humor. Darryl understood them. Hell, he'd known them as long as he'd been alive. A hardware owner, a pharmacist, a grocer, a dentist (the one who put gold crowns in everybody's mouth), a used car dealer, a wrecker driver. Just good old, down-to-earth, practical guys he'd known since first grade. They didn't have a spiteful bone in their bodies. And not much gumption, either, he decided. Still, every month he liked going down there to complain, and he figured he could wear them down eventually.

Then finally the city did something. One morning when he was leaving the house to go to work, he saw a brand-new orange traffic cone in front of the pond.

Mrs. Bertha Wilcox, ninety-two, who lived a block away up Beech Street, always drove that way going to the store. She was the first to knock the cone into the water. She had driven that road all her life, and she'd be damned if she was going to twitch the steering wheel even an inch to avoid hitting something that didn't belong there. Darryl watched her coming down the street and knew she was going to hit it, and sure enough, a great sheet of water splashed up on his yard, flooding a dozen or so crawfish chimneys, and Mrs. Wilcox drove on by like nothing in the world had happened. The cone was lying almost completely submerged in the pond, where it stayed unmolested by city workers.

Darryl worked, when he wasn't fishing, and nothing changed with the pond except it kept growing. Then one Friday morning when he left the house to go to work, he saw a great blue heron strutting through the water where the curb had once been, lifting its claw high and slowly into the air, peering at the water with first one eye and then the other, then putting that claw down and slowly lifting the other for another step.

"Naw," Darryl said to himself. "That heron is fishing in that pond. If he's fishing, then there are fish in it."

He dropped his tool belt on the front seat of his pickup and went out and stood in the yard, staring at the pond now covering more than half the street and most of the sidewalk for a block. The orange traffic cone was still lying on its side where Mrs. Wilcox's car had left it, about halfway across the street, submerged in the water. Since twelve inches was the minimum (legal) length to keep a catfish, Darryl was certain the cone was resting in more than a foot of water. He didn't need a tape measure to tell. He stared for a long time at the pond, while from a neighbor's yard down the street the heron patiently waited for him to go away.

Then he went back in the house. Even though it was a workday, Darryl decided he had more important things to do than earn a living that day. Mary could just stretch the money, anyway. He didn't mind another meal of boxed macaroni and cheese with a can of tuna mixed in. Hell. Darryl was going fishing.

"Hey," he yelled at Mary, who was sitting at her potter's wheel out on the back porch swatting mosquitoes with her muddy hands, "sell more coffee cups. I'm going fishing."

The old woman, stooped and shabby, walked slowly through backyards taking laundry off clotheslines. Nobody in Whitmire had a fenced yard in those days. Dogs, pigs, and people wandered as they wished. She tucked the stolen clothing under her rags—sometimes underwear, sometimes shirts. None of it could fit her thin frame. She never spoke. Eventually she would return to her dark house invisible in the shadows of overgrown shrubs. At least once a week, one of the town's women would stop by and leave a casserole on her porch. They understood dementia and forgave her pilfering, that broken woman.

Sarah Bibber liked to extend her lunch hour by visiting with her jolly friend, Jane Tappan, in the sewing shop next door to the Standard. *One day Jane dropped a cutter on her foot and blood spurted ten feet. Sarah ran screaming from the shop into the women's clothing store next door. "Gimme a Kotex," she yelled, "gimme a Kotex! Jane is gonna bleed to death!" The handful of customers and clerks all looked at one another in astonishment. BoMac, hearing about the incident later that day, wondered what must have gone through all the minds of those church ladies.*

Miss Susanna Andrews ran a small dry goods store near the elementary school. A devout member of First Fundamentalist Church, she often lingered by the door of her business in the afternoon to entice children into the store, where she would read them a Scripture lesson and give them candy. Usually the children, mostly Black, would wait patiently for her to finish, then grab the candy and disappear down the street. Those who asked for another lesson got another piece of candy. Her apostolic candy ministry was popular in Whitmire, and some local businesses helped by donating chocolates and peppermints.

CHAPTER
TEN

Darryl Stewart was growing fond of the pond in front of his house. One weekend, he netted a bunch of perch and some minnows from the lake, which he set loose in it. By the weekend, the great blue heron he'd named "George" had a companion stalking along the sidewalk, hunting for fish. On another weekend, he brought a mess of catfish home from the lake and let them loose in the water, to keep the minnows and the perch on their toes. Figuratively speaking, he chuckled to himself. He started sitting on his extensive lawn in a folding aluminum chair and just staring at the pond, watching the people narrowly missing the hole. He'd tried plumbing the hole's depth, but his piece of string only went to twelve feet and it hadn't touched bottom, so he quit. He also brought a piece of equipment home from work and drove some pilings into the ground along the sidewalk next to the pond, to keep the water from eroding his whole yard. He figured if he was going to have waterfront property, then he might as well plan for it. Besides, he suspected that hole, actually a spring by now, might be eroding up under his yard and he didn't want it to get any closer to his house. It could carry off some of his front yard, which would lower his property value. He began designing a small pier for himself, now that he'd stocked the pond with fish.

"Whatcha doing, Darryl?" the police chief said one day, driving by.

"Hi there, Trey," said Darryl, "come on in and have some coffee, and I'll get another chair."

It was Saturday after the cartoons, and Mary had gone back to bed. When she got up, she'd go out to the porch to throw pots on her wheel. Darryl had thought he might spend the afternoon working out at the deer camp but liked the idea of sitting and watching the water more. Also, he was tired. Three roadrunner cartoons were two too many. He welcomed the intrusion of the chief.

They microwaved stale coffee from the percolator in some of Mary's garish mugs, the ones she couldn't sell, and went back out to sit in the chairs. After a while of shifting and grunting, Trey nodded at the pond.

"Where's my road cone?" he asked.

"It sank," Darryl said. "I watched the water getting deeper and deeper and then one day, I'm sitting out here and that whole section of street just disappeared under water."

"No shit."

"Yeah."

"Guess we need to put up another cone."

"Maybe wait. It's getting cold weather. Might freeze over."

"Somebody told me you been fishing in it."

"Yep. Stocked it with fish from the lake. See that great blue heron over yonder? I call him George. George comes over and fishes in it every afternoon."

Trey nodded, took a sip of coffee, then looked over at Darryl and slowly poured the coffee out on the ground. "Hope you don't mind," he said. "Remind me not to drink coffee with you on Saturdays."

"Raunchy, ain't it." Darryl grinned.

"I value my teeth, and that Cajun stuff you drink gnawed off half the enamel. I could feel my teeth getting all edgy and like."

"Does the same to me," Darryl said.

"So how deep you think it is?" Trey was looking at the pond again.

"I dropped a twelve-foot plumb line down in it and didn't touch bottom."

"Really?"

"Yeah. I've been telling the city council this for three years, but they just grin and say they don't have the money to fix it."

"They got the money. They're just cheap bastards."

"Why they're elected," Darryl nodded. Trey reached into his shirt pocket and pulled out a can of snuff, took a pinch, and offered the can to Darryl. Darryl shook his head. He liked Trey, but he preferred not to wad tobacco into his cheek. Lots of guys did it, but he wasn't one of them.

Darryl sat there for a bit waiting for Trey to get to the point. The police chief doesn't just stop by at noon on Saturday if there's nothing on his mind, and it must be big because he wasn't talking, so Darryl just figured he would wait him out. They'd known one another since third grade. Darryl and Trey understood one another. Besides, it was Whitmire, Texas. Nothing ever needed doing in Whitmire in a big way. You survived in Whitmire by just easing along, taking your time.

Finally, Trey spit out onto the grass.

"You know John Coleman?" he asked.

"He that boy works for Hogleg in the woods? Lives on Railroad Avenue?"

"That's him."

"Never heard of him." Darryl didn't crack a smile or even blink.

"Me either," said Trey.

They sat in silence for a while.

"My man went over to evict him from one of old Miz Elkins's shacks," Trey finally continued. "She went along to make sure it was done properly, and it seems he insulted her."

"I heard that," Darryl said.

"Thing is, it's not illegal to insult somebody," Trey said.

"Trey, old buddy, are you letting your conscience get to you? This is Whitmire, Texas. Some people you don't insult. You can rob them, but you can't insult them. You know that."

"Yeah, I know it." Trey spat again, a long stream of brown juice. Wiped the back of his hand across his mouth.

"But that's not your problem," said Darryl, lifting an eyebrow at Trey.

"Naw, it ain't. Because see, she claims he was late with his rent, but that's because Hogleg didn't write checks to his men on Friday. He couldn't because the mill held up the checks that day. Somebody sick or something. So she evicted him."

"He raise his fist at her or anything?"

"I got some folks that will say so, but I don't believe 'em. I've been watching Coleman. He's okay people. Works hard, stays out of trouble. You'd think he'd already been to the pen the way he avoids trouble, but he hasn't."

"He's not from around here, is he." Darryl was making a statement, not asking a question.

"He told me his family lives up north, St. Louis and Chicago. But they have relatives down here and he wanted to know them. That's why he's here."

"Can't have much money if he's working for Hogleg."

"Don't know. He was holding thirty-seven thousand cash when we ran him in for disturbing the peace."

Trey fiddled for a bit.

"He's paying fourteen dollars a week rent, doesn't have the cash when Miz Elkins shows up to ask for it like she does every single week at the same time, and the next day he's sitting on almost forty thousand he says he took out of the bank that morning. Betty Parris, the teller—you know her?"

"Pretty girl, black hair, about five-feet-six tall, nice teeth, little pug nose, blue eyes, not married, about twenty-three years old?"

"That's the one."

"No. Never seen her before either. Leastwise, not that Mary knows, and I'd like to keep it that way."

"Betty verifies that he withdrew the money from his checking and savings accounts that morning. I don't get it."

"Where'd a boy like Coleman get that kind of money?" Darryl asked. He had never held that much money at one time in his whole life.

"Lots of questions here," Trey admitted. "He says he earned it, and Hogleg says he's been the best worker he's ever had. I guess he just works and saves and doesn't get in trouble."

"Until now."

"Yeah, until now."

"What kind of trouble is he in?"

"Well, that's the thing, ain't it." Trey fiddled for a bit. Darryl waited for him to change the subject, which meant he would move on and Darryl could go on out to the deer lease after all and get a nap. But Trey didn't change the subject.

"So there's laws and there's laws," said Trey.

Darryl nodded. Trey wasn't through yet after all.

"And Coleman didn't break any of them that we know about." Darryl nodded.

"But I've got laws, too, and if I break any of them then I could go to prison, or get fired, or even have the state come down on me."

"Sounds like you need to do the right thing," Darryl nodded. Now he knew where this was going.

"I can't arrest a man who didn't do anything," Trey said. "And he didn't do anything. He didn't even disturb the peace, and the JP won't accept the charge. But I can't refuse to do what Miz Elkins tells me to do, because she holds all the purse strings in this little town. All of 'em. And that includes my job."

"Where's Coleman at now?" Darryl asked.

"That's what I'm telling you. I had to let him go. Can't find anything to charge him with. I told him to stay close, and he will. I think he's moving over to Piney Creek. Knows somebody or something. Besides, his first call was to that lawyer in Beaumont. The Black one."

"Bad news. He's the civil rights lawyer. What's his name? Always getting his name in the paper."

"Charles Goldsby. They call him Charlie. He's bad news. We don't want him poking around up here in Whitmire."

"So, what you thinking?" asked Darryl. Finally he understood why Trey was there. Trey was trying to figure out how to keep his job and not get prosecuted for misusing his office.

"I could arrest him on suspicion of racketeering," Trey said.

"That's a new one," said Darryl. "Black boy arrested for racketeering, in Whitmire, Texas. What is he racketeering over?"

"Selling drugs. Only explanation for why he had that much cash."

"Drug dealers don't usually put their money in the bank," Darryl said. "It's too hard to explain to the feds."

"Best I can come up with."

"Ain't no law about holding a bunch of cash, Trey," Darryl said. "Where's that cash now?"

"I took it as evidence," Trey said.

Darryl looked away from the pond and stared at his friend.

"You took it?"

"It's in the safe of my office," Trey said.

"That safe only about a hundred and fifty people know the combination to," Darryl said.

"Only safe I've got." Trey sounded like he was beginning to wonder about the wisdom of his action.

"Why'd you take it?"

"Suspicion of racketeering. I told you."

"That's a crime?"

"Could be."

"You shitting me."

"What? Why you say that?"

"Trey, I'm no lawyer, but you can't take a man's life savings as evidence of a crime that don't exist."

"Who says it don't exist?" The tone of Trey's voice betrayed the real reason behind the visit. Darryl had put his finger on it. Search as he had all night long, nowhere in the Texas Code of Criminal Procedure had Trey found a "suspicion of racketeering" reference. But reading was not something he did often or well, so he figured he had just skipped it. Besides, he told Darryl, if the law didn't already exist, then it should.

"Trey, Trey, Trey," Darryl said, wagging his head. "The question is not whether there's a law. The question you and I both want answered is, How do we keep this money for ourselves. Right?"

"It's Saturday," Trey said, standing up and handing Darryl the empty cup. "I'm going to take the little wife and drive over to that seafood place in Livingston for oysters. Probably leave about six, can't be back before ten. Later, if we go to a movie. All the boys are off on Saturday. That sheriff and his deputies are the only ones on duty, and I think they cut the staff down to one or two at most on weekends. You got a police scanner?"

"Don't everyone?"

"You'll hear 'em reporting in to dispatch off and on. They will likely be

55

fourteen, fifteen miles away from town all night."

"I hope you and Mabel have a really nice supper," Darryl said, standing up. "Don't do anything I wouldn't do." He grinned and reached out his hand to shake with Trey.

Trey backed his police car out of the driveway and headed down Beech Street, hitting the edge of the pond just enough to splash up on Darryl's lawn.

Guess I better go to the deer camp, Darryl said to himself, afore I get sent to prison.

CHAPTER
ELEVEN

Different small towns in the South have different ways of addressing social and racial issues. Most try to ignore these issues because to do anything would be to change and they hate change. Some actively deny issues like economic and racial disparity, while many assume that all of the crime is committed by persons of color, because White people "never do anything wrong." In some small towns, racial parity is so skewed to one or another race—Hispanic, White, Black—that the few representatives of difference are inevitably the scapegoats. Vast differences in wealth are generally not a source of social conscience, because making a lot of money at the expense of the environment and other people is the essential ingredient of the "American Dream." Basically, that means the more wealth you can accumulate, the more important you become and the more you can expect to be treated like royalty. As others have noted, rank hath its privileges. Americans in general and small towns in particular are fiercely devoted to their habits and their caste system of neo-nobility. As long as nothing ever changes the balance of misery and no new enemy arises, they are as content as they are going to be.

Piney Creek, the county seat of Cypress County, had the benefit of some political geniuses early in the twentieth century in learning how to cope with racial unrest. The Black people of Piney Creek, many of them descendants of slaves and the rest refugees from the North, made up about forty-seven percent of the electorate and were often a powder keg of anger. But the same politicians who manufactured federal support for the largest impoundment of water in Texas, Lake Ralph Yarborough, also advised the city council and the local police in a unique arrangement. The local White evangelical Protestants were opposed to the sale and consumption of alcoholic beverages, but much of the working-class Black population was not. Acknowledging this distinction, Piney Creek allowed the Black population to have two nightclubs where illegal liquor could be sold and consumed. At the first hint of trouble, however, the police would shut these illegal establishments down and they would remain shut down until the trouble stopped. Then they would be allowed to reopen.

For example, over ninety percent of the starring players on the Piney Creek High School football team were Black, but only White girls were cheerleaders. When some Black mothers went before the school board to protest this blatantly racist policy, looking to have their daughters at least be given a chance to try out for cheerleading positions, the nightclubs were closed and stayed closed for two weeks.

Lesson learned.

Officially, therefore, everyone turned a blind eye to this arrangement, and that made the enterprise open to various kinds of manipulation, including avoiding local and state sales taxes, laundering of money from various criminal enterprises, and the sale of narcotics. Even the Texas Alcoholic Beverage Commission, charged with regulating the sale of alcohol where legal, was significantly missing from the locale because, in theory at least, it was a dry county and no alcohol was sold. So special was the arrangement, that in Piney Creek the police would protect the property and park outside the establishments to prevent disruptions of the peace, but not interfere with the illegal commerce carried on inside. It was a cozy, profitable arrangement, and everyone on the city council, in the police department, the county government, and particularly the political geniuses who devised the scheme were taking a profit. A huge profit.

As these things go, eventually word spread out around the region about the Piney Creek enterprises and wormed its way via the East Texas Black network into the shady parlors of Houston's gang-infested Third Ward, where an enterprising drug cartel boss named Melton Carr was looking to expand his reach.

Carr's grasp of the free enterprise system had taught him a few things about dealing with competition. In an unregulated free enterprise business, for example, information, bribery, and extortion were keys to success. So, he chose an assassin, Ben Pickett Jr., and a small-time distribution chief named Abbie Morton to go on an exploratory expedition to Piney Creek. They had all the money they needed, and more available, but Carr was strict with them.

"If you spend my money, you get me results," he said, leaning back in his leather office chair to gesture at the wall behind him. Nailed to the wall were over a hundred human ears, some mummified and some still bleeding. Both Morton and Pickett still had two ears. Some of Carr's other workers had only one.

Carr referred to his collection of trophies as workforce training, an important part of any capitalist enterprise. He even had an HR department to supervise this training, as well as a number of other lieutenants handling such important functions as operations and finances. When you run a business making about $100 million a year illegally, you use successful management models from other businesses exemplifying the free enterprise system. Exxon, for example. He even had a vice president for public and government affairs, and another for investor relations, namely some Central American governments who were heavily dependent upon Carr's business kickbacks. Decisive, quick, intelligent, and disciplined, Carr learned from the mistakes of others and kept himself both well connected and informed.

"My sources tell me a US congressman and a federal district judge are involved in some way," Carr told Morton and Pickett. "They don't know how. But if the top of the food chain is corrupt, then we have an entry. Find out."

"Any contacts we can know about?" Morton asked.

"One of my sources told me to look for a drug pusher named Clarence Thomas and a bartender named Chillers Banks."

"Got it," said Morton. "We'll get on it."

"Also, a honky used car dealer," said Carr, "but I don't know his name. Apparently, he is the distributor. Go up there, blend in, get to know people. Let me know."

"Leaving now," said Morton.

"Congressman's name is Rip Johnson," said Melton Carr.

Three and a half hours later, Abbie Morton and the silent Ben Pickett Jr. drove from Houston under wet February skies into Piney Creek. Brief inquiries from Black cashiers at convenience stores helped them locate one of the nightclubs at the end of a potholed street that dead-ended at the chain link fence of a predominantly Black elementary school. Children just out of school at the end of the day were coming through the fence gap by the nightclub, passing in front of a porch full of lounging Black men.

"Some of those boys got a view," muttered Pickett.

"Looks deliberate," said Morton.

But they also saw teachers patrolling the playground and watching for the children. "Those women over there in the school know what's going on," said Pickett. "They've already spotted us. And look there, that one is writing down a description of this car, I bet. They're on sharp lookout."

59

"This look like it?" asked Morton.

"Humpf," grunted Pickett. He cut his eyes at the other houses on the street, checking to see if any of the dawdlers on the street were carrying weapons and saw two or three people peeking out at them from behind curtains or standing on their porches watching for the children to come home. "Could be," he said.

"Think those boys are dealing?" asked Morton, nodding in the direction of three Black teenagers who had obviously skipped school.

"Nah," said Pickett. "They're waiting. Maybe spotting. They ain't dealing."

"Go in?" asked Morton.

"Too soon," said Pickett. "Drive around, see if we can find that used car dealer. Come back after dark. Maybe buy a local car to blend in or steal some plates. Small town like this, better not steal plates. People might recognize them."

"Yeah," said Morton.

It had been raining for a week, that sporadic, dark February rain, and the woods were soaked, the gray rain splattering against the potholed street, running in muddy rivulets. The two splashed down the street in their "company car," jostling over the uneven pavement. But for the moment, the rain had stopped, just in time for the school children to get home to safety and dinner.

Tobacco smoke drifted in a silver cloud from the open door of the nightclub, like a snake.

Coleman went over to Whitmire on Friday to see the police chief, and Trey Green handed his money to him in a paper sack from Sonic. They counted it out together at the chief's desk, in neat stacks still in wrappers from the bank.

"That's a lot of money," the chief said to him.

"Yessir," replied Coleman, not looking directly at him.

"Where'd you get it?"

"I earned it. Some of this here money goes back to when I was twelve years old and sacking groceries."

"Where'd you stay before you came to Whitmire, John?" Green asked.

"I was in Oakland for a long time, then LA. Before I moved here, I worked at an iron mill in Birmingham, but them Blacks over there lack respect."

"Respect is an important part of living in Whitmire," the police chief said, not taking his steady gaze off of Coleman. "Know what I mean?"

"Yessir," Coleman nodded. "I does." He was trying to use the Black dialect that was common in Whitmire and hoping it didn't sound like he was pretending. "You reckon I ought to apologize to that old White woman for laughing at her?"

"I 'spect not," said the police chief. "No good can come of it. But you've moved out of town, right?"

"Yessir. I stays in Piney Creek now."

"Not to make a big deal out of it," Green said, "but it's best if you stay over there."

"I knows what you mean," Coleman said. "I takes that as friendly advice."

Wade Felder and his best friend, Clay Ford, sometimes swapped wives. One night, he made love to his own wife. When she fell asleep, he got up, took his .410 shotgun from the closet, held the gun point-blank an inch below her left ear, and pulled the trigger. Afterwards, he walked two miles to the sheriff's office and laid the shotgun on the dispatcher's counter. "I murdered my wife," he said simply and sat down to wait. Three years later, imprisoned, he married Ford's ex-wife by proxy. Six months later he was paroled and back in the woods, cutting timber.

CHAPTER

TWELVE

The new high school social studies teacher was Black, and from up North. Everybody in Whitmire was uneasy about him. Charles Henniker had that way of moving that telegraphed danger, but he was friendly and bright-eyed. He said hello. He looked people in the face when he spoke to them and smiled. He always wore a clean shirt with a tie, and his shoes were always polished. He held out his hand to shake. He was learning how to duck his head just right, so as not to be offensive. In Whitmire, they'd never seen any Black man like that before. Some people resented his manners but couldn't find anything wrong with him. Except, of course, that he was a different kind of Black.

Like every small town, what they didn't know about someone they just made up. The only reason a Black man would move to rural East Texas had to be to get away from some kind of trouble back where he belonged, they supposed, so they made stuff up. Before he'd been in Whitmire a week, he had a fictional backstory of brothers in the state prison for rape and murder. He was accused of hijacking eighteen-wheelers for the mob. He was thought to be a drug runner. Some people said they just didn't trust him because they didn't know his people.

What they didn't know, in other words, was that his family had lived in San Augustine since the 1600s, during the time of the Spanish. They had farms along the El Camino Real de los Tejas that ran through the major settlements in the Spanish colony of Texas. Some of them had become wealthy. Some had married into White families, and some had not, but the bonds of family were strong among the Navarros and Hennikers and Kings and Ybaros of that part of the world. A single wedding held in 1976 drew over a thousand members of the family, who camped out around the Ebenezer Church and enjoyed "dinner on the ground" for three days.

Charles Henniker had just finished defending his master's thesis on political conflict in Somalia when his aunt called to say his grandmother wanted to see him again, and also that she still made the best damned banana pudding in the world. Also, the world's most wonderful pecan pie. He had more than a hundred cousins living in and around San Augustine, some of them as White as any resident of Whitmire, with blue eyes. Some of them with blue eyes and coal-black skin.

Race was complicated. Ignorant people thought it was all one or the other, but nothing on the planet was that way from Charles Henniker's point of view. He drove to San Augustine to visit, was welcomed back into the dense thicket of blood and kin, and made up his mind to leave Ohio. He wanted to teach. He liked teaching. He had cousins who were teachers and he talked to them. Eventually his officer training would propel him into administration, but he liked the whole idea of dealing with young kids while they could still learn to think, and that meant interacting with them in the classroom.

The complexity of the world is why he loved studying political science. How on earth could ignorant people get along with one another? he wondered. And then of course the obvious answer was, they couldn't. Ignorance is intolerant. The only way to make a difference was to teach. When the answer had hit him in the middle of the night, it felt like his beloved Celia had leaned over and whispered it in his ear. In fact, he was certain that she had. He had heard her voice, felt her sexy breath on his ear, the squeeze of her hand.

During his interview for the job with Arthur Shelby, the Whitmire school superintendent, Henniker was told at least half a dozen times there was no racism in Whitmire, and no racial unrest. Henniker learned that Superintendent Shelby had several good friends who were Black, and he had the highest respect for Black people in general. For example, he loved jazz and barbecue. Henniker did not ask him to name his Black friends. Henniker was smarter than a bucket of fish bait.

The superintendent wanted Henniker to know he was hired on probation as a first-year teacher, and the quickest way to lose his job was to make waves. Not once did he ask Henniker why he was applying for a job in a forgotten corner of rural Texas, so he had no way of knowing about Henniker's grandmother or his extensive family only fifty miles away. Also, Henniker figured, he'd be damned if he'd bring one of his grandmother's pecan pies to share with this Arthur Shelby.

Then Shelby stood up and extended his hand to shake. "Good luck. You'll be replacing old Ben Shelby, my great-uncle, who has been teaching this subject here for fifty-five years. I expect you'll find his shoes hard to fill."

"I do sincerely hope I am capable of living up to your expectations," replied Henniker, dropping his gaze and grasping Shelby's hand gently. "Thank you for the opportunity."

"I just hope I don't regret it," Shelby replied, reaching for his alcohol hand wipes as Henniker left the room.

Henniker knew better than to roll his eyes, only nodding pleasantly to the unibrowed and bespectacled White secretary acting as door guard for the big, Negro-loving man fond of jazz and barbecue.

The school board had quietly explained to those who asked that it was part of an effort to racially diversify the teaching staff. They said the state had been putting pressure on them. Next year, maybe they could recruit a quiet Black female. With ninety-two teachers on the staff, that would give them five Black teachers. The student population of 1,103 was forty-nine percent Black. It would help, the board members quietly explained, to have a Black male instructor who might be able to discipline the Black boys so important to the athletic programs. Besides, qualified Black male teachers were hard to find.

Henniker found a small three-bedroom brick house with a garage on the edge of that part of town traditionally occupied by Blacks and adjusted to his new neighborhood in Whitmire with caution. As an unattached Black man, the neighbors watched his every move but didn't speak. No family, no way to visit with him. They didn't know about his San Augustine connections, though Henniker was sure that sooner or later the Black network would place him. People visited, they talked, they attended one another's churches, they carried food to their own relatives. The network was very much alive, and he was curious how long it would take the network to make him out as old Momma Henniker's grandson. Meanwhile, he'd need to start the conversations, if he wanted, and then he'd keep his distance until they knew him a lot better. A whole lot better. In the South, Black men stayed near their mothers for the most part, and their mothers and grandmothers were the social network. An unattached Black man was a nobody, feral and maybe dangerous. Until the network identified him, he was to be avoided.

Nobody knew for sure about Henniker's past. Even his relatives only knew he'd been in the military, but not what he did or his retirement rank as lieutenant colonel. He had appeared in Whitmire with a teaching certificate and a master's degree from Case Western Reserve. He kept to himself, never gambling or drinking or talking to the women, but he had a past he told no one about.

Henniker had served twenty-three years as an Air Force officer and commando. He had a decent retirement salary. He had a Silver Star, a Bronze Star, and a Purple Heart in little boxes in his dresser drawer. He knew a thing or two about discipline and keeping his head down to keep from getting shot, so East Texas was no worse than Vietnam or Cambodia. In fact, if you substituted race for religion, they were about the same: same kinds of conflicts, same kinds of arguments, same kinds of tactics, same kinds of ignorant fundamentalist zeal. In the Middle East, you killed people over their supposed religion. In East Texas, you killed them over the supposed color of their skin. The subject of the conflict was different, but the conflict was the same. He'd seen it. He'd survived it. He'd survive it again. East Texas was okay, and much wetter than Somalia or Mali, which was fine. At least in East Texas they spoke a kind of English.

Also, he was alone. He liked to tell himself he needed no one. He needed a can opener. Period. And his knife would work if he didn't have a can opener. Charles Henniker was exactly the type of person who would be the most feared human in East Texas: a capable Black man with training and honed skills, who had an extensive education in a variety of fields besides political science, including survival and self-defense, and was able to think for himself. He was accustomed to command, he had the bearing of an officer, he was quiet spoken, and he was impossible to intimidate. White power meant absolutely nothing to him, except he didn't want to draw attention. He just wanted to teach, stay to himself, be humble and quiet. That's all he wanted. He didn't want a woman, a loud lifestyle, or a car. He outgrew those things on the ground in North Vietnam, trying to rescue those poor pilots. He wanted to make a decent living and mind his money. It kept his mind off some of the things he'd lived through, and that was better. Henniker had come to recognize that the world's safety depended on education. Educated kids able to think and reason were the ones who could prevent war. All war was the result of ignorant people doing ignorant things, and the only real defense was education.

Besides, he enjoyed working with kids. They had energy, they were creative, they played. The difference between a kid and an adult was play. And their play, if you shaped it right, could lead them to important questions, and more importantly, to answers.

Henniker was used to moving into new neighborhoods. He'd moved often in the military, and he knew how to make friends. In the early years, he'd had a dear wife to move with him, and to wait for him to come back from deployments to dangerous places. They had loved one another deeply, but not well enough to prevent the breast cancer that claimed her life. Childless, Celia had died at just thirty-four, and he had mourned her for the last nine years, lying awake at night sometimes to remember how she had held his hand and encouraged him to do more, be more, to get his graduate degree, to think about a future she might not share.

He wasn't interested in friends these days, and only slightly more in his family obligations. He was interested in doing his job. He did not want a lot of attention at any time, and especially not now. Sometimes on his slow drives back to Whitmire from San Augustine, he listened to the National Public Radio station. The radio signal came and went, but it kept him up-to-date with the world. Now that he was actually teaching, the chess game of politics held a professional fascination for him, and National Public Radio was a reliable and interesting source.

You could not say the same for the *Beaumont Enterprise* newspaper, which appeared to be struggling to stay afloat mostly by cutting its news staff, or the *Whitmire Standard*, which was so parochial. But he wanted to avoid entanglement with people if he could. He'd done a lot for the hegemony of the Western White world in poor places around the planet, and none of it had been conclusive or original. Spreading education, food, and medicine would have been original. Shooting people was not original and accomplished nothing.

Sometimes he thought he might finish his PhD in political science. He had the GI bill and a standing promise of scholarship at Case Western, but it meant having to hassle with bureaucracies again, and he didn't want more of that. He just wanted to be alone and not be bothered and to go about saving the world one child at a time.

More than anything, he wanted to mourn for Celia.

CHAPTER

THIRTEEN

Another brutal interview with Mrs. Jane Elkins. He stood. She sat in front of her eight-foot-tall antique Chippendale secretary desk and behind a matching Chippendale table. He was not allowed to stand on the costly Persian rug in front of the desk, but he noted with a sense of irony the ball-and-claw feet of both pieces of furniture. Typical for her to prefer predatory claws in this room that smelled of genteel Victorian dust and lemon-scented furniture spray. BoMac knew the interview in her home office—a room at the back of the house where hired help and merchants could be met without allowing them into the front part of the house—would be bad. It was hard to pull off a "white" sale in January in Whitmire, since exactly only one store sold the kinds of sheets and towels that were typical of that sale, and there was no snow. The President's Day sale was likewise a flop. The post office and bank were closed that Monday, but everybody else was open. Even the schools. It was just another ordinary day everywhere, and was the day Mrs. Elkins wanted to interview him about his future with the *Whitmire Standard*.

"Somebody told me you were in the county clerk's office looking up my deed records," she started off. "Why?"

"I was sorting through all the prominent people in Whitmire, looking for family relationships and property associations. I think I don't know as much about this community as I should if I don't know whose granddaddy sold the family farm to whom."

"Whom?"

"Whom."

"Every single person in Whitmire except you would say 'who.'"

"And they'd be grammatically incorrect, even if they were the English teachers at the high school or the librarians at the memorial library."

She waved her hand at him, like she was shooing away a fly.

"You made it into the black in December," she continued, looking again at the financial accounts, "but so far this month you've already wiped out all that profit. What are you going to do to keep from going out of business at the end of this month?"

"January is a tough month," he said. "We've got the Miss Sweetgum County pageant at the end of the month, of course, but that ad revenue will all come in February. We have Valentine's Day in February, and our three clothing stores might do something. The car dealers. Mostly, though, people will get their Christmas bills in January and not be able to spend much during February."

"I'm not looking for excuses, Mr. Maclean. I'm looking for solutions."

"Yes, ma'am."

"The *Whitmire Standard* has been a part of this community since before the Civil War, but times change. Maybe it has outlived its purpose."

"How would we know?"

"You will not know, Mr. Maclean. That decision is mine."

"Yes, ma'am."

So far, he had heard nothing new. This was almost verbatim the same interview he had heard every January for the past three years. Basically, it was comforting in an odd way that she wasn't coming up with new stuff. He could live through the old stuff, and money would start flowing in Whitmire again in the spring, when the winter rains stopped and logging could resume.

Except readers bought groceries every week. So the grocery ads were an integral part of his survival at the paper.

"Why don't we look at some of these other newspapers around the country, see what they're doing?" Mrs. Elkins asked him.

"I go to the press association meetings," he replied. "Everybody says the same thing. Some publishers are mailing the grocery store ads free to their entire counties, but the grocery stores aren't paying more for that. I'd need some help at the office if we tried to create any new products, like a special monthly historical review of the county. I think that's a good angle for readership, but I can't do it myself. I'm already working seventy and eighty hours a week."

Mrs. Elkins snorted.

"This backwater doesn't have a history. Damned jayhawkers refused to defend the South in the Civil War, and then died of yellow fever. Served them right. And nothing much has changed since. Forget the history thing."

"Your family figures prominently in that history," he said quietly. "And it's all good, as far as I can tell. Some positive press might be good for the bank, and all."

She looked up at him for the first time. He thought there was a glint in her eye, but it was quickly snuffed out. Despite her reputation, he realized, she would be a really bad poker player. She was easy to read. And that made sense. How could a woman of this wealth and influence keep from being bored absolutely to death? And there he had hit on it. She drew breath because of her pride, and nothing else. She had nothing else to live for.

He'd start making some inquiries into her own family in Houston, see if he could find something to make her feel better about herself. After all, she owned the Elkins name and property in Whitmire, but it was her husband and his prominent family who were fondly remembered. A call to the Houston Post, another to the Houston Chronicle, and he'd have some photocopies or microfilms from their morgues. Or he could go down to Houston. And maybe to Galveston. Somewhere he'd picked up rumors of connections in Galveston. He'd figure out how to squeeze all this in between the obits and the quilting clubs and the grocery ads. He'd do it.

"I'll give you until the end of February, Mr. Maclean, to show a profit. If you aren't in the black by March 1, I will need to look around for someone who can get me there. Is that understood?"

"Yes, ma'am," he said, just as he said every month.

"Your year-end figures are not going to be great," she continued. "I'm not running a charity here. If you can't make money, you don't have a reason to exist. And this newspaper doesn't have a reason to exist. I need to see profit."

She slapped the financial report on the table and looked away. "Sarah, get in here," she commanded.

Sarah Bibber, the *Standard* secretary/spy, came sheepishly into the room.

"I've asked Mrs. Warren to be a witness to this statement," she continued. "Sarah, did you overhear what I just said to Mr. Maclean?"

"Yes, ma'am."

"You heard me tell him that he would be fired at the end of February if he was not showing a profit?"

"Yes, ma'am."

"Mr. Maclean, do you have anything to say?"

"Of course I do. I wish you would use your great power to make the rains stop so the loggers could get to the woods. If they're not cutting trees, no money at all is being made in this town. So just this year, please, dry out the woods so our loggers can work and so I can keep my job. If they don't work, they don't buy, and the merchants don't spend their money buying ads in the paper. It all comes down to rain, Mrs. Elkins."

"You are making an excuse for your own shoddy work," she huffed.

"I like being a journalist and being close to the lifeblood of the community," BoMac replied. "But I don't think I have the power to stop the rain. I'm sure you do. So stop it."

And with that, he excused himself and left the house without looking back.

With Sarah Bibber out of the newspaper office for a few minutes, he'd be able to make some phone calls without being overheard. He rushed to his office and closed the door, first calling the morgue at the Houston Post to ask for anything on the marriage of Michael Campbell Elkins in the 1950s. They said they would look, but they might like him to sign a cooperative agreement with the paper to supply them news from time to time. He agreed.

Then he called Ellen Etheridge's apartment.

She was at school, of course, which he'd momentarily forgotten. He hoped to talk to her in the evening after Sarah Bibber had gone home, or back to her nest, or wherever a gorgon went. And sure enough, seven hours later Ellen called.

"Hey," she said, sounding happy.

"Hi," he said. They had been talking for months, and they found a lot to talk about. Her classes in the ninth grade at the high school, his work at the paper, his observations about the people, her observations about his observations. The conversations were easy and continuous. They had been out a few times, driven to foreign countries together, like Beaumont, Texas and Lufkin, Texas. Mrs. Elkins had still not followed through on her threat to fire him, but she repeated it at every monthly meeting when he finished in the red. The first time she'd threatened he had become nervous, but now it had become yet another common thing—and something he and Ellen could laugh about.

The third time they left town together, however, Commissioner George Brown had taken him aside at a meeting and quietly told him that the only way to keep things quiet was to, quote, "cross three rivers," un-quote, before meeting up. "You cross three rivers in Texas, you can do anything you want with anybody and nobody will find out. Less than three rivers, and it's the talk of the town."

"What are you talking about?" BoMac had asked.

"You and Ellen Etheridge," grinned Brown.

"What about her?"

"You must be screwing her because you were with her in Lufkin last week. Boy, that's only one river away. I've already told you people in this town have small minds. They hear about the two of you together so close by, and they will pass judgment. I'm your friend here, you piece of shit. Just be forewarned." He paused and leaned back, squinting at BoMac through his good eye. "I'm not just your friend. I'm your best friend"—he grinned again—because I'm your only friend." He gave BoMac a tap on the shoulder and walked to his Precinct Two position behind the desk just as the clock ticked to ten, the official starting time for the Commissioner's Court.

BoMac tried to keep his feelings out of his face, but it was hard to do. Then he thought, so what? It didn't matter what people thought. The rumor mill was busier than a Singer sewing machine.

A common theme between Ellen and him was how little they actually knew about the community. Neither of them was native to rural East Texas. He only had his experiences in the piedmont of Virginia, and she with the high-White, rich, and suburban city of Sugar Land, southwest of Houston. They were strangers in rural East Texas, and they knew it. So, they had a lot to talk about, much of it couched in complete wonder. "It's like a frontier," said BoMac over the phone. "I thought civilization had spread all over this country, but some of these people . . ." His voice trailed off.

"I have their kids," she said. "Today I learned that one of my students lives with six other kids in a one-room house with dirt floors. They spread hay over the dirt every Saturday, and the dad somewhere got a monkey that lives in the rafters of the house."

"A monkey?" BoMac was incredulous.

"A monkey," she replied. "There's no reason to doubt it."

"I went to a fire last week," said BoMac, "and learned the true meaning of a dogtrot house. It's two cabins joined by a walkway under one roof. The walkway is for the dogs. The old man kept his goats in one of the cabins, and the rest of his family in the other one. There was an outhouse in the back, hand dug and not very deep. The chickens roosted in it. I guess every morning they go out there, do their business, and gather the eggs for breakfast. Sort of a hand-to-mouth existence."

A comfortable giggle came over the line, brightening his whole world. What a nice person, he thought to himself.

"But the fire was bad for them," he added. "Any fire in a place like that is bad. I heard their church was already taking care of them, but they didn't have much to lose."

"Sometimes I think the people who are worst off in the world are the ones who don't go to church," she said quietly. "Nobody comes to their rescue when they're in trouble."

Despite the rumor mill, they agreed to meet at Dairy Queen in the afternoons when she got off work. It was obvious to everyone they liked one another, and the one women's store in town began stocking clothing for a trousseau. They all knew she would buy her wedding gown in Sugar Land, with her mother, but having a nice selection of traveling clothes and lingerie in her size was always a good idea. Patty Cannon, who had worked at the store for most of a generation, had a good eye for women's sizes and tastes, and she placed her orders appropriately. She figured out they were meeting at Dairy Queen and often stopped by on her way home to observe them. It would be an expensive wedding, she concluded, because the bride obviously had family money. Nobody could afford those shoes on a teacher's salary, she knew. In fact, many of the local teachers were collecting food stamps or other government assistance if they had dependents. Nobody got rich off of teaching, and few students got smart. Patty figured it was a fair trade. Who needed smart children?

In 1921, a Texas A&M agronomist told civic-minded leaders in Whitmire that hogs could survive on pine needles. Pine needles were a foot deep in the woods, so they raised the huge sum of ten thousand dollars for a champion boar to improve the breed of hogs wandering the gardens and streets of the community. Two men rode the train to Pennsylvania, where they purchased a state champion Duroc boar. He was brought back, turned loose, and promptly disappeared into the forest. About once a year someone would spot him trotting from thicket to thicket. They named him "Pathfinder."

CHAPTER

FOURTEEN

Jesse Grinder finally had transportation. It had taken him three months, but his boss at the used car lot, Bob McKinney, allowed him to have a twelve-year-old Ford pickup with a dented fender and bent rear bumper. It was not much of a truck, but it was a truck. He could drive to work and back, and that saved him a lot of effort. Of course, he was in debt, too. Now he needed to pay the note on the truck as well as what he gave his momma. They were still paying off the doctor's bills for his wreck and would keep doing that for another five years. Minimum. He was still living in the trailer park. Well, hidden away at the back end of the trailer park away from everybody else. But the truck meant he could get to the locksmith shop a whole lot easier, and it also meant that Wilburn, the locksmith he helped out, didn't need to drive him home in the evenings.

He'd enjoyed the free ride, but he could tell that Wilburn Hall's heart was not in it. Wilburn did it as a sort of obligation when he'd rather be doing other things, so he grinned when Jesse told him he'd finally got a truck.

"Good for you," Wilburn beamed. "I'm happy for you. Don't wreck this one."

"Oh, I won't," said Jesse, hoping that was true. Walking about fourteen miles a day had been good for him and he was lean. Also, his brain seemed to be working better. Most weeks he could go without having one of his spells. So far, he'd not had another one while he was driving, only that one time when he was out delivering McKinney's brown paper package to Mrs. Johnson. He had not been back out there after the shotgun incident because Bob McKinney claimed he enjoyed doing it himself. But Jesse delivered a lot of packages all over west Piney Creek to houses that were not nearly so grand as Congressman Rip Johnson's. McKinney

75

always gave him a different car off the lot, and always told him the same thing: "If you get arrested, you're on your own. Got that?"

Jesse had no idea what he was talking about. He assumed it meant that he was to stay out of trouble and not get into any fights or rape the clients, and he obeyed those instructions. He also made his deliveries.

Some of the women who came out to meet him in the driveway were pretty fat, which he liked. Some were pretty thin. One woman might have weighed no more than eighty pounds, and her ribs showed under her tee shirt where she had tied it up. Her hip bones stuck out above her cut-off jeans and her thighs looked like little sticks of dry spaghetti. She didn't smile. She just snatched the package and handed him an envelope with a kind of desperate look, then hurried inside.

Most of the women never spoke to him. None of them. Not even to say "thank you." Most of them didn't smile. None of them showed him their boobs, either. He got the feeling that he was invisible to them.

But he'd learned a lot hanging out around Wilburn Hall's locksmith shop. He'd learned how simple it was to jimmy a lock, for example. You didn't really need to figure out the whole combination of pins on most locks. If you got three of the four or even five pins right, it'd open. And he practiced on the lock of his own trailer until he had it down.

Then one night after he'd been sitting in the dark and he'd thrown his empty bean can into the unused bedroom—throwing it hard against the far wall so it wouldn't roll back toward the door—he thought he might try out his skills around the neighborhood. He walked up to the trailer park office like he was just taking an evening stroll, but there was nobody around. Everybody was asleep or inside watching television, the blue flicker of their screens bouncing on drawn shades. The park manager's office was dark. Jesse didn't know where the manager lived, but it was obviously not in his office. He figured the manager must have a different home somewhere else.

He strolled by the office a few times looking things over. A hundred feet away from the office, out over the main drive into the sparse circle of mobile homes, was a lone security light, but the light didn't get up under the shade of the carport awning over the office door. He walked around for a bit, like it was the most natural thing in the world, but nobody saw him. He went back to the office and slipped into the shadow and up the three steps to the door. He had his tools in his hand already, and in about a minute he was inside the dark office.

He hadn't thought about that. If he turned on the lights, someone might see and get suspicious, and it was so dark inside that he couldn't see anything. Well, ain't I dumb, he said to himself, slipping out and re-locking the door. Next time he would bring a flashlight.

Still, for a first time it was exciting. He felt it in his groin, like that big girl Sue stroking him with her eager touch. Back at his own trailer, he took off all his clothes and lay down on the bare mattress.

Eventually he went to sleep dreaming of Sue, who had somehow become that little short woman Annabeth with the toddler, the one he saw his first day in the park.

Wonder what she did with that manager? he asked himself as he drifted off to sleep.

CHAPTER FIFTEEN

Tropical Storm Beryl lingered over Deep East Texas for three days in late April like an unwelcome maiden aunt, raining steadily. The pine-covered hills loomed darkly in the overcast, vegetable gardens drowned, and great swaths of clear-cut timberland shed millions of tons of virgin topsoil into creeks and lakes. By the time she moved on to visit her lugubrious cousins in Louisiana, she had dropped twenty-three inches of rain, leaving behind a morass of bogged vehicles, washed-out bridges, and ruptured dams.

In Whitmire High School on Monday during the storm, with half the students unable to get to class because of rising water, new social studies teacher Charles Henniker asked his tenth graders to enumerate the ways this storm could affect the local economy.

His students had become accustomed to his creative thinking and adored him for it. They would rather go to his classes than stay home, and that made Henniker extremely unpopular with other teachers. They were jealous that a first-year teacher could have that kind of influence over children they had carefully instructed in obedience to authority, and the smarter ones worried he would break the tradition of privilege by getting students to think for themselves. For Henniker, it was about not being bored to death with a state-mandated curriculum designed to subdue independent thought. He covered the mandated materials, but he related them to the lives his youngsters were living. Hence the assignment: think of the economic impact of a storm of this magnitude.

"So how do we measure some of these effects?" he asked them.

One student suggested that the rushing water in the creeks was really muddy, so the class brainstormed why it was important to protect the soil and how to measure the suspended particles in the floodwater using mason jars from their mothers' pantries. Another suggested that the flow rate of the water needed to be measured in order to estimate the amount of dirt being washed away, and they talked about how to do that. Henniker noted that during the days of sailing ships they used something called a "log" they would throw over the side and then count the number of rope knots that passed out during a known period of time. Possibly something like that could help.

Several of the students, including a tiny Black girl with wild curls bunched into tuffs on either side of her head and a cute smile, said they needed to talk to the math teacher about how to measure water flow.

"Also get him to talk about turbulence," Henniker said. "That water is twisting all around. The amount of sediment in it might be affected by where you gather your sample."

"Oh right," said several bright-eyed students. "Right, right."

"This sounds like science, not economics," commented the tiny girl.

"It is," replied Henniker, "and we need math to make sense of it. Math is our tool to understand, but science is what we call that understanding."

"Huh," she grumped. "I thought this was economics."

"Economics is a science," he replied with a grin. "All knowledge is part of all other knowledge. You don't know what you need to know if you don't understand it. That means you've got to be able to talk about what you know, which is why you study English."

"Tell that to old Ms. Newton. That crazy woman is nothing but worksheets. Nothing!" the tiny girl said.

"We could put a bicycle wheel with paddles on it in the water and measure the spin to get an idea," said one boy with big glasses. "I have a bicycle wheel. What do you think we could use as paddles?"

"Does your bicycle wheel need some kind of support for the axle?" asked Henniker.

"Well, yeah, or maybe I could get close enough to the water to hold it myself."

"Sounds dangerous," said Henniker. "What do the rest of you think?"

The class proceeded in that manner until he just took all of them down to the library. Some would research turbulence and water flow. Some would see what they could find about measuring suspended soil particles. Some would figure out how to measure the depth of the water so they could calculate volume moving through. Some began looking at soil preservation and the causes of the dust bowl in the 1930s. Some looked at copies of the *Whitmire Standard* for grocery ads and copy prices. Everyone expected the prices to be higher since no trucks were resupplying the stores. They made a list of common items: bread, ground meat, chicken legs, gasoline, sodas, gummy bears. The way the group broke into collaborating teams amazed him. He'd seen recruits showing up for basic training who had no idea how to collaborate. Remarkable, he thought to himself. If you just give them a chance to think—

Henniker was pleased with himself. He thought he was finally getting to teach the way teaching ought to be, and he enjoyed watching all of the students working together, excited, sharing information, even shouting at one another.

The noise evoked stern looks from the school librarian, but when two of the boys began shouting to one another through the stacks of books about what they were finding, she dropped her glasses to the end of her nose and stared at Henniker. He ignored her, and she got up from behind her little fortress of a desk and disappeared.

Henniker had closed and locked his room at the end of the day and was just leaving with his bag of teaching materials and notes when he was accosted by a gruff voice from behind.

"What the hell were you doing taking those kids to the library?" It was Mr. E. P. Allen, the principal.

"We are using the rain to teach economics," Henniker replied, a little testily, and moved on.

"Get back here," demanded Allen. "I want to talk to you in my office."

"Now," he said a moment later, sitting down with a huff in his overstuffed office chair, not offering Henniker a seat, his bulk audibly squeezing air from the complaining cushions, "we have state testing next month. I want every student in this school taking practice tests every day until then. They have no business in the library."

"I prefer to educate," Henniker said.

"I prefer that our school be recognized by the State of Texas as an exemplary educational institution," Allen retorted. "That means the students ace the tests. Nothing is allowed to distract us from that. Do you understand?"

"I think I understand education," Henniker said, then decided to keep his mouth shut for the rest of the interview.

"I'm not going to debate educational theory with you," Allen said. "But I don't think you do understand education." The principal glared at him. "If you did, you'd keep those students practicing their tests. Your salary is tied to their performance. My salary is tied to your students' performance. Every teacher in this school gets paid on the basis of our school's overall test performance. Stop slacking off and do your duty. I want those kids doing practice tests every day, all day, in every class, until they learn to

81

ace the exam. That's education. Acing the exam. It's all the state expects, and it's all this school expects. Forget the rain, the library, everything. Nothing matters but the state test. Either you will be a team player, or I will get you off the team."

Henniker stood with his mouth shut, wondering why any educator would think taking old exams would teach students to analyze information or learn history.

"We are near the end of the fifth six-weeks of the year," Allen continued when Henniker stayed silent. "You've had almost twelve weeks to teach them 'Economics with Emphasis on the Free Enterprise System and Its Benefits' as required by the state of Texas, and the second half of US history since 1877. Now they get ready for the tests. Only the tests matter. Each day, you give a test and then go over the answers. Got it? If there's time, you start the next test. I want them to do a hundred tests before the exam. How many have they done?"

Allen reached into his desk drawer and pulled out a can of snuff, unscrewing the lid. He put a wad of the fiberglass-laced tobacco product into his cheek and pulled a white foam cup over from the front of the desk. Henniker knew it was for his spit. He hoped he'd be gone before Allen did that. The idea of keeping a cup full of tobacco-stained spit around on your desk, little brown beads weeping through the flimsy polystyrene, was disgusting.

"So? How many?"

This time the principal glared at Henniker, his left cheek bulging as he worked the tobacco.

"About ten," Henniker finally admitted.

"Uh-huh," said Allen, nodding and reaching for the cup. He squeezed a stream of brown juice from his mouth, causing the spit in the cup to foam up, the wintergreen odor of the flavored tobacco cascading out into the office's stuffy atmosphere. "How many of your students could tell me who Samuel J. Tilden was? Do you yourself know?" Allen paused, staring at him. "You've had your chance, Henniker. Your kids better outperform the state average. I'll do better than that. Your kids better outperform the state's average by twenty percent. If every single one of your students fails to achieve at least an 80 on this year's exam, you're history. Got it?"

He did not look at Henniker this time when he spit. Instead, he swiveled his groaning office chair to stare out the window at the line of students huddled out of the torrential downpour under the walkway awning waiting for the buses, watching without expression as two senior boys pulled up a ninth-grade girl's blouse to show off her bra, one of them snapping the elastic as she screamed and tried to get away.

"And I'm not happy about your classroom management, either," Allen went on. "Absolutely too many of your students are allowed to go to the bathroom. I've already told you that your quota for bathroom breaks is two. No more than two students are allowed to go to the bathroom during any one period. They have to hold it, and they have to concentrate on those tests. I'm going to write you up for letting three students go on Friday after lunch, and I'm going to write you up again for violating school policy about mandatory test-training today. Have you got anything to say? No? Then the next step is to assign you to remedial training for classroom skills. You'll report at 6 a.m. tomorrow to watch the video again, and to take the test on it. If you violate school policy again, you will be terminated, and a substitute teacher will take your class. Obey the rules and support the team. It's in your contract. If you don't believe me, read it. In fact, I'm not required to give you a third chance, so think of this as a gift."

Henniker turned and walked from the office. The office door had been left ajar, and Allen's secretary averted her eyes when Henniker walked by, a smirk twisting the hatchet scar of her smile.

Before he escaped into the hall, however, Allen called to him again.

"I forgot to tell you that you have bus duty for the rest of the month. Be here at 6 a.m. tomorrow morning and also plan to stay after school."

Ms. Hatchet-smile dared a triumphant glance at him, then dropped her eyes to her work.

"Terrific," muttered Henniker to himself. "And I suppose tomorrow he will add cafeteria duty."

Allen did not add cafeteria duty the next day, for the next day was when Tropical Storm Beryl's water finally broke into Toby Creek and the principal could not get to school. By 6 a.m. on Tuesday, the creek was four feet out of its banks even though it had stopped raining during the night. By noon, it was ten feet over its banks, and rising. Allen was trapped at home, and his phone was out. All over the county, waterlogged ground was releasing its grip on trees, and they were falling across power lines, shutting down power and telephone to large segments of the population. Allen's family farm was in the dark, cut off from the outside world.

The school was cut off, too. Every road leading into Whitmire was under water, and the state had closed highways. Brother Lyncefield Burk, the preacher at First Fundamentalist Church, called for a prayer meeting at noon to ask for deliverance from the rising waters, and all of the teachers except Henniker went. He had not joined a local church, but he was pretty sure First Fundamentalist would not be on his list. Besides, he had cafeteria duty because he, the cook, and the janitor were the only adults left at school with several dozen students while everyone else went to the prayer meeting. Henniker realized the school had no way of knowing which students were where.

"Oh great," he thought. "And I'm here, so if anything happens, it will be my fault."

The prayer meeting lasted two hours, and then students and teachers with solemn faces began arriving back at the school, almost all of them headed to the cafeteria for a cold lunch. It was 3 p.m. before anyone realized that Annie Putnam, the junior varsity head cheerleader, was missing.

By late in the afternoon on Tuesday, every bridge into the city of Whitmire was flooded by angry brown water frothing and foaming down both forks of Toby Creek: Little Toby to the north and east pummeled clay banks and toppled centuries-old cypresses, and Big Toby to the west and south thundered through the lower neighborhoods, flooding the Walmart and Dairy Queen. If you were not already in Whitmire, you would not be getting into the city. Even boat traffic was impossible in the raging floodwaters. The two forks of Toby Creek could be heard clearly in the background over all the hushed murmurings of students and teachers, but when roll was taken for the final period of the day and Annie was not found, panic gripped the school.

Ms. Hatchet-smile, who had assumed authority in Principal Allen's absence, called the Whitmire City Police, 9-1-1, the sheriff's office, and finally, Annie's mother, Miranda, a teller at the bank.

Miranda's shrieking over Hatchet-smile's phone could be heard clearly in the hall outside, and it was only moments later that the distraught mother roared up to the front door of the school, leapt out leaving the car running, blocking the entire bus lane, and came screaming into the building. Henniker, whose room was at the far end of the hall from the office, heard the commotion and glanced out his classroom door to see her flailing two hundred pounds of powdered and plastered body on ridiculously small high heels into the office, screaming for the mercy of Jesus. Other teachers along the hall abandoned their rooms and students to go help, while Henniker just firmly closed the door and turned back to his seventh-period class.

"So, we know how much water fell on the thousand square miles of this county," he said, resuming his discussion. "How do we calculate the economic cost to our future? Do you think this relates in any way to the benefits of our free enterprise system?"

But students had heard, and recognized, Annie Putnam's mother, and they all knew that Annie was missing. The blonde, blue-eyed cheerleader with the fabulous makeup and the sexy clothes just bordering on scandal was the school's most popular girl. Everybody who didn't hate her for being beautiful loved her for being beautiful, and that was all of the males and about a quarter of the females. None of them cared about the rain anymore. They wanted to talk about Annie's kidnapping ("and worse," some of the older boys whispered to themselves).

All of Whitmire's cops showed up at the school a few moments later. Both of them.

The police chief, Edward "Trey" Green, III, was stranded in Piney Creek thirty miles away, where he was caught by the floods, unable to get home.

Lucy Dougherty was fourteen when she married. She and her twenty-six-year-old husband wisely decided to delay having children until she finished high school. He operated the movie theater and sold popcorn, candy, sodas, and automatic weapons. His best seller was the MAC-10 in .45 caliber. Lucy was smart and beautiful, and to see her married was to know the look of joy. A minor, she had to get him to write her an excuse note whenever she missed school. But she caught him secretly dating several ninth-grade girls, and the sound of their confrontation made a war movie sound tame.

85

CHAPTER SIXTEEN

The Justice of the Peace read the affidavit from Miranda Putnam accusing Charles Henniker of kidnapping and rape and then went home to cook dinner. She was hungry and loathed waiting for the police to bring in the suspect.

Sure enough, Henniker was booked into the county jail as soon as the last bus departed the campus. He had been read the Miranda warning, however, and knew from experience to keep his mouth shut no matter how angered he was by the baseless charge. Although he could have physically destroyed the two policemen, he allowed them to handcuff him and duck his head down so he could sit in the filthy rear seat of their patrol car while they muttered to themselves. At the jail, he met Sheriff Lee Davis, a short, pudgy man missing part of a digit on his right hand, who told Henniker that the JP might or might not come in for a while after dinner to tend to business. If she didn't come in, he would have to spend the night.

"Do I get a phone call?" Henniker asked, wondering if his cousin Calvin in San Augustine would come get him, then realizing he couldn't because of the flood.

"After we get you booked in," the sheriff replied.

He turned Henniker over to the county jailer, who led him into a small examining room and told him to strip, snapping on a pair of blue gloves. Henniker's underwear was bagged separately, and then his body was carefully investigated, including his body cavities. His genitals were swabbed, and the swabs collected in a numbered evidence bag. He remembered feeling thankful that the deputy examined his mouth before he investigated his rectum, and not vice versa.

"At least there's that," he thought.

Eventually, stripped down and clad in an orange jail jumpsuit, he was led into the hallway outside the booking room and told he could make one phone call on the ancient dial-up phone with a short, armored cord, but when he picked the phone up to call Calvin, there was no dial tone. All the phones were out because of the flood.

"No line," he said to the jailer. "Phone's dead."

"Heh heh heh," chortled the pudgy deputy. "We know, ha ha."

"So now what?"

"You want your eggs fried or scrambled in the morning?"

"I'm spending the night?"

"Probably. But I'm just joking about eggs. You don't get no eggs in jail, MISTER Henniker," he sneered, emphasizing the "mister." "And now you've had your phone call, I don't have to let you have another one. Not my fault all the phones are out, so you are most likely going to be the guest of the county. Hang up and come on."

The electronic lock clacked like a dry-fired gun when there's no shell in the chamber, and the jailer escorted him through the first set of doors. A second click, and he was ushered into what the jailer called the drunk tank. It was occupied by one other prisoner, an elderly man with wild white hair and a scrawny beard, who stared at him.

"Ain't got no drunks in here tonight, yet," the jailer said, "so we just holding everybody here until the judge sets bond. Isaac," he said to the old man, "this here's your cell mate. Name's Henniker. You two get along now, you hear?" And he left.

The holding cell was capacious and completely exposed to the on-duty jailers and anybody else who wandered into the jailer's office. A stainless-steel toilet unit sat in one corner, offering no privacy whatsoever.

"Glad I don't have a shy bladder," thought Henniker, studying the old man, who was studying him.

Finally, he spoke.

"Hi," said Henniker. "Your name's Isaac?"

"Knight to f3," said the old man.

"What?"

"I said knight to f3. King's side knight. You play chess, don't you?"

"Oh, ok. So, you're white. That means I'm black."

Isaac looked at him like he was a lunatic.

Henniker loved chess when he was in high school. It was exactly the geeky kind of thing he liked to do. "Then king's knight to f6," he replied.

"Ha!" said Isaac. "Old trick." He looked at Henniker and scratched his chin. "What's he gonna do?" he asked with a stare at no one, and then, "pawn to c4."

"Um hmm," mumbled Henniker, visualizing the board. "Pawn to g6."

"Aha," Isaac said, "old Grünfeld Defense. Then queen's knight to c3." When Henniker didn't speak right away, Isaac added, "You don't mind me saying queen's knight or king's knight? Throw some people off."

"It's useful at the beginning of the game. Hard enough to keep it all straight in your head."

"So, are you lucky, or what?"

"Apparently not."

"Well?"

"What?"

"Move."

"Oh," Henniker said. "Bishop to g7."

"Sheesh. What for you do that?"

A minute or two elapsed in silence.

"Pawn to d4," Isaac said.

Henniker studied the board in his mind. Isaac now had two pawns side by side in the middle of the board, supported by two knights. Not quite centered. One square off to the queen's side. It was a clever opening. But his black king could castle, and Isaac's white king could not. Castling was nearly always the right thing to do. In war, you put your king in a castle and defend him.

"Castle," said Henniker.

"Who the fuck do you think you are, goy boy? Bobby Fischer?"

"No. And you're not Donald Byrne either," Henniker retorted, smiling, "but you play like him and I'll beat you like Fischer did."

Isaac stood up and stomped off across the cell, sitting on a metal plank set into the wall that served as a cot at night. He turned his back angrily to Henniker and said nothing for a long time, his arms folded across his chest.

Henniker watched the deputies and jailers through the bars and bulletproof glass partition. He spotted cameras in the corners of the cell and an intercom speaker set behind a heavy grille in the ceiling, about nine feet up.

"Shtik drek," Isaac finally said to no one.

He turned around and glared at Henniker from one eye.

"Shvantz," he spat.

"It's a famous game," Henniker said. "Played in 1956 between two of Collins's chess prodigies in Brooklyn. Fischer and Byrne. Fischer was thirteen years old."

"Collins I know. Him I studied with," Isaac said. "He would not waste time on you. And he was Fischer mentor, not teacher. He fed Fischer, set up games, but Fischer was ahead of him."

"I studied the game in high school. Fischer's queen sacrifice was magnificent."

"It was drek," said Isaac, "but it caught Byrne by surprise. Fischer, he let queen sit there and sit there, and Byrne would not take it. And finally, it was too much, and he took it. After that, Fischer one more move needed, and he had it. He stay one move ahead of Byrne, and he windmill Byrne into checkmate."

"Stacking those bishops, that rook, and that knight amazed me," Henniker said, reimagining the end game. "Brilliant."

"Bah, not so much. Fischer had plenty more brilliant moves. But he always punk. Good riddance."

"Yeah, his later years were embarrassing."

"Once a punk, always a punk."

Isaac had cooled off, but Henniker wondered how mercurial he would be. He also wondered whether he would be able to call a lawyer. He had not even been charged, yet. He was completely in limbo, jailed but not charged, arrested on some bogus claim, locked up with a Yiddish-speaking lunatic. And what was all this about some girl raped? Surely not. Several strangers entered the jailer's office and stared at him through the partitions. One of them wore a state trooper uniform, one wore a cheap suit with a narrow tie, a plainclothes cop or prosecutor. They spoke to one another. Reading their lips, Henniker could tell that the trooper said, "That's him." And the plainclothes said, "I don't like the looks of him."

A few minutes later, an overweight middle-aged woman entered, looking intently at Henniker through the glass.

"Why are you in here?" he asked Isaac as the crowd in the jailer's office began gesticulating.

"Every Tuesday I walk by their stupid church and laugh at them," Isaac said. "And every Tuesday they arrest for loitering. But how can you be loitering if you keep walking? Still, they arrest me. Every Tuesday. And they bring me here, and they give me ham sandwich for dinner, with white bread and cheap mayonnaise, and they give me bacon for breakfast, and they laugh at me, and then they let me go."

"Do you live in town?"

"You call this town?"

"Well, it's where we are."

"You call this living?"

"My wife would have hated it here," Henniker said. "She would have felt all closed in, claustrophobic, like she was suffocating."

"Her you listen to," said Isaac. "Listen. Leave this sty for pigs." His command of English did not clue him to Henniker's use of the past tense, so he didn't realize that Henniker's wife Celia was dead.

"Why don't you go?" asked Henniker.

"Go where? This as far I can get from synagogue. Sixty mile any direction."

"You're Jewish." It sounded like a statement, but he'd meant it as a question.

"I am Jew who studies God," Isaac said. "You know proverb: The closer to synagogue, the farther from God. This as far as I can get."

"Are you finding God here?"

"Not me. And not no one else, I think, either. I love trees and green things. They make me happy. But God, I no find him on these streets."

"Henniker!" a voice screeched over the intercom.

Henniker stood up.

"Come to the door. We are taking you out."

He obeyed, having no other choice, and the obese jailer waddled toward him. When he was in place, the cell door clicked, and the jailer pulled it open.

"This way," he snarled, pointing Henniker toward the barred doors at the end of the corridor.

He was led into a small courtroom, actually just a desk with file cabinets against the wall. The jailer stood with him and the judge came in. Justice of the Peace Teresa Lewis was about five-five with breasts the size of peach baskets. They were so large that they'd be dangerous to innocent bystanders if she whirled around suddenly.

"Mr. Henniker," she said after studying him with obvious distaste. "You have been arrested on suspicion of being involved in the disappearance and possible rape of Annie Putnam, and for using profanity to a peace officer."

Henniker said nothing.

"Do you wish to give a statement?"

"You mean, in writing?"

"If you prefer. But you can tell me in your own words."

"Can I have a lawyer present?"

"Do you have one?"

Shit, he thought.

"No, ma'am."

"Can you afford a lawyer?"

"I think so."

"Have you called a lawyer yet?"

"No, ma'am. I tried but the phones are out."

"I see," said the judge. "Well, I will not formally charge you at this time until you have been interviewed by the deputy and you have given a statement, but I will remand you to personal recognizance while we sort all this out. Apparently, the girl has been found."

"Whew," said Henniker. "That's a relief. I'm glad for her and her parents."

"Yes," said the judge, raising an eyebrow. "Mr. Henniker, what church do you and your wife attend?"

"I am no longer married, your honor. My wife died of breast cancer about nine years ago. I moved here from Cleveland," he replied. "I'm not sure I will stay, so I haven't joined a church yet." He kept all expression out of his face and tone. In this town he thought it was probably a good idea not to discuss his lack of religious conviction.

"I see." Her face resumed its appearance of distaste. "Cleveland is fairly close by. You could commute to work here if you wanted."

"No, ma'am. I meant Cleveland, Ohio. Where I was doing graduate work."

"Oh, I see," she said. "A word of advice, Mr. Henniker. It doesn't help you out at all to sound uppity." She stared at him as though her words carried a weight of significance that would cause him to cringe. They had the opposite effect, of course.

"I knew I had not seen you at First Fundamentalist," she continued. "Jailer, take him back to the cell. I will wait here for another thirty minutes for the report from the hospital, and then we will consider whether to charge him with insulting the police. Dallas comes on in thirty minutes," she added, as though that explained everything.

Shuffling back to the cell in his loose jail slippers, Henniker pondered the judge's words. Hospital? Had something actually happened to Annie? She was egotistical and a bit of an airhead, but not any more so than most girls that age. Still, he didn't want anything to happen to her. Kids like her were the reason why he served so many years in the Air Force, trying to keep the country safe from bad guys.

What the shit, he asked himself as the cell door clanged shut behind him.

"Bishop to f4," said Isaac, grinning through his brown teeth.

"Pawn to d5," said Henniker, absently.

Miss Abigail Fanninburgh was the much-loved fourth grade teacher in Whitmire. When report cards came out, she loved flipping the cards to the students. One day, one of the spinning cards caught Jeff Mikel in his left eye, blinding him.

Years later, the elementary school burned down during the Lions Club Fourth of July bass tournament while all the volunteer firemen were fishing. The following Fourth of July, the high school burned down. The arsonist struck other structures, then Mikel was arrested for burglary and confessed to the fires. It was past the statute of limitations, so he wasn't prosecuted.

CHAPTER
SEVENTEEN

Edward "Trey" Green, Whitmire police chief, talked to his office by radio from the Piney Creek police department, since the phone lines were out, and he couldn't call his wife. His dispatcher in Whitmire had hand-carried a message to his wife, though, so he was in the clear until the waters went down. Every once in a while, he thought, the world aligns just right to give a hardworking man a break and lets him go and have a little fun. He decided before he'd ended the radio message that he'd drop in on Belle Guinness, if she were available.

Piney Creek had not suffered as much flooding damage as Whitmire did from Tropical Storm Beryl, so the phones in that county still worked, though most of the highways were closed. As the waters gathered fury, everything in Piney Creek would close and people would just wait until the floods receded before going about their ordinary habits of kindness, extortion, and thievery.

But one thing Beryl did for Belle was bring her a phone call from an old acquaintance now working the floor at the Coushatta casino in western Louisiana. Once you're in the game, you have friends who watch your back. Her friend had just called to tell her that her husband was messing with Black Widow, the name they called an African American prostitute whose real name was Betty. She just wanted Belle to know that the man had strayed off the reservation.

"Yeah, not surprised," replied Belle. "Thanks, honey." And she hung up. Almost immediately the phone had rung again and this time it was Trey Green.

"Oh hey," she said brightly. "Where are you?"

Ten minutes later they were clutching one another in Belle's kitchen, and eleven minutes later she was unzipping his pants. Twelve minutes later he was snoring, and she was plumb bored with life.

So, she called Bob McKinney.

If that asshole husband of hers was going to leave her, she'd need to lose about twenty pounds to be competitive, and McKinney could help. Also, he might have some other stuff to help ease her through this crisis.

McKinney said he'd send his man around in about thirty minutes. Belle stared at the ceiling in the kitchen for a few seconds, hugged the phone to her bosom, listened to the snoring from the bedroom, and agreed.

"And add some stuff, okay?" she breathed.

"Only the best," said Bob McKinney, looking up from the girlie magazine he had spread out on his desk and licking his lips. "But you owe me."

"Oh honey, you know you can count on me when you need it," she said in her sexiest voice. Even to her it was not convincing. I gotta work on that, she reminded herself.

Jesse Grinder pulled into her driveway thirty minutes later driving a yellow Oldsmobile sedan. When he made the turn at the end, he saw Belle's Cadillac and the rear end of another car sticking out of the carport, but Belle was standing there in her robe. He rolled the window down.

"Hey, stud," she breathed, the flap of her bathrobe slipping a little.

Grinder was floored again. He was staring. Nothing else in the world existed but that flap in her robe.

"I'm supposed to get a package from you," said Belle. She held out her hand, turning it over to reveal the blue veins of her wrist. It was a small hand, and it looked soft to Jesse.

"Sure. Okay," he said, reaching over to the passenger seat for the sealed brown paper package.

"Thanks, sugar," Belle said, taking the package and stroking his arm with her other hand. "Y'all come back now, y'hear?" She slipped him a sealed envelope.

Grinder's jaw had dropped about six inches at the touch of her hand, and also, of course, Belle had let her bathrobe slip open another few inches. She knew a live one when she had him on the line. Besides, that fucker Richard was going to divorce her in about ten minutes anyway. Why not?

She turned away and flounced back toward the door while Jesse just stared at her. But when she put her hand on the doorknob, she realized her predicament.

Oh shit, she thought. I've locked myself out.

She jiggled the door and hollered but got no response from inside. Trey-the-fuck Green was completely zonked out on her spare bed.

Grinder put the car in reverse, but he was still staring at Belle. She turned around.

"Help me," she said, drowning out the noise from the motor.

Grinder turned off the car.

"I've locked myself out," she whined, going over to him.

"I can unlock it," he said, grinning his ruined smile.

A man who eats beans every night and rarely bathes does not pay a lot of attention to his teeth, and this impressed itself on Belle, not in a positive way. But hey, she thought, I've seen worse.

Grinder got out and shuffled over to the door. Belle's first impression was that he was a much larger man than he seemed in that sedan. The other thing that impressed her was that he was a good bit more feral than most men she'd played. Well, she thought, we'll see how this goes.

From inside the house, she heard the ding of the fax machine turning on.

What if that damned fax machine wakes up Green? she thought. But it didn't. She rattled the door again, and called to Trey Green, but got no response.

"I can open this door," Jesse said, grinning at her through his stained teeth. "What you give me?"

"Open it and we'll see," she grinned, flapping the front of her bathrobe just enough to keep his interest up. She was wearing little purple bikini panties but no bra, and she hoped this man would get a glimpse of the color. Playing men was like playing fish, she thought. You give them something, then set the hook. Then you reel them in.

He ambled back to the car, reached through, and pulled out a packet that looked like a wallet. A few minutes later he put away the lock picks he'd lifted from Wilburn Hall's locksmith shop and opened the door.

"You're a savior," she said, grinning up at him and acting all flustered. "Why don't you come in for a bit?"

"Is that a cop car in your carport?" he asked, hesitant to enter.

"Yeah, but the guy's sound asleep. He came by for a visit and passed out. Not my husband," she added holding the door open.

She led the way toward the master bedroom at the other end of the house. It was a large house. Her husband made a lot of money selling tires in Piney Creek, which is why he could afford to marry her. But he also lost a lot of money gambling. Overall, he didn't make a dime more than he earned, but he didn't know that. They passed the office on the way down the hall and she saw the fax machine with a queue of paper spilling out of it. What the fuck, she thought. But she led Jesse on down the hall.

"Now honey, I'm just going to go make that policeman go away," she said to him, stroking his chest. "You go in there and take a shower while I get rid of him."

"Guess so," said Grinder. He figured Bob McKinney didn't really need him back at the car lot anytime soon.

"Be right back, sugar," she whispered, and off she went down the hall, pausing to go into the office on her way. When she looked over her shoulder, Jesse was still standing in the doorway of the bedroom staring at her, so she shooed him on in. "Take that shower, honey," she cooed, shooing him with her hand. Then she ducked into the office to retrieve the fax.

Sure enough, her sorry-ass husband had faxed her a set of divorce papers.

"Well, that m-f," she muttered. "A fucking fax machine. Of all the cowardly things to do." She wadded up the papers and threw them in the wastebasket, then went back to Trey Green, still snoring in the spare bedroom.

"Trey honey," she said, "Trey. Hey. Wake up."

He rolled over.

"Trey, baby, you got to get up. My husband is coming home."

Those were the magic words and Trey Green opened his eyes.

"Where he at?' he asked, staring around.

"Just go, baby. We'll get a happy ending some other time. You gotta get out of here now."

"Okay, okay," he said, trying to get his brain in gear. "Is he here now?"

"No, not yet, but you've been out a long time. You are one tired bunny, honey. Go on, now. Zip your pants up and go on."

"Okay, okay," he muttered, gradually waking up. "Anybody else here?"

She thought maybe he had heard something from the master bedroom or the office.

"Just go on, okay?" she pleaded. "Get going. It's for your own good."

He fumbled for his zipper.

"How long was I out?" he asked.

"All morning," she said. "Now git."

He stood and was stumbling toward the bathroom when the bedroom door flew open. Jesse Grinder was standing there nude, dripping wet, the water steaming off his body like he was a furnace.

Trey Green threw up his hands in defense, but it did no good. Jesse hit him five times, and the Whitmire police chief fell to the floor, unconscious.

Belle screamed, shocked, but almost immediately it occurred to her that maybe nobody else knew Trey Green had been with her. In fact, she was sure of it. A smile spread over her face.

"Aw honey, are you fighting for me?" she purred as she got over the shock. "That makes me so hot!"

Grinder looked around, confused, like he didn't know where he was. Belle's robe slipped open, and then he came to, his gaze so narrowly focused on a swatch of purple cloth that he didn't see the man on the floor.

"But look what you've done, big guy. Maybe you killed a man."

Grinder was blinking like he didn't know where he was.

"I did?" he finally asked.

"Yes," she said. "You did. Now what?"

"I don't know," said Jesse.

"We need to get rid of this body," she said. "I don't see any other choice. And the car."

"Okay," he said. "I guess you're right."

He dragged the unconscious form of Edward "Trey" Green through the bedroom and into the carport, where he manhandled the body into the trunk of the police car. Belle went out to the street to see if anyone was coming. Like all suburban neighborhoods on a Tuesday morning after a weekend of bad storms, nobody saw anything. It was a desert out there. Green had parked the car out of sight of the street anyway. Grinder slammed the trunk lid shut on the patrol car, then went back inside to get his clothes.

"Follow me," he said to her, handing her the keys to the yellow sedan. "Going to a boat ramp on the river." He climbed in the police car and pulled into the street.

Grinder turned off the pavement onto the damp sandy road about thirty minutes later and followed the track through looming woods and steady rain to the river. The boat ramp was unused, and brown floodwater swirled and thundered past, foaming and looking angry. Occasionally a tree swept past or submerged to breach like a whale a hundred yards downstream. He angled the car at the top of the ramp and turned it off. Belle pulled in next to him and he opened the trunk. The policeman was struggling to rise, frantically trying to get the tire iron loose to defend himself. Grinder hit him several times and a foul stench filled the trunk. Then Grinder dragged him out.

Belle joined him. She was breathless and excited, her breasts heaving.

"You better put him in the driver's seat," she gasped, one hand holding her breast. "We gotta make it look like he drove in."

Grinder nodded but said nothing. He grabbed the limp policeman around the neck and jerked him into the driver's seat, positioning him behind the wheel. For good measure, he hit Chief Green again, hard, slamming his head sideways. He didn't fasten the seat belt, just propped the unconscious man up behind the steering wheel, inserted the keys in the ignition.

"Turn the car around," he said to Belle.

While she was doing that, he reached through the open driver's window and started the car. He checked the limp body again, positioned Green's foot on the accelerator pedal, then slipped the car into gear and saw it jump down the steep ramp toward the water, gathering speed. It splashed into the river and the current caught it, turning the car around and around until finally it inverted and submerged.

"Guess you better come back in," she breathed when they pulled back into the carport, a sly smile playing at the corners of her mouth. It had been a long time since two men had fought over her, and she liked it. It was exciting to see the way this big guy took down that police officer, and when that car disappeared in the river, she got wet all over again. Before he left, she screwed his brains out, humping him over and over.

After an hour with Belle, Grinder got dressed and drove the yellow sedan back onto the lot at Bob McKinney's used car lot. By then, he had forgotten about Trey Green but not about Belle Guinness. Grinder's life was pretty simple, regardless of what angle you chose to look at it from. Mostly it involved the dark places in a woman, and titties.

Back at the house, Belle unwrapped McKinney's package and found the pills. She also found a neat little dime bag of white powder she instantly recognized.

"Bob McKinney, you dear man," she smiled, and went to draw herself a bath. She popped two of the so-called diet pills, and poured herself a big glass of white wine. She dropped her bathrobe on the floor along with her soaking panties and stuck a tentative toe into the water, taking a large gulp of wine. It was perfect. She rummaged around in her makeup kit and found a glass pipe and some matches, and then eased herself into the warm water, swallowing another gulp of wine and thinking back over the delightful day. Not even evening yet, but it had been a full day. And that stud of a man. Wow, she thought. So strong the way he'd gripped her, lifted her, tossed her around. He made her feel so feminine! Oh yeah, she thought. Nice day. Scary, but nice.

She settled into the warm water, struck a match to her little glass pipe, and inhaled the heroin deeply.

Belle was still in the bathtub on Saturday four days later when Richard came back from the Coushatta casino with fifty thousand dollars in his wallet and the Black Widow on his front seat. He wanted to pick up some clothes and his guns before he abandoned the place.

"Spooky," the Black Widow said as they pulled in the driveway.

A dozen buzzards were sitting on the roof of the house, strutting around in their ungainly way and a solid mass of flies inside made the house vibrate.

"We gotta call the cops," he said to the girl. "Right now."

CHAPTER

EIGHTEEN

The judge was getting restless. Her show would start in ten minutes, and here she was at the jail. She'd seen the preliminary report from the hospital: nothing had happened to Annie, but her mother had been admitted under sedation.

"That's right," she muttered to herself, leaning forward to rest her weaponized breasts on the desktop and sighing. "Best place for her. About time."

She called the duty station at the jail.

"Have you interviewed Henniker yet?" she asked.

"No, ma'am, the patrolman hasn't come back from the bridge yet. You know, the bridge that's out."

"Has Chief Green written out a charge against this Henniker?"

The silence at the other end of the line told the judge exactly what she already knew. Chief Green was in Piney Creek, trapped by the flood. So of course, he had not written out a charge, and Patrolman Davis, if he was still in the building, would take about an hour of sucking on a pencil and erasing to get out fifty words. She would not see a statement from the police this night.

"Okay," after the silence had gone on for a minute, "bring Henniker in here and get his things ready. I'm letting him go."

Henniker appeared a few minutes later.

"Sit down, Mr. Henniker," Judge Teresa Lewis said.

"Now," she continued, "I have reviewed the allegations made against you and read a statement given to me by Miranda Putnam, Annie's mother. Do you know Miranda Putnam, Mr. Henniker?"

Henniker shook his head. "I might have seen her at the school this afternoon. Large woman. Unfortunate preference for tight dresses and

103

strapless black heels? Was that she?"

"Maybe. She says that you have been hanging around their house."

"I have no idea where they live. How could I be hanging around?"

"Big house? Long concrete driveway? Big pine trees? Two story? Does that ring a bell?"

"There's a house like that on the street where I rent a house."

"What's your address? Oh, never mind, here it is. You're at 124 Park Street. Right?"

"Yes, ma'am. The little three-bedroom brick house in the bend where Park turns. I walk to school most mornings."

"Well, that explains that," said the judge. "Of course she's seen you. You walk by her house twice a day."

She looked up at Henniker and then sat up, trying not to groan with the effort. She tapped a pencil eraser against the desk pad.

"Mr. Henniker, I am going to drop the charges against you. I think it's safe to say that the people nearest and dearest to Chief Green's patrolmen use language every bit as foul as any you might have used. And I think Miranda's suspicion is misplaced. Obviously, nothing happened to Annie, and you were at school all day. Annie herself told the police that she'd spent the day sleeping in her own bed. Apparently, she has so many pillows and stuffed animals on the bed that her mother didn't see her when she looked in and assumed she'd been kidnapped. So I think this has all just been a mix-up. Her fear that Annie had been raped was misplaced, according to the hospital. Sometimes people do strange things when they're gripped by fear. I'm sorry. I'll tell the jailers to give you back your things and let you go."

Henniker stood. "Thank you, ma'am," he said, "I wonder if you'd let me borrow your phone to see if we have service again."

"Sure," she said, rising and stepping around the desk. "Take your time." She left the door to the office open when she stepped out, but she was on her way home.

The phone was still dead, so he headed back toward the jail where the jailer gave him his possessions and opened an interview room for him to change in.

A few minutes later, he was sitting on a bench in front of the jail swatting at the moths that were swarming around the overly bright lights overhead. He sat for a long time, thinking through what he should do next. Patrol cars came and went. A black-and-white state trooper's car pulled into the drive in front of the jail and sat there for a time, the trooper just staring at him. When a deputy pulled his car in behind, the trooper eased off back to the highway. The deputy got out and walked over to Henniker.

"Nobody come to get you yet?" he asked.

"I'm thinking I better walk home," Henniker said. "I'm just sitting here trying to sort things out in my mind."

"You call anybody?"

"Phones are still dead."

"Yeah," said the deputy sitting down and taking out a cigarette.

They sat in silence for a few minutes, the deputy blowing smoke at the moths.

"Tell you what," he finally said, "I can drive you home if you want. You're bound to live in town. Nobody's getting in or out of town right now."

"I would appreciate it," Henniker said. "It's been a long day."

"Where do you live?"

"Park Street."

"Oh," said the deputy. He looked off across the street at the dimly glowing line of pine trees lit by the mercury vapor florescence of the jail's lights. "That's the street the Putnams live on."

"I just learned that."

"Yeah. It's probably not a good idea for you to be walking on that street after dark. Not tonight. Come on, get in. I'm going to drive you. Jack Lewis, by the way," he said, holding out his hand.

"Charles Henniker," said Henniker, shaking the hand. "Are you kin to the judge?"

"She's my uncle's stepbrother's second wife, so she's what? An aunt? It's hard to follow sometimes, but yeah, we're kin. In this town, though, everybody's kin."

"Like Pitcairn Island," Henniker said, settling into the worn front seat of the patrol car cluttered with cop gear.

"What's that?" asked Lewis.

"Oh, nothing. Just a place where some sailors were marooned for a couple of hundred years."

"Yeah," said Lewis, "that's us. Ain't nothing ever changed here. No new blood. No new jobs. Shit, half my job is tracking down people for hot checks, and the other half is hauling people in for not paying their bills. Some days I bring one fellow who wrote a bad check to another fellow, and the same day I bring in the second fellow for not paying a bill he owed."

"Vicious cycle."

"Yep. The honest ones don't pay, the dishonest ones try to fool the system, and that's about the whole population. Honest, and dishonest. But nobody has money."

"Some folks here have money."

"Well, yeah, the Putnams. He has money. The woman that owns the bank. She has money. Mostly, it's two or three rich folks, and the rest of us."

They had driven slowly through dimly lit residential neighborhoods and were finally on Park Street.

"That's Putnam's house," Lewis said as they slowly drove by. "You might want to stay away from there for a while. He's been talking."

"What about?"

"About what he's going to do to anybody who messes with his baby girl. His wife said it was you. The hospital thinks she hasn't been messed with, and that's what the girl says. But the bad blood has been stirred up. Just stay out of sight, if I were you."

"Good advice," said Henniker. He'd just drive over to the school and do his six miles on the track every morning instead of jogging through town. It was a lot more boring that way, but it would be much safer, and he'd be alone.

Solitude was sounding pretty good to him.

Then maybe one day he could get together with old Isaac and they could finish that game and talk chess. That'd be a nice break.

Before he went to bed, Henniker went to his garage and backed the car out. Then he did his evening calisthenics and spent half an hour kicking and punching at his Wing Chun wooden-man dummy. When he'd lathered up a sweat, he bounced over to the martial arts mannequin and spent another half hour practicing his kicks.

"Too slow," he thought to himself as he went inside to shower. "Too slow."

CHAPTER
NINETEEN

On Thursday, Annie's father, Henry "Hogleg" Putnam, went down to the high school and asked Assistant Principal Lonnie Cline if he could speak with Henniker. The principal, E. P. Allen, was still stuck at his ranch by the floodwaters.

"Can't have violence in the school, Henry," Cline said. He had been Putnam's eighth-grade science teacher and did not accept the nickname "Hogleg" to refer to his former student. He expected Henry to address him as "Mister Cline," and wasn't disappointed.

"Well, Mr. Cline," Putnam said, "I want to apologize to him for all the trouble yesterday. My wife was wrong, and I want to own up to it with him. I'm just down here to see if he would accept her apology."

"Now that's an extraordinary thing," Cline said. "You know he's Black? He might not know what an apology is."

"Now, Mr. Cline, you know that's not how to think. I work with Black men all day long. Been working and sweating with them for years and years, and they've made me a bunch of money and I've made them a bunch of money. One thing I can tell you is that black don't rub off on you. They are people like the rest of us."

Cline nodded. "Well, if you say so. I just wanted to be sure you weren't going to kill him or something. Let me check his schedule."

"I'd like to see him right now while I have my nerve up," said Putnam.

"I worried about this all night, but Miranda and I talked it out this morning and we're agreed. So, the sooner the better for me."

"I see. Well, he has a prep period in about thirty minutes."

"I might not be here in thirty minutes," said Putnam. "I want to get this over and done with right now. And also," he added, "I want you to be there when I speak to him."

"Of course," Cline nodded.

They strolled down the silent hallway. With so few students and staff in the school, the janitors had achieved a world-class shine on the freshly buffed floors.

"Can you tell me what room Annie's in?" Putnam asked.

"We are keeping an eye peeled for her, you know," Cline said. "She's in English right now. Do you want to pull her out?"

"No, no, it's probably best for me to do this by myself. She and her mother will go personally apologize later today if Mr. Henniker will accept it."

Cline looked over at him again, amazed at this evidence of character. This was not the Henry Putnam he'd paddled in the eighth grade for sneaking cigarettes into the boys' bathroom.

In fact, Cline reflected, nothing he knew about Henry Putnam would have predicted that he'd be here doing this.

"Here we are," Cline said stopping by a door near the end of the hall. "I'll just call him out."

He opened the door and stuck his head in, beckoning to Henniker.

"Mr. Henniker," he said, closing the door. "This is Henry Putnam. He is Annie's father."

Putnam stuck out his hand. "Mr. Henniker, sir, I'm glad to meet you."

Henniker looked at the proffered hand and then at Putnam.

"Why?" he asked, not taking the hand.

Putnam lowered his hand.

"Well, yes. Okay then." He swallowed. "Mr. Henniker, I came to apologize for my wife's behavior. She was wrong to make an accusation against you. In fact, everything about that was wrong. We know you had nothing to do with Annie. In fact, nobody assaulted her at all. It's just, well, we love her so much and her mother is very protective, and the flood and all got everybody so riled up. So, I'm sorry."

Henniker looked at him, judging him, assessing the sincerity of the apology. He had a good lawsuit for defamation against the Putnams, but was that what he wanted?

"Mr. Putnam, thank you for that apology. I will mull it over and decide whether I can accept it. I was insulted and jailed. I was given a body-cavity search in the jail. I was denied a phone call. Some of that is just the ineptitude of the local sheriff and his staff, but all of it happened because of you and your wife."

"I know that, Mr. Henniker." Putnam hung his head. "I just want you to know that we are truly sorry. We are sorry for all of it."

"Yes," Henniker said. "You should be. And you should be ashamed."

"I am, Mr. Henniker. Believe me, I am."

"Well, then. I will think about it. I will discuss it with my attorney. I don't mind telling you that I have contemplated bringing legal action against you. If I had not seen you today, I most certainly would. Now I will think about it."

"Thank you, Mr. Henniker. And my wife would also like to come by and apologize in person. Would that be possible?"

"I will hear what she has to say. Where should we meet?"

"I thought maybe we could stop by your house this afternoon after school. Me, my wife, and my daughter Annie."

"Do you know where I live?"

"It's a small town, Mr. Henniker."

"I will be at home around five."

"Thank you, Mr. Henniker. And again, I do sincerely apologize for all we put you through. It was unfair and unjust. I'm sorry."

"Those words mean a lot to me, Mr. Putnam," Henniker said. "I will reserve judgment until I hear from your wife. I don't think you need to bring your daughter. She is a victim in all this."

"Thank you, Mr. Henniker." Putnam held out his hand again. This time, Henniker shook it, drilling his eyes into Putnam's.

He had made his choice as the large White man had stood there, as red-faced as a Japanese saru monkey. If he was going to be a teacher in this town, in fact anywhere in Texas, he had to negotiate these kinds of events. Nothing required Putnam to offer an apology, and his prospects of winning a defamation suit against a man of Putnam's influence in a town of this size were not good. If he could establish a relationship based on equality and mutual respect, then he won. That was worth more than a million-dollar judgment he might never collect. On balance, accepting Putnam's offer was the smartest thing he could do, provided he was able to keep his dignity.

To keep his dignity meant giving Putnam a way to keep his own. Everybody needed to save face. And while a jury in Whitmire might decide for Putnam anyway, if the two could work it out between them, then everyone was better off.

He would see if he could get his neighbors to come over to his house to be there when the Putnams arrived. He did not want to meet the Putnams without witnesses. Or maybe that English teacher, what's her name, Etheridge, Ms. Etheridge, would stop by. He'd ask her during lunch today, encourage her to bring a friend, explain. It was a lot to ask, but she would be a reliable witness and not obligated to Putnam. His neighbors might be working for Putnam and want to stay out of it.

Ms. Etheridge might want to stay out of it, too. He couldn't blame her. Still, they had visited quite a bit during lunch periods. They had the same prep periods, when they could go to the teachers' lounge to write lesson plans, catch up on grading, call parents, and grab a cup of coffee. He felt they had a mutual respect for one another. He'd ask her. He'd encourage her to bring a friend.

In-line skates became popular with some high school students who could afford them. When the Crooks Bros. Grocery store closed at 9 p.m., they would go down to skate in the empty parking lot, and skate until the moth-swarmed lights went out at midnight. The boys brought ramps and obstacles to jump, often falling. The girls practiced skating backwards, making long, swooping circles, arms outspread like swans. The boys wanted to be like daredevil Evel Knievel; the girls went home to watch ice dancing on television and dreamed they were Jayne Torvill skating with Christopher Dean. No one did homework.

CHAPTER

TWENTY

Ellen Etheridge finished class and packed up a stack of essays to take down to the teachers' lounge.

"Going for coffee?" Henniker asked, sticking his head in her door. "Mind if I walk with you?"

"Sure," she said brightly. Actually, she would be having mint tea and sitting as far away as she could from the gratuitous brownies on the counter. Every day somebody brought sweets of some kind to the teachers' lounge. It was not a lounge, actually, but a workspace with refreshments, a copier machine, a grading machine, pencils and pens collected from teacher meetings around the state, and softer chairs. One day there would be an anonymous cake, another there would be a pile of chocolate-chip cookies. Sometimes she would see a teacher bringing a plate of something to share. Regardless, it was bad for her figure. On some days, however, just knowing she could find something down there brightened an otherwise difficult day. Working with hormonal teenagers all day long every day was exhausting.

"I need some help," Henniker said as they walked along.

"In class?" she asked.

"No, outside of class. You know what happened yesterday."

"Awful. Unfair and ridiculous," she said. "I couldn't believe it."

"Mr. Putnam came to see me a few minutes ago, to apologize."

"He did?" She was amazed and just stopped to stare at the handsome Black teacher. Wow, she thought. I didn't expect that.

"He did," Henniker said. "He brought Mr. Cline as a witness."

"Cline was a teacher here for more than forty years before they made him assistant principal. I bet he had Putnam in class at some point."

"He's had some experience with the people here," Henniker nodded.

111

They had arrived at the so-called lounge. One of the ninth-grade math teachers was running a pile of forms through the Scantron machine, getting test results. The machine clattered at the process.

"Mr. Putnam asked to come over to my house tonight with his wife so she could also apologize," he said to Etheridge, under the clatter of the machine.

"He did?" She put her hand on Henniker's forearm. "What did you say?"

"I told him I would be home about five. He wanted to bring Annie also, but I think I dissuaded him from that."

She moved toward a table in the back, nodding at him to follow her. "What can I do to help?"

"I really hate to talk to these people without witnesses," said Henniker. "You never know how it is going to go. Mrs. Putnam was hysterical. I mean, hysterical in a bad way. Out of her mind."

"Some people cannot handle stress," said Etheridge.

"I believe she had cracked. I've seen this before in people with shell shock, and in soldiers under fire. Sometimes they recover. Sometimes they don't. I'm just uneasy about it. I don't know these people and can't predict what they will do."

"Do you think it's wise to meet them?" she asked.

"I think so. I don't know. What if she pulls a gun on me? What if he does?"

"That's a risk. He's got a reputation as a tough guy, but I don't worry about him. I'd worry about the wife."

"You think?"

"She's the unbalanced one. I don't think Mr. Putnam would carry a gun unless he was in the woods or something, but Mrs. Putnam is a tad unpredictable."

"Can you get a friend and come by my house about 4:30 this evening? I'm asking you to be a witness. I'd ask my neighbors, but some of them work for Putnam and it could put them in a compromising position."

"I'll ask BoMac to join me, the guy from the paper. That ought to keep things civil, or at least I hope so. And the Putnams will certainly know who he is."

"Thank you, Ms. Etheridge," Henniker said, standing. "This is important to me, and I owe you."

"The two of us would like to know you better anyway," Etheridge said, smiling and spreading out the essays.

"Thank you," he said. "I'll have some tea for us."

Henniker returned to his classroom with a much lighter heart, and immediately put the whole matter out of his mind. He focused instead on the mason jars of floodwater with the sediment settling out. This was going to be a devastating flood.

He settled into the chair at his desk, wondering how he could shape this disaster into meaningful assignments for his students. Anecdotes, surely. He'd have them interview their parents and others in the community about past flooding. He'd have them collect stories about it, stories about the economic impact. He'd ask them to form opinions about the benefits of the free enterprise system based on their observations and collections of data. How was this flood made better or worse by businesses competing with one another in the logging industry? How did current logging practices affect long-term sustainability of that industry, which was so important to the survival of Whitmire and Sweetgum County? By the end of the semester, he hoped he could gather all his classes together in a symposium to share their ideas. He'd record their sessions. He'd figure out how to grade their products and their discussions.

He needed to get more information about how to grade discussions. Did anyone else at the school do it? His mind's eye flashed at the math teacher running those stacks of data forms through the scanning machine earlier. He thought about the state's mandated year-end testing system, with millions of similar data forms running through similar machines, designed to resemble a giant Trivial Pursuit game asking for random bits of knowledge. An educational system designed like a Henry Ford–inspired assembly plant was creating a whole line of children exposed to similar ideas but none of them were learning anything but trivia.

You needed to participate to learn. You needed to have fun, get involved, and most importantly, think. And he would see if he could make that happen in Whitmire, Texas. If it wasn't involved and fun, it wasn't learning. You could teach recruits all day long about throwing grenades under fire, but until you took them out to the range with bullets firing at them, they didn't know. Kids in classes were the same way. He could figure this out. He still had six weeks left in the year, and whatever he did now was something he could start off with next year.

His mind did not give the Putnams another thought until he got home from school at 4:15 and went inside to prepare to make tea in his $2000 Japanese teapot.

A tropical storm drowned East Texas in 1926 with about thirty inches of rain, then wandered up over Arkansas into the central Mississippi basin, where it caused the devastating flood of 1927. All East Texas cotton crops had been planted but the rain stripped the ground bare. Farmers were bankrupted, local businesses were bankrupted, and many people facing famine and ruin abandoned their farms and moved away. The economy in seven states was destroyed, preparing the way for the stock market crash in 1929. Progress, measured by telephones, radio stations, and electricity, halted in East Texas, not to return until 1956.

CHAPTER
TWENTY-ONE

BoMac was intrigued by Ellen's call. They had planned to have a coffee or iced tea at the only other cafe in Whitmire, a hamburger and barbecue place called John's, because they still could not get across the creek to the Dairy Queen. But he had seen Charles Henniker at various school functions and was hoping to meet him. The man looked disciplined, reserved, and educated. Sometimes you could just tell by how a man held himself and dressed what kind of man he was. Henniker looked like he was unflappable and in charge. That made him different from everyone else BoMac had met in Whitmire.

He arrived at Ellen's apartment in the old Dodge truck, the engine purring gently, and she came out. She'd seen him pull in the driveway.

"Have I told you how much I love your truck?" she asked as she climbed in, all smiling. She'd changed from her teaching clothes to jeans and a blouse. Because the sky was still overcast, she added a light jacket and carried an umbrella.

"I think he lives on Park Street," BoMac said, slipping the truck into gear. "How was your day?"

"Except for this, quiet and uneventful," she said, slipping under the seat belt. "I have a stack of essays to finish grading, but fewer than half the students were there today so I'm getting caught up. How about you?"

"This is going to be another bad week for advertising. At least we have the festival coming in a few weeks, so the merchants try to cash in on the excitement. We always get a little boost in advertising around then. But this month is going to be another washout, I'm afraid, both for the city and for its newspaper."

"I'm sorry it's so hard," she said. "I know you do your best."

"Thanks," he said, "but it's the job, you know. I'm not alone. The businesses support the paper, but the businesses are struggling too. I help them get customers in the door, but this whole place is marginal. It's just too small."

"I love it here. It's so much calmer and easier than Sugar Land. We don't have restaurants and entertainment, but we don't have the traffic jams and the pollution either. I'm happy here."

"Oh, it's challenging," said BoMac. "I've learned so much here. But I wish it were easier to make a success of the paper. A community needs a paper like mine."

They detoured around a large puddle at the corner of Beech Street and the highway, and she pointed to a great blue heron strutting in the yard of the corner house.

"You think there are fish in that pothole?" she asked. "That bird is fishing, it looks like."

"I think that's where Darryl Stewart lives. He has been telling the city council for years that they needed to do something about it. He claims they've put it off so long that now, yeah, it has fish in it." He laughed. "Most months he and I are the only two people at the council meeting. Sometimes we'll get somebody else who doesn't want to pay taxes or needs to complain about a streetlight or something, but he's there every time trying to wear them down about that pothole."

"That's funny," she said, chuckling. "And so typical. You'd think this was the last meager outpost of civilization, the way these folks behave."

"Oh," BoMac said, "I'm convinced it is. Right there," he pointed out the window at a patch of pine trees and undergrowth that came out to the pavement, "right there is where civilization ends, and the wild world begins."

She nodded, her eyes bright.

"Okay," he said a few minutes later, "here's the address. Looks like he's expecting us."

Henniker was standing on the small front porch up two steps from the sidewalk. He had set up a small table and additional chairs, enough for five people. The table held his teapot, porcelain cups, starched white napkins, a small tray of cookies. Ellen was impressed. This was not what she expected from a man who lived alone.

"Thank you for coming, Ms. Etheridge," Henniker said, holding out his hand. "And you are Mr. Maclean, I think."

He and BoMac shook hands.

"You are both welcome. Please be seated. I believe we will wait for a few minutes. Perhaps the Putnams can join us. What do you think?"

"Is this a social visit, then?" Etheridge asked.

"I hope it is at least civilized," Henniker replied. "I will give them a chance to rise to that level after what they put me through. So, we'll see. Nevertheless, I am so happy to have you both here."

"Nice teapot," BoMac said, looking around.

The porch was spotless. No dirt dauber nests, no spider webs in the corners. No dead moths in the porch light, and no dust. The front door was freshly painted or looked that way. Even the porch railings were clean and dust free.

"Thank you," said Henniker. "My wife was fond of Japanese customs and manners, and we shopped for several years until we found one we both loved. It was made by a little gnarled Japanese man with the softest hands, maybe a hundred years old, in a pottery studio he kept at his house."

"When you were in Japan?" BoMac asked. Even in social circumstances he was a journalist.

"Well, yes, of course. Celia and I lived there for four years."

"Tell us about the teapot," said Etheridge, admiring the delicate work, "and its potter." Something about it struck her as very beautiful.

They chatted about Japan for a few minutes, and then the Putnams' long Cadillac appeared coming down the street.

"I think this may be our visitors," Henniker said, rising. He went and stood at the top of the steps while Hogleg and Miranda pulled into his driveway.

Hogleg got out first and nodded at Henniker, then went around and opened Miranda's door. From Miranda's reaction, whose hand was already on the door handle, BoMac assumed Putnam did not do that all the time, maybe never.

"Hello, Mr. Henniker," said Hogleg, speaking first. "This is my wife, Miranda." Miranda carried a casserole. They were dressed in their Sunday clothes.

"Mr. and Mrs. Putnam, may I present my colleague, Ms. Ellen Etheridge, and her friend, Beaumont Maclean." He gestured with an open hand.

Then he turned to face the Putnams and waited.

Hogleg Putnam went red in the face. "Well, yes, I believe you are the fellow from the paper," he said to BoMac. Then to Henniker, "No need to involve the press, Mr. Henniker."

"I invited them to join me for tea, Mr. Putnam."

Putnam looked around as if wondering what to do next, swallowed, then stood up straight and said, "Mr. Henniker, I met you this morning at the school to apologize. I have now brought my wife to meet you and she wishes to apologize also."

Henniker looked at Miranda Putnam, who was sweating profusely. It was clear to him that she had spent the day crying, but now she was just nervous.

"Mr. Henniker," she began, then sobbed. "Henry," she whispered, "I can't do this."

They exchanged looks, and after a moment she turned around to face Henniker again.

"Mr. Henniker," she began again, "I acted foolishly the other day, and I am afraid I said and did things that insulted you. I falsely accused you of something you did not do. I'm sorry for that, sincerely sorry. I was wrong." Her voice cracked, tears tumbled from her bloodshot eyes, and she was unable to go on.

Hogleg took the casserole from her and stepped up to the porch.

"Mr. Henniker, she made this for you. Will you accept it along with our apologies?"

Henniker took the casserole, coming down the steps to do so.

"Mr. Putnam, nothing can repair the degradation and insult I suffered, but I accept your apology." To himself he calculated that a casserole and apology in front of witnesses was worth about a million dollars, give or take, in Whitmire, Texas. He was willing to move on. "Mrs. Putnam, thank you for the casserole. I'm sorry we have not met before now, and of course I accept your apology. I am willing to forget this ordeal and forgive you. I know you acted out of deep love for your daughter. Will you and your husband join me and my guests for a little tea on the porch? Please, come up the steps while I take the casserole inside. It's still warm, I see. I'll put it on the range."

The Putnams had surrendered all of their pride, so what did they have to lose? They joined Ellen and BoMac around the small table, shaking hands while Henniker was inside.

"Have you known him long?" Miranda inquired of Ellen in a low voice.

"Oh no. We met at school. He only came in January when Mr. Allen retired. The children seem to adore him."

"How's business, Mr. Putnam?" BoMac asked.

"All this rain, I don't know. Depends on how soon it dries out so we can get the trucks in the woods again. Right now, ain't no business."

Henniker rejoined them with a black iron kettle of steaming water, which he set on a trivet on the table. When it stopped blowing steam, he carefully lifted the lid from the beautiful teapot and spooned in several teaspoons of aromatic tea. Then he poured in hot water from the iron kettle. He replaced the lid swiftly and sat back.

"Now we will wait a few minutes for the tea to brew," he said.

"I always use a tea bag," said Miranda.

"I learned to make tea in the orient," said Henniker, "where it was first discovered. I always thought iced Lipton's tea was the only kind of tea there was, with a dozen spoonfuls of sugar in each glass. But did you know there are more than a thousand different kinds of tea?"

"Tell us about the potter who made this beautiful teapot," Ellen said, going back to an earlier question. "You said you met him, and he was about a hundred years old."

They chatted about the potter and the pottery, about Japan, about tea ceremonies, and about a host of other things from faraway places and cultures, sipped their tea, and finally the Putnams went home to see if they could find Annie.

"Stay and help me eat this casserole," Henniker urged Ellen and Bo-Mac.

Around 10 p.m., Henniker watched as his two new friends left the house and climbed in the red and white pickup with the camper shell on the back.

He was happy. Or anyway, happier. He could make a life here.
And now to see if he could find old Isaac. The next move was white queen to b3, and he would answer with pawn to c4. It was a famous game, and he'd memorized it during a very long winter at 17,000 feet in the Himalaya.

Until Eisenhower's second inauguration, despite programs put in place by the federal government in the 1930s, electricity in Whitmire was provided by the city's single-cylinder diesel generator. In their wisdom, the city fathers determined that the city's residents did not need electricity before 11 a.m., in time to start lunch, or after 8 p.m., which was bedtime. The sawmill ran on steam power coming from the burning of lumber by-products, and more rural households either had storage batteries for crystal radio sets, or no electricity at all. Most city residents remember listening to the gasp of the "one-lung" generator.

CHAPTER TWENTY-TWO

On Friday morning, Sheriff's Deputy Jack Lewis squeaked his beat-up Ford LTD patrol car into Darryl Stewart's driveway and got out to look at the pond. Several blue-teal ducks were paddling happily around, diving and bobbing up, on their annual migration from the Yucatán back to the defrosted tundra of northern Canada.

Huh, he thought, you don't usually see ducks in a pothole. Two males and a female. Story of my life.

He stood there for several minutes, watching the game birds and wondering about putting decoys in the pothole in late August when the season opened up, maybe putting up a blind in Darryl's front yard.

Nah, he decided, the city probably doesn't want people firing off weapons inside the city limits. He decided he would check, though, just to make sure. If he could bag some ducks right here out of Darryl's front yard, it would save a world of trouble.

Because of the pothole, or rather pond, Darryl had stopped parking his pickup on the street. He had it nestled into the chain link fence at the end of his driveway, almost in the backyard where his pair of beagles were setting up a din to welcome Deputy Lewis to the property. And moments later, Darryl came out of the side door, his jeans fastened but barefoot, with two cups of coffee in his hand.

"You're here early," he said to Lewis, handing him a cup of coffee.

"Well, yeah," said Lewis. "Just covering the bases. Have you heard from or seen Trey?"

"Trey Green?"

"Yeah, Trey Green. Police chief of Whitmire. Not too tall, not too bright, kind of pudgy, about fifty years old, capable of being a real mean son of a bitch. That Trey."

"The one with the wart on his nose like a size-ten boot?"

"No, the other one. The one with the double chin and size forty-eight khakis, wears his belt about twelve inches below his navel. Got short arms."

"Oh, that one."

"Yeah. Police chief."

"Name rings a bell."

"He told people you were his best friend."

"If I didn't feel sorry for him before, I do now."

"I'm just repeating what I heard," said the deputy, raising his cup. "No offense."

"Oh," said Darryl, as though he suddenly remembered. "Oh, you mean that Trey Green. Why sure. Why didn't you say so?"

"You seen him?"

"No. Why?"

"He ain't been heard from since Tuesday is all. He radioed the office over here from the police station in Piney Creek, said he couldn't get home because of the floods. Nobody believed him, except his wife, which was good enough. But he hasn't been heard from since. Thought maybe you'd heard something."

"No, I ain't heard from Trey all week. Kinda strange, actually. I think he's got a thing for Mary, the way he keeps stopping by."

"This here is one of her mugs, I'm guessing."

"How can you tell?"

"Lumpy, misshapen, off center, garish glaze, lopsided handle, uneven lip. Just little things like that tend to give it away."

"You are one observant investigator, Deputy Jack Lewis."

"Thanks," said Lewis, pouring the rest of the coffee out on the ground. "Sorry," he said, handing Darryl the mug, "but I ain't no fan of that chicory shit you put in your coffee. Where'd you pick up that nasty habit?"

"I worked offshore out of Terrebonne Parish when I got back from 'Nam," Darryl said. "My first couple whores taught me to like it. Never went back to plain black."

"They must have been hot hot hot," said Lewis.

"They were. And by the way, I'd appreciate it if you didn't pour my coffee out on the lawn. It kills the grass. Just pour it on the concrete instead and let it kill the black mold."

"Oh, right. Sorry. Wasn't thinking."

"Works better than bleach," Darryl said.

"So, everybody is wondering where Trey is," Lewis continued. "Last heard from on Tuesday. Today is Friday, and no word. He could be up to anything, of course."

"Sure could," Darryl said. "But the better tittie bars are closer to Houston, on US 59, down south of Humble. The other way from Piney Creek."

"I'll write that down in case I need to know," Lewis said.

"No telling what he's doing in Piney Creek, if he's still there. This here flood has pretty much shut everything down so far this week, so he can't have gone far."

"Nobody knows why he went to Piney Creek to begin with," said Lewis, "but the radio message definitely came from the police station there. The dispatcher remembers letting him use her mic and all, so he was in there on Tuesday morning."

"I might go to work today," said Darryl. "But maybe not. Mary has found a television channel that shows Roadrunner cartoons all fucking morning."

"How are you and Mary doing?" asked Lewis.

"Oh, you know. I been screwing with a limp dick so long I could row a boat with a rope."

"Bullshit," said Lewis. "You can't row a boat."

"Now don't get personal."

"Naw, I mean it. When was last time you rowed a boat?"

"Been awhile, that's true."

"See?"

They paused and looked out at the happy ducks gabbling away at the edge of Darryl's lawn.

"I'm thinking I'll put in rice this summer," Darryl said. "Maybe I can get me some snow geese in the fall."

"Good plan," said Jack Lewis. "Thanks for the coffee. Such as it was. Sorry about that smoking spot on your lawn. Maybe it will settle down after a while."

"Oh, I'll take a hose to it," said Darryl. "Never you mind."

"If you hear anything about Trey," Lewis said, "let us know. Okay?"

"Oh sure. That depends, of course, on what I hear. Man hears a lot of stuff about his friends. Some of it don't bear repeating. What makes a friend."

"You got that right."

Deputy Lewis made a wide swing around the lake in front of Darryl Stewart's house. He didn't like the way the pavement had cracked around the edges, and that sucker looked like it was way deep. He figured Darryl already had catfish living in it, along the bottom, feeding on chicken bones and the stray cats that fell in.

Now that the ice plant had finally failed, Jane Elkins decided she needed an ice maker. Either that, or she needed to buy a new refrigerator. Also, putting money into getting exactly what she needed was appealing, so she told Fletcher Holden at the bank to order her one. First, plumbers and electricians came to work in her garage, then it began producing ice. She discovered it made five hundred pounds of ice a day and instructed Henry Forbes, the caretaker and chauffeur, to dump the ice in the driveway first thing every morning. Nobody needs ice in the morning.

CHAPTER
TWENTY-THREE

A Hispanic couple who lived about fourteen miles north of Piney Creek bought a car from Bob McKinney on Friday morning. The husband worked night shift at the plywood mill, she cleaned houses, their five children went to school in Piney Creek. They drove off the lot with big grins and a loan charging them seventeen percent interest. Plus the down payment.

"Suckers," smiled Bob McKinney as he waved them goodbye.

Now see, he said to himself, that right there is why being in business for yourself is worthwhile.

The yellow sedan Jesse Grinder had driven over to Belle Guinness's house on Tuesday was also sold on Friday. It went to a Black man from Houston named Abbie Morton, who'd walked onto the lot.

McKinney always loved it when somebody walked onto the lot. It meant he would have another car sale, probably within minutes. Nobody who walked onto his lot ever walked off of it. They drove off.

But Morton was a disappointment to him. He bargained well over the yellow sedan, knocking McKinney down to a mere thousand-dollar profit on the sale. When he was satisfied with the price, he started going over the car carefully. He looked under the hood, removed the air cleaner and looked at it, cranked the car up and removed the oil filler cap to see if exhaust fumes were whirring by, indicating piston ring problems. He examined the glove box and looked under all the seats. He pulled the cushions out from the back seat to look under them. Then he opened the trunk and his face changed expression.

"Smells like something died in this trunk," he said to McKinney. "What've you been doing back here? Killing hogs?"

McKinney's expression took on a well-practiced look of concern as he examined the trunk and sniffed. Seven years of cocaine had destroyed his ability to smell, so he didn't notice anything unusual.

"I see some stains on the carpet," he said. "But that's nothing. Come out of there with a little soapy water. As for the smell, I don't smell anything, but if you do, then I can fix that right now. Jesse!" he shouted into the shop, "bring the air freshener out here and spray down this trunk. Gentleman wants it to smell fresh."

He led Morton into his shabby office while Grinder emptied a can of air freshener into the trunk.

"I don't want that car now," said Morton. "It stinks."

"It's just a temporary thing," said McKinney. "My man Jesse out there is fixing it right now."

"Not good enough," said Morton.

"What might make it good enough?" asked McKinney, all smiles.

"Come down a thousand."

"No. But I'll come down $250."

"Come down $500 and I'll clean the damned carpet myself."

"You drive a hard bargain, Mister, uh, Morton. How about I come down $350?"

"Four hundred or nothing," said Morton. "I don't really need a car. I'm just buying this for a friend."

"Let's talk about financing," said McKinney. "I'll come down $500 if you'll finance it with me."

"What's your interest rate?"

"Well, your monthly payment would be, here just a second while I add it up, about, uh," he fiddled with the calculator on his desk, "right at $250 a month, actually $251.39 for only three years. I know a man like you can afford it."

Morton did not grow up in Houston's Third Ward ghettoes without learning how to deal with pricks.

"I asked you what your interest rate was."

McKinney looked hard at Morton and decided not to risk it. "Eleven percent."

"Bullshit."

"If you've got good enough credit, I can probably get it lower."

"What's my walk-out price?"

"With tax, title, license, and insurance, it comes to," here McKinney fiddled with his calculator some more and recited a figure.

"What makes you think I'm going to buy insurance from you?"

"You can't drive it without insurance. Do you own a car now? I saw you walk onto this lot. I assume you aren't carrying insurance, and besides, I have a good plan and it's cheap."

"Cut the crap, Bob McKinney," Morton said, reading the name off the cheap desk plate. He had plenty of experience with small-time merchants who thought they were clever. "Here is what I'm going to do. I am not going to buy your insurance. I am not going to pay you to register this car. And I am not going to pay you for the title. I will go down to the county clerk's office and do all that myself. I will give you $1,500 for that yellow sedan, in cash, right now, and I will drive it off your lot. The police are too busy harassing other people to notice me, and even if you call them, I will already be gone. So, I don't need insurance to drive away with it. Take the cash or forget the sale."

Morton stood up.

McKinney's look turned pure hatred.

"I think you are a son of a bitch," he said to Morton, who towered over him.

"What I think of you is not worth saying," said Morton, "but I made you an offer. In two seconds, I am walking out of here."

"Okay, okay. I'll take it. You know I'm not making any money on it at that price."

"You're not paying property tax and it's not taking up space on your lot. Count your blessings."

"Hand over the cash."

Morton reached in his pocket and handed over the cash without counting it.

McKinney realized he'd been had. Morton had known what he was going to spend on the car before he walked in off the street.

"Okay," said Morton, folding up the title and putting it in his shirt pocket, and taking the keys. "One more question."

"Anything for a customer, even one who drives a hard-ass bargain," said McKinney, all fake smiles.

"Where can a man buy some crack?" He fake-smiled back at McKinney with the kind of look designed to make a smarter man shiver.

Bob McKinney wasn't that smart. He just acted like he had no idea what this "crack" was.

Morton looked at him with a lifetime full of rage and hatred bred in the worst ghettoes of Houston, and then turned away without a word and went to drive the car away. Air freshener and all. Before he was off the lot, all the windows were down.

After their first information gathering expedition in February, Houston drug lord Melton Carr had sent additional teams to Piney Creek, and now had sent Morton and Ben Pickett Jr. back to move ahead with his takeover. Piney Creek was about to become the crack center of East Texas and western Louisiana, and McKinney was in the way.

Two elderly sisters in Lufkin read a Whitmire Standard *story about a pregnant nineteen-year-old being burned out of the old school bus that was her home. They decided charity was needed and collected clothing, food, utensils, and hundreds of dollars in donations, then drove some sixty miles to Whitmire. Joyous at the wonder and gratitude that filled the young woman's eyes, the sisters started home in a golden glow of happiness. Topping a hill, they wandered across the median into the oncoming path of a loaded log truck. Investigators spent three days determining how many victims were in their car.*

CHAPTER

TWENTY-FOUR

About twice a year, Darryl Stewart got a call from a rich oil-and-gas attorney in Houston about mowing his ranch. The man never went to the ranch because he was too busy, but he had picked it up for a song about a decade before and hoped one day to retire there and raise horses. It was a nice ranch. About 350 acres on a hill sloping toward the north, well drained, good soil, and near the highest point in East Texas at about 700 feet above sea level. The longer the attorney lived in Houston, the more convinced he was that he wanted to move to high ground, away from the Gulf coast. He was not a complete dumb-ass, Darryl thought. Besides, it was a nice piece of property.

Darryl had a 52-horsepower John Deere tractor with a six-foot rotary mower locally known as a "bush hog" he kept at the deer lease. Most of the year he just used it to whack down the weeds and brush along the roads at his lease, and toward the end of summer he used it to put in his oat patches to bait the whitetail deer. But twice a year he would load it up on his lowboy trailer and haul it out to the attorney's property to mow down the 350 acres of unused pasture.

At some point in the distant past, previous owners had built a drive-through barn out there, pretty much in the middle of the pasture, with a few oak trees and a nice grove of pecans nearby. The moss-covered remains of a burned-out house still stood in the shade, its stone fireplace sticking up like a "fuck-you" finger. It would make a pretty site for a new house, Darryl thought, if a man wanted to have a house without a lake in his front yard. The way the land sloped, it would be possible to bulldoze a lake at the bottom of the property near the paved farm-to-market road, and the subsoil would probably hold for a few decades. Darryl could see the lake in his mind's eye, but he already had a lake he fished in. He didn't need to build one. And besides, he had the pothole in front of his house.

He reckoned one day he would put trotlines in that pothole, see if he could land some of those catfish he'd stocked in there.

For folks who don't know, a trotline is a submerged fishing line that runs out across a body of water. It has hooks hanging down every so often, tied to the main line. Most people suspend the line from floats so they can find it, but some don't. Plastic gallon milk jugs are still a popular type of float, but some fishermen just tie off the ends at the bank on either side of a river, or between bald cypress trees if they are fishing in the syrupy waters of East Texas. Sometimes they drive stakes into the riverbed to suspend the line. You don't want a trotline that drags on the bottom, because it snags things. But if you're fishing for catfish that live on the bottom of lakes and rivers, then you want the hooks hanging low, nearly all the way to the bottom. There was an art to placing a trotline, and Darryl was a Renaissance master at it.

But Darryl had a lot of practice with trotlines. He routinely checked about seven miles of trotlines he had strung in the Corps of Engineers lake near Whitmire, and his deep freeze back home on the porch next to Mary's pottery wheel was always filled with hundreds of pounds of fish. What room was left in the freezer was stocked with venison from the deer lease. Those were the two main protein sources for the Stewart household. He never bothered shooting squirrels or raccoons, which he considered plebeian and beneath him.

That Friday evening, the Houston attorney called Darryl.

"How they hanging, Darryl?" the wealthy, aristocratic, Harvard-educated attorney asked.

"Lemme check," said Darryl. A moment later he said, "I reckon I'm still in business."

They bantered for a few minutes, and the attorney asked him if he'd been up to the ranch to mow yet that year.

Darryl said he had not and lamented how the whole county was drowning in the remains of Tropical Storm Beryl.

They talked about the weather for a bit, and then the attorney said he was thinking of getting an architect up there sometime in August and asked him to have the place mowed by then so they could find it. Or at least find the property lines.

Darryl assured him that would not be a problem. He was busy busy these days, making money hand over fist, but he'd be happy to take a couple of days off to drive the tractor up there and bush hog that property. As always, he added, it would take the better part of two weeks, unless the man wanted it butchered as well as mowed. In that case it would take three weeks.

"Just the mow is all I want this time," the attorney said. "And send me a bill. Same address as always."

"Yes, sir," Darryl said. He kind of liked this job. It got him outside all day, he wasn't supervised, he didn't need to work during the hot hours of the day, but he got paid for them anyway. Overall, he wondered why all jobs weren't as easy and satisfying as this one.

"Darryl," called Mary from the kitchen. "Do you want the arsenic or the cyanide on your green salad tonight?"

"This is an arsenic kind of evening, I think," he replied. "And by the way, I'm leaving early in the morning to go run the trotlines. No telling what kind of fish those floodwaters washed down the river."

"That's nice, dear. But it is Roadrunner morning."

"I'll be back before you even open your eyes," he said, going in to pinch her butt.

"Stop that, you fool," she giggled as she slapped his hand away, "and come sit down to eat."

"Pour me some buttermilk to dip this cornbread in," he smiled. It was shaping up to be a good time of year. Fully stocked freezer and it was only the end of April. Good-paying jobs. Plenty of work if he wanted it, but a man had to be careful how much he wanted, or he'd wear his ass plumb out.

All things considered, Darryl Stewart was happy with his life.

Now, some boys in East Texas dream about getting the largest buck of the hunting season. They will sit around the cafes drinking coffee and bragging or listening yet again to how so-and-so killed a twelve-point buck. Or about the seventeen-point buck, a freak, killed up near Cherokee. And other guys will talk about the size of the bass they caught out of the Corps of Engineers lake, or about the thirteen-pounder Florida hybrid bass that fed their family for a week. For most East Texas guys, size mattered. The biggest antlers, the most squirrels, the largest fish. If you could measure it, they'd compete against the record. A man who held a record might keep it for decades before somebody came along to better it and go in the record books. If you held such a record, you'd likely keep it the rest of your life and die knowing you were better at something than anybody else. It was what passed for fame in East Texas. Success was measured by size. And the guys at the cafe knew the records, and many of them knew the record holders, or were descended from them.

One calm summer morning at dawn, Darryl had almost got his name in the record books when he hauled in a 118 pound 7 ounce blue catfish from the river channel at the bottom of the Corps of Engineers lake. But that huge fish, more than six feet long, had been two pounds shy of the lake record and three pounds shy of the state record. Darryl had hung that fish in his backyard to gut it, like a deer, while all his neighbors and other friends came by to take pictures and admire it. Then he cut it into two-inch thick catfish steaks he shared with the neighborhood, which were the best eating he ever had. But the fish had done something else to Darryl. Whereas prior to catching that huge fish he had just been running his trotlines a couple of times a week for the sake of bagging fish for the Lions Club Fish Fry, held each July Fourth, now that he had come so close—so close!—to the state record, he was obsessed with catching another one. A bigger one! A state record! He'd be famous. People would ask him for his autograph, television stations would come interview him. Hell, he might even get a lucrative sponsorship from some boating company or tackle maker.

And if there was a 118-pound 7-ounce fish in that lake, he was just positive there would be that fish's bigger brother weighing enough to set the state record. Maybe the national record. It was a great lake for catfish.

Darryl was bound and determined that he would be the most famous trot fisherman in the history of Texas, and it drove him to wake up every morning, hook up his boat to his work truck, and drive out through the morning fog to the lake to run his trotlines. Every morning. Mary never even knew he was gone, and the peace and tranquility on the lake before dawn was like opium to him.

Darryl was addicted. At 4 a.m. every morning, his eyes popped wide. He needed his fix.

News budget April 24: Taylor Ake harvested a large turnip that looked suspiciously like Commissioner George Brown—short, fat, pasty-white. The turnip weighed forty-two pounds. Brown said he was proud to be recognized by the good earth of Sweetgum County and assumed the resemblance was in honor of his careful management of the county's resources. Ake said he'd consider whether to mash it or roast it but promised Brown a bite. The turnip could have been a world record if he'd weighed it officially before dicing it up. This elicited an ironic laugh from Darryl Stewart at County Court Cafe.

CHAPTER
TWENTY-FIVE

Morton parked the yellow Oldsmobile on the street near the dead end and went into the nightclub alone around 6 p.m. on Friday, but the place was slow and not many people were there. Pickett had returned to Houston to take care of a small "human resources matter" in Baytown, and Morton was relieved to be away from his companion, who was silent, humorless, and fatal.

The club was just a converted row house with several interior walls removed. It had an armored door, a long bar down one side, and a set of furniture brand-new since Morton's last reconnoiter. Liquor bottles padlocked in stout wire cages hung on the wall behind the bar, which had a row of coolers for beer and wine along its length. Unlike many places, no snacks or food were available. This place was strictly for drinking and visiting, and Morton approved of that focus. He thought most places tried to do too much and missed the central issue, which was to sell overpriced alcohol.

"You're back," said Chillers Banks, the bartender, wiping his hands on a dirty rag. Banks was so black that even his gums were dark blue. In his mid-fifties, he wore his pants hiked up above his navel and had a bulge in his right pocket that Morton suspected was a pistol. A ring of keys dangled from his belt. Morton also figured he had a shotgun under the bar somewhere. Security cameras witnessed everything that went on inside the club, and three of them from different angles were focused on the cash register alone, including one that pointed straight down from the ceiling. It occurred to Morton that wherever the feed from those cameras went, it was probably not to any place inside the club, which had no spare rooms or closets, just a single bathroom with a dirty brown sink in a corner in the back.

"I forgot what you drink," said Banks. "I also forgot your name, Third Ward."

"Third Ward does okay," said Morton. "I drink Budweiser."

"What's your real name?" asked Banks, handing him the can. Bottles were too dangerous.

"Skip it," said Morton. "I'll sit over there and wait."

"We don't want any trouble in here, bro," said Banks, swabbing the bar with the rag. "But we can deal with trouble."

"Not here to cause trouble," replied Morton, who moved over to a small table next to the wall and sat with his back away from the window, keeping his eye on the bar and on the front door.

Patrons began entering the bar around 8 p.m., mostly men, some women in groups and one or two unattended women, all of them Black. Somebody dropped change in an old jukebox and music started, mostly rhythm and blues. Morton noticed one smartly dressed woman, more self-confident than the others, join a small group of women at the bar. They all seemed to treat her with respect and a kind of deference, and that set her apart. Banks handed her a small bottle of white wine and a white plastic cup, but she did not twist the cap off the bottle for some time. She was there to visit, obviously, not to drink. She said something in a low voice for the others to hear, and they all broke into raucous laughter, then she glanced his way.

He was intrigued, but unmoved. She looked like an academic with her square, clear-rimmed glasses, her tasteful gold chain around her neck, her dark gray silk shirt over a matching pair of modest pants. She was obviously a woman who was more intellectual than she was sexy. Morton liked sexy. He didn't care for women who were thinkers.

Still, his most useful distributor was an innocent-looking little high school girl, about ninety pounds and a sweet, cherubic face. She moved more crack than anyone else on his squad. The woman at the bar did not appear to be the kind who tolerated drugs. After fifteen years sizing up customers, Abbie Morton had become an expert at discerning that peculiar odor of bored desperation that always seemed to ooze out of users. She was clean, and he was the bored one.

He looked back at the door, ignoring the little knot of women at the bar, and waited. He was as still as a copperhead camouflaged in fallen leaves waiting for a squirrel to scamper by.

But such waiting has its limits, and a warm beer makes a lousy dinner. By 8 p.m., he had been nursing the one overpriced Budweiser for two hours, and it had completely lost its appeal. Still, he waited, and almost exactly at 9 p.m. a tall man in a loose leather sport coat entered the club carrying a duffle bag. That was Clarence Thomas, he knew. With a gentle flick of his fingers, Morton pushed the beer aside and watched for Thomas to gather his bottle of sweet wine at the bar—no charge—and go to a seat in the back, in the shadows on the other side of the busy pool table. Most drug pushers like to be closer to an exit, but Thomas obviously felt comfortable, even protected, in this place and at that spot. A security camera's red light pointed directly at the table.

Thomas busied himself for a moment, putting his duffle bag between his feet, unscrewing the cap on the bottle of red wine, getting himself adjusted in the seat, then reaching into his bag to pull out several clear plastic baggies of what appeared to be marijuana. The dealer was in business, and soon enough, first one customer then another ambled over to the table, money changed hands, and the baggies disappeared. Finally, one loud man who had been gesticulating and laughing over by the pool table went over and spoke to Thomas, who reached into his duffle and brought out a small bag of white powder. Morton recognized it instantly. That was East Coast heroin, produced at labs between Baltimore and Annapolis. You could tell it anywhere from the gold foil sticker sealing the bag shut.

Maybe it's time for me to visit with Mr. Thomas, he thought, shoving his chair back.

Walking past the bar, however, the smart girl in the gray silk shirt stopped him.

"Say," she said, "tell us something."

"What?" he growled.

"Me and the girls, we want to know your name and where you're from."

"Why?"

"Because we never see new people around here, and we're curious. We just want to know."

"Third Ward," he said.

"No it's not," she said. "That's not your real name. The way you walk, I bet your momma called you Prince."

"Or Little Emperor," laughed one of the other girls.

"Don't mess with me," he said, "and I won't mess with you."

"But we want to," she said. "We hardly ever see anybody new. Besides, there's only one King in this place and that's me. So you can't be in charge."

"What do you mean?" he asked, stopping.

"She's Lizzie King," laughed one of the other girls, "and she rules with an iron fist. You don't want to piss off the king."

"That's right," said another girl, "she'll have your head taken plumb off."

He shoved past them, but not rudely, leaving them to their private hilarity, and approached Thomas.

"Hello, brother," said Thomas. "What do you want?"

"Crack," said Morton.

"No crack allowed in here," said Thomas. "I've got weed, meth, a few others, but you got to ask for them."

"What you are getting for your smack?" asked Morton.

"Depends. You want cut or uncut? You want the sealed or the open? You gonna shoot it, sniff it, or smoke it?"

"You got uncut?"

"Five spot per five grams, and it don't come any smaller."

"What is it cut with? Not baby powder or powdered sugar?"

"Why that matter?"

"Wanna know what I'm sticking into myself."

"You are sticking heroin, fool. Nothing else matters. But I'll tell you my lab cuts it with powdered glucose. Or you can also get it with glucose and powdered Benadryl. That one is sort of pink and you don't want to smoke it."

"I've seen heroin before from the East Coast. That looks like what you're selling."

"I think it's time for you to put money on the table or get the fuck out of here," said Thomas, raising his chin toward the door.

"Oh? What are you gonna do? Call the cops?"

"I don't need to call them. My good friend Mr. Chillers Banks will turn you into smoked sausage tomorrow morning, bones and all. Don't mess around where you don't know what you're doing."

"Hey, honey," said Lizzie King as he shoved through the throng at the bar. "That your yellow sedan out front?"

"Why?" he asked.

"You might better be careful with it. Old Clarence over there, he's as mean as a rattlesnake. Just telling you for your own good. I like the look of you, but you need to stay clear of him if you don't want a world of trouble."

The lighting strike blew up a pine tree, scattering splinters in a hundred-yard circumference. It dug a foot-wide trench from the base of the tree about fifty feet to an old metal washtub half buried in leaf mold, heating it incandescent. In a split second, the howitzer-like explosion was all gone but the ashes and debris.

"Scared me bad," said Virgil Stalcup. "I was sitting there on the porch rocking and watching the storm go over and worrying about my roof, and bam! Danged near took my head off with that piece of wood." He pointed to a four-foot-long splinter.

CHAPTER
TWENTY-SIX

Jesse Grinder got sent home early on Friday. McKinney didn't give him a reason. He just sent him home. No deliveries that day; the garage was empty; the flood had gone down; nobody was buying cars. The truth was, McKinney decided he did not care for Jesse Grinder too much and would be happier if he quit. He'd think about it over the weekend, and probably fire him on Monday, unless he thought of some reason to keep him on. The only two things Grinder had going for him was he probably was too stupid to know what was in those packages he was delivering, and he was honest about bringing back the money. That was a lot, considering. That might be enough, he thought, tapping the steering wheel with his fingers as he drove along the oak-shaded streets.

McKinney was driving one of the cars off the lot out to Belle Guinness's house. She had said she owed him, which she did, and the big bosomy woman had ways to pay a debt that any man would find satisfying. But he had more on his mind than that. He wanted to find out why she hadn't said anything about the little extra gift he sent along, and he wanted to be sure Grinder had not screwed things up with Belle the way he screwed things up with Congressman Rip Johnson's neurotic wife. He wondered if old Rip might like a stronger dose for his wife. The man had younger women in stables somewhere he could replace her with. He'd feel him out on that next time they had a moment alone.

Which was probably going to be tomorrow afternoon, when he drove out to make his monthly payments.

He turned onto Belle's street and immediately sensed there was some kind of trouble. A big black buzzard was sitting in her front yard, like he'd been there all day. Overhead, way up, he saw a dozen more buzzards circling the neighborhood. Buzzards don't usually just sit in people's yards, he thought to himself. They move off if anybody's around. Nobody's come or gone from that yard for a bit.

Even the grass had gotten shaggy despite the rain. It was sending tendrils out across the sidewalk, and worms were wiggling out of the drowned earth. Belle's Cadillac, one he'd sold her almost brand new, looked like it had not been moved all week, all the windows yellow with pine pollen. The house had the distinct air of being unoccupied, despite the car being there.

He made the turn at the end of the cul-de-sac and drove back, getting a glimpse of the backyard with standing pools of water. A few egrets were foraging for bugs, their extreme white plumage a stark contrast with the death-black buzzards overhead.

Nobody is living in that house, he concluded. I guess I'll just have to wait to find out what happened to her.

Maybe Jesse knows, he thought. Hope he didn't kill her. Be just like him, stupid son of a bitch.

Jesse, however, had driven slowly back to the mobile home park, and then even more slowly through the park itself. About a hundred trailers were scattered around, most of them out of sight of one another, which was one of the selling points of the place, according to the manager. Privacy. "Where else are you gonna get privacy plus a place to park your mobile home?" he'd asked Jesse when they were discussing the rent. "Folks live out here like their privacy. Hell, ever-body does, ain't that right, boy."

He spotted the bright color of Annabeth's blouse moving away from the manager's office, and slowed even more to watch her from a distance, intrigued. He knew exactly where she lived. He'd even been over in the dark to look at her trailer, wondering, stalking. Sometimes he'd even gotten close enough to the back side of her trailer to hear her television through the walls, or her talking to her three-year-old daughter.

One night, he'd been startled by a sudden burst of activity from inside the thin walls, and then a car had pulled in front, the lights sweeping across his legs through the underside of the home. Cries of delight, door slamming open, little girl shouting, "Daddy! Daddy!"

The lights scared him, and he scampered back to his own trailer. What if he'd been seen? That husband of Annabeth's was a really strong-looking guy, big neck, big arms, tattoos, but short. He'd watched him, too. Judging. Maybe he could take that guy in a fight. He figured that offshore job on the oil rig kept him pumped up. Probably those guys had nothing else to do but work hard and then exercise. He decided he'd lie low whenever that husband showed up.

Still, he was gone three weeks at a time. So that gave Jesse an idea, and he hunted up some scratch paper and a stub of pencil and made himself a calendar. He crossed out the days the husband was home. Then he couldn't help himself, so he put question marks in all the other days. This weekend was one of the question mark weekends. The last one for a while. He sat in his stuffy place staring into empty space, the calendar in his hand, and started thinking about Belle Guinness, the things she'd done to him. Then he went away. It had been a few months since he'd gone away, but this one segued into a full night of sleep.

He woke up in the morning hungry. One can of beans left in the place, so he would need to go buy more. He had his pay for the week, which wasn't much because McKinney had docked him for a few hours on Monday and again on Friday. He'd need to get more food from somewhere, and it gradually dawned on him he could maybe open Annabeth's door while she was gone, get some food from her refrigerator, and test out his locksmithing skills at the same time. He'd watch and wait for her to go somewhere like she always did on Saturday morning, shopping or something, and go try the door.

Beautiful Whitmire cheerleader Annie Putnam, sixteen, had a stimulating summer. Her father put in a swimming pool, and she spent almost every day hosting "swimming" parties with her friends. They competed to see who could wear the most attractive bikinis, as measured in the interest shown by neighborhood boys. By the end of June, their new bikinis were threatening to bankrupt their families. It's amazing how much four square inches of cloth and a few strings can cost. Removing body hair became a full-time preoccupation for these girls, and sunshine on skin and hair did all the rest. They glowed.

Charles Henniker was walking through downtown Whitmire early on Saturday morning before the businesses started opening up, cooling off from his six-mile run. It was one of those mystical days, when the air was heavy with humidity and oxygen breathed out by the trees overnight, and the birds were the only sounds. No actual daylight yet, just a kind of semi-gray light in the east, that time of day when the birds wake up hungry and talkative. He saw a red pickup pulling a fishing boat stop at the light in front of the courthouse, the only vehicle moving on the street in any direction for miles, and watched the driver yawn. Under one of the oak trees on the courthouse lawn he spotted Isaac from the jail and went over to say hello. He wondered if Isaac would remember where they were in their chess game.

"Ah," said Isaac as he walked up. "Make move."

"Hello, Isaac," Henniker said. He wiped the sweat from his brow with the sleeve of his tee shirt. It had been quite a week: storm, flood, missing girl, jail, new friends. Maybe his world was expanding a little. It felt good. It felt like he was moving into a real place in it, gradually being shoved and pulled by some universal force into the place he needed to be. His instincts told him to meet as many people as he could. Learn as much as he could about them. And it genuinely pleased him to see Isaac. This was one of the world's more interesting eccentrics.

"So, you heard news?" he asked Henniker.

"No, not since the other day when they found that girl."

"Silly girl," said Isaac.

"Just young," said Henniker. "The young ones don't need to think to survive. Maybe she will grow up."

"They lost police chief," said Isaac. "Lost him. Can't find him nowhere. Look and look. He not seen all week."

"Queen to b3," he added.

"Pawn on d5 takes your pawn on c4," Henniker replied.

Isaac sputtered and cursed. "You still play that game? Not think for self?"

"From the crowds of pickups parked over there, I think the County Court Cafe is open across the street," Henniker said. "May I buy you a cup of coffee?"

Indeed, the place was full of men, or almost. A few tables remained near the door, but the long bar in front of the cook was elbow-to-elbow with the town's workers and small business owners. Most were smoking, many were laughing or thumping the tables with their index fingers as they made one point or another. The surly waitress was obviously reluctant to come to their table, pretending to be busy behind the counter, but eventually she came over with two cups dangling from one index finger and a Bunn coffee pot in the other hand. You could tell from her expression that she'd be damned if she would bring them menus, until the owner, who was the cook, saw them. He spoke to her, she hissed at him, and he raised his spatula to her with a threat. Then she stalked over to the table and dropped menus on the table with a slap and walked away through the clouds of cigarette smoke. Isaac and Henniker ignored the young woman and chatted briefly about chess while they sipped at their coffee. After a few minutes, BoMac came in, his camera slung across his shoulder.

"Hey," Henniker called, "BoMac. Come join us."

"Say, Mr. Henniker," BoMac began, but Henniker held up a finger.

"I asked you to call me Charles." He smiled.

"Oh right. Yes, you did. I enjoyed our get-together the other night and meant to ask you about the research project you had your kids doing. What did you come up with?"

For the next ten minutes or so, Henniker and BoMac discussed the massive erosion caused by Tropical Storm Beryl, and the lasting effects of the flood. As of Thursday night, the town had finally been liberated by falling creek levels, and people could drive in and out of town over the still-swollen creeks. Grocery supplies had resumed, including deliveries of toilet paper that had mysteriously disappeared at the first hint of a shortage. Now it was Saturday morning, and last weekend's storm was fading into memory.

"Isaac was telling me they've lost the police chief," said Henniker, changing the subject.

"He's missing," agreed BoMac. "Whitmire being the kind of town it is, there are plenty of rumors." He smiled at Henniker. "You better check your alibis before they come after you again."

Henniker laughed. "Again!" He sputtered, smiling. "You might be right. I hadn't thought of that."

"Nobody know where he be," said Isaac, "No car. No nothing. Car and Trey Green, both gone."

"That car could be a problem," said BoMac. "The city's revenue is not that good and buying a new patrol car isn't in the budget. They're going to argue about that at city council meetings from now on." BoMac was about to make a lame joke about "eating greens" when Darryl Stewart burst in from the street shouting at the top of his lungs, his pickup still running, stopped in the middle of the highway.

"Lord help me! Lord help me!" screamed Stewart to the crowded cafe. "Come quick! I found him!"

CHAPTER
TWENTY-SEVEN

Henniker was through the door before anyone else, hustling a sobbing Darryl Stewart by his elbow back to the truck. "Call the sheriff's office, the police office, whoever," he shouted back at Isaac, who had risen from his chair in the commotion. "Where are we going?" he demanded of Darryl. "Corps of Engineers lake," he shouted again at Isaac. "Boat ramp." It wasn't easy understanding Stewart's panicked mutterings, but he'd dealt with traumatized men before.

"I'm with you," BoMac called to him, rushing to catch up. "Let's get him in the truck and take off."

Henniker nodded and surrendered Stewart to BoMac, who managed to shove the wilting man into the truck's passenger seat and then slide him over to make room for himself. Henniker took the wheel and they were off—Henniker's squealing U-turn leaving smoke behind, and the empty boat trailer fishtailing. He braked slightly for the light at the highway crossing, leaning on his horn and blinking the lights, then blew through the intersection. No one was coming. Moments later they were hurtling through the gradually brightening dawn, mailboxes on the side of the road whipping by.

Stewart began to revive while BoMac plied with him questions, and checked to be sure he had film in his camera and the lens was clear. Henniker reached for the dashboard, flicked the air conditioner to defrost, and opened his window.

"Cold air fogging the windshield," he explained with the wipers going. "Too humid for A/C right now." That's all he said in the full fifteen minutes it took to reach the boat landing, wheeling off the highway with more screeching and complaining of tires, the headlights bouncing across the concrete landing, revealing where Stewart's boat was tied off to a cypress knee. A swirl in the water at the end of the boat and two triangular orangish-red lights about six inches apart reflected back at them.

"Goddamned alligators got to him already," said Stewart, struggling to get out. "He was too heavy for me to get him out the water. I had to drag him completely across the lake."

"Tell us what happened," BoMac insisted.

"I was running my trotline," said Stewart. "Just pulling out across the lake, one hook at a time every ten or fifteen feet. The really big fish live on the bottom of the river channel, down about maybe fifty feet, and just as I got to my hook in the channel, I felt something heavy tugging at the line and thought I'd got another big catfish. So heavy I thought it was a state record. Thought I'd have a state record!"

He broke down as Henniker waded into the water at the back of the boat, dragging on the heavy fishing line where it trailed off underwater.

"I was so damned excited!" Stewart got out before he started sobbing again, clutching at BoMac's shirt. "Gonna be the greatest day of my life, I thought. Gonna be a record for sure. And then, you know, I felt this knocking on the bottom of the boat, something kicking at it, like a big fish struggling, and I pulled up one more time and Trey's face floated up in the water, all bloated and white."

Henniker had the body partly out of the water, but just laid it to rest on the concrete. He looked around in the boat and found a towel he draped across Trey Green's face, then leaned to put his hand against the boat and panted. In the distance the three men heard sirens heading their way.

"Couldn't lift him," Stewart repeated. "I tried to grab him by his shirt, but it tore. Then by his belt, but his mouth opened and bubbles came out. His eyes were open, looking up out of the water. After that, I just towed him by the trotline. 'Fraid it might pull out, and every once in a while, I'd run over a stob or a log and have to slow down. Didn't have the heart to touch him."

"That alligator didn't do much to him," Henniker said at last. "I think we rescued him just in time, or what there was to rescue. The little fish already got his eyelids and the skin under his jaw."

The first police car wheeled into the entrance and slowed when the headlights showed the scene. A dozen or more cars followed, including the volunteer fire department rescue truck with its famous and very expensive piece of hydraulic equipment called the "jaws of life." They used it to pry accident victims out of wrecked cars, but obviously had no need for it at this scene. Other supplies in the truck could have come in handy, but Trey Green's body had been in the cold water at the bottom of the river channel for some days, it looked like. Not much they could do for Trey.

Everyone looked at the towel-draped corpse, examined the body with their flashlights, just staring, shaking their heads, muttering quietly. They would have to wait for the Justice of the Peace to come out and pronounce him dead, and then help the coroner load him into the hearse to transport his body to the morgue. He didn't need to be seen by a doctor, not yet.

BoMac took pictures, some with flash and some without to capture the mood of the scene. He wouldn't publish photos of the body, but the gloomy, skin-crawling scene might make a good feature shot. Maybe a good shot of the boat bobbing on the water. A photo of the alligator's eyes would be a knock-out prize winner, but the gator was gone.

"Gonna do an autopsy?" BoMac asked the volunteer fire chief.

"Tell you what," Henniker said coming over, "his jaw is all out of shape, like it was broken. You are going to want to autopsy."

"Who's going to pay for that?" the chief asked. "County can't autopsy everybody."

"What I'm saying," Henniker said slowly, "is my bet is that he was beaten and might have already been dead when he went in the water. I'm guessing this will prove to be murder."

The chief stared at him a minute without speaking.

"Who are you?" he finally asked Henniker.

"I'm the new teacher at the school," said Henniker.

"Best stick to your own business," the fire chief said. "We can always use good help, but we don't need smart-asses making decisions." He turned and walked away.

"Charles, man, I'm sorry for that," whispered BoMac.

"It's okay, BoMac. It's okay. Man needs to get off his high horse, but this is not the time or place. Go ask some questions and I'll just go keep watch over the body so that alligator doesn't sneak up out of the water again while we squabble."

"Need a weapon or something?"

"Nah. Just an alligator. I'll take him home and make a pet out of him if I want to or cut off his tail and eat it." He smiled his big smile, licked his lips, and went back to sit on the gunwale of the boat.

Justice of the Peace Teresa Lewis arrived with C. L. Turner, the district attorney. Everyone called him "cock lover" to his back, and he knew it, so he compensated by wearing the most ostentatious weaponry he could: shoulder holster with a 10mm caliber Colt Delta Elite pistol, another pistol at his waist along with some smoke and flash grenades, and a variety of weapons in his bullet-holed truck, including a sawed-off 12-gauge "riot" shotgun with buckshot and a fully automatic M16 with 300 rounds of ammo. He kept a .38 snub-nosed revolver with a shrouded

145

hammer in one commodious boot, and a Bowie knife with a saw-blade cut into its spine in a shin-scabbard on his other leg. To hold his pants up with all that weight of threatening metal, he wore his karate black belt across his shoulder like a bandolier. He cut quite a picture for a district attorney, especially when he appeared in court wearing all this armament.

"I thought he knew how to swim," Turner said loudly, with a chuckle, to no one in particular.

People liked Trey Green, in general. He was just a guy, someone they grew up with, not special except he was police chief, and Turner's remark seemed to them the kind of statement that probably should have been saved for the County Court Cafe, where irreverence and insolence were expected—not here in this solemn location, spoken over the corpse of their friend.

"Who found him?" asked Turner when he didn't get a rise out of the men.

The fire chief nodded his chin at Darryl Stewart, who was leaning with his head down against the fender of his pickup.

"You find him?" asked Turner in his best prosecutorial courtroom voice.

Stewart nodded.

"Was he dead?"

"He was under water, he wasn't breathing except to have bubbles come out of his mouth when I tried to lift him, and he was swollen and pasty white," Stewart replied. "His eyes was open in the water, but they weren't moving. That's what I saw."

"Maybe he was dead," said Turner.

"You reckon?" asked Stewart.

Meanwhile the judge had walked over, and one of the deputies lifted the towel from Green's face. The judge bent down, shone a light in Green's waterlogged eyes, and stood up.

"He's dead," said Judge Lewis. "Let's let Mr. Quick take him. John," she said speaking to the black-suited undertaker standing nearby, "you can take him. Some of these men will help you lift him."

"Thank you," Quick replied in a voice that sounded like crude oil pouring from a Coca-Cola bottle. "Shall I determine a cause of death?"

"Oh, he probably drowned, don't you think?" she replied.

"Maybe," he said. "I'll let you know. Hard to tell if he's been in the water a long time, which it looks like. If I see anything suspicious, I'll let you know."

"Might be handy to have a time of death while the body's still this side of the ground," she said.

"Gonna be hard to get an internal temperature. Might be the same as the bottom of the river. I'll go drop a thermometer down there this afternoon, get a base reading," replied Quick, moving the gurney into position and reaching down to hold the towel out to Henniker. "Little help?" he asked.

Henniker dropped the towel back into Stewart's boat and waded into the alligator-infested water to lift Green by his slimy, alligator-savaged ankles. Several others helped get the soggy corpse up, dripping, onto the gurney.

"Sorry to get your gurney wet, John," said Judge Lewis.

"That's okay, your honor. Not the first time."

All four county commissioners decided to attend the inauguration in Austin and invited BoMac to ride along. With him in the car, the trip couldn't violate the state's Open Meetings law, and helped save on gas. To save more money, they booked rooms in the Stephen F. Austin hotel, which had fallen into disrepair, and the heat went out during a rare Austin winter night when the temperature fell to twenty-one degrees. "I went to pee this morning," said Commissioner George Brown, "and my poor old peter was so cold it looked like a little wren sitting on a nest."

CHAPTER
TWENTY-EIGHT

When Charles Henniker got home from the lake, the phone was ringing.

"How's my fav'rite cuz?" asked a deep male voice.

"Calvin?"

"Lemme tell you what," said Calvin King. "Momma came home from the store with a whole case of Nilla wafers. Know what that means?"

"Banana pudding?"

"She's making banana pudding for hundreds. Has maybe fifty pounds of bananas, maybe a hundred. Got more damned eggs than you can count, but you know those chickens. Laying all the time. I say it looks like she's having a party."

"Isn't tomorrow Mother's Day?" asked Henniker.

"Of course it is. And I have the smoker going. Been going since dawn. I'm putting half a ton of beef and pork on there in about five hours and I'm going to cook it all night. We are planning to serve about two tomorrow, after church. You coming up?"

"Sounds great. I don't have anything going on down here and I'd like to get out of town for a bit before these people dream up something new."

"Heard about your night in jail."

"Pretty brief, actually. They locked me up, then dropped the charges and let me go. Was only in there maybe an hour."

"Still. Jail. No fun. Been there myself."

"Yeah."

"So, you coming?"

"I can go down to Crooks Bros. Grocery store and buy them out of three-liter bottles of Big Red and Grape soda. I'll bring as much ice as I can."

"We have the ice. Bring about four hundred plastic cups and all the soda you can haul. The whole family will be here for Mother's Day."

"Why is Momma cooking on Mother's Day?"

"For all her daughters and sisters, Charlie. All her daughters and sisters, and daughter's daughters and their kids. And everybody is bringing something. We are going to have enough food to feed the whole county."

"Hell, our family IS the whole county."

"You got that right. Miss you, cuz. Gotta call some more family. See you tomorrow?"

"Yes, sir," said Henniker. "I'll be there with a trunk load of sodas and cups."

He was smiling when he hung up the phone. "Momma" Henniker was the grand matriarch of their huge family, a great-great-grandmother to the youngest children. She had over a hundred direct descendants, plus all their husbands and in-laws. Some had moved off, including a few living in Los Angeles, Baltimore, Chicago, some in federal agencies in Washington or holding elected office. She was short, round, and in her late eighties, but she ruled the large clan with invisible power and love. Her infectious smile comforted and encouraged everyone, and they were drawn to her sweetness like bees to honey. She was literally everyone's momma. That was the only name they had for her.

Calvin had played NFL football like four of his other brothers and now bred whitetail deer to go along with his prize-winning herd of longhorn cattle. He farmed about a thousand acres of soybeans as well. Not bad for a guy whose salary in his twenties gave him enough cash to retire to luxury and sloth for the rest of his life. But of course, Momma would have none of it. He was her grandchild, and she got all up in his face the first time he showed up with a Lamborghini. She made him go trade it in on a Massey Ferguson tractor, and even went with him to the dealership. When the tractor dealer tried to rook him, she got all up in the dealer's face, too. One did not trifle with Momma. One did what Momma said. And Mother's Day weekend was a gathering day. Everybody came. The only other day of the year that was a gathering day was June 19th, which was the day in 1865 when the slaves in Texas were told they were freed from slavery, and an official holiday known as "Juneteenth."

It was also, as the local preachers were happy to point out, the day when the Nicene Creed was adopted by the Christian church in 325 AD. "Important day," Momma told them all. "We observe that day. That is the day we honor all things visible and invisible, the light of light, and above all, the hope of freedom."

Momma was too deep for many of her children, but her heart was open to all of them. It was mystical, almost magical, how her invisible influence bent and shaped the lives of those who loved her.
And who loved her banana pudding.

On the walls of her kitchen were printed the names of her eight children and all their spouses and children, arranged by generations. She had gone to great effort to get everyone's name and order of descent properly placed. Stepchildren were included. Adopted children were included. At a gathering, everybody at some point walked through her kitchen to see their own names. It was an affirmation of belonging and place. Charles's name was there, with the names of his mother and her mother and the names of all his brothers and their wives. Calvin's name was there, with a gaggle of kids of his own and another of his half-sister's kids. Momma's kitchen wall was a standing memorial to the large family, and she often told people that when she ran out of room for her kids' names, then she had come to the River Jordan, and it was time to cross over to the promised land. "Gonna be my time to wade in the water," she said, "praise Jesus."

Lavinia Fisher's new boyfriend was seventy-nine years old. He lived near the lake and took Lavinia to cook and clean. She wasn't much of a cook, but she slept hard and let him do anything. One day after a hearty night when it had rained, he went out to drive them to town for his meds. His van's tires slipped in the mud, though, so he got out to rock the vehicle back and forth. It went into reverse and backed over him. "That van smushed the old man's head like a rotten orange," the patrol officer told BoMac.

CHAPTER
TWENTY-NINE

Jesse Grinder woke up hungry at about 4 a.m. He lay on his mattress for a time, staring up at the dark ceiling, and then remembered he had nothing to eat. He did have a little cash but getting in the truck and driving back to Piney Creek was too much trouble. He drank some water, and then waited for Annabeth to take her little girl off to the grocery store, where she went every Saturday morning. She was bound to have some food in her place, and he knew now he could get in through the back door of her mobile home, out of sight of anyone else in the neighborhood. He'd wait for her to pull out, then go quietly up to the back with the short stepladder he'd hidden in the brush. This time he would remember to wear gloves and he would let himself in by picking her lock. He'd get in, find some food, and then leave. He already knew the door could be locked from the inside then pushed shut. He'd be out and gone, and she'd never know he'd been there.

About 9:30 on the morning before Mother's Day, with the sun already up and bright, he was hiding in the brush, watching through the underside of her trailer, when he saw her bare legs coming down the steps from her front door. His stomach growled and his mouth watered as he watched the little girl's legs follow her mother, the two talking away to one another in happy tones. A moment later, her Chevy Nova cranked up and he saw the tires of the car move down the driveway. He waited about three minutes and then went up to the door, propped the ladder against it, and in under two minutes opened it with his lock picks. He smelled her presence, and it clouded his mind, something almost fog-like coming over him. He was in the utility room and all their dirty laundry was sitting there in front of the machines in plastic baskets, waiting to be washed. The front-loading washer was already humming and thumping with a load of the weekly chore. He fingered her and the baby's soiled underwear, smelling it as the washing machine switched loudly to the spin cycle. He held the panties to his face and inhaled deeply, closing his eyes, staggering a little as he was overcome, his heart racing, bracing against the dryer.

He didn't hear the front door open or see her until he heard her scream.

Grinder parked Annabeth's Chevy Nova back in front of her mobile home and went inside. No one saw him. With the washing machine finished, the deserted home was silent. Only the smells of her and her baby remained, like ghosts. Hungry, he took a package of meat out of her freezer and a mason jar from the kitchen counter half-filled with loose change, mostly pennies. With the jar of pennies and the frozen meat, he left through the back door, and that afternoon he walked up the road past her mobile home several times, his heart beating faster and faster.

CHAPTER
THIRTY

Every year, in a show of collaboration unusual in Texas, the school districts of Sweetgum County moved their graduation ceremonies to coincide with the annual Mayhaw Festival in Whitmire. Every graduating senior in the county appeared in the lengthy ceremony, which always drew a huge crowd. Instead of black gowns and mortarboards, all of the graduates wore tuxedoes and ball gowns—or their mother's wedding dresses if available—and they competed for various prizes long-established over the eight decades of the festival. The chief prize went to the Queen of the Mayhaw and included a unique gold ring, a hefty college scholarship, and the honor of representing Sweetgum County at all celebratory county and state events. She was even invited to Austin to meet the governor and visit with politicians, where she was expected to ply her feminine charms in the most innocent way among the drooling dogs of the legislature.

Of the five school districts, three had graduating classes of twenty or fewer while Whitmire had the largest graduating class of around ninety. With consistent commercial encouragement and public pressure, every graduate received some kind of prize and a chance to walk the stage in front of a crowd numbering in the thousands, composed of all the county's families. It was a happy, innocent time.

For the most part, academic achievements were the featured honor of the evening, but for the Queen of the Mayhaw, a different set of rules applied. Senior girls interested in being crowned the queen were expected to interview five times before a panel of thirty or forty judges made up of White male business owners in the county to demonstrate their maturity and sense of poise. By simple majority vote over five evenings, the senior girls were winnowed to one girl from each district, with runners-up receiving ranks such as "duchess" or "princess." No girl who had won the "Miss Sweetgum" beauty pageant in February was eligible for the "Queen of the Mayhaw" title, much to the chagrin of certain competitive spirits; tradition was tradition. It just didn't happen. Best not to ask why.

The surprise coronation ceremony occurred at the beginning of the evening, requiring family and parents of all the other graduates to wait for their senior to cross the stage before leaving, thus ensuring the lengthy graduation process would remain fully attended. The queen presided over the awarding of diplomas, blessing each graduate with a nod and a metaphorical sprinkling from her ceremonial trident. Nobody knew why the queen carried a trident. It made no sense to BoMac or to anyone, but again, tradition was tradition. She did not poke at the graduates with the trident, no matter how tempted, and had been warned that even a lighthearted gesture in that direction was grounds for being dethroned, first by a bucket of water over her head while the crown was yanked loose from her hair. The bucket of water was actually carried onto the stage with the crown, appropriately decorated. After all, the mayhaw is a tree that grows in boggy ground and is often harvested by shaking the fruit into the sluggish waters of bay galls and bayous. The relationship between buckets of water and mayhaw fruit is well understood, whereas the symbolism of dumping water over the head of a misbehaving queen is not.

It was a custom that kept BoMac chuckling for weeks before the ceremony, hoping that this would be the year the combined wisdom of the county's merchants failed to elect an obedient and compliant female as queen. It had never happened. He was sure, however, that sooner or later some rebel would slip through the bars and there'd be a standoff in center stage. Think of the photos! he chuckled to himself. He imagined some valedictorian all-state athlete holding off the coronation committee with her trident, cleverly eluding the scrambling committee armed with the decorative water bucket. Would the local police use a taser on her and then drag her offstage by her heels? The people of Sweetgum County were pretty fierce in defense of tradition, which is really all they had.

To pay for these ceremonies, the school districts contributed about $100 per graduate, the commissioners court added another $12.50, the two incorporated cities added another $25 per graduate, and the unincorporated communities, Lions Clubs, and volunteer fire departments all added what they could, which wasn't much. But with careful negotiation and untold hours of haggling, a Lufkin clothing rental outfit would always finally agree to take the thousands of dollars of fees in exchange for the business of supplying the county's graduates with ball gowns and tuxedoes.

After the graduation ceremony, the graduates were hosted at a dance in the Whitmire High School gym, served refreshments, and entertained until the chaperones were ready to drop from exhaustion and it was too late at night for the graduates to get drunk and speed up and down the county's roads, killing themselves in wrecks.

Public life in East Texas is always about available funds, and most residents really did not have the money to contribute to much extra stuff, like one-night clothing rentals. As late as the turn of the twenty-first century, many people were subsistence farmers or day laborers, or both, and cash was scarce even if food was not. Often, food was also scarce. Consequently, the dress-up night for graduates was a big deal. For most, it would be the first and only time they attended a formal function of any kind. Some planned weddings on that weekend to take advantage of the rented clothing.

BoMac felt these financial difficulties acutely. Working as the editor of the Whitmire *Standard*, he knew firsthand what abject poverty felt like. He knew what it meant to live on a diet of oatmeal, beans, and corn tortillas at the end of a month, which for him was most months. He knew that he needed to use his own limited funds to buy film and darkroom supplies, to pay for office supplies, just like the teachers who had to use their own limited salaries to buy teaching supplies. He had gone many months where he had nothing to eat during the last few days, and yet he had only his gasoline and groceries to pay. The money was just not there. A town the size of Whitmire did not have the number of merchants necessary to keep a newspaper alive, and near the end of the month he felt like an indentured servant rather than an employed and skilled administrator. Still, after four years he felt committed to the town and to the county, aware of the important role he filled. It may not seem like much to be the newspaper of record of such things as weather, weddings, funerals, and Boy Scout awards, but it was. Even during his four years he had attorneys and courts seeking his records of weddings and deaths, of weather and traffic accidents. True, no one cared much about the Eagle Scout awards, except the recipients, or the killed rattlesnakes featured most weeks during the spring, or the outlandish tubers pulled from local gardens, but clippings of his newspaper accompanied a large number of college and job applications. He felt a deep responsibility to the county and was careful to preserve his papers in a way that would benefit future generations, to illustrate the full panoply of life with all its quirks and inanities. "This was life in Whitmire," he wanted to tell the future. "This is what it was really like."

This was not a responsibility shared by Mrs. Jane Elkins, his employer. Her interests did not include the welfare or history of a community she considered her thralldom. BoMac chafed at that but could think of no way to change her mind and finally decided that a self-righteous bigot was probably not going to change. So, he did his job and left her out of it as much as he was able. And Ellen Etheridge was such a help! She supported him morally even though she could not support him financially, and their friendship blossomed over shared beans and corn tortillas, for she, too, found the financial reward of being a public-school teacher in a rural district was not large. If she had been a mother, she would have qualified for food stamps, and many teachers made it because they did collect food stamps and some form of welfare. Poverty was and still is endemic in East Texas, a land of pine forests and the brutal lumbering industry.

BoMac knew he could buy the paper from Ms. Elkins, but it would take a lot of money, more than he was worth, and he did not want to negotiate with a bank for that. His father's bankruptcy in Virginia had tainted him, he felt, and his family's squabbling had further undermined his financial background. He was on his own, to make or lose what he could, without his family to rely on, and his prospects were not good. Unless Ms. Elkins would finance his purchase of the paper, and agree to give up control, his chance of owning a struggling rural newspaper in East Texas was nil. It just wouldn't happen. In the long run, he admitted to himself in the dark hours before dawn, it was actually a very difficult job and not a really good investment. The future of newspapers was diminishing as the population of the nation slipped back into illiteracy. He could see it coming.

Besides, if his friendship with Ellen developed beyond the Dairy Queen stage, owning the newspaper would not make much difference. If she wanted to stay in Whitmire and continue teaching, then he would do that. If she wanted to move back to Spring or Sugar Land, he could do that. He had skills now and awards from the Texas Press Association that would make him employable in other markets, but Ellen's affection was not yet sufficient to build a life on. He would just go on, week by day and issue by week, staying up all night on Monday to get the paper finalized for final proofing on Tuesday and off on Tuesday night at 10 p.m. to be printed, back at 4 a.m. Wednesday for addressing and bagging for the post office and for distribution to the news racks, and then a new week beginning on Wednesday afternoon.

For the Mayhaw Festival, however, he had what was called a "special section" of the paper. This would be a sixteen to twenty-four-page tabloid with color, which was expensive, folded into the main paper. He wrote up biographies of each of the five finalists for queen, he recited the academic achievements of the county's graduates, he sold advertising. He included photos of every graduate with their family trees, he noted the scholarships already awarded by such organizations as the Sweetgum County Beauty Pageant, the so-called "University Interscholastic League" for things like debate, one-act play, extemporaneous speaking, "ready writing," and other nonsporting, that is, academic events.

The final state baseball and track-and-field championships were also well underway by the middle of May and drawing to a close. It was always possible that a student athlete would win a regional or state title, and that needed to be a special page in the Mayhaw tabloid, even though he would attend most of the contests personally, take hundreds of photos, spend dozens of hours in the darkroom hoping the chemicals would not make him sick, writing up the stories. The Mayhaw tab wrapped up the school year for everyone, the news cycle ended, and a languorous summer of little activity or news stretched ahead in boring heat and unmoving air, with an occasional snagged catfish for dinner.

For one very slim issue the preceding summer he had written a story with the headline "Killed and Butchered!" He wrote it to sound like a sensational murder of an innocent victim, kidnapped by barbarous heathen. It was, of course, if you read to the end, about the theft of a calf from a local farmer. Cattle rustling was still dealt with by lynching in East Texas, so it was a risky act. Still, the thieves had gotten away with a hundred pounds of meat, enough to get them through a long summer if you added catfish and frogs to the diet. And cattle rustling was rare despite the prevalent hunger of malnourished and unemployed people, so it deserved a story. If it happened every week, he'd ignore it. But if it bled, it led. Front page, top story, column one.

With few exceptions, the only view of the horizon was from the top of the Whitmire water tower. Aboriginal pine forest screened off the distance everywhere else. So illegally climbing the tower appealed to teenagers, something about the view, or about getting away with the challenge, or about being away from parental control. One night Annie Putnam and seven of her friends climbed during a full moon. Transfixed, Annie stared at the moon as if hypnotized, out over a silver sea of pines. Hours later, only she and Willie Dickerson were still on the tower, and he was sound asleep.

CHAPTER
THIRTY-ONE

Charles Henniker pulled his car into the long driveway in front of Calvin's brick palace around 10:30 on Sunday morning, parking in a shady spot beneath the trees, and went looking for Calvin and some help carrying in the fifty three-liter bottles of soda he had secured from Crooks Bros.

Calvin was pushing a trolley through the kitchen loaded with a large tub of pork and venison sausages when Henniker walked in. The big man threw his hands in the air, letting the trolley careen into one of the marble counters, and bounded over to give him a big hug, lifting him from the floor. Calvin had been the all-pro linebacker for Detroit and retained a lion-like posture and attitude toward the world and everything in it. Charles Henniker was his favorite, a man so completely different from himself and yet blood kin—short, scholarly, deadly. He truly loved Henniker. But then, he truly loved most people, which was one of the more endearing things about him.

"Charlie, Charlie," exclaimed Calvin. "I'm so glad to see you. You've been retired what, three years, and I have not laid eyes on you."

"True. I've been up here a few times since I moved to Whitmire, but you weren't here. Folks said you were off at some whitetail deer auction or something."

"I must show you my deer," said Calvin. "You won't believe how large those antlers can get if you feed them right and keep them safe."

"Give me a hint."

"How about nineteen points, with a thirty-two-inch spread?" asked Calvin.

"That's impressive."

"Damn right. And folks will pay a lot of money to hang those horns on their den wall, or the entry to their law firm. You have no idea what a set of horns like that is worth, if you let the man kill it. Probably a hundred thousand dollars, or more. Most ridiculous thing I ever saw—and remember, I played pro ball."

They laughed and visited. After a bit, Calvin threw his massive arm around Henniker's shoulder.

"Tell you what, Charlie. I want you to meet my wife's baby sister. I don't think you have."

"Are you trying to set me up?"

"Have you got a woman at the moment?"

"No, you know that."

"Do you have a boyfriend?"

"What do you think?"

"I've known you and loved you since you were shitting yellow, Charlie, and I don't think you are the kind to have a boyfriend."

"Right."

"But if you don't have a woman, then you probably need one."

"No."

"Oh, come on. She might not like you anyway. And I'm not sure she wants a man. Besides, you know, you're kinda short. She might not like that about you."

"If that's how she makes up her mind, then I'm really not interested," said Henniker. "I don't need a woman in my life."

"If you don't have a woman, you need one," said Calvin. "I'm just saying that for your own good and because I love you."

"What's her name?"

"Lizzie King. If I can, I'll introduce you. If not me, then Cheryl will. No expectations. You two might hate one another at sight. But it would be fun if you hit it off. Family holidays and all. Juneteenth. After school gets out." Calvin was grinning his irrepressible grin, as big as a summer moon.

Henniker helped Calvin load a hundred pounds of sausage into the smoking grill, arranging the links just so over exactly the right spots between the brisket and the ribs to get just exactly the right amount of heat to be ready to eat in three hours. Calvin did nothing haphazardly, so he created a very exacting science to the fine art of smoking meat. Since he also raised most of the meat himself, he felt more than a common interest in achieving perfection in the finished product. Last to go on were a hundred pounds of chicken, arranged at the top of the grill where the heat was highest. The heavy slathering of barbecue sauce prepared with root beer, molasses, pepper, and ketchup for the most part scented the rest of the meat.

Later, after the first three or four hundred people had made their way past Calvin and his altar of barbecue, Charles Henniker and Lizzie King did meet. They were standing in line together as they got to the great chef's serving station.

"I'll take a sausage and a chicken," said Lizzie.

"Same," said Henniker.

"Well, look here," gloated Calvin. "You two have met up already and I don't need to introduce you."

"Introduce me to whom?" asked Lizzie.

"To Charles Henniker, my favorite cousin," chuckled Calvin King. "You two have been standing in line together this whole time, and you haven't talked? Lizzie, meet Charles, and be nice to him, if you can."

"What makes you think I won't be nice?"

"You are your own woman, Lizzie. Cheryl says so and I believe her. Anyway, this is Charles. He's a good man. Say hi and go eat together."

"Are you ordering me around?"

"Let me handle this," said Henniker, stepping forward. "Are you ordering this young lady around?"

"Never," said Calvin, who was rescued at that moment by his wife.

"Lizzie, you're beautiful," said Cheryl, taking Lizzie by the hands. "Thank you so much for being here!"

"I'm trying to hook her up with Charles," said Calvin in a loud, hoarse whisper clearly heard by everyone within twenty yards.

"Oh shush," said Cheryl, "honey you look great. Want to come sit with me at my table?"

They went off together while Henniker sulked along with Calvin, who loaded his plate with more meat than he could possibly eat.

"Okay," said Calvin. "I tried."

"Yes, you did," said Henniker. "I might like her. She's got brains and spunk, I think. I'll take my plate over there and see if those two will let me join them. If not, I'll meet you in the pool hall later and whip your ass."

"Not many people can beat me on my own pool table," said Calvin, "but if anyone can, it will be you."

The family gathering in San Augustine was exceptionally happy. Calvin had a rhythm and blues band come down from Shreveport, the Olympic-sized swimming pool was packed with kids, the smoke from his forty-foot-long grill wafted an aromatic perfume over the entire countryside. The day was hot, the girls in their sundresses and the boys in their slacks and polished shoes congregated by groups, dancing and eating and laughing at one another. Around 4 p.m., the balls came out and teams formed for baseball, basketball, and football. Some of the girls played, too, not happy to let the boys have all the fun.

The adults gathered on Calvin's huge patio around large tables under shady umbrellas, and every member of the family did something to serve the others: carry in food and drink, carry out dirty dishes, pass around bowls of pudding. Momma held court in the center of the gathering, like a queen bee surrounded by workers though she had been up since 4 a.m. baking the pudding and getting exactly the right brown tips on its meringue topping. A stirring three-hour worship service at the Bethsaida A.M.E. Church that morning had cleansed her of every earthly worry, and her spirit beamed like a lighthouse among her hundreds of relatives as they praised her pudding, her great-grandchildren crowding around to thank her.

Henniker and Lizzie spent some time talking, and even walked off together to look at the prize deer for a while. He remembered her from Calvin's wedding, where she had been the maid of honor, but he was married at the time to Celia, so they had not talked. Lizzie seemed to strike all the right chords in him, and he thought perhaps she would be a friend he could trust. He found himself warming toward her.

For her part, she was conscious that they were the same height, whereas she preferred men to be taller than her. She liked the feeling of confidence and understanding she sensed in his pleasant banter, and the height thing became completely unimportant. As they were strolling back up from the deer pens, though, she asked him if he'd heard about the drowning of the police chief, Trey Green.

"I did," said Henniker. "I was there and helped pull him out of the water. Looked to me like he had a broken jaw, but the other guys there just passed it off."

"I heard they found his badge wallet under a bed in a dead woman's house in Piney Creek," said Lizzie. "Nobody knows how it got there, but the Rangers have been called in. Killing of police gets all of them out."

"I heard they were looking for a sedan of some kind, maybe yellow."

Lizzie stopped, her heart giving a little flip as she remembered the Houston man at the nightclub Friday night.

"Yellow?" she asked.

"I heard at the cafe this morning before everybody went to church," Henniker said. "Somebody had heard them saying maybe a yellow sedan of some kind had driven down the street a couple of times, but they weren't sure what day it was."

"Oh my God," she sighed. "I hope they're wrong. The man I met Friday night was driving a yellow sedan. Said he'd bought it that day. He said he was from Third Ward in Houston, and that's the name he went by. Third Ward. I hope it's not the car. We do not need a Black man arrested around here for killing a white policeman."

"The police will find every yellow car in East Texas," said Henniker.

"And arrest every driver. I don't think they've got much to go on. How did the woman die?"

"Another mystery. Apparently went in to take a bath, did some drugs, and died in the tub. Her husband found her when he came back from the Coushatta casino in Louisiana. Rumor was that he'd already faxed divorce papers to her, but they're not calling it a suicide. They don't know. A body dead in a warm tub for five or six days can be difficult to autopsy, but it might be connected with Trey Green. They're looking at everything."

They had stopped walking and were looking at one another, worry showing in Lizzie's eyes.

"Tell me about this man," said Henniker, taking her gently by the elbow. "Are you okay? You look really concerned."

"I'm terrified. Piney Creek is a hard enough place to live without some kind of Black-involved police and drug murder," she said.

"You think that's what it is?"

"You said she had taken drugs, and the police chief was probably murdered. It doesn't take a lot of imagination to link all that to some Black man from Houston's Third Ward driving a yellow sedan. Besides, he spent time talking to Clarence Thomas."

"You're right about being Black in East Texas," said Henniker. "It's easy to feel like you're hunted all the time, especially if you draw attention to yourself. It's one of the things I admire about Calvin, being able to get past that by being a hero on the football field."

"Listen," she said, "I'm leaving. I've got to go to work in the morning and I still need to do some things before that. Grocery store, ironing, that kind of thing. Besides, if this murder sets off the powder keg, none of us will be safe in East Texas. Do you mind telling Calvin and Cheryl I said thanks?" She walked swiftly away toward the large field where the cars were all parked. Henniker ran after her.

"Lizzie," he said, catching up, "Lizzie, wait up."

"Charles," she said, "I've got to get home and get things done before it gets too dangerous. You need to get home too."

"Can I come with you?" Henniker asked.

"No." She was firm and out of breath. "That's sweet, but no."

"Call me," he said, pulling a business card out of his wallet. "My number is on here."

She looked at him for a minute, smiled a little, then hurried off, but turned and called his name.

He went towards her and she caught him by his hand, pulling him close into a hug. Then she kissed him on the cheek.

"What's that for?" he asked.

"For the family. They are all watching," she said. "But also, for thanks. Now let me go. I've got to go."

In the early days of the century, all the roads were gravel, but the state built nice, level concrete bridges over the creeks. A popular pastime was to drive out to the bridges on Saturday nights, dressed in zoot suits and flapper dresses, to listen to car radio music and dance in the enchanting moonlight. Some just sat on the bridge railing smoking their cigarettes, drinking Cokes. Cooler air rising from the creek was a welcome respite from the day's heat, the shimmering water enhanced the moon, and the night sounds of bullfrogs and peepers filled in conversational gaps.

CHAPTER
THIRTY-TWO

Carroll "Shorty" Fike was exhausted. He'd worked extra shifts on the rig so he could get off in time to go surprise Annabeth for Mother's Day, and now the helicopter had broken down. Everyone leaving on rotation had to wait, and the line was growing. It was not an uncommon thing for the helicopters to need last-minute servicing, or for the pilot to be drunk, or something. The company did a pretty good job getting reliable choppers to the rigs, but things happened. Now instead of six crew members rotating off, the twelve-hour shift change had happened and another six had joined the throng leaving.

That also meant the rig would close down. You couldn't operate this huge rig if you were twelve men short. They only had eighteen crew on the rig to begin with. Shorty had already worked back-to-back shifts to get off a day early, and the delay was frustrating him. At just under 178 cm, about five feet seven inches, Shorty had long ago developed a rooster-like attitude toward the world, and that included a short fuse. His fellow rig workers respected him, some even liked him, and all of them gave him space. He had the personality of a bantam-weight, world-champion boxer, say one of those seriously dangerous Mexican fighters you sometimes saw on television, who never backed down or quit. And most of the last twenty-four hours he'd spent high over the rig on the monkey board guiding a stubborn column of pipe up and down the hole. It was exhausting work, and he was ready to lie down. It was one of the more tedious and arduous jobs for a deckhand, but it had gotten him off shift early enough to surprise Annabeth and their little three-year-old girl, Maria, for Mother's Day, and it had been worth it.

Now he was stuck with no chopper in sight, with the sun going down. He intended to sleep on the ride to shore before getting in his Dodge

Magnum with its 400-cubic-inch V-8 engine and roaring the two hours up to Piney Creek, hoping to be as refreshed as possible for the drive. He expected he and Annabeth would embrace passionately, as always, when he walked in the door.

The chopper finally came, and he slept for an hour on the way back to Houma, Louisiana. He got into the car after dark, about 6 p.m., stopped in Orange at a Krispy Kreme donut shop for a little extra surprise for the girls, then angled north from Orange up through the dark pine forests on the eastern flank of Texas.

He pulled into the trailer park a little after 9 p.m. expecting to find Annabeth and the baby already in bed. Her car was parked in front. A light was on in the kitchen. But the trailer was silent when he opened the unlocked door.

He wandered back toward the bedroom calling her name, noting she had been doing the laundry. Wet laundry in the washing machine, dirty laundry in a pile on the floor. But no Annabeth.

It was so unlike Annabeth to leave a job half-done. She never did that, and Shorty had his first sinking misgiving about her absence. He'd been away for three weeks, and he hadn't told her he was coming back, but still he was surprised. She should have been there. Besides, her car was out front.

Maybe she was out visiting with some friends, playing cards or something. She liked doing that.

He ate a donut from the box, and collapsed on the mobile home's short sofa, where he went sound asleep, a half-eaten donut in his grease-blackened hand.

He woke up on the floor to dead silence. No Annabeth, no little Maria, no coffee. His heart flipped. Had she left him?

He went to search the bedroom. All her clothes were there, except the ones in the laundry. All of little Maria's clothes and toys were there, her favorite blanket, her stuffed animals she couldn't sleep without. No note. Nothing indicated that she had intended to leave. Shorty had been left before by other women, and it was always after weeks or months of cold shoulders, sharp words, or sharper silence. But they'd had none of that. He went to the front door and looked out at the park, what he could see of it. Not much, actually. Each little lot was well hidden from the others by overgrown brush and litter, white plastic grocery bags snagged by the wind on trees and thorns, all lying in what shade tall pines could provide, which wasn't much. It was Sunday morning. Nobody could be seen moving around.

He went back inside trying to think about his next move. He was confused. Should he call the sheriff's office? What would he tell them?

The more he thought about it, the more he felt panic building in his chest. He was having a hard time breathing and a harder time focusing.

He stared around the small sitting area, the small kitchen. Something was missing, but what? He couldn't remember. Something wasn't right. He looked and looked. He looked in the refrigerator and saw neatly wrapped leftovers. The place was spotless, as always. She liked being his wife, she liked taking care of the things that made their life together. It was part of the way she showed how much she loved him. Spunky Annabeth, little short Annabeth, so sweet. So feisty, like himself. As energetic as a terrier. And always saving money so they could move. Always. On everything. Nothing wasted.

By noon, he was frantic. He called her mother in Minneapolis, not a cheap call, but she had not spoken with Annabeth since Thursday. She had heard nothing about weekend plans, no, she didn't know. No, Annabeth was not on her way to see them. Try her brother in Houston.

Her brother had not talked to her in two months. Even if he had, he would not have remembered the conversation. Her brother was not a reliable witness about anything, just happily living minute to minute.

He called every acquaintance, but no word.

Then he started going to the neighbors.

"Have you seen my wife, Annabeth?" he'd ask. "Yes, the short one."

Even the park manager, who was lounging around in his baggy underwear with his eyelids sewn up with catgut, had not seen her.

"Nope," he said. "Saw her last weekend when she came with the rent. Haven't seen her since. No idea." He grinned, his stained teeth casting a beige shadow on his meaty lips.

Jesse Grinder saw Shorty coming and decided not to answer the door. He had nothing to say to Shorty Fike. He just sat in the shadows of his trailer waiting for the little man to go away.

An hour later, he drove his pickup out of the trailer park, making a detour around the end of the park where Annabeth's trailer was, and headed west toward Sweetgum County. It was Mother's Day. He figured he'd go see his mother, maybe get a biscuit or two if his father and brother had left any. Besides, the trailer park was feeling oppressive. And later, maybe he'd drive down to the county line and look up one of the girls, if they were still around.

Annabeth had really nice titties, he muttered to himself, driving down the narrow, two-lane paved road past the barn about thirty miles from the trailer park.

Nobody was there, no cars or trucks.

So far, so good, he thought.

Hogleg Putnam worked hard and was gone from the house plenty, but he was no fool. He saw the burgeoning intimacy between Annie and her boyfriend Willie around the swimming pool in his backyard and collaborated with the high school coach to find a summer football training camp. Just when Annie had decided that she had invented sex, pretty evident from her irrepressible grin and the way she clung to Willie, he managed to get the boy out of town for the rest of the summer. "Whew," he thought. "I hope I was in time. Three more years of this."

CHAPTER
THIRTY-THREE

The Cypress County sheriff's office deputy who answered the phone on Sunday evening was not particularly interested in a missing person's report. He wrote down a few details, took Shorty Fike's name, and relayed the message to the dispatcher. The dispatcher radioed for deputies who had time to go take in the details of the report at the mobile home park, but the place was not classy enough to warrant much real interest. Nobody of any consequence or influence lived out there, unlike the death of Belle Guinness and the sudden spotlight on the discovery of Whitmire Police Chief Green's wallet under the dead woman's bed. The Texas Rangers were crawling all over everything, reviewing logs of calls and listening to tapes, even trying to find a connection to a yellow sedan that had been seen on the street the first of the week. That was where the interest was. Some man's wife run off from him, that was not news. Wouldn't even get a write-up in the local weekly, the *Piney Creek Crier*.

The deputy who eventually showed up to interview Shorty the next day was one of the ones the Rangers had said they would not work with. They'd taken one look at him and his law enforcement background and told the sheriff, Bishop Adams, he could keep that one on traffic surveillance for all they cared, but to keep him away from the Belle Guinness site they were investigating.

Sheriff Adams didn't need an explanation. An overweight mouth-breather, Deputy Jasper Rhodes was his wife's nephew and was only on the force because Adams had taken the law enforcement exam for him and forged his signature. And because he needed a job and no one else would hire him. County law enforcement, like county politics, tended to stay in the same families in East Texas, with often multiple generations of one family holding on to various offices like a large family reunion

171

every day, including the same affiliations and feuds you'd find in any large family.

Deputy Rhodes squeaked and bumped his cruiser into the mobile home park around 10:30 on Monday morning, counting the sagging lot numbers covered in red clay dust. But he didn't need to worry about missing the place. Shorty had cleaned off the house number and was standing in the drive nervous and jumpy as a rabbit in daylight.

Deputy Rhodes decided that Shorty Fike was going to be his chief suspect, if anything had happened to his wife. He was convinced that Shorty's appearance and energy was proof of guilt, so he wrote up his report that way, something that took him the better part of the afternoon. But first he dusted for fingerprints, leaving black dust all over the house. He found plenty of fingerprints everywhere, and Shorty admitted he had opened the refrigerator and probably touched lots of surfaces. He had even put the clothes in the dryer to keep them from mildewing, piling the clean ones on his daughter's made-up bed. Deputy Rhodes outweighed Shorty by two hundred pounds and stood almost half a foot taller, so he tended to treat Shorty like a kid and ignore him and his ideas. But eventually he said, "Well, Mr., uh, Fike, we don't have much to go on here. These women, you know, sometimes they just up and leave. Happens all the time. If we find out something, we'll let you know."

"She didn't take her purse," said Shorty. "It's in the car. Her keys are in the car. She didn't take anything with her. She had a shopping list in her purse, and I know for a fact that she always went shopping on Saturday morning. I'm telling you, something has happened to her."

"Well, I hate to say this, Mr. Fike, but if something has happened to her, the husband is usually the first suspect. You realize that, don't you?"

Shorty stared at Rhodes, his astonishment quickly changing into rage.

"Her money's in her purse!" exclaimed Shorty. "Her checkbook! She did not run away from me! I love my wife and I love my daughter. She loves me! Something has happened to them!"

"Okay, okay," said Rhodes, taking in rasping breaths through his mouth, "I'll go talk to the neighbors, see if they saw or heard anything. Most of them didn't though, I can tell you already. Still, I'll go door-to-door for you."

"I've already done that," said Shorty. "Nobody saw anything."

"Well, you ain't exactly a police officer, are you?" replied Rhodes. "People tend to say things to the police they don't say to their neighbors. I'll talk to a few of them, see what I can find out."

"Start with that sumbitch park manager," said Shorty. "That man was lying to me. He said he had not seen her since she came in to pay the rent on Monday."

"Anybody else?" asked Rhodes.

"Not everybody was at home," said Shorty. "There's one trailer way back in the back of the park where nobody goes. His pickup was in front of his trailer, but he wouldn't come to the door when I knocked. Maybe he'll talk to you."

"Yeah, I'll drive back that way, see what I can see. If his truck is there, I'll get him to the door. If not, I'll leave a note for him to contact me."

"He's not going to contact you," said Shorty.

"I'm not going to arrest him, either, just because he don't come to the door," said Rhodes. "Unless he's Black. Is he Black?"

"Might be. He's dark. Might be suntan and dirt."

"You got plenty of that. What do you do for living?"

They talked for a few more minutes, Deputy Rhodes proud of his sharp investigative skills in questioning a suspect. He'd write up his notes to show how smart he was being. Then he snapped shut his notebook and bid Shorty goodbye. Told him they'd be in touch if anything turned up.

Nothing turned up. Not that day, or the next, or the next. Shorty's girls were just gone, and he was certain it had not been deliberate. Too much evidence showed that they had not left deliberately. She loved him; he knew she did. But she was gone.

At night in the silent mobile home, Shorty brooded. His mood turned dark and foul. He quit his job on the rig to stay home and wait for word. He questioned every neighbor again and again. He visited the grocery store where she shopped, to see if she'd been in that day. He asked if it were possible to trace her purchases and learned that she'd written a check every time. They were always happy to take her checks because they were never returned by the bank for insufficient funds. Annabeth Fike was a careful, precise manager and a pleasure to do business with, said the grocery store manager. That little girl was just precious, so happy all the time, Shorty was told.

At home, he pulled out the bank statements and pored over them, noting when she had paid each expense, looking at her signature on the canceled checks. He was interested that the rent for the mobile home lot was so low. He thought that was odd, but it was saving them a bunch of money. She had been paying only a hundred dollars a month for their lot, which was saving them, best he could recall, a hundred fifty dollars a month for a down payment on a real home.

Shorty's eyes teared up as he thought how careful she had been for their future. She had not left him. His fists clenched and he held his breath to keep from screaming, and then screamed anyway, a long, wailing scream that went on and on, pounding the flimsy table and bouncing items onto the floor.

Then he collapsed forward and wept for hours, hatred gnawing his heart out.

Nelson Mitchell was attacked by the deer while he was walking on a forest road. The six-point buck charged him from the underbrush, knocking him down and tearing him with his horns while slicing with his hooves. "I had to grab those antlers with both hands," he said, "to keep 'em away from my eyes. Couldn't go for my knife." He was rescued when two hunters drove by and scared the deer off. They got him in the pickup, but the buck charged again, leaping into the truck bed. One of the hunters shot him through the back window glass.

CHAPTER
THIRTY-FOUR

When Charles Henniker got home from the family reunion, Deputy Jack Lewis of the Sweetgum Sheriff's Office had left a note for him on his front door. It asked Henniker to call him, which he did.

Deputy Lewis had some questions of a friendly sort and wondered if he could just stop by.

"As long as it's a social visit, sure, come on," said Henniker. "If it's official, you'll need a warrant. But you know that. Still, the house is always open to a friend, so stop by and I'll pour you a cup of tea."

He was just finishing his exercise routine in the garage when he heard the car pull up outside. He walked back in through the kitchen, turning the fire on under the kettle, and went to the door, mopping his brow.

"Hi Jack," he said, opening the door.

"Charles," nodded the deputy. Lewis had left his gun on the front seat of his car. "Thanks for meeting me."

"Anything for a friend," said Henniker, ushering him into the tiny living room. "The water is getting hot and will be ready in a moment."

They chatted for a bit about the weather, the way the week had sorted out since Henniker's arrest and dismissal. After the tea was steeping in the exquisite Japanese teapot with the conical handle on the side perpendicular to the spout, Lewis got down to business.

"We got the preliminary report back on Trey Green," he said. "I thought you'd like to know."

"Sure thing. What happened?"

"Two things we know for certain right now. He didn't drown is one of them."

"I thought so. Darryl said he saw bubbles coming out of his mouth when he tried to lift him by his belt. Not much air left in a drowned man, in my experience."

"I'd like to know more about your experience," said Lewis. "But in a minute."

He paused to take a sip of the tea.

"This tea is extraordinary," he said. "I've never had hot tea before. Only tea I've ever had was on ice with a cup of sugar in it, but this is delicious."

"Tea is an important drink in some parts of the world," said Henniker, "and in those parts, the weedy stuff Lipton sells is never brewed. It's a matter of taste. And refinement, of course. But mostly taste." He took a little sip of his pale green tea. "This is a tea called 'sencha' and is very popular in Japan, but they have plenty of other varieties. And not every brand of sencha tastes the same, either. It's kind of like a vintage wine—type of soil, elevation, sunshine, moisture, all of that figures into the flavor. And the carefully developed varieties, too, of course. If you're interested, we can sample some in future visits."

"That might be fun," said Lewis, "if it doesn't kill my taste for station coffee. I need to have that coffee they make down at the S.O., even if I put salt in it to kill the bitter."

Henniker laughed. "I understand. If you're drinking that stuff, your taste buds might not appreciate subtle flavors."

"Subtle is not my main suit," nodded Lewis, grinning. "But you already know that."

Henniker nodded.

Lewis paused, then went on. "The other thing we got from the autopsy report was Green had a broken jaw, just like you said at the dock when you pulled him out of the water."

"I know," said Henniker. "I figured a professional would see that."

"He also had a cracked skull. Can't tell what he got first, but maybe they can figure that out in Houston. He also had a cracked vertebra in his neck. Trey Green was in one helluva bar fight, looks like."

"Didn't know there were any bars in East Texas. I thought all these counties were dry."

"Well, yes and no," said Lewis. "A man needs a drink, he can usually find a place to sell him one. Two places down at the county line south of here make a killing getting people drunk. Piney Creek has a couple of places, and some of the pharmacies have drive-through windows where they'll sell porn and booze to people they know. Playboy magazines and whisky. That kind of thing. They keep all that under the counter so their religious customers can't see it."

"I wondered how people were getting liquor," said Henniker. "Driving all the way to Beaumont or Houston for beer seems like a real waste of money."

"Also, if you're out driving to get booze, you're drinking it in the car on the way home," said Lewis. "We have a god-awful lot of drunk drivers and car wrecks because of it. But some folks, and you know who they are, want to keep up the appearances of being a righteous community without sins like booze and porn."

"And for some of them," said Henniker, "we are. Takes a certain kind of blinders not to see humans as they really are, but some people do it."

"Yes, they do."

"So, his jaw was broken, and we're looking at a murder," said Henniker, returning to the subject.

"Right. And there's more."

"I heard some stuff at the cafe this morning," said Henniker. "Something about a wallet and a yellow sedan?"

"Man comes home from gambling all week in Louisiana with a fine-looking whore on the front seat and a wad of cash in his pocket. He's faxed his wife some divorce papers and was just stopping by to pick up his guns and some clothes but finds her dead in a tub."

"Was she murdered?"

"No, she'd been dead in that tub all week. House was stinky stinky."

"I know what you mean," said Henniker, images of war flashing in his mind.

"Thing is, they found Trey Green's badge wallet under a bed on the opposite end of the house. No apparent marks on her. She might have been having sex, but again we're waiting on autopsies to tell us what they can. Too early to say."

"You think Trey Green was visiting her for sex and got caught?"

"Husband has a solid alibi," said Lewis. "We even have video footage of him in the casino with that whore almost all day every day for the whole week until he checked out on Saturday. Wife must have died while he was away enjoying himself."

"Any other evidence?"

"Well, yeah, but you know this is all confidential, right? I'm not even supposed to know this stuff."

"Of course, but the whole state knows all that so far," said Henniker. "Every busybody in East Texas is listening to police scanners. It's a lot more interesting than watching daytime television or listening to what passes for local radio."

"I know," said Lewis. "And some boys, they just aren't very discreet about what they say on the air. I know the story's out."

"How does the yellow sedan figure into it?" asked Henniker.

"One of the woman's neighbors said they saw the cop car come down the street to her house Monday morning. Then about an hour later, the yellow sedan came down the street. They had seen the cop car down there before, but nobody drives a yellow sedan. The car was strange, and it caught her eye."

"Then what?"

"Then a little later, the cop car drives off and the yellow sedan follows it. An hour later, the same neighbor noticed that the yellow sedan was back in the garage, but no cop car."

"Any way of telling what time all this happened?"

"We have an earliest time, because Green used the Piney Creek PD radio to get a message to his wife. But the end time was when Darryl pulled on his trotline. The neighbor can't give a definite time. She says it was about 10 a.m., or about twenty minutes after Green placed that radio call, but she can't swear to it."

"As I see it," said Henniker, putting his fingertips together in front of his nose, "we have Trey Green alive at this woman's house, where he drops his badge wallet, then she's dead, and the same day we find her is the day Darryl Stewart snags Green's dead body on his trotline. I observe the broken jaw, and other head injuries and assume he was dead before he went in the water. Is all that right?"

"So far, that's what we know," agreed Lewis.

"We can assume that Trey Green and this woman were both alive at the same time in her house, I think," mused Henniker, "but something happened to Green. If a jealous lover came in on them and killed Green, then the woman's corpse would show signs of injury as well. But you say it didn't?"

Lewis shook his head. "So far, no injury we can see. But she was doing some drugs in the tub, apparently white wine and smoking some kind of powder. We also found a package of diet pills, or we think they're diet pills. We're looking at that, but the chemical analysis will take a while. The powder was either heroin, or crystal methamphetamine. If she was mixing two kinds of amphetamine with wine in a hot bath, it could have been enough to do her in."

"Heroin would have done it, too," said Henniker. "Straight-out heart attack time, if you mix up those drugs. If she was hyped up on amphetamines and drinking, she might have been too active to sit in a tub of water for more than a few seconds. My guess is heroin. I could be wrong."

"Right," said Lewis. "That's the thinking."

"And the yellow sedan might have held either the lover or the drug dealer, or both," said Henniker. "Finding that sedan is important to unwinding this case."

"That's what the Rangers are thinking," said Lewis.

"The only snag in the yellow sedan story, though, is it might not have been driven, or even owned, by the same person on Monday and now." He remembered Lizzie's comment on the yellow sedan.

"We are looking through all the title transfers," said Lewis. "The only older model yellow sedan we've found was purchased by Jeff's Used Autos about a month ago. No transfers since."

"You ought to see if he's still got that car," said Henniker. "Don't they have thirty days to register a car purchase? I think they do. A new owner might not have registered it yet."

"Right. And here's my big question," said Lewis, "now that we have all this out of the way. My question is how do you know all this? Most guys just don't know how to recognize fractured jaws, murder, that kind of thing just right off like you did."

"I have some background in it," said Henniker.

"Law enforcement?" asked Lewis.

"Military," said Henniker. "Air Force commando training."

"No shit."

"Yeah. Twenty-three years. You learn a lot of stuff and see a lot of things when you're in special forces for that long."

"Like different kinds of tea," said Lewis.

"Also that," said Henniker.

"Then you were not guessing about the broken jaw when you pulled him out of the water."

"I've seen lot of broken jaws. I've broken several. After the first one, I learned not to use my fist, but yeah, I've had experience I'd rather not talk about."

"Got it," said Lewis. "Did you see anything else yesterday morning that the rest of us might have missed?"

"It's hard to tell how much blood he had on his shirt," said Henniker. "After all that time in the water, it's hard to tell blood from mud. It did look like his shoe and pockets were filled with mud, so I assume he was dragged along the bottom of the riverbed by the current. That alligator got his other shoe, I'm guessing."

"Nobody's thought of that," said Lewis. "I'll have them look into it. Anything else?"

"You might find out if his car keys were in his pocket. And what about his money? Was he robbed? Did an active police officer carry a gun when he wasn't in his home city? I didn't see a holster on his belt, so the gun might be a clue. Did he leave it in his car, like you left yours?"

"How'd you know I left my gun in the car?"

"You're wearing your badge, so you're on duty. The waistband of your trousers is canted down to one side instead of level, and that's the side where you wear your pistol. When you walk, you tend to hold your right hand out a little farther than your left so it can swing without bumping against the gun. Little things like that give it away."

"Are you sure you're not a detective, Mr. Henniker?" Lewis asked laughing.

"You learn to stay alive by being observant," said Henniker. "And keeping your head. Two things: look, be cool."

"That's hard for some people," said Lewis.

"It's a learned skill," said Henniker. "We had a lot of training in it, and a lot of opportunity to practice it."

"Do you think you would recognize the drugs if you saw them?"

"I've also seen a lot of drugs," said Henniker. "I'm no expert, but if they are military grade drugs, like combat drugs, I can tell you at a glance what they are."

"I'll pass that on to the Rangers if you don't mind."

"Again, I'm available for consultation as long as it's civil and informal," said Henniker. "I've had all the insulting from the local law enforcement I can tolerate this week and will not officially speak to anyone without a lawyer present. Generally, you get one chance to have people cooperate with you, and this bunch blew it on Tuesday. But for you, anything."

"I understand," said Deputy Lewis, standing. "Thank you for the tea and your service and thank you for being willing to talk to me."

Henniker stood and held out his hand.

"I hope I was helpful," he said. "I'm happy to be helpful when I can be."

A favorite hymn at First Fundamentalist Church had always been "Take My Life and Let It Be." Brother Lyncefield was amused at the earnest, blank look on the faces of his parishioners as they sang those old words, completely unaware of the irony. In a later verse they sang, "Take my silver and my gold, not a mite would I withhold." This, too, was true music to the good reverend's ears. He always said a secret prayer to himself at that juncture to remind himself to raise more money for the church's work, including, of course, his own blessed ministry.

CHAPTER
THIRTY-FIVE

BoMac was sitting at his desk in the *Whitmire Standard* office on Sunday evening trying to piece together the Trey Green story and the rest of the news budget for the coming week. Last week had been all about the flood, and he had made the decision to ignore the Annie Putnam fiasco. Though an amusing bagatelle of local color and ultimately trivial despite the sound and fury of its passage, it would be better left to oral history. Maybe. If it went into print, he could not really use the girl's name since she was technically a minor, and using Charles Henniker's name would just expose him to mistrust and ridicule. Besides, the charges were dropped, so it was not an official case. He'd let that go.

In other news, one person was swept away crossing a flooded bridge. That always happened, because the bridges did not have guardrails; but the county commissioners refused to budget extra construction money for that safety precaution. "People ought to know not to drive off into a creek, even if they think the bridge is there," said Commissioner George Brown. "Not our fault if they're stupid."

"You lose a vote when they drown," replied BoMac.

"I lose more of them if I raise taxes," retorted Brown. "Somewhere you've got to have common sense. If they don't have it, we can't buy it for them."

BoMac had nodded. Brown was probably right. Still, it was an obligation to help people avoid killing themselves by accident. And if they could see the guardrails above the water, then they'd know how deep the water was and that the bridge had not been swept away. He thought of that too late to tell Brown, though, whose attention had already been distracted by another huggable vote walking in the door of the meeting room.

Every news budget involved a brainstorming session, and he was taking notes of his ideas, marking where he needed to beef up his research and sources, starring stories he could write without gathering more info. And he had a stack of obituaries from the local funeral homes, all of White people. The Black funeral homes never submitted obituaries to the newspaper—they didn't need to. Their churches printed up the obits and circulated them on Sundays along with prayers.

When he was through with that, he'd go on to make up his ad budget, but he pretty much already had that lined up. He would be short on ads again, despite the mayhaw graduation tabloid coming in two weeks. Did he have time to do another valedictorian profile before he set to work on this week's issue? Maybe, but it'd cost him sleep. In-between mentally composing news stories in the morning, he would try to squeeze another few dollars out of the local merchants with some small ads, something that would maybe get a few customers in their doors.

The phone rang and he picked up. Thank God, he breathed, it was Ellen. Just the sound of her voice was so relieving.

"I'm hearing things," she said, "about Trey Green. How much do you know?"

"I've been hearing a lot of things, too," he said. "I've got photos of him with his feet still in the water and Charles standing nearby. Won't run that, though. I've got a profile shot of Darryl Stewart that's pretty good and might run that. But I'm shy on details. Tell me what you've heard."

"Betty Parris and I were chatting," she said. "Do you know Betty Parris from the bank? Somehow we kind of got to be friends. Anyway, she said she'd heard that Trey had been hanging out with a woman in Piney Creek, and that's why they found his wallet over there under her bed."

"I'd heard about the wallet. I guess it's easy to put two and two together. But we don't have any proof of that, do we? And the woman's dead, too, right?"

"Do you think it was a double murder?"

"Maybe. Probably. The autopsy report won't be public until after deadline, though, and they'll wait to give it to the television stations in Lufkin and Beaumont on Wednesday after we've gone to press, so we can't break it. But maybe they won't release it, after all."

"Why wouldn't they release it?"

"Ongoing investigation is what they always say, although an autopsy should be public record. In fact, I think by law it is a public record."

"Then it should be available to us when it's ready. How long do you think it takes them to get it ready?"

"A couple of hours for a preliminary report, say drowning or obvious injury. But maybe they will want to do a more thorough autopsy of Green. I'd say they do. Charles was right—his jaw was broken."

"That's what I heard."

"He might have been dead before he went in the water, that's what I'm thinking."

"Have you to talked to Charles?"

"No, he was gone all day today. I think he said something about a family gathering somewhere. I'll swing by over there in a little."

"He's home. I drove by a minute ago and a deputy's car was just pulling away. I hope they didn't arrest him again."

"Good grief. That's a good man. I hope so too."

"I tried to see if anybody else was in the car with the deputy but couldn't be sure."

"I'll call him. I think I have his number here somewhere."

"On your secret Rolodex?"

"Yeah. I have a public one for that witch to browse through when she's going through my desk, and then I have the other one hidden in the darkroom. I don't think I'll put Charles's number in the public one. It'll be in the phone book anyway next year, and besides, the school has his number, I'm sure. Still, I'd like to visit with him, get his insights. He might be able to give me some information I can use in the story."

"Want company?" He could hear her shy smile in her words.

"With you? Always," he said. "I want your company, and a sandwich. I haven't eaten since early this morning."

"BoMac, you need to take better care of yourself. Exercise, proper diet, sleep. You need that. Constantly pushing yourself like you do will kill you."

"Thanks. Come see me. We'll get a burger or something and swing by Charles's house, see if he's home."

Not one green thing so much as waved in the direction of any of the kitchens of the places to eat in Whitmire. The closest you got to a vegetable was some form of potato, either mashed or fried. At least the Dairy Queen put shredded iceberg lettuce on their thin hamburger patties, and more lettuce than the overpriced McDonald's. Also sliced tomatoes. And pickles, which only count as a vegetable because at some point in their limp lives they were growing out of the ground as cucumbers in some remote South American nation. When Ellen was choosing, they went to Dairy Queen for the extra lettuce. BoMac was convinced you could starve to death if you only ate food from Dairy Queen, but knew he was just prejudiced. At his father's farm, they had a cook who prepared three meals a day and did a superb job with everything from okra to beans, yeast rolls, biscuits in the morning. Whenever he thought about what home once was, BoMac sighed.

"Did your mom cook?" he asked Ellen. "I mean, when you lived at home, did she cook and so on? Take care of the house? Tell me about your parents."

"Mother could cook," she said, "but I don't think she much liked doing it. She sometimes made waffles in the morning. Sometimes on Saturdays she would make me a sandwich for lunch, usually a peanut butter sandwich with sliced bananas inside. But when I got older, she stopped. My dad grilled a lot of meat outside in the backyard and seemed to do that every night when it wasn't raining, but mother was one of those people who just wasn't much interested in food. Why?"

"Just wondering." He told her about the cook named Jane Champion, hired by his father when she was still in her early teens, maybe fourteen or fifteen, and worked for the family for the rest of her long life, until his father died bankrupt. "I wish I could make some money to send to her. She was like a mother to me."

They pulled up in Henniker's driveway and were met at the door.

Henniker confirmed that he had heard the same rumors but declined to be quoted about Green's broken jaw. "My word was disputed at the boat ramp," he said. "The same people would dispute it again. No point in aggravating junkyard dogs."

"Can I say that you drove Stewart's truck?" asked BoMac.

"That is an observable fact," said Henniker. "It's not a judgment made by me, so sure, you can say that. I just don't want any of my opinions or observations printed. You've got a good story without it, because you were there. You can confirm everything you saw with the fire chief and Darryl. How is Darryl, by the way? He was pretty shocked."

"Can't get in touch with him," said BoMac. "I'll try again tomorrow. I'm told that Trey Green was a friend of his."

"In a town of this size, you are friends with everyone you are not fighting, and even then, you're friends. All that means is that they didn't fight." BoMac nodded.

"I've got some of my grandmother's banana pudding inside," Henniker said after a minute. "It won't be as good tomorrow. Want to come in and help me finish it?"

Later, BoMac and Ellen agreed that it was the best thing they had ever eaten. BoMac said that such a pudding served to the right people at the right time could create world peace.

Ellen giggled at his silliness, but she didn't disagree.

The Sweetgum County sheriff's wife had three sisters. One of the sisters was the county clerk. One was the wife of the commissioner for precinct two. One was the county treasurer. The sheriff's sister was a Justice of the Peace. The sheriff's younger half-brother was the only person the sheriff approved as a bondsman for jailed prisoners. All of these relatives hated one another and feuded constantly, often running for election to one another's jobs. One of the more amusing pastimes in Whitmire was laughing at who would run against whom and guessing how long they would stay in office.

CHAPTER
THIRTY-SIX

In the morning, no one at the Whitmire police station would comment on Trey Green's death, except to say that they had a death certificate from the coroner. He was legally dead. They said they were treating it as accidental drowning.

It mystified BoMac that they would create such a fiction. At least two dozen people had seen him as they pulled the body out of the water, and Henniker had pointed out the broken jaw. The Whitmire police, scattered and unnerved as they were about the death of their chief, were silent. Basically, they knew nothing. They didn't even know if it was being investigated.

"Cock-lover" Turner, the district attorney, also refused to be drawn into the story. He refused to say whether Green had a broken jaw, just claiming that he didn't notice it himself. BoMac suspected that Turner wouldn't know a broken jaw if he saw one, but admitting ignorance was not Turner's style. When he didn't know something, he just lied and made something up. Also, Turner was busy stroking the barrel of his eight-inch-long chrome-plated .44 magnum revolver with a soft cloth while BoMac interviewed him. He did things like that when he wanted to distract people. The gun was huge and terrifying, and it got your attention when he waved it around fully loaded or knocked it on the desktop for emphasis. He also made a point of loading and unloading the gun in front of BoMac, paying as little attention to the newspaperman as he could.

But Turner fully focused his attention on BoMac about one thing.

"That Black man at the boat ramp," he said, "that man needs to learn to keep his mouth shut. Also, if I ever find him driving like that again, I'll lock him up and throw away the key."

"I thought the sheriff was the head of law enforcement in this county," BoMac replied, ignoring Turner's threat. "I thought you were an officer of the court."

"I'm the law in this county," replied Turner, standing up and holstering his gun. "If you see that Black man again, tell him to watch his step. He's been in jail already this week, and I don't think it will be the last time. And next time," he leaned over the desk to shake his trigger finger at BoMac, "he might not be treated with as much civility as last time."

"May I quote you on that?"

"Absolutely not. When I have a statement I want in the paper, I'll write it out for you so you don't get it wrong."

"What have I gotten wrong in the past?" BoMac asked.

"Too many things to count," replied Turner. "Your paper is nothing but a pile of false facts."

"I will retract any statement in the paper that can be proved false," said BoMac. "So far, no one has brought anything to my attention."

"I bet they've complained, though," said Turner.

"Sure. They hate being identified as convicts or being arrested for drunk driving, so they complain. But those are verifiable facts, not falsehoods."

"Your paper is still full of lies," said Turner. "And I have nothing else to say to you."

BoMac stood. "Hey," he said, as he prepared to leave, "I've been meaning to ask you. Doesn't that Bowie knife on your shin cut into your ankle?"

"My legs are long enough," claimed Turner. "Are you implying that I have short legs?"

"You have small hands," said BoMac, grinning. "I figured it would cut into you. Glad it's not. Hate to see the district attorney bleeding out on the courtroom floor."

"One day I'm going to whip your ass," scowled Turner. He was not joking.

Inside, BoMac just laughed at him. He was an elected official. He would run for reelection in a year or two. BoMac thought that the good people—the ones who voted and did their civic duties, went to church, that kind of thing—might not reelect this man if they had a reason to doubt him. And Cock-lover Turner was not well-loved anywhere. People knew a jackass when they saw one. Usually.

BoMac finally had to call the Piney Creek police office to confirm the investigation into the death of Belle Guinness. They referred him to Sheriff Adams, who was busy but returned his call quickly.

"Well, Mr. Maclean," boomed Adams. "What can I help you with?"

"I'm calling to see what you can tell me about Belle Guinness and Chief Green's wallet," said BoMac. "Is it true that Belle Guinness was found dead in her bathtub?"

"Sure was. She had been dead for several days, and you can imagine what this heat had done to her body. We sent her for autopsy. Sometime this week we should get the results."

"Any sign of foul play with her?"

"None that we saw. The local funeral home that handles our unexpected deaths said her body appeared to be undamaged. They did not want to give an opinion on the cause of her death."

"Right. Can I say that she expired in her bath? Would that be accurate?"

"That would be accurate as far as it goes. That's all we really know right now."

"Do you suspect any additional causes? Drugs? Accidental drowning? Anything like that?"

"The Texas Rangers forensics team is investigating her death," said Adams, "so I am not at liberty to tell you what their thinking is. We did find some drug paraphernalia in her house, but we cannot connect that with her death. That will need to wait for the autopsy. So right now, all we can say with accuracy is, as you put it, she expired in her bathtub."

"What can you tell me about Trey Green's badge wallet?"

"We found his badge wallet and blood splatters in a bedroom on the opposite end of the house from Mrs. Guinness's bathroom," said Adams. "We have no idea whose blood it was, or why the wallet was under that bed. We won't even know if he was in the house until we get the analysis back on the blood samples."

"When do you think you will have some kind of report?" asked BoMac, thinking that this story might be a better lead in next week's paper. Give the investigators another week and hound them, maybe he'd have the full story next week. As for the blood, the old saying was "if it bleeds, it leads." That's journalism. Break the story this week, full follow-up report next week. He'd have time to do that.

"We expect to have something back on Wednesday or Thursday, but whether we can release it is up to the Rangers. They are fully in charge of all this. You'd have to talk to them."

"Can you give me a contact number for the Rangers?"

"Why, no, I can't. You can call headquarters in Austin, see if they can patch you through to someone, but I don't have any numbers I can give you."

"If you had to call them about something, could you?"

"Oh sure. I'd call on the radio and they'd get in touch. Or I'd ask one of the local state troopers to call them. They don't like to be bothered by trivial stuff, though, murders and such. That's local business."

"You know we pulled Trey Green out of the lake on Saturday morning. Do you think he was murdered?"

"Why would I think that?" asked Adams.

"You found his wallet," said BoMac.

"Man might drop his wallet at Belle Guinness's house for a number of reasons," said Adams. "Including distraction."

"What if that's his blood in the bedroom?"

"Well, then we will rethink how that wallet got under the bed. The only person we know of who could tell us died in her bathtub, though. It's a hard case with no clear answers."

"Anything else I should tell people over here?" asked BoMac.

"Mr. Maclean, just say that Sheriff Adams and the entire Cypress County Sheriff's office are heartbroken about the death of Trey Green. He was a fine lawman, a good family man, and an outstanding example for his community. Our heartfelt sympathy goes out to his wife and the good people of Whitmire."

BoMac scribbled all that down while rolling his eyes. He read the statement back to Adams and received his approval.

"That's pretty good, isn't it," Adams stated. "Right off the top of my head like that."

"Nice statement," said BoMac. "Thanks. Please call me when you have any updates."

"Oh sure," said Adams, hanging up. "You bet."

The rest of the day went just like that. BoMac either encountered hostility or platitude from everyone he asked. No one ventured an opinion. No one wanted to be quoted. Everyone said it was a season for waiting and watching while the secret gears of law enforcement ground slowly along.

BoMac wondered why they wanted law enforcement to be secret but kept that to himself.

Even John Quick, the undertaker, who had been friendly with BoMac since that summer day last year when BoMac helped him look for the missing eyeball, said he couldn't confirm anything. It was all pending. Even when BoMac offered to go off-record with him, just for some background stuff so he wouldn't get anything wrong, Quick demurred. It just wasn't possible at the current time to say one way or another.

He did not pass on a warning to Charles Henniker about Cock-lover Turner's threats. Henniker was teaching school, the students adored him and were excited by his classes, Ellen thought the world of him and admired his grip on classroom management. Henniker was a good man.

Solid, strong, disciplined, and intelligent. He was smart enough to know that being a Black man in East Texas was not for the faint of heart; being a forceful, educated, and intelligent Black man in East Texas was a dangerous role, but Henniker was up to it. BoMac thought Henniker had probably seen enough in his lifetime that would have broken lesser people, so the trivial threats of two-bit politicians would not bother him.

"I wish he'd gone to law school, though," thought BoMac. "He'd be a perfect candidate to run against Cock-lover in the next election."

One day the Piney Creek sewer system backed up. In a town of seven thousand, this was a notable civic catastrophe. The city's emergency response team determined all of the wastewater plants were functioning normally and traced the problem to a clogged two-foot outflow pipe where the treated water flowed through creeks into the Corps of Engineers lake to nourish the catfish. Workers discovered a 110-pound alligator snapping turtle, probably a century old, had crawled into the pipe and somehow turned sideways, plugging it. Once they got the snapper out, their first stop was the newspaper office for a photo.

CHAPTER
THIRTY-SEVEN

BoMac hung up the phone after trying unsuccessfully to get more information on Trey Green's death, only to find Brother Lyncefield Burk, the pastor at First Fundamentalist Church, waiting to talk to him with an announcement of Trey Green's memorial service.

"Your paper will come out on Wednesday, I think," said Brother Lyncefield, handing BoMac a three-page, single-space typed announcement. "The memorial service will be held on Thursday, and we expect a big crowd after the floods and all. Will you run this announcement on your front page? It has obvious value to the public."

BoMac took the announcement and scanned it, taking three or four milliseconds to spot four typos, several run-on sentences, and an opening line of at least ninety words.

"I'm glad you brought this in," he said. "I'll just clean it up a little and stick it in. I think we will have room on the front page for the announcement, although not in its entirety. We will jump the story to an inside page."

"Oh, no," said Brother Lyncefield. "It's perfect the way it is, and I think you need to run the whole thing on the front page."

"Well, it will take up the whole front page," said BoMac. "I can't do that. But as a public service, I will certainly give the announcement prominent placement."

"I see the announcement as the most important thing happening in Whitmire this week," said Brother Lyncefield. "Surely you can accommodate this important public event."

"I will place the announcement in the newspaper," said BoMac, again, wondering how Brother Lyncefield would react to him walking into church service on Sunday morning to commandeer the pulpit and preach his own sermon. He couldn't see Brother Lyncefield being accommodating. But who knows? Maybe he would try it.

"I expect we will have several thousand mourners," added Brother Lyncefield. "Most of the state troopers and the uniformed police from surrounding communities will attend and follow the procession out to Memorial Haven. We could have several hundred motorcycle patrolmen leading the procession."

"Will you have a jazz band, too?" asked BoMac. "Like one of those New Orleans funerals?"

"I don't believe the family were much fond of jazz," said Brother Lyncefield. "As you will see in the story," he gestured at the typed pages, "they have chosen appropriate music for the occasion. I admit, though," he added with a small, satiric grin, "I was able to dissuade Mrs. Green from having the "Bridal Chorus" from Lohengrin as the processional music. She is quite fond of that piece of music."

"The 'Bridal March'?" asked BoMac. "The 'Here Comes the Bride' song? That's what she wanted?"

"We have persuaded her to accept 'His Eye Is on the Sparrow,'" said Brother Lyncefield. "Although she is truly fond of the Bridal Chorus. I believe she plays it on her tape machine every night during dinner. Quite charming, actually."

BoMac refused to shake his head in disbelief. As a journalist, it was his job to take the world as it really was, to report what he saw. He made a mental note to store away this oddity for the great American novel he was writing.

"I'll ask Sarah Bibber to type this into our news copy," said BoMac. "Meanwhile, Brother Lyncefield, could you answer some questions for me about Chief Green's death? Have you viewed the body to confirm it was he?"

"I'd rather not get into that," said the good pastor, "not at this time. Perhaps after the service or next week. My focus now is on giving Trey Green a good Christian funeral and in comforting his widow. But it is typical for law enforcement to request a minister to confirm an identity when next of kin are unavailable for whatever reason."

"Didn't they have children?" asked BoMac. "Can you tell me?"

"I believe the chief had two small nephews he and his wife were raising while the parents were occupied."

"Occupied?"

"Well, the mother is temporarily in jail, you know, on a variety of shoplifting and petty theft charges. The father is unable to care for the two boys. I think they are ages three and five. The whole family are members of my church, and you would have met them if you had ever joined us."

"May I attribute this fact to you, that Trey Green and his wife are raising their two nephews?"

"I think you should be careful to say that they are raising two of their nephews. I believe they have several additional nieces and nephews whom they are not raising."

"Ah, thanks for that clarification." BoMac made another mental note. Raising someone else's kids is high on the list for human interest, and it shows a dimension of Trey Green's personality that might otherwise not have been evident.

"I did take the liberty of talking to Mrs. Elkins this morning about the announcement," Brother Lyncefield continued. "She told me she had no problem with placing it on the front page."

"Thank you for checking with my employer," said BoMac. "I will make a note of that. Is there anything else you think I should know about Trey Green or his death besides the official report?"

"Accidental drowning, of course," said the pastor, assuming a particularly grating tone of unctuousness. "In high school, he was a state champion in swimming before integration closed the state swimming contests. The fact that he drowned seems, shall we say, ironic—but alas. It can happen to anyone. It's not everyone who can walk on water."

BoMac sighed internally. At least this week, he would need to go with the accidental drowning story line, even if it was probably wrong. Meanwhile, he knew the Texas Rangers would be coming to their own secret conclusions, which they might share with bigger news sources than the *Whitmire Standard*. But he believed Charles Henniker about the broken jaw. Everything he had learned about Henniker was consistent with a truth-speaking, knowledgeable man. He would accept Henniker's word over just about anyone's.

The rest of Monday was successful with ad sales. The merchants intuited that this week's paper would be a sellout, and they looked to boosted circulation to generate more income for themselves, and they placed larger ads. Merchants who only occasionally ran ads bought space in this week's paper also. By late afternoon, BoMac had a hefty newspaper, which meant he had room for more local news. That also meant he needed to find more local stories, or anyway, get some ideas in case it turned out he needed to add pages to the paper. You couldn't add just one page. You had to add four pages if you were going to add any, and the cost of printing four additional pages was less per page than the cost of each page in a shorter press run. It was one of the quirks about the newspaper business. Still, four additional pages would increase the overall printing bill as well as the cost of postage on the thousands of mailed copies, and add to the weight of the mailbags and the number of bags—which were restricted to a maximum weight by postal regulations. It was a complex business and difficult to know the break-even point. Still, BoMac guessed that they would have a profitable paper this week.

And since many of the businesses had asked about Brother Lyncefield's announcement on the front page, he knew that the First Fundamentalist Church network had been active throughout town during the day. Whatever, he thought. He'd take it. Maybe Mrs. Elkins would not be quite so bitter and cruel, with a banner week early in the month like this and the mayhaw graduation issue coming at the end of the month, always a money-maker for the paper and its supporting merchants.

A tropical storm drowned East Texas in 1926 with about thirty inches of rain, then wandered up over Arkansas into the central Mississippi basin, where it caused the devastating flood of 1927. All East Texas cotton crops had been planted, but the rain stripped the ground bare. Farmers were bankrupted, local businesses bankrupted, and many people facing famine and ruin abandoned their farms and moved away. The economies in ten states were destroyed, preparing the way for the stock market crash in 1929. Progress, measured by telephones, radio stations, and electricity, halted in East Texas, not to return until 1953.

CHAPTER
THIRTY-EIGHT

Monday was warm, a day reaching into the mid-nineties and cloudless. After the tropical storm two weeks earlier, the still-flooding creeks and bay galls were saturating the warm air with humidity, and the millions upon millions of pine trees were pumping that excess moisture up their tall stems and out into the atmosphere like giant misters blowing invisible but dense water vapor. Because of the humid haze, visibility was down to around five miles. Still safe for flying under visual operations rules, and no hazard to driving, the close air and lack of breeze meant the actual heat in Whitmire was much less than the felt heat. It felt like it was more than 110 degrees F.

BoMac pulled into Henniker's driveway a little after 6 p.m. The garage door was open, and Henniker was exercising. He had a forty-pound dumbbell in each hand and was jumping onto a stool, then off again, then touching the dumbbells to the floor, then hoisting them over his head, then repeating the routine when BoMac walked in. His face was shiny with sweat, and his tee shirt was soaking. A fan in the corner helped, but not much.

"Mind if I watch?" asked BoMac.

Henniker nodded, breathing hard. "Set is twenty," he panted. "Then I do something else."

BoMac found a place to sit, watching the exercise. He was not sure he could even pick up a forty-pound dumbbell, much less one in each hand. And as far as jumping up on a stool with them, there was no way. This Henniker was one very strong man.

Eventually, Henniker finished and set the weights back on their rack, grabbing a towel to wipe his face and drink from a glass of cold water.

"Hello, BoMac." He grinned. "What brings you over?"

"Oh, just wanted to visit," smiled BoMac. "But don't let me interrupt you."

"I won't. But you are going to press tomorrow night. You wouldn't be here if you weren't fishing."

"I might." BoMac acted offended.

"Okay. You might," smiled Henniker. He had caught his breath. "Let me finish my workout and then we can sit around for a little bit. But I have classes to prepare so we can't visit long."

Henniker went over to the mat on the floor and did fifty-five one-handed pushups, alternating hands, then without stopping, twenty-five pushups where he slapped both hands on his chest. "Those are fun," he said, breathing heavily again. "The trick is moving your hands fast enough." He rolled on his back and did a hundred bent-knee sit-ups, touching an elbow to alternate knees, lifting his feet from the floor.

"Okay," he said, hopping up and grinning again, "floor work is done. One more thing, then we can talk."

He took another large swig of water, wiped his face again, and strolled over to the Wing Chun dummy. Ten minutes of rapid practice on the wooden arms, his hands moving faster than BoMac's eyes could follow, and Henniker seemed to have caught his breath.

"Ah," he said at last, "so relaxing. I love my workouts. Such a buzz."

He wiped off with his towel again and invited BoMac into the kitchen, where they sat at the white-enameled kitchen table and drank water together.

"You're right, you know," BoMac finally said. "I'm on deadline here. I'll be up most of the night anyway trying to get everything together. We have a lot of last-minute ads to build, and the lead stories are still not written. I'll work on those most of the night while I've got the office to myself."

"I figured," said Henniker. "What do you need to know?"

"I have heard a lot of rumors about Trey Green, but I have no one who will confirm anything. All the law enforcement are clamping down on information about his death."

"That's what they do," said Henniker. "They will only talk when they think they have someone they can win a trial against."

"That's the case," nodded BoMac. "But I think people need to know that Green was probably murdered. Hell, he was a swimming champ in high school. Even overweight and in his 50s, he would still know how to keep his head above water."

"I don't want to be quoted, even as an unnamed source," said Henniker. "I need to bring as little notice to myself as I can, especially after what happened last week with the Putnams. You can't mention me at all in any way in the paper."

"I didn't think you'd mind if I credited you with driving Darryl's truck."

"I don't want to be associated in any way with the death of a White police officer," said Henniker. "I expect you to honor my request. Leave me completely out. After the comments I heard that morning from the fire chief, I realize that I am in a lot of danger from people who resent me getting noticed. If you put me in the paper, that level of danger increases."

"Okay," groaned BoMac. He knew the story would get national press coverage as soon as the facts emerged, and the facts would emerge. He needed to be the one breaking those facts.

"But I'll give you the number of a truthful deputy who might be able to help you out," continued Henniker. "Jack Lewis. Here's his number. He came over to talk to me yesterday, and he confirmed everything you and I think we know. Maybe he will talk to you. If it's the truth, you can't go wrong with publishing it."

BoMac called Jack Lewis from the now dark office, Sarah Bibber, that spy, having left at 4:30. She figured her work obligations were no greater than those of the secretarial staff at the courthouse, who all went home at 4:30 every day. Why should she work to five? And some days she left at 4:00 just because—usually on the busiest days, when she might have been some help at getting the paper to press. By suppertime, the office was deserted except for BoMac, and the only sound was the clatter of his typesetter's keyboard as he worked through his news budget for the week.

Jack Lewis was on duty. He stopped by the *Standard* office at the time of day known as "dark thirty," that twilight between sunset and full nighttime. On this day in May, it was about 7:45, and BoMac had just finished the layout for the last ad of the paper and turned his full attention to the news stories. His strips of black and white film were already processed and hanging like flypaper in the darkroom to dry. He'd work on the stories for a while, then go run the film strips through the enlarger to see what he had, make up his mind, go back to write the stories to go with his photo art, and so on for the rest of the night. Around midnight he would be pulling prints of the shots he'd include with the stories, and by 2 a.m. he would be pulling the front page together.

With the ads already stacked on the inside pages, you had to lay out the news on the front page first. All of the other pages would be affected by the stories you jumped inside. Despite the increasing frenzy of deadline, however, BoMac was delighted that Lewis stopped by.

"Nobody told me I could talk to you about Trey Green," he started, "but nobody told me I couldn't. Ask away."

"First, can I quote you?"

"Sure. Why not? I'm responsible for what I say."

They had a lengthy discussion of the condition of Trey Green's body when found, confirming not only the broken jaw but other relevant injuries, like a broken neck and cracked skull.

"You reckon he was in a fight?" asked BoMac.

"The injuries are consistent with a fight with, say, a gorilla," said Lewis. "But we can't know that. All we know is his condition when we found him. He'd been underwater for several days, probably since Tuesday."

"Did he drown?"

"You'd suspect that somebody underwater for almost six days would have drowned," said Lewis, "but it will take a coroner's report to know. We are still waiting for that. The bigger question is how he got into the water to begin with. Did he slip and fall and get bashed around by logs and such? If so, then where's his car? We will know more later in the week when the water goes down some. I bet we eventually find his car somewhere."

"Where have we looked?"

"Well, the obvious place would be along the shore of the lake upstream of where he was snagged. So far, none of the game wardens have seen anything, and they've been riding up and down the river and lake shores since Saturday. On land and in boats. Something will turn up. But it might not tell us much."

BoMac had his story at last and was ready for Lewis to leave.

"One last thing, deputy," as they parted at the door of the office. "What do you think of Charles Henniker?"

"We are lucky to have him," said Lewis. "I mean lucky. But he's going to have trouble from some old-timers here in town. If you see him, tell him to be on the lookout."

"Right," said BoMac. "Will do."

Her ex-husband wielding a heavy wrench knocked out Lavinia Fisher's teeth. Afterwards, she became a paranoid schizophrenic with persistent lung congestion. She moved into a garage apartment wearing her only prized possession, her dentures, but one day in the bathroom she was taken with a coughing fit as she turned to flush. The dentures splashed into the swirling toilet and disappeared. A neighbor helped her get the toilet off the floor and fish around in the drainpipe, which dropped fourteen feet straight to the sewer, but no dentures. BoMac always wondered if losing the dentures was worse than finding them.

CHAPTER
THIRTY-NINE

The funeral at First Fundamentalist Church drew a huge crowd, and a collection for the widow almost matched the church's whole budget for the quarter. The entire town of Whitmire arrived hours early at the church to get the best seats, and the sixty-person church choir made quite an impression in television news broadcast on all three national networks. For weeks afterwards, the church was flooded with mail requests for recordings of the choir. Unfortunately, no sufficiently sophisticated sound equipment or sound engineers existed in Sweetgum County to make the recordings.

Brother Lyncefield stormed and shouted for days until he was hoarse about the parsimonious board of deacons who did not fund his requests for upgraded sound equipment when first requested years prior. The church had plenty of money, and Brother Lyncefield was a master at raising more. But the reluctant deacons had dragged their feet and dragged their feet, and this was the result. The one chance for First Fundamentalist Church to break into the big time, to prove that church choirs in small towns in rural Texas could be just as good as those—in his words—"non-Christian choirs in spurious religious institutions such as one could find in Salt Lake City" had come and gone.

"The Good Book says that opportunity knocks but once," raged Brother Lyncefield. "But some people won't open the door!"

"It's the story of this whole region. One opportunity after another lost because of lack of vision!" he shouted at the deaf walls of his office.

For the next six weeks he preached on the theme of a stitch in time saves nine, which was his interpretation of Jesus's Sermon on the Mount. "Blessed are those who think ahead and prepare," he intoned. His parishioners ate it up. So true, they nodded to one another.

BoMac was kept informed of these pastoral opinions partly because he was given a summary of the week's sermon each week for publication in the paper, to be printed on the same page as notes from the quilting guild and the garden club, and also because the general breakfast talk over omelets served with bacon and cigarette smoke at the County Court Cafe could not help but be overheard. Civilization was being hammered out without much artistry in this way in Whitmire, but it was being hammered out just the same, an ongoing project. BoMac loved that about this job. He got to see the whole nation trying to get itself together and become something, right down here at the low end of culture as far from New York City as a man could get. This was the nitty-gritty of what being American really meant: basically good people just trying to understand, and with damn poor tools to do the work.

The Mayhaw Graduation Festival was a distant memory by the middle of June, but the Trey Green story continued to nag at people. Every once in a while, somebody would ask around the cafe if anybody knew an update, and then everybody would look at BoMac as though he was in charge of knowing everything. The blood spatters in Belle Guinness's had matched Green's blood type, but they also found blood that did not match either Belle or Green on Belle's sheets. They had no idea who that was from, and speculation was rampant. The blood match with Green seemed to place him in Belle's house, alright, but didn't explain why. Somebody suggested that he was serving a warrant on Belle for a hot check, and that seemed like the most plausible excuse anyone could imagine, and also explained why he might have been bloodied. And that's where the story stagnated. If the Texas Rangers had learned anything new, they didn't say so.

The owner of a yellow sedan was interviewed at the Motel Six in Piney Creek, but he showed investigators papers dating the sale to the Friday before Green's body was found on Saturday. Besides, Bob McKinney had removed it from his roster of used cars the day he sold it, and that was enough corroboration to let Abbie Morton escape being arrested for murdering a White police officer. The Texas Rangers behind their opaque Ray Bans had given him back to the Piney Creek police, and Piney Creek had let him go with a brief warning about learning to stay in his place. Besides, other than the yellow sedan, nothing tied him to the murder, and nobody knew for sure that this particular car had been the one seen. His blood type was different from both Trey Green's and from the unknown person in Belle Guinness's house. They gave him a pass. "This time," they told him. "You should count your lucky stars."

The third week of June, a fisherman casting for bass in the Corps of

Engineers lake thought he spotted something in the water upstream from the dam. The water had receded from the flooding and the lake level had dropped back to its base reservoir pool height. The Corps had closed the floodgates at the dam to keep the lake level steady, and some small islands that had disappeared in Tropical Storm Beryl's inundation had reemerged. Snubbed up against one of them still underwater, where the bass fisherman had snagged his lure, was the missing Whitmire police car. Trey Green's car. The rooftop red lights could be seen just below the brown water's surface. Later, investigators found the keys in the ignition. His gun was not in the car. The driver's side window was down.

The story was sensational, and even caught a short notice in the national press, but it didn't draw in any more advertising for the *Whitmire Standard*. The only thing worse for advertising revenue than the January lull after Christmas was the lull of summer, when everyone quit work and went fishing or took family vacations. Just keeping the newspaper publishing during those months was difficult, and some weeks the paper was no more than six pages. BoMac did not need to hear from Jane Elkins that he was losing money again, or how worthless he was as a newspaper publisher.

Besides, Ellen was not teaching for the summer but had returned to Sugar Land to take graduate classes and study while lounging around the pool at her mother and father's house. So not only was business bad, but news was also spotty, and emotionally BoMac was not having a very good time.

To be completely fair, thinking that some workers could not afford to be laid off, the manager at the local aluminum lawn-furniture plant announced a partial shutdown for July and August, but allowed workers to volunteer for the layoff. His reasoning was that layoffs according to seniority unfairly discriminated against some newer workers who really needed a paycheck. He made the announcement over the plant's public address system, inviting workers to volunteer for summer layoff. They could apply during lunch on Friday. By noon Friday, the line stretched outside and around the plant. Every single employee, including foremen, applied.

CHAPTER FORTY

With Ellen out of town, BoMac found himself spending more time with Henniker. They visited almost every day, and BoMac began exercising with him. Sometimes Jack Lewis, the deputy, would stop by, and they'd talk. Like Ellen, Henniker was not teaching for the summer, but he was engaged in correspondent graduate classes with Case Western. This summer he was studying the Dred Scott decision and its social ramifications leading to the Civil War. He intended to spend August planning his fall classes on the 1877 compromise that removed federal troops from certain Southern states and caused the collapse of Republican state governments there. Henniker did not talk about his research with his two White friends, but sometimes went down to the courthouse square early in the morning in hopes of bumping into Isaac to talk chess.

One evening, Lizzie King called him from Piney Creek.

"Why have you not called me?" was the first thing she said to him, not even saying hello or telling him her name.

She didn't need to. He knew.

"Hi Liz," he said, settling down in a chair "How's it going?"

"It's not going," she fretted. "The police talked to that Houston guy about his yellow sedan, and that's all. And now you haven't called, and it's been almost three weeks. It's not going at all."

She fretted and fumed for a bit, then seemed to thaw out. An hour later, they were still talking, and Henniker had switched the phone from one ear to the other three or four times. He was not accustomed to talking—and listening—on the phone for that long. By the end of the conversation, they were exchanging stories about the family in San Augustine and laughing out loud. It was good to have someone who shared some of his history. It was comfortable, and that rod of tension he'd felt since the police hauled him down to jail on the word of some mad White woman finally began to unwind and relax.

Finally, he asked her how things were going in Piney Creek.

"I heard from some friends that they got the autopsy report back on that woman who died in her bathtub," she said. "Some pretty serious drugs in her system. Meth, heroin, and a whole lot of alcohol. They think the meth gave her a heart attack."

"It sure could," he said. "It sure could. Where'd she get it?"

"My guess is a local supply," she said. "I see it being sold at the club sometimes by a Black man named Clarence Thomas."

"He ever get busted?"

"Looks like the cops are protecting him," she said. "He goes inside with a duffle bag of goods and they're all parked out on the street to keep the peace, and then he comes out with his bag empty and walks away and they're just watching. Hard to tell what they do and don't know, but my guess is that they're getting a take. The club's got video cams everywhere, so somebody is watching."

"Sounds like a mafia thing."

"Lots going on in East Texas," she said. "They are uneducated and ignorant, but they tracked a yellow sedan back to a used car dealer named McKinney. But now who knows. The car was in his inventory when Green and that white woman died. But nobody is looking at McKinney. Something is going down over here."

"Sounds corrupt as hell," agreed Henniker. "I wonder where it leads."

"My guess is it leads all the way to the top," she said, "and nobody's safe. The men running the nightclubs were both tried in federal court and sentenced to twenty years for interstate transportation of drugs, but then they were freed on bail while their convictions were appealed, and nobody cares. All the federal prosecutors were transferred to other jobs right after the trial and those two have been out on bail for almost twenty years."

"You're kidding."

"I am not kidding," said Lizzie. "No, I'm not kidding. And Congressman Rip Johnson put up the bail money."

"Nobody looking into it?"

They talked for a while longer about the property owned by the congressman and the judge, and Henniker just whistled.

"If Trey Green was onto something, no wonder he got knocked off," said Henniker.

"How well did you know Trey Green?" asked Lizzie.

"Didn't know him at all. The one time I met any police, he was out of town."

"If Trey Green had been bright enough to add two and two without counting on his fingers, he might have been onto something. My guess is that he was too damned dumb to figure out anything. Trey Green was the kind of man who took orders and didn't think much, or at all."

"Do you think it could have been an accident? Is that what you're saying?"

"I work in the county clerk's office and have friends in the police department. I got to look at the blood analysis from that woman's house. It was a match for Trey Green's blood. I think he got the shit beat out of him in that house, but that old fat woman was not one to do it. She would have had trouble lifting a cast iron skillet. Besides, they found semen in her in all the places it could go, and blood on her sheets that don't match hers or Green's. Some other male was involved, but they don't know who. I'm not sure they're really looking. If Trey Green stumbled on a drug sale going down to that woman, it would have been enough to do him."

Henniker thought about that.

"Stay safe, Lizzie," he said at last. "This is dangerous stuff, and nobody can help. The FBI could do something, but if it is all circulating around a federal district judge and a US congressman, they might not want to get involved."

"I know. That's why I'm telling you. I need someone to know about it in case they kill me next."

"I wish we could tell the newspapers or somebody, but they'd be silenced too."

"Also, they've got to keep their advertising and their readership. If something threatens this congressman, the advertisers might just pull out. He's like a redneck god to these people. A crude, mean, self-serving little deity. And I mean little. About five foot five, but powerful as all hell."

"I'll talk about that with my friend from the newspaper, BoMac, when he comes over tomorrow. We've got an exercise routine."

"Stay healthy, Charles," she said. "I gotta go. Call me, damnit."

She hung up, and Henniker sat still in his darkened room for some time, staring out the window at the dark street dimly lit by a single streetlamp on the corner.

One Saturday morning, a pickup hauling nearly seven tons of sweet potatoes on a lowboy trailer bound for the farmer's market braked at the Toby Creek bridge. The forward surge on the overloaded trailer's hitch broke it in two and the trailer careened across the highway and into a ditch on the opposite side of the highway, where it overturned. Luckily, no traffic was coming the other way. Word of the wreck spread rapidly through Whitmire, and by sunset so many people had swarmed the spill that only a few small pieces of broken sweet potato remained in the ditch.

CHAPTER
FORTY-ONE

Darryl Stewart had not been fishing again since pulling Trey Green out of the lake. The sight of that swollen face rising moon-like from the dark water in predawn twilight would not leave his mind, and he trembled every time he thought about it. The Lion's Club social organization, however, insisted on holding its Fourth of July fish fry as always, and his fellow club members had counted on Darryl's frozen fish all year. They were going to clean out his freezer for him, and then there he would be, without any fish.

He sat out in his front yard studying the pond in the middle of the street, trying to wrap his head around it all. His head was not wrapping very well. Sometimes he would swivel to look at his boat in the driveway for a while, then turn back to the pond. He could park that boat in the pond, he thought. That might finally get the city council to do something. Just tie the boat up to a stake in his yard and let it float there. He could go climb in it sometimes and crank the 200-horsepower outboard engine up, rev it a few times, get the oil to circulate, swirl some oxygen into the water. It's good for an engine to be cranked and run. Like me, he thought. It's good for me to get cranked and run.

The Beech Street Lake, as he called it, had now been a neighborhood presence for five years. During Tropical Storm Beryl it had grown considerably, and most of the residents who typically had used Beech Street as their main route to the post office were now detouring down Redbud Street, a block over. Besides, Darryl's attitude toward it changed once he stocked it with fish. But Darryl was done with fishing. He was not going fishing again. The Lions Club could come clean out his freezer if they wanted to, and he'd try to figure out how to supplement his and Mary's diet with something else. Deer, maybe. Some folks ate raccoon, but those rascals were sly and hard to get. Maybe the wild pig population would take off and he and Mary could live off pork. He could build a chicken coop out near Mary's kiln and they could raise chickens. He kept thinking of alternatives, but nothing really appealed to him. Basically, he liked fish.

Also, he could work harder and make more money, distasteful as that seemed, so he could buy more meat at Crooks Bros. Grocery.

Darryl, he muttered to himself, boy, you can't let a little thing like Trey Green getting himself killed change your whole life.

Darryl, in fact, did not know a single person who thought Trey Green's death was a great loss to the world. Sure, thousands of uniformed policemen from around the state had swarmed Whitmire for the funeral, but then they left. And when they left, Trey's wife also left, returning those two nephews to their father. Nobody knew where she was, but some people thought she'd taken the insurance payout and gone to Vegas. Frankly, nobody cared. Sooner or later, they'd find somebody to take the police chief job, but why did they need a police chief? Whitmire did not really need police at all, except maybe down at the bank and the bank could hire private guards.

Old Miz Elkins wouldn't hear of it, though. Darryl knew that. She regarded her bank as a public service, despite its rapacious lending practices. She would want the city to pay for protecting it. Darryl understood would-be royalty. East Texas was full of would-be royalty. Miz Elkins wanted to be treated like royalty, and mostly she was. She had a lot of money, and nearly everybody wanted some of it.

Maybe, Darryl thought, if he just bought himself a new boat. He could get a fancy new rig in Lufkin, then he and Mary could spend their weekends drifting around Lake Ralph Yarborough, that huge lake built with federal funds won for East Texas by those powerful people in Piney Creek, chiefly US Congressman Rip Johnson. It'd mean a new note to pay, and that would mean needing to work more, but if he had a new boat, maybe he wouldn't be reminded of Trey Green's face every time he looked at the boat he had now. Maybe the nightmares would go away.

He poured the rest of his coffee into one of the brown spots already in the lawn and went back inside for his tool belt. He was going to work today. He was going to make enough money to buy that new boat. He had made up his mind.

When he got home from work, he'd figure out how to dock his current boat in the Beech Street Lake. He could a put a "For Sale" sign on it, and who knew? Maybe somebody would buy it and he'd be able to argue Mary into going along with a new bass boat—one of those sparkly fiberglass numbers from Ranger, cost about $50,000. He could probably swing a loan, if he sold his current boat first.

But damned if he'd try to borrow money again from that Elkins witch.

In Piney Creek, Lizzie King found a chest full of old deeds in the courthouse basement, deeds that were notarized but not in the county clerk's official records. The discovery sparked mischief in her mind, soon blown into full flame by a lifetime of resentment at a White community that targeted and robbed Blacks of absolutely everything of value: their money, their land, their honor, and even their bodies. Almost all of the county clerk's record books had been destroyed by a fire that started when thieves tried to blow up the post office safe with dynamite in 1899. All of these deeds would have been recorded in those burned books. She had figured that she'd keep the discovery to herself, just slipping copies of the deeds into the property records, a guerilla action that might eventually cause tremendous problems for certain wealthy people when they discovered clouds on their titles to land and minerals.

The East Texas Field had been a very productive oil find in the early twentieth century, and a lot of local wealth could be traced to it. Now possibly some of that wealth could eventually go to the people who owned the rights to it, instead of the anti-Reconstructionists who stole it from Black families.

With the help of a local genealogist, she was able to identify the family connections of both the Black and White neighborhoods. Records were spottier for the Black neighborhoods, and some birth certificates gave the date of birth as "berry-picking time," or "turnip planting." Lots of Black children and quite a few White children had grown up, gotten old, and died without ever having a birth certificate. When cotton disappeared as a widely grown crop in the 1920s, most of the cotton fields went back into native pine, which gave rise to the lumber industry. The loss of cotton also meant the loss of a way of life for both White and Black communities, and they had to scramble for other ways to stay alive. Some managed to keep their land and farm it. Most left for the cities and their property was vacuumed up by others. But here she was completing the record, quietly and thoroughly. At least they had that, her people. At least they could know the truth of their robbery and loss. Next, when she was ready, she would quietly and unobtrusively start chaining title to the mineral and surface rights of the land back to their original owners and notifying the descendants of their good fortune. Then she would sit back and watch the roar, enjoy the circus as petroleum land men and attorneys started tearing up the courthouse with suits over titles. Oh my, she chuckled to herself, if

I can get away with this and not get caught, it's going to be quite a show!

She liked thinking that the trees always came back, given time. In her own backyard, she'd noticed that if she scraped a place clear of leaves to expose bare dirt, like she did in her little kitchen garden, by summertime the next year a pine tree would have taken root in that little patch. It happened all over East Texas. Bare dirt and sunshine and you'd have a pine tree. She hoped other Black people could do the same, if they got their own little patches of dirt to grow on.

She also stopped going to the nightclub. Her relationship with Henniker supplied the socializing she needed, and she had never liked the place. The fear she felt when she heard about a stupid White police officer being killed had become anger and it focused her. She'd uncover more of the old records, just keep going. Nothing had been computerized or scanned, not even microfilmed, and every day at least three or four petroleum land men would be working through the volumes to chain titles. They would be the first to know, and it might escape their notice altogether until they started trying to renew leases or expand holdings. Then all hell would break loose.

She started writing letters to her brother-in-law Calvin, explaining what she was finding and asking him to keep it safe for her. They might come for her, they might not. They might think they were untouchable, which they pretty much were, but they might not be. If she could present the story so it was something along the lines of continued slavery in the South, the New York Times would probably publish it. It would be fun to see if the lost deeds she was putting in the old handwritten volumes of the abstracts would make an impact, but she was pretty sure they would.

And that for sure could get her killed.

But sometimes you wake up in the morning knowing the truth is worth dying for.

One day Darryl Stewart sprained his ankle on the job and couldn't mow the grass, so Mary mowed it instead. Darryl made himself a large glass of iced tea and hobbled out to the front porch to make sure his wife was doing it right, propping his leg up on pillows in front of the old steel glider couch. Darryl, the first generation of his family to live in a town, had been raised on a farm with a mule. It amused him to holler "Gee" and "Haw" at Mary as she mowed, reminding her to turn right or left.

CHAPTER FORTY-TWO

Bob McKinney sat in the dark shadows of his office at the used car dealership in Piney Creek tapping a pencil eraser on his desk. He was alone, and mostly he was thinking about Belle Guinness, about the dime bag of smack he had given her as a gesture of goodwill, and about Jesse Grinder. The more he thought, the more he worried. Should he keep Grinder on so he could keep an eye on him, or should he fire him? That yellow sedan he sold to that Houston Black had been driven by Grinder when he went to Belle's house, and Grinder was late coming back. Texas Rangers had already been by about the car, looked at his bill of sale. At least the yellow sedan Grinder drove was not the only one in town. He might be safe if they didn't have any better information than that, but those Rangers were scary. He felt his tighty-whiteys filling up with cold sweat as the Rangers sat in his office, their chiseled chins and slow, controlled movements telegraphing danger.

What were they after? he wondered. Were they investigating the murder or the drugs? The Rangers were probably investigating the murder of the policeman, taking over from the local dumb-asses. Were the Rangers even thinking about the drugs? The autopsy probably would not show drugs in the police chief, since Belle was not the kind to share. Besides, she was probably out of drugs when Grinder got there and couldn't have shared any. But was the police chief there when Grinder arrived, or did he show up later? That's a big question, but maybe not important. What did Grinder do?

Still, maybe the cops were closing in on him and his cozy little side business. If he got rid of Grinder, would that protect him? Maybe Grinder needed to speak with the thousands of catfish on the bed of Rip Johnson's catfish pond.

But today he was supposed to go over to Fort Polk in Louisiana. Just because the fort was named for a Confederate general was no reason why they might not be filming everybody on base. And hauling a shitload of drugs while being filmed was such a bad idea. So far, though, it had worked. Still, Belle.

Damn, he thought. I'm going down for this.

His first instinct was to run, which is everyone's first instinct. If he could make it to Mexico, he might be able to disappear into Central America somewhere. Getting his cash out of his various banks might slow him down. His dealership account was tidy, with some well-managed creative accounting by the congressman's in-house tax attorney, which involved a public set of books and a private set of books. They had to hide the drug income somewhere, McKinney thought, muttering out loud, "Drugs, liquor, those girls he keeps over in Leesville outside Fort Polk, crazy real estate deals, that old boy is sure into a lot. How's he have time to go to Washington and still run all this stuff? And he's got what, five hundred acres of cattle and a thriving ranch? At least three girlfriends decades younger than his skinny witch of a wife. Damn. I'm not smart enough to keep all that straight. Don't know how he does it."

"I can tell you this, Bob McKinney," he said to himself, "Congressman Rip Johnson will hang it all on you if he can. That son of a bitch will feed you to the law one piece at a time."

He stood up, shuttering, sensing the hounds of hell rising around him.

"And Jesse Grinder might be the only one who knows what went on in Belle Guinness's house that morning," he said through clenched teeth. "I gotta get Jesse Grinder first."

Burrell Oates watched seventy-year-old Mary-Eleanor Pearcy's house until she left for church. Then he broke in and rummaged around, but lost track of time and Mary-Eleanor returned. She had the Sunday collection with her in a Citizens National bank bag, intending to deposit it the next day. He raped her and ran off with the collection, but deputies knew he was the only Black man nearby so they whipped him bloody with a garden hose until he confessed. At his trial, defense counsel made him tell what happened. "Chambers," the judge pointed at D.A. Cock-lover Turner, slamming his gavel. "Mistrial."

At the trailer park, Shorty Fike was coming to the same conclusion about Grinder. So far, the man had managed to elude him. Everyone else had been open and frank with him, but Grinder was hiding. The more he hid, the more Shorty's mind moved toward thinking Grinder had something to do with Annabeth and Maria's disappearance. The stupid Cypress County sheriff's deputies were doing nothing. They were all trying to best one another finding clues to the death of that dumb Whitmire policeman. As far as Shorty was concerned, until he had spoken with Grinder, he would not have a single idea about the disappearance. Even then, he might not. Still, it was all he had to go on.

A clue, any kind of clue, is what he wanted right now.

He contacted a series of private investigators in Beaumont and Lufkin but didn't find anyone willing to take his case. He admitted to himself that it sounded shady, like he was trying to set them up as a cover for having done away with his women himself. That's what the Cypress County assholes thought and had even told him. But he kept looking. Somebody somewhere, some private investigator, would be hungry enough to make his own investigation of the mobile home and the car. He knew it would cost a lot and he did not have a lot, or they would have moved away from here before this. But still, whatever it took was worth it. If the cops wouldn't do their job, he'd hire it done, somehow.

CHAPTER

FORTY-THREE

The high spot of the news cycle for BoMac in June was his report on finding the police chief's car in the lake. He was there taking pictures when they lifted it from the lake and got a dandy picture of it with water streaming out, the open driver's-side window showing. The doors were all locked, which was odd, BoMac thought. If the window was down, then Green could have been conscious and rolled it down himself trying to get out. But what about all the damage to his head?

Besides, it didn't take a genius to see that the damage to the patrol car was pretty superficial. It had not been in a wreck and then gone in the water. Except for small dents in the hood and roof, the car was waterlogged but not wrecked.

The ignition was switched on, also, and the gearshift lever was in drive, so the car had probably been running when it went in the water; and it could not have been going fast when that happened because of the lack of damage. BoMac could not piece it all together. He and Jack Lewis talked about it for hours driving around the county in Lewis's patrol car, going over every scenario. They finally decided between themselves, with no evidence to prove them right, that Green had been dead by the time the car hit the water, that whoever had killed him had set it up to get rid of both Green and his car. But why?

"I don't think it was planned, myself," Lewis finally said. "I think it was all pieced together, that one thing led to another. There's lots of ways to get rid of a body without throwing him in the water."

"What do you mean?" asked BoMac.

"Well, you know, bodies float sooner or later. They might not float for long, but that Corps of Engineers lake is not that big. It's mostly just a frog pond. It's not even very deep. The old river channel is deep, but most of the lake is only eight or ten feet. It's a bad place to hide a body. You're better off burying a body. Either that or figure out how to keep it in the water. You know, concrete boots or something. Weights."

"You don't think he was already dead when he went in?"

"Oh yeah, I think so. They still aren't letting ordinary people know about the autopsy, but I'm pretty sure our man Henniker nailed it. Trey Green was dead before he went in the water. The window was down because somebody put his body in the front seat then reached through and put the car in gear. My guess is he used a boat ramp somewhere and let the car drive itself off into the water during that flood. That's the best I've got, but I can't make all the pieces fit any other way. Trey Green was murdered, and the whole car in the water thing was a way to get rid of the body."

"And didn't they find his wallet and money still in his pockets?"

"Yes, they did. He left his badge wallet on the floor of that woman's house, but it was in his shirt pocket, or maybe on his belt. His money was in his hip pocket wallet, and it was still buttoned up in his pants. He wasn't robbed. He was just killed."

"Jealous lover?"

"You know, I've been looking at photos of that woman. I think it's been a couple of decades since she might have had a jealous lover. But you never know."

"Some people I talked to over in Piney Creek said she might have had a steady trade in boyfriends. She was married, but her husband was hardly ever home, they said."

"He's lucky he got out of that," said Lewis. "I'm not speaking ill of the dead, but some people you don't much miss."

"I got that impression," said BoMac.

"You talked to Darryl at all?" asked Lewis.

"I dropped by the other day, but he'd gone to work. I'm not seeing him at the County Court Cafe much. In fact, not at all."

"He's taking this pretty hard," said Lewis. "He and Trey were friends. Well, friends the way Trey was friends with anyone, if you understand me."

"I thought everyone in town was friends with everyone else," said BoMac. "You never hear people bad-mouthing one another in Whitmire."

"Lots of people keep their thoughts to themselves," said Lewis. They came to the top of a long hill that bottomed out crossing one of the numerous creeks of the county, and Lewis let the car just drift down the hill slowly gaining momentum. As they passed over the bridge, BoMac marveled at how high the floodwaters had risen during Beryl, leaving debris fifteen or twenty feet above the normal creek level. It was difficult to imagine how the lazy little foot-deep creek oozing along through the dark shadows of the forest could have raged like that, reached such a level of destruction.

"If he went in the water on that Monday, the flood stage was at its highest," added Lewis. "The water in that Corps of Engineers lake was overflowing the spillway by three or four feet by Monday, and I've never seen that much of a flood. They'd opened the flood gates all the way, and the whole river downstream from the dam was flooded. Lots of folks lost their homes along the river, and it's still got some of the petrochemical plants in Beaumont shut down."

"Lots of people without homes, and lots of people without jobs," said BoMac. "This is not a good time for East Texas."

"No, sir," said Lewis. "It is not. But you watch, some people will get richer off the poor people who ain't got nothing. I expect we'll get a lot of burglary calls now, too."

"Full moon?"

"No, full moon is when we get rapes and shootings. When people lose their jobs, they start needing to get stuff from their neighbors. Food, things they can sell. Of course, some folks do that all the time anyway. Just the way the world is."

"Where are we going?" BoMac asked.

"Oh, no place special. I just like to drive down some of these roads, look at things, see if anything's unusual. Check on the houses, make sure the right people are in them. Let people see their law enforcement is looking out for them."

"This is a big place over here," said BoMac, looking at the hundreds of acres of unmowed pasture. "Got a big barn out in the middle of it, but no house."

"House burned down. You'll see the brick chimney back there on the other side of the barn if you look, out among those pecan trees. The man who owned it threw his support behind one of the sheriff candidates about twenty years ago, and someone burned his house down. Ruled an arson, so he couldn't collect on the insurance. He moved off to Houston, I think. Anyway, place is owned by a Houston attorney now. That's all I know."

"Damn, that's a story," said BoMac.

"It was at the time," agreed Lewis. "It's not now. It's been forgotten, all those sheriff candidates are dead, so it's dead too, I reckon."

"Yeah, maybe so," agreed BoMac, wishing Ellen were back in town so they could visit. He'd call her tonight. And he would make sure she was getting the paper in the mail. She liked talking about that, even the obituaries and the notices. She said it kept her in the loop.

One year, the Whitmire chamber of commerce thought the city's employment outlook would improve if the state built a prison nearby. The chamber organized a group of citizens to tour the prison in Huntsville, and BoMac tagged along. It was newsworthy, or at least as newsworthy as yet another ribbon cutting. The state warden explained that new prisoners were given a battery of tests, and eighty-seven percent had learning disabilities, as though incarceration were not proof enough. BoMac mused that the state could save a lot of money with better public education. But then, what about the other thirteen percent?

CHAPTER
FORTY-FOUR

Darryl Stewart stared at his empty twenty-two-cubic-foot chest freezer, studying the patches of ice and dirt left on the floor when the Lions Club boys cleaned it out. The fish fry had been a success, earning the club about four thousand dollars to go to scholarships and other civic projects. That was about twice what the women's clubs could make on their big events like the Christmas tour of homes and such. It was always a point of pride with the club to make more money than the women's clubs. But now that was over. Somebody else would need to be catching the fish, Darryl told them.

He dropped the lid of the chest freezer and thought about unplugging it. Then he decided to leave it running. He'd be stocking it with something soon enough. If not fish, then something. He had built some hog traps out at the deer camp, even though he had not told the landowner about them. If he started catching some hogs, he would. If he didn't, he'd just keep quiet. He was pretty sure something would get in the trap to eat the corn, even if it was only town ants.

Wild pigs were not a protected game animal in Texas, so he could hunt them year-round. Also, they bred year-round, so there were always young to capture and feed up. He'd think about that, too. The result of all this was that instead of getting up before dawn every day and heading out to the lake, Darryl now got up every day and headed out to the deer lease to check his traps and throw out a little more corn.

"Darryl, honey," said Mary as he walked through the kitchen with his empty coffee cup, "I'm out of clay. I need to go in to Tyler to buy some. You want to come with me?"

"I'm gonna work today," he said. "You go on and have a good time."

"Okay. I'm going to do a little shopping, too. You need some new underwear. How are your socks?"

"I'm okay on socks. I could use a new bass boat, though." He tried to grin at her, but his grins had mostly drowned during the last two months. It came off looking like indigestion.

"We could use some fish," she replied. "You need to get over Trey Green and go fishing."

"Okay," he said. "I guess."

He left through the kitchen door with his tool belt. He'd work until the end of August, then he'd take a break and go mow that man's pasture. The steady hum and vibration of long hours on his tractor would be comforting, and he could always take a snooze out under those pecan trees during the hottest part of the afternoon. Nobody cared if he took a break. He was being paid and he'd get the job done. But that was a month away. He needed to make as much as he could between now and then.

If he put out new trotlines, that would mean going down to the lake every day or so. You could catch more fish, but you had to put in the time. If he abandoned trotline fishing, he could sit out there on the water and doze while he waited for a bite on his line. He'd catch bream that way. Or he could go to casting and join the ranks of scorned bass fishermen. Bass fisherman were hated by trotline fishermen, because they were forever getting their lures caught on the trotlines and cutting the trotlines to free their own lures, creating a lot of animosity among the trotline fishers. Lord help the bass fisherman who needed rescuing on the water if only trot fishermen were out. The feud was reminiscent of the old frontier feuds between cattle ranchers and sheep farmers, or between sailors and soldiers, or between Democrats and Republicans. Either way—casting or float fishing—the fish would not be catfish, and he loved fried catfish. When it didn't remind him of Trey Green's face.

By the middle of July, the air in Whitmire became hot and steamy. Although the temperature never exceeded one hundred degrees when clouds were in the sky, it was always over a hundred when the skies were clear. This pattern persisted through the month, with the oppressive heat and humidity making outdoor activity tedious, but by the end of the month the daily afternoon showers began. About 4 p.m., almost every day, a brief rain shower caused by rapidly rising humidity from the forest would condense and fall, rinsing the streets and washing the dust away. These daily rains cleaned the air and the whole town, and sometimes in the late afternoon after they had passed, the sun would come out again in blinding radiance. Toward evening, sunshine on the wet streets would pave them with gold while evening meal preparation began in homes and children started wandering home from play.

Jack Lewis and BoMac began spending every evening with Henniker, exercising and chatting. On nights when Lewis was on patrol, he would stop by briefly to check in on them, and sometimes BoMac would ride with him. Sometimes he would stay with Henniker and just talk. They talked about all kinds of things—the weather, of course, but also local politics, Jane Elkins, Hogleg Putnam, you name it. Henniker refrained from expressing any opinions, just discussing known facts, while BoMac was burning to pronounce judgment on people like Cock-lover Turner. But Henniker kept him in check. Whenever he began to wander in the direction of a judgmental statement, Henniker would warn BoMac to remain objective.

"Lots of ways to see things," he would say. "Lots of different attitudes. You can't see any alternative when you make a judgment, so back off."

"But he wears a goddamned Bowie knife into the courtroom," exclaimed BoMac, "and a shoulder holster."

"If the judge doesn't mind, then you don't either," said Henniker. "Remember that."

"He's also a son of a bitch."

"Well, of course he is. If he was a halfway decent lawyer, he wouldn't be working for peanuts in Whitmire, Texas. Remember that, too."

"Well, shit," said BoMac.

"Yeah, okay," said Henniker. "Now let me show you how to properly execute a kick to a chin."

By the end of July, BoMac, still in his twenties, had packed on a lot of muscle. His neck size was up from fifteen inches to seventeen, his stomach had that six-pack every older man wants, and his thighs bulged through his jeans. He had grown strong, and it had happened quickly, as it always does with young men. He felt good. And Henniker approved. The two of them bonded deeply, BoMac unconsciously adopting Henniker as the father figure he'd lost.

Junior Brown and Jackson Bunch, both seventeen, enjoyed evenings smoking with girlfriends atop the white-painted tanks in the sluggish East Texas oil fields. One evening, Junior wondered what was in the tanks and unscrewed a lid to look. "Hey Jack," he said, "hand me that lighter so I can look in this hole." The explosion blew both of them off the tank, giving Junior third-degree burns on both his arms. He pulled the unconscious Jim into the front seat of his pickup and drove them seventeen miles to the hospital, flesh dripping from his arms. The girls drove themselves home.

CHAPTER

FORTY-FIVE

Jesse Grinder sensed something was up. He'd seen those signs before from his bosses. They wouldn't look at you, they didn't want to talk to you, they closed the door to their offices when you were around. He thought he might as well quit, but who would McKinney get to run those packages out to all the housewives? Would he do it himself?

Besides that, Jesse had no idea what was in those packages. He understood beer. He had a nodding acquaintance with wine. That was it. He would not have recognized the contents of those packages even if they were labeled. Which they were not. All he knew was that he traded wrapped parcels for stuffed envelopes, and for the time he was in the car he was able to sit in air conditioning.

Still, there was McKinney.

Since that shooting across the street from the congressman's house, he had not been sent out there again. Instead, he saw a resentful McKinney driving off, losing potential car sales.

Jesse decided he needed to pick up his relationship with Wilburn Hall at the locksmith shop. He was still going over every morning early to sweep out and carry the trash, polish the front windows, dust the cabinets, and polish all the goods. He'd done a lot of good for old man Hall, he figured. Maybe it was time for Wilburn to employ him full-time, teach him how to do the locksmith business. Besides, Jesse had watched a television show about somebody opening a safe, and he wanted to learn how to do that. That looked like fun. That was the kind of intellectual stimulation Jesse Grinder desired.

His more important part needed the stimulation of large titties, but he was kind of avoiding women right now, since Annabeth and her daughter. Shorty Fike was his other problem. McKinney and Fike. Those names haunted him all night when he let them. So far, he'd avoided Shorty as well as he had avoided McKinney. He wasn't ready to get fired by McKinney yet, and he really did not want to confront Fike, who gave off the air of a man with a gun in his pocket.

Wilburn Hall was bored with Jesse Grinder. What had started as an act of Christian charity had become a chore. He really didn't make enough money to pay Grinder to sweep up and clean. Besides, he had literally zero walk-in traffic. When somebody had trouble with a lock, they called, he went, case unlocked. Sometimes they even paid their bills. At least those on the less expensive streets paid. He had yet to collect a bill from some folks in million-dollar homes, even though he could unlock all their doors and their cars and their office safes if he wanted to. The would-be royalty of Piney Creek did not owe money. Everyone else owed money to them, for creating the society. That was their attitude, and that was pretty much Wilburn Hall's attitude also. Sometimes he got recognized at Christmas with a fruitcake or a turkey. After thirty or more years working in Piney Creek, he expected no more from the would-be royalty. But at least the others paid.

Wilburn was sure Jesse Grinder would not understand any of that, so he didn't bother to explain. He just said that no, he could not afford to put him on full-time, and so, no, he wasn't going to be able to teach him how to open a safe. "Thanks for all you've done, Jesse," Wilburn said. "But business is just not good for a locksmith, even if he's the only one in the county."

"I unnerstand, Mr. Hall," mumbled Jesse. "Thank you for all you done for me and all. Want me to keep sweeping?"

Wilburn took a deep breath then let it out. "Jesse, I care about you, but I just can't pay you anything. Not anything. I haven't got enough income in the summer to buy my own groceries, and I'm living alone now."

"I know what you mean," said Jesse. "You can forget about last week then. I'll stop by sometimes to check on you, see if things pick up."

"Thanks, Jesse," said Wilburn, impatient for Grinder to be gone so he could replace the locks on his doors with the new unpickable kind. When Jesse Grinder disappeared past the storefront window, he shuddered and then turned to remove the lock from its packing material.

"Fun," he thought.

226

July melted into August, and the first of August melted into the last of August, and one day Darryl Stewart woke up and decided that this was the day he would go mow that pasture for the Houston attorney.

"Mary," he hollered, cheerfully adulterating his chicory blend coffee with sugar and fat-free creamer, "I'm going up to that place on Farm-to-Market Highway 755, gonna start mowing that man's pasture."

"Okay, honey," she yawned from the bedroom, "don't go driving that old tractor off into a hornet's nest or something."

"It's a big place," he said, going to the bedroom door with his steaming mug of pretend coffee. "Gonna take at least two or three weeks, or more."

"Yay," she said dreamily, "steady income." Then she rolled over and pulled the covers over her head, her shapely butt sticking up under the blanket.

Darryl Stewart stared at that enticing hump for several minutes while he sipped at the mug's contents, then sighed and went out to the truck. He wouldn't need his tool belt today. Just a drive out to the deer lease to hook up the trailer and load the tractor and he'd be off to the north, to the ranch on FM 755.

He saw Henniker and BoMac, the newspaper editor, jogging past the First Fundamentalist Church, then he was off, turning right at the red light and going south out of town, past Crooks Bros. Grocery, the NAPA car parts place and Walmart, the feed store, and down into the bay galls and sluggish sandy-bottomed creeks of East Texas, where he'd hunted deer since he was six years old.

Lavinia Fisher began hanging out at the Standard *office because sometimes BoMac would listen to her while he drank his fourteenth cup of coffee of the day. Sometimes she would carry out the trash or wipe down the counter where the coffee pot lived. She looked to BoMac for protection, since no one else cared about a toothless paranoid schizophrenic, and she knew she needed help. To show her appreciation, one day she made him a present of a knitted refrigerator magnet that looked exactly like an Oreo cookie. "I thought you needed more fiber in your diet," she explained.*

CHAPTER
FORTY-SIX

The first day of mowing is always the most critical. You want to get along the fence lines without busting the fence posts or getting snagged in the barbed wire or running off into an overgrown ditch, or any of a number of things. Also, Darryl knew from long experience that the first day of mowing a big tract set the pattern for the rest of the job. You cleared up the fence lines, evened up the rows, and then you just basically sat up there on the tractor and let it rumble along without any effort, just correcting the steering wheel a little. Because his tractor was a 52-horsepower John Deere, that meant continually turning the steering wheel a half-inch to the right to keep it going straight. Every once in a while, he would run over a fire ant bed and his six-foot brush hog would bang around a little, kicking up a cloud of dust, but for hour after hour, not much happened.

Darryl loved mowing. It was almost as relaxing as fishing, and at the end of a row you could always look back and see your progress. It was a repetitive activity, like knitting or weaving, and Darryl was proud of how evenly the rows were forming, how good the mowed pasture looked.

It takes some time to mow 347 acres of pasture, especially when you need to mow around the clumps of shade trees left for the cattle, and a six-foot mower doesn't make that big a swath. You always need to watch for low-hanging branches that reach out to grab your hat or swipe the sunglasses off your nose. And sometimes you'd see a stump of "lighter" pine—the decades-old remains of a pine tree rock-hard with crystalized turpentine, immune to decay or wood-eating insects. You could hang up on a stump like that and lose control of the tractor. Darryl never trusted his machines, so he paid attention.

That first day was hot, and the grass was tall, almost three feet in places, making it hard to see where he was going. By early afternoon the browning grass was reflecting heat into his face under his hat and he was dirty all over from the dust—dust sifting down his collar, up his sleeves, into his work boots. When he wiped his face with his bandana, it came away grayish brown with dirt. By 3 p.m., with the sun just getting good and cranked up for the afternoon heat, he had made one full pass along two of the fence lines and figured he'd quit. He had enough room for U-turns at both fences, so he wouldn't need to slow down or stop and back up, and the irregular shape of the tract meant that mowing in a circular pattern was a waste of time. He would come back in the morning and start mowing again after the dew dried off, and tomorrow he would bring a cot to pitch in the bed of his pickup where he could take a nap after his sandwich until the sun settled down.

Getting up to go to the lake was not on his agenda for tomorrow. Fish he'd caught would live on the trotline another day, even in this warm weather. He'd go early on Friday and run those lines, then come back. He figured he might be about half through with the pasture by Friday. And tomorrow he would carry his .223 caliber ranch rifle in case he spotted any of the hogs whose wallows he'd found near the back fence of the property. A little ten- or twelve-pound piglet would make a good dinner over the weekend. He hoped he'd get a shot.

Sure enough, it took buying a new boat to get him on the water again, but he got a slick one this time. Some people would look at a boat like that and think it was a high-end bass boat, rigged to run fast and far, racing other bass fishermen to the sweet spots at the shotgun blast that started a bass tournament. And for a lot of bass fishermen, that boat was the epitome of all their wet dreams. But Darryl got the dealership in Lufkin to paint the name of his boat on both sides of the bow: "Trotline King." Darryl was convinced this properly conveyed his sense of right and wrong when it came to fins.

And he was fishing for the big-un again, too. He figured Whitmire was likely to have only one police chief stupid enough to get in a barroom brawl and end up dead in the river. The chances that he'd catch another murdered man on the Corps of Engineers lake was much less than his chance of going in the record books forever as the man who caught the biggest catfish ever caught in Texas. Those were odds Darryl could live with, he convinced himself, just shortly before taking out a loan for a $63,000 boat with multiple sonars, twin 150-horsepower Evinrude outboards, onboard radio, and a refrigerator. One option he did not choose was the portable television. He could read Mary's mind, and he'd be damned if he would ruin a good day of fishing with Roadrunner cartoons.

He parked his tractor under the large pecan trees that shaded the remains of the burned house with its one chimney sticking up like an insulting hand gesture. A few hundred yards away was the old clap-sided barn, a door standing partially open and warped in the sun. He wondered idly whether the Houston lawyer would tear that barn down when he moved up to the country, and decided he was sure of it. Maybe he could salvage that old wood. People were paying a lot these days for barn wood. The big pecans were in full leaf, deep green, the leaves spiraling up against the sky like so many concentric circles, and the swelling nuts beginning to bend the branches toward the ground. It was peaceful there on the hilltop, so far from the coast that the afternoon rains rarely disturbed the dust. Darryl sat and listened to the quiet for a bit, his hat off, mopping his forehead and relishing the still and quiet of the place, the deep shadows, the buzzing of harmless insects and the call of distant crows crowding together over the mowed strips of grass to eat the exposed insects and decapitated remains of snakes and field mice butchered by the heavy mower blades.

  He liked it there up under the dark trees, looking out past the barn to the distant paved road empty of traffic and then off across trees as far as the eye could see. Actually, a fellow could see all the way to Arkansas if the air was clear enough, because this was the highest spot between the Gulf and the Ozarks. Somewhere out there rivers ran through all those pines and their shadows, with their mighty fish, but not a trace could be seen from this hilltop refuge. Darryl liked that. It was his kind of place. It was why he came back to East Texas after Vietnam.

  His stomach rumbled, the sun declining toward the west and his wristwatch showing almost 6 p.m. Time to go home.

CHAPTER FORTY-SEVEN

Shorty Fike had moved into a tent outside the trailer, next to Annabeth's car, on the third day after he decided something criminal had happened to her. He did not want to disturb the crime scene if he could avoid it. Of course, he still used the mobile home's refrigerator, the dishes, the bathroom and laundry, but he left everything else untouched. Who could tell?

He also spent most of each day studying the trailer from all angles, even crawling underneath to see if something was out of place or odd. On one of his inspections, he found two indentations in the ground at the back door. He mused about these indentations for a long time, just staring at them, then up at the door, which was about three feet off the ground at that spot, then back at the indentations. He had never opened that door. Had Annabeth? Why would she? It was too high off the ground for anything but an emergency exit, and she was so short that it would be a long jump for her. But those were not footprints. They were rectangular, narrow, and short. If a man propped a ladder up against the mobile home, that's the kind of marks they would leave.

Shorty's heart skipped a beat.

"I'll be a goddamned son of a bitch," he muttered. "Was that door even locked?"

He rushed back around the trailer and went up the stairs to the front door, then down the hall. The door opened outward, so he couldn't tell if it was locked or not. But he didn't want to test the door handle for fear of obscuring any fingerprints. That fool deputy who made such a mess in the kitchen and bathroom had not bothered with the door handle.

"How long will fingerprints last?" he wondered out loud. "Has it been too long?"

He retrieved his disposable camera from his tent and took pictures of everything. The inside of the door, the outside of the door, the indentations in the ground, some additional indentations he suspected were boot prints. Then he drove into town to get the film developed at the drug store. While he was there, he walked over to the sheriff's office to see if he could catch Deputy Jasper Rhodes. The dispatcher was sitting behind a bullet-proof glass shield that had a fist-sized hole drilled through it for speaking that completely did away with the usefulness of the bullet-proof glass. She looked up at him as he walked down the hallway, suppressing a smirk at his short stature. She knew about short men. They always needed to prove something.

"May I help you?" she asked, taking off her headset.

"I have new evidence for Deputy Rhodes," said Shorty. "I think I can prove my trailer was broken into."

"And so?" asked the dispatcher.

"What do you mean 'and so'?" asked Shorty. "My wife and daughter are missing, and I think I can prove my trailer was broken into at the time they went missing."

"Oh really?" asked the dispatcher. "Well, that's interesting. Give me your evidence and I'll see that Jasper gets it."

"I don't have it with me," said Shorty. "He needs to come out so I can show him. I keep calling for him but he's never in."

"Oh, you're the one," said the dispatcher. "Well, we'll see. I'll take a note and put it in his box. He will probably contact you when he gets back from his break. He's on duty tonight. Will you be home?"

"Yes, but ask him to call me before he comes out." He gave the dispatcher his phone number.

"Oh, I sure will," she said, her overly red-lipsticked mouth making a sort of unenthusiastic smile and blinking her false eyelashes at him. She scribbled something on her notepad. "You all have a nice day now," she said, ending the conversation and turning back to her silent radio, replacing her headset.

Shorty left the sheriff's office and strolled over to the *Piney Creek Crier* office, to see if he could talk to someone on the news staff. He'd like to discuss his view of the way the sheriff's office was handling his missing persons case, and maybe get some advice from the editor. As angry as he was, he was not stupid. He would listen, and he'd learn. If he couldn't get the deputies to take him seriously, maybe the newspaper would.

As it happened, BoMac was visiting the *Crier* offices just then, touching base with the editor, Ed Nichols. They traveled together to state meetings of the Texas Press Association and always enjoyed talking shop when they were away from the office. When the two newsmen heard Shorty's story, they were both surprised that nothing had been done.

"I've been to the sheriff's office at least two dozen times in the last two weeks," said Nichols. "Nobody said anything about a woman and little girl missing."

"They won't even return my calls," said Shorty. "I don't know what to do."

"Did you say the deputy handling it was Jasper Rhodes?" asked Bo-Mac, making a note in his reporter's pad.

"Well, no wonder," said Nichols. "He's the most worthless piece of shit ever to carry a badge."

"What am I supposed to do?" asked Shorty. "I've been living in a tent so I won't disturb the scene in case we can prove a crime. But I can't even get them to go out there. That Rhodes dusted for fingerprints in the kitchen and bathroom and picked up a lot of prints, but I'm pretty sure they were all of Annabeth and me. He did a really lousy job. I don't know nothing about fingerprinting, but I can tell you he didn't do much."

"I bet he told you that you're the chief suspect, too," said Nichols. "He's not the brightest guy in the S.O., and that's a really damning statement." He grinned. "I bet he spread fingerprint dust all around with that flimsy little brush, but then didn't remember to even use tape to lift them so they could be analyzed."

"You're right!" said Shorty. "He spread that black shit everywhere, and that was all he did. I never saw him use any tape or anything. I wondered what the hell he was doing."

"Oh, he didn't know," said Nichols. "Sheriff's nephew or something. If he wasn't working for the S.O., he'd be an inmate in the jail. He's too stupid to stay out of trouble. Mostly the uniform means people watch out for him, help him remember not to shoplift, or just ignore him when he does, that kind of thing. Can't spell his own name some of the time."

"I think it's an interesting story," said BoMac. "But it's your county, Ed. What do you think?"

"I think I'll go over to the sheriff's office and ask around," said Nichols, "but I've got a lot on my plate this week. You want this story? It could be a good one, and Lord knows you don't have much going on in Whitmire."

"Bass fishing contest this weekend out on the Corps of Engineers lake is all," nodded BoMac. "This might be a good human-interest story for next week. Mr. Fike," he said turning to the short man. "Would it be okay for me to write up a story about this? I'd like to look into it." Something in BoMac's brain was buzzing, some puzzle he'd been thinking about but not thinking about. Mostly it was a gut reaction. Missing wife and daughter: that could be a news item, and it was close enough to the communities in his own county that it might actually do some good. Maybe somebody local had seen the two, knew something.

"Tell you what," said Nichols, "I'll do a little piece about them missing. Run their picture, ask for info. Let's get all the information from you now, names, dates of birth, and so on. We'd both like to have some photos of them, if you've got any. What do you think, BoMac?"

"Yeah, and I'll go back out with you to your home," said BoMac. "I've got my camera with me and I can probably take some photos to share with Ed here."

"Okay," said Shorty, "I appreciate your help. I'm waiting for the one-hour processing at the drug store, and then I'll be ready to go. I can maybe show you some of what I think is evidence."

"Right," said BoMac. "And when we get out to your mobile home, maybe we can get some more photos. You want to come along, Ed?"

"BoMac, I'm swamped. We've got that special back-to-school section coming out this week. I've got to go sell some ads, write up some copy. My reporter, James Fisher, is doing his best, but you know, he'd do better if he would shower sometimes. I'm the one who needs to talk to the teachers. Just keep me in the loop, okay?"

"You bet," said BoMac. "Will do."

CHAPTER
FORTY-EIGHT

BoMac's pickup, as reliable as sunrise, squeaked behind Shorty's showy Dodge Charger, heading west toward the county line. About five miles before the bridge over the river, Shorty turned off on a narrow paved road, and then right into a gravel drive with a tilted sign advertising spaces for rent in the Camelot Mobile Home Park. After twisting through looping roads and along washboard gravel paths, they arrived at Shorty Fike's home. His tent was pitched near the front door, next to Annabeth's Chevy Nova. Shorty had run some extension cords out of the mobile home to hook up fans for his tent, and he had built a cooking table with a camp stove and a bucket for washing dishes. Shorty was serious about preserving the supposed crime scene as much as possible, and BoMac wondered about that. Was it all a show to cover up his own guilt, or did he really believe someone had taken his wife and daughter?

The two discussed what kind of pictures BoMac would take. He'd share some of them with the *Piney Creek Crier*, others he'd keep for the *Standard*. He imagined one caption for a photo of Shorty standing next to his tent: "Waiting for justice."

Shorty provided good photos of Annabeth and Maria—one pose for BoMac's paper, and another for the *Crier*. He would also give the *Crier* a summary of his notes, while he would keep the fuller story for the *Standard*. Then he went around the trailer with Shorty to see the indentations in the ground.

They looked like the legs of a ladder to BoMac, who agreed with Shorty. Then he suggested to Shorty that maybe they should look around a little, see if they could find more evidence.

After Tropical Storm Beryl, the ground had been saturated and the clay soils had absorbed a lot of water, but by Mother's Day those soils had begun to dry out. The result was that boot prints left in the clay would have solidified into hard impressions, and sure enough, they found several clear boot prints behind the trailer. The prints led down the hill to a little thicket of yaupon, and there they found a short stepladder lying in the brush and the indentation of a large body with more boot prints. BoMac, whose own shoe size was about a ten, guessed the boots were a size fourteen. They were distinctive because the heel prints on the right foot were much shallower than those on the left foot, something he remarked on with Shorty. He photographed them from various angles, trying to get a good raking light to show the contours and sole impressions as best he could.

They tracked the boot prints down the hill toward a little natural drain and across and up the far hill.

"Who lives that way?" asked BoMac.

"Man named Jesse Grinder," said Shorty. "I've been trying to talk to him since I found Annabeth missing, but he's the only one out here who won't talk to me. Ask me, that's suspicious. I figure I can tell if a man lies to me, at least most of the time. But when he flat out refuses to talk to me, then I've got a problem."

"Might not mean anything," said BoMac. "Hard to tell."

"I want my wife and little girl back," said Shorty. "I'm going to find them." The tone in his voice was flint-like, dark. BoMac didn't want to suggest that something might have happened to them. It was obvious that Shorty Fike was aware of the possibilities. It was also obvious to BoMac that Shorty Fike was not the kind of man to give up on anything. Sooner or later, Shorty would corner Jesse Grinder.

"Can you think of anything else about the situation that maybe you've not said anything about?" asked BoMac when they got back to the trailer, sweating in the summer heat.

"Something's not right," said Shorty.

"Yeah," said BoMac.

"No, I mean, I go in the house and something's not right. I can't put my finger on it, but something's not right. It's like I ought to see it, but I don't."

"You mean something's missing?" asked BoMac.

"Yeah, but I don't know what. Sometimes I stare at the kitchen for an hour just trying to think, but I keep getting a blank. Sometimes I go sit in Maria's bedroom and talk to her, you know, like she's there, and I talk about something not being right, but I still can't figure it out. So, I don't know. Maybe it will come to me."

"I hope so," said BoMac. "That might be important."

"I got a list of all her purchases from the grocery store," added Shorty, "since the last time I was home."

"You work offshore, right?"

"Not anymore. I quit when all this happened."

"Oh, right. Sure," said BoMac, making another note. "So why did you go over the grocery purchases?"

"Well, you know, we were very careful with our money. We hated living out here and wanted a real house with a real foundation and a yard for the girl. I don't know if you've ever lived in a mobile home, but they creak and shift all the time. You feel every step someone takes, hear everything. The walls are thin, the floors are weak, the roof is hardly better than tin foil. It's good if it's all you can get, but I was beginning to get good money and we wanted to move to Louisiana to be closer to work and have a real house, not this cheap thing."

"I understand," said BoMac, taking notes. "Go on. Why the groceries?"

"The groceries were the only thing that varied in our budget. Our electricity bill was the same every month, our rent was the same—although it was less than I thought. The only thing that varied was how much she spent on groceries, and that didn't change by more than five or ten dollars a week. I just wanted to compare what she had bought with what we had left. Don't ask me why. Just something to do."

"Okay," said BoMac. "And did you find anything?"

"Well, I know it sounds silly, but yeah. Everything she had bought was either in the refrigerator or freezer, or I found the empty packages in the trash. Except for one thing."

"Oh?" asked BoMac. This was sounding interesting.

"Yeah, I can't find a two-pound package of hamburger. I've looked and looked. Annabeth was the most orderly person in the whole world, and if she'd cooked that meat then I would have found the package somewhere in the trash. It's not there."

"Have you told Deputy Rhodes about that?" asked BoMac.

"I've called a dozen times, but they won't call me back," said Shorty. "Just like tonight, I bet. I walked over to the sheriff's office today and left a message in person with the dispatcher, and she said she'd get it to Rhodes, and he'd call me. But you can spend the night sitting with me right here, and I guarantee he's not going to call."

"It's like they don't care," said BoMac.

"Exactly," said Shorty. "They don't care. To me it's the most important thing in the world, but they don't care."

"I'm going to quote you on that," said BoMac.

"Oh, do it," said Shorty. "And I'd be happy to give you more quotes, but you probably can't print them."

"I understand," said BoMac. "I might quote you on that, too. I mean, the not being able to print them. I think that will convey the situation effectively to my readers."

"I just want my wife and daughter," said Shorty. "That's all I want. That's all I care about."

BoMac scribbled that down also and took his leave. Driving back toward Whitmire he passed a large pasture with an old barn in the middle and observed that someone was beginning to mow it. A flock of startling white egrets were poking along a mown strip near the barbed wire fence next to the road.

CHAPTER
FORTY-NINE

All sheriffs in Texas are elected by their counties. The other countywide elections are for county judge, county treasurer, and county clerk. These are the elected elite of the county, second only to the governor of the state in power but not nearly so politically powerful. With 254 counties, most county officials are pretty insignificant in the grand scheme of statewide politics, although you'd never hear a state official say so. These low-level politicians provide the votes that keep the state politicians employed. Just as County Commissioner George Brown hugged voters every time he saw one, the state politicians hugged county sheriffs and county judges. It is a well-established back-scratching system, the purpose of which is mostly to make sure the roads and creeks are passable so ranchers and farmers can get their produce to market. Every county government deals with dirt, literal clay and sand dirt. The metaphorical implications of dirt also apply but are perhaps somewhat less obvious. The bottom feeders of state politics, the judges and sheriffs, and so on, had relatively little impact on the reelection of august personages such as governors, perhaps depriving them at most of a few thousand votes in an election that polled millions. But one word from the great white shark in Austin could demolish the political careers of judges or sheriffs.

The symbiosis between county government and county media is a long and complex one, but generally speaking, public opinion is shaped by two major factors. One of these is the charisma of the local politician, and it may be the most important. But the other factor shaping public opinion is the news of what these politicians are doing with the power of their office. Plenty of people are charming, charismatic, and frauds. They use the power of their offices, which cannot be taken away short of revolution or a quadrennial vote, to enrich themselves and their friends. This is true at all levels of politics. Some few actually try to meet public expectations of common sense and fiscal responsibility. Those who respond to public opinion are generally honorable and honest. Between the two extremes—those who are only in for what they can get out of it, and those who are trying to do the job according to moral and ethical principles—is a lot of gray territory occupied by most elected officials. This is true nationwide, not just in East Texas. It may be true worldwide.

The *Piney Creek Crier* article on the disappearance of sweet-faced Annabeth Fike and her exceptionally cute three-year-old daughter, Maria, had a galvanizing effect on Piney Creek and on its elected officials. They woke up on Wednesday morning as they always did, taking coffee and chatting with neighbors, to be broadsided by the story. A description of the sheriff's office response to the disappearance was not viewed with favor by the reading pubic, and Sheriff Bishop Adams could be heard grinding his teeth from the depths of the century-old masonry jail on the courthouse lawn. He was not happy. Neither were his constituents. All four of the county commissioners came by the jail to see him and ask about why he had sent that fool Jasper Rhodes on such an errand. "He was on rotation," was not a good enough answer. "That's a pretty good-looking girl, there," they said to Sheriff Adams. "What the hell?"

Sheriff Lee Davis of Sweetgum County in Whitmire was less affected. The missing were not, after all, people who voted in Sweetgum County. His tune changed, however, when a certain official from the Texas Department of Public Safety called his office to inquire whether he was working with Cypress County to locate the pair. He was not. His office knew nothing about it, he said, trying to laugh it off, sliding the blame fully over onto Bishop Adams. That was when he learned that Annabeth's uncle was deputy director for the south Texas region of the Department of Public Safety. He was a man who met weekly with the governor, who supervised vast stretches of Texas along the southern border, and who held almost mythical esteem in the state. Sheriff Davis swallowed hard.

"I'll be more than happy to devote resources to helping Sheriff Adams crack this case," said Davis. He was sweating visibly by the time he hung up. In all his years as Sweetgum County's chief law enforcement officer, he had never had to deal with a missing persons case. Most years, hunters went missing in the woods and would be found, sometimes days later, starving and dehydrated. Once an elderly couple drove off to play pinochle with neighbors but took a wrong turn and ended up stuck on a sandy track miles out in the woods. They died. But there was no mystery to it.

After hanging up with Sheriff Davis, the Department of Public Safety officer made a few more calls, and by mid-morning a forensics team from the regional office of the Texas Rangers was headed to the mobile home park.

It is as true in East Texas as it is anywhere that who you know makes all the difference. Shorty Fike was pleasantly surprised when the first of ten police vehicles pulled up behind Annabeth's Chevy. He regretted not going to the paper earlier.

"Are you Mr. Fike?" asked a Department of Public Safety highway trooper.

"Yes, sir, I am," said Shorty.

"We've come to help out investigating the case of your missing wife and daughter."

"At last," said Shorty, fighting back tears. "Thank God."

"I'll need some information from you, and you might as well get used to the idea that you are going to be repeating the same information most of the day to different people. This can be exhausting and frustrating, but I assure you that it is best if you cooperate in every way that you can."

"I'm ready," said Shorty. "I've waited weeks for something to start, and all I can think is it's damned time. I'll do anything to find my wife and daughter."

"Yes, sir," the trooper said, "I think we all understand that."

More cars arrived, photographers climbed out, and Shorty gave the investigators all the information he had. He pointed out the indentations in the ground, the stepladder he and BoMac had found, the boot prints, the apparent path of the boot prints. Plaster casts were taken of the boot prints and the indentations, the stepladder was dusted and then fluoresced for latent prints, and the whole tedious business of a full-scale investigation ground into gear.

The Rangers who were leading the investigation were the same ones who had conducted the investigation at Belle Guinness's house, where they had lifted the fingerprints of at least a dozen Piney Creek men. Only two or three sets of those prints had not come back matched to local residents, and all of those identified had provided proof of alibis that kept them out of Guinness's house at the critical time. Although they weren't saying, the Rangers' search for the murderer of Trey Green had narrowed down to three sets of unidentified prints, and they were pretty sure that eventually those prints would be identified. Meanwhile, they kept trying to match the prints with every database they could find.

While they were conducting the search, Shorty was taken back into Piney Creek for a battery of interviews, including a voluntary polygraph test. They wanted to rule out Shorty as a suspect as soon as possible, but they intended to keep an open mind. Some husbands are damned clever and set up puzzles very difficult to solve.

Sooner or later, though, most get solved.

CHAPTER
FIFTY

The story that appeared in the *Whitmire Standard* ran near the top of the front page and was much more complete than the one that ran in the *Crier*. In keeping with their gentleman's agreement, BoMac had shared his notes and photos with Ed Nichols. In fact, BoMac appreciated Ed sharing the story with him, since the *Crier* had a prior claim because it had walked into Ed's office in the person of Shorty Fike. He had printed a thousand more papers than usual, expecting the copies to disappear off newsstands as soon as people looked at the attractive image of that young woman and her child.

He was not disappointed, and copies were sold out in some stores, but many more copies were gone than were paid for. He expected that too. It happened every week. Because of the higher press run, he also had several hundred more copies than usual to throw away at the end of the week. That was something else he expected. DA "Cock-lover" Turner was fond of saying that the dumpster was where the paper belonged, but since you had to print at least a thousand copies, that always meant you had some hundreds of copies left over. Cock-lover didn't care. All he wanted to do was pick a fight so he could show off his fancy weapons.

The day the story about a missing White woman came out in the paper, Betty Lou Beets and Henry Forbes were sharing an intimate tête-à-tête in Mrs. Jane Elkins's kitchen. They were leaning in over cups of late-morning coffee and whispering so Elkins couldn't overhear them. It wasn't their business to care about the woman and her child.

"My nephew's second child is a CPA," said Betty Lou. "He knows what's what. If you've never filed a tax return, then you've never put any money into social security. Why have you never filed?"

"I thought it was a White man thing, and I ain't got no truck with that," said Henry. "I stay in my place. You know that. That's why I've been working here so many years."

"How many years?" asked Betty Lou.

"Well, let's see, I got hired by old Mr. Elkins when he went on the bench. That would have been around 1930. I've been working right here for about fifty years."

Betty Lou shook her head.

"They've been paying you all those years and never gave you any tax documents or anything?"

"Not sure I could read 'em if they did," said Henry. "You know that. Man can't read, can't get ahead. I taught all my children that."

"Where are your children now?"

"Well, they all went to college. That was a struggle. I've got one dentist, one lawyer, two businessmen—one of 'em owns that big insurance company in Port Arthur—one of them just raises her kids and her husband owns a tire dealership. They all live in Houston, except the one in Galveston. He's the one who told me about Miz Elkin's nephew and that queer place." Henry sat up with a look of disgust on his face. "They ought to make places like that illegal."

"He's the doctor, right?" asked Betty Lou.

"Yep. Works at that big hospital there in Galveston. You know the place. Where they take poor people."

"Yeah. I know it. My uncle went there." She took a sip of her cooling coffee, rich with cream and sugar. "He died."

"I'm lucky," said Henry, "I've never been sick a day in my life. But my wife died. She had the cancer."

"Let's get this straight. You've worked here all this time and they never gave you anything to prove you worked?" Betty Lou asked, looking around to be sure Elkins was not listening at the gap of the swinging door that led into the dining room.

"Never anything, except sometimes I'd get a Christmas gift from old Mr. Elkins. I kept all the cards and wrote on 'em the amount of money he gave me. And then I kept a list of all the money I got every week after we collected the rent so I could show my wife. It made her feel good to know I was bringing something home for her and the kids."

"You still have that list?"

"Tacked up on my bedroom wall. I'm about to run out of room."

"You need to keep all that safe. A bedroom wall is not the best place. Get yourself a fireproof box and store all that in it. You will need them if you ever retire."

"Why would I retire? I don't have anything else to do."

"Because you might get sick. Or she might fire you. Then what? You think you can support yourself raking and mowing lawns?"

"I always just get up and come to work and do what needs doing, then go home and do what needs doing and go to sleep," he said. "Been that way for seventy-four or -five years."

"She's going to get rid of you. That woman has no heart. You need to be ready. I'm ready. She hasn't given me a wage statement or paid my social security in twenty years. I bet she hasn't done that for you either. Isn't one of your kids a lawyer? Ask him. Or is that a her?"

"Got two lawyers," said Henry proudly. "Boy and a girl. The girl's married to that boy used to be a fireman, Fletcher Mann. He's the one with ads on all the Houston stations."

"Is that man your kin? You need to talk to him."

"What about?"

"About not ever getting any kind of tax document or wage statement or anything in all the decades you've worked here, you fool."

"Why do I want to do that?"

"Because she owes you the money. And she's got plenty. That White woman will steal it from both of us if we let her, and she doesn't need it. You know she's got no heart."

"No, not much heart in that shriveled up thing," nodded Henry.

"Henry?" Jane Elkins's shrill voice called from the drawing room. "Henry? Go and get the car."

"Yes'm," answered Henry raising his voice to be heard. "Yes'm, right now. I be waiting at the back door."

Betty Lou nodded at him, then stood and took their coffee cups to the sink. No point in leaving evidence that they were drinking Mrs. Elkins's leftover breakfast coffee. She'd get a tongue-lashing for that, and she was having a difficult time keeping her own temper these days. This summer heat was hard. You work all day in an air-conditioned house, go home at night to a house without air conditioning and a half-dozen fighting youngsters. It's hard to adjust. But Lord Jesus gave her patience and loved her despite her trials and temptations. She could sleep at night because of that. At least no matter how hard life was, at least they weren't crucifying her like they did him, and he did a lot less to deserve it than she had. At least she had that, even if that was all she had.

She hadn't told Henry, but right now Mrs. Jane Elkins owed her about $225,000 in unpaid taxes and medical insurance, according to the accountant in Piney Creek where she went on her one day off. Plus, he smiled, a triple penalty to the federal government, and overtime pay to her for that sixth day of extra work every week for more than twenty years. One day, she'd get that money for her children.

Some people didn't know the world had changed since the Civil War.

CHAPTER FIFTY-ONE

Late summer has its special, golden heat. The sun slants against the tall grass in the morning, glowing green and sparkly with dew. In late afternoon, the sun's slant softens the contours of the grass, now seen as shivery stalks of brown light bowing in the languorous, heated air rising in shimmers from the fields. Nothing stirs. The black wings of crows part the air, but the turbulence of their passing never reaches the ground. Only the man on the tractor methodically mowing another fifteen or so acres every day stirs the breeze and causes the grasshoppers to take their buzzing flight. But for him, the light breeze on his face from the tractor's movement is a relief and a pleasure. Sometimes he will pause at the end of a row to turn the tractor off and let it cool, wiping his face and letting the air get to his sweaty hair under his cap. Other times he will change his plans and turn to mow one more circumference around the uneven contours of the field, gradually spiraling in toward the old barn. But for hour after hour, he sits on the tractor seat, adjusting his speed with the lever on the steering column, just watching out for hidden ditches or caved-in fire ant hills, leftover stumps, carcasses of long-dead cattle. Toward sunset, his gaze drifts to the shadows of the surrounding pines, hoping to catch the stealthy movement of deer, or the black, jerking movement of wild boar.

He could drop a wild boar at three hundred yards if he needed to. His stainless-steel Ruger .223 caliber rifle rode comfortably in its padded scabbard strapped to the tractor's side, a twenty-round clip loaded into the magazine. He might also shoot a coyote, if he saw one. That would help this man clean the varmints out of his pasture.

A hawk rode the invisible thermals well overhead, turning its head right and left trying to spot any mouse flushed from cover by the tractor. Other birds had been overhead all day, but they had quietly gone away when the hawk came. Alpha predator of the air, the large hawk was not too proud to take a crow or a blackbird if he was hungry. But hawks tended to have the same attitude toward lesser birds like crows that Darryl had toward lesser fishermen like bass fishers, mainly that they were low class and not worth the effort. The hawk preferred a live mouse or rabbit. Darryl Stewart preferred a young boar, which would be more tender than its six-hundred-pound mother. Unlike the hawk, Darryl knew if he wasn't hungry at the moment, then he'd be hungry later. He'd take whatever came to hand. The hawk, by contrast, would just finish its meal for the day and go to roost, satisfied and sleepy.

Off in the distance to the southeast, Darryl saw thunderheads building in the slanting sun. They were piling up, dark underneath, turning pink in the evening light. Their dark masses swirled upwards, sparking lightning, but they were far away. At least a hundred miles. Too far to hear the rumbling of their thunder. He knew he could only see the massive clouds at that distance because they were probably twenty thousand feet in the air, maybe higher. They posed no threat to him or his tractor. They would pass over to the northeast, bringing rainfall and maybe hail and a tornado to some other community. For him, though, the majesty and glory of the clouds were beautiful, reminding him of how insignificant his own life was in the grand scheme of things and how blessed he was to have it. But he was glad the clouds were not coming his way. Rain would complicate the mowing tomorrow, and lightning was always a threat when a man is out in the middle of a field on a tractor. But it was time to quit for the day. That Houston fellow had gotten his full day of labor out of Darryl this day, and he had probably two more weeks to go. Tomorrow night, Darryl would call with an update on his progress, but this night he would spend inside with Mary and her casserole.

Life was good for Darryl Stewart. He was rich in the ways that mattered and had no obligations that he couldn't meet. He wasn't the richest man in Whitmire, but he might have been the most content.

Besides, he had a new Ranger Bass Boat rigged for trotline fishing. Who else could make that boast?

Twenty-five miles to his east, closer to the boiling thunderheads, Jesse Grinder was trying to think through his options. McKinney had not actually fired him yet, but Wilburn Hall had changed the locks on his locksmith shop. Jesse was beginning to think maybe he should look for work somewhere else, in some other town. Whitmire was out. Whitmire was much too close to his mom and pop, and besides, it was their town. They shopped there, got work there. He'd need to go looking somewhere else. But he was still paying McKinney for the truck, and he was sending part of every paycheck to his mother, so he was not exactly free to move around. Where would he find another place to live as cheap as this? he wondered. Beaumont was out. Conroe was out. Lufkin was a maybe. Athens was a maybe. Palestine was a maybe. Tyler was out. Maybe he should take the plunge and just move to Arkansas, find a job sweeping a Walmart up there somewhere. But still, it took some kind of money to move and Jesse Grinder had no money. Besides, what if he just drove his pickup away and never paid McKinney again? Would that sorry bastard file a criminal charge against him? Jesse had heard enough about jail that he never wanted to see the inside of one. Maybe he feared jail most of all.

Jesse could not think these things through. His mind seemed to be getting worse, not better, and dealing with problems was bottom of the list of things he could do. Satiating his hunger took precedence over everything. Then sex, specifically titties, then sleep. After that, everything else. Jesse Grinder was not a complicated man, and he knew it. Food, sex, and sleep. That's all he needed. Maybe in that order. He thought he could steal enough food to keep that part covered. And sleep was okay as long as he kept the trailer. If he needed to go back to sleeping in the pickup, that would be a problem. He was too big for the pickup. And sex, well, there was no easy answer for sex. Not one woman in the trailer park would so much as look in his direction, much less say hello. And the longer he went, the more he thought about those magnificent tits on Mrs. Rip Johnson, the congressman's skinny wife.

"Nah," he said aloud lying on his bare mattress, "she's got all that security." He lay in the dark musing. "Big difference between a rich man and a poor man is how much protection he can afford for his titties," he finally shrugged. "Not like Shorty Fike."

CHAPTER
FIFTY-TWO

In the first week of August, schools began reopening. Football squads met on the practice fields beginning at 6:30 in the morning, going nonstop until 11. After a two-hour rest, they would meet again for wind sprints and endurance from 1 to 3. Then, at about 4 p.m. at the peak of the summer heat, the varsity football players would drag into the showers under the stadium, gulping salt tablets by the handful, while the first strangled hoots from the junior high marching band forming up on the vacated field could be heard squealing all over town. One sousaphone player, Dewey Hunt, was famous for his lung power, and went by the nickname of Tubby. In the eighth grade, he already weighed over 240 pounds and was in danger of becoming too large for the instrument to fit around his body, but he certainly had the lung power. While the other instruments faded out as one got farther from the field, Tubby could be heard for miles tooting in time to unheard drums. Sometimes the varsity football coach would linger to watch Tubby, trying to visualize a class 3-A star center for the football team. Then Tubby would stumble, or his glasses would slide off his nose, and the coach would turn and go get in his pickup, kicking the gravel as he went.

Junior high marching band practice ended around 6:30, just as the sun's hottest slant was burning into their faces. They exited the field to board buses back to school, and meanwhile the senior high marching band was arriving on other buses, disgorging hundreds of happy youngsters, jostling and laughing. Every night, the 200-member senior high band marched under the football stadium lights until after 10 p.m., or later if band director J. Paul Collier, notoriously impatient and extremely picky, was not happy with the practice. He stood on his elevated platform looking over the field, directing the band like a dyspeptic emperor, and sometimes forced the youngsters to repeat a single phrase and marching formation dozens of times until neighbors in nearby houses finally gave up watching television at full volume and just loaded up everyone to go stroll the air-conditioned aisles at Walmart. Walmart closed at 9 p.m., though, and Collier might still be making those kids march and play the same six measures of music for another two hours before giving up for the night. The noise and the glare of stadium lights were as symbolic of the coming year as any deified volcano to a primitive Polynesian tribe, and required similar sacrifice.

Ellen came back to Whitmire, tanned and enthusiastic, around the end of the first week of August, and she and BoMac had a grand reunion. He had changed, and so had she. She glowed, he towered. Henniker could see the romance blossoming and was glad. His own relationship with Lizzie King had also developed during the long summer, and Lizzie knew exactly what the compromise of 1877 was all about, and the Dred Scott decision. The two of them also had much to talk about. Her research at the Piney Creek courthouse had revealed some new and interesting information, namely that both the congressman and the district judge were partners in a large number of shell corporations, all based in Piney Creek.

"Pretty stupid, actually," commented Lizzie on the phone one night.

"Depends on who's looking," said Henniker. "My guess is that you don't have to turn over very many rocks in East Texas to find snakes."

"I do wish," replied Lizzie, "that you'd at least consider your metaphors. Except for places like Rockland, there are no rocks in East Texas. Everything is clay or sand, and trees. You don't find any rocks in Piney Creek, for example, except the ones people bring in for landscaping. But we have a lot of logs lying on the ground."

"Point well taken," said Henniker, grinning. "Of course. I will rephrase: you don't need to turn over very many rotten logs in East Texas to find a snake."

"Now that right there is the statement of a genius," said Lizzie. "Why don't you come see me?"

"I've been busy working on my thesis," he replied.

"Bullshit," she said. "Come over tomorrow night and I'll introduce you to the nightclub and Chillers Banks."

"You think he will be there?"

"The nightclub doesn't exist without Chillers," she said. "And Clarence Thomas is probably going to be there, too. He usually shows up here on Friday night."

"Where is he on Saturday night?" asked Henniker.

"The other place. We aren't going there. Just come over here. I'll make a chicken-fried steak or something."

"Nice offer," said Henniker. "But don't put yourself out. I'll be happy with something simple like a sandwich or spaghetti. You don't need to go to all that trouble."

"Depends on what you're bringing to dinner."

"What do you want?"

"I swear, Charles Henniker, why do you always have to fog everything up? What do you think I want? Okay, I'll tell you. I want a diamond ring and a proposal, but if you aren't ready for that, then bring something we can eat together. Just tell me so I don't make a duplicate dish."

"Mashed potatoes? Candied sweet potatoes?"

"I swear. Sometimes you are so dense. Bring a diamond ring or a dessert. Those are your choices."

"Okay," he said, grinning, knowing his grin was transmitting at light speed through the line. "One or the other, then."

"Right."

"Same result?"

"You are some kinda fool, Mr. Charles Henniker."

"Lieutenant Colonel Charles Henniker, please."

"You are so full of shit. Be here at six." She hung up.

Henniker stared at the phone for at least fifteen minutes, lighted by the glow from the football stadium through his front windows with the ungodly racket of the Whitmire High School marching band learning a new piece at full volume.

"Daddy gave me a couple of nice rib eye steaks," said Ellen Etheridge into the phone. "Do you want to come over here and help me cook them?"

BoMac was distressed. He'd seen steak before. He'd watched his late father cook steaks on the grill. But he himself had never had enough money to afford a real steak. How do you cook a steak?

"Uh, sure," he said. "I've never cooked a steak before."

"Neither have I," she replied brightly. "We can figure this out together. Besides, if both of us try, then we will probably learn something."

"Maybe you should call your dad for instructions," he suggested.

"Okay, but meanwhile, come over here and help. I hear that you are supposed to drink wine with steak, but I don't know the first thing about wine either."

"Neither do I," he said. "Do you think Dr Pepper will do?"

"Maybe," she said. "I'd actually rather drink Dr Pepper, but you know."

"Yes, I do," said BoMac. "I know. But call your dad early and get some advice in case I need to drive down to the county line and pick something up."

"Sure," she said. "We talk every morning. An hour with dad, then an hour with mom, who corrects any misconceptions I might have gotten from dad."

"I love your family," he said. "I'm not sure my mother and father spoke two words to one another after my sixth birthday, and my memory is too foggy before that."

"They're pretty close, in a certain way," she said. "I'm not sure it's entirely healthy, but they get by."

"I'm so glad you're back," he said, changing the subject. "It's been a lonely summer."

"I know," she said, "for me too. Come early so you can bring me up to speed."

"How about I come now, and we talk until tomorrow when it's time to put on the steak?"

There was a long pause on the phone, during which BoMac dared not interrupt.

"Okay," she said at last.

Nobody shoots off rockets or fireworks in August, but BoMac saw them.

Accompanied by Tubby Hunt's grunts on a sousaphone.

CHAPTER
FIFTY-THREE

The rain from Tropical Storm Beryl had been good for the pasture, but it was proving bad for Darryl. The grass and weeds had grown so high that he was forced to go half the speed he had gone in other years. Instead of two weeks, it looked like the project would go on into the middle of September.

"I'm not coming until the end of September," the Houston lawyer said. "My architect got tied up on a job in Colorado and won't be available until September 29."

"That's good," nodded Darryl into the phone, "It might take me that long to get through. You can't believe how much growth you've had up there. Most places are at least three feet, and a lot of them four or five feet deep. The grass is over the hood of the tractor as I go."

"Just keep it up," said the lawyer. "How much have you done so far?"

"I've got in fifty-five hours," said Darryl. "All of last week and half of this one."

"And how much have you mowed?"

"I'm just now making the third cut from the fence," said Darryl. "About sixty acres. I'm guessing it's going to take at least eighty more hours of mowing to get it nearly done, and that's not certain. We should have cut it early in the spring."

"I understand," said the lawyer. "That storm dumped a lot of rain here, too, and caused a huge number of problems. Freeways flooded, big trucks floated into one another and overturned. You can't believe how much work a lawyer can get out of that kind of storm. But I want my house built in two years, so this is the time to push ahead. Just do your best."

"Thank you, sir," said Darryl.

It was not quite as dire as Darryl represented, but a man can't make money telling the truth most times, he figured. He might be through in another week, if he stopped taking naps in the afternoon, which was unlikely. He loved lying down under those big pecans. Still, he was right about one thing. That pasture was a bugger. It was tall, dense, full of small pines and brambles, some areas were absolute thickets of inch-thick sweet gum seedlings standing five or six feet tall, and it had eroded from the heavy rains in April. He could run his brush hog through those thickets, but he'd leave behind a deadly stand of sweet gum punji stakes sharpened by the blades, and those sticks would just be brushy sweet gum saplings again in three months. Eventually, the man would need to figure out what he wanted to do with this pasture. If he didn't have cattle eating the greenery, or goats, or something, in under three years the whole place would become a young forest. In ten years, he wouldn't be able to find the fences.

Darryl liked musing about what could happen to the man's place. It had a top-notch soil index, was fertile, and it would love to grow pine trees again, like it had for millions and millions of years. But all the water drained off or soaked into the sandy soil. If it was his piece of property, he'd put in some ponds first thing, then some patches of oats and millet for the deer, and maybe build himself a kennel for dogs. Man could always use a dog in this country.

The tractor chugged along, scaring up clouds of grasshoppers and rattling over thickets and brambles, and August turned into September. The Whitmire football team won its first game, a practice game, against a much smaller 2-A school from the south part of the county, a district located down near the river and largely occupied by people who fled integration in areas farther south. In other words, they were not natives. It was a small school but had a scrappy attitude and the game had been a good one. Whitmire won by one point on a thrilling point-after kick. That quarterback Dickerson scored a touchdown and hit for two more on long passes. Darryl and Mary had season tickets, of course, and joined the happy crowds sweating in the pre–Labor Day heat, swatting mosquitoes, chatting, and cheering. Little Annie Putnam looked like Miss America in her skimpy cheerleader outfit. Overall, the winding down of summer was a fun time, full of anticipation and excitement and story. Darryl loved this time of year.

The ducks were already coming into the rice paddies along the coast, and teal duck season would open this weekend for those who wanted to brave the twenty-something different kinds of mosquitoes drifting in clouds among the saw grass and mangrove marshes. Darryl had been teal duck hunting, recalling that hunt as he sat on the vibrating tractor steadily moving ahead at no more than two miles an hour while the big mower shuddered against sweet gum and young pine or stalled in a stand of blackberry brambles. That had been an enjoyable hunt, in the sense that no comfortable hunt ever produced anything worth bragging about. Darryl had most of his luck freezing on a deer stand, slogging through soft-bottomed marshes with seventy pounds of duck decoys on his back while being eaten by insects and chased by gigantic water moccasins, or walking miles through rattlesnake-infested grass in search of quail. It was, however, one of the biggest reasons why he liked to fish, and that new boat—

Darryl's mind drifted off to the new boat, the surge of power from 300 horsepower of outboard motors, the refrigerator, the comfortable seats a man could recline in. He even had a coffeemaker in it. If he could, he would just live in that boat.

The second football game of the season would be this evening, it being Friday, and Whitmire was playing another staunch rival but from a 3-A school, so the contest would be even closer than last week. He would finish up at the pasture early, then he and Mary would have a quick dinner and they'd head off fifty miles up the road to the game. With no kids of their own, he and Mary had pretty much adopted all the kids in Whitmire and they wouldn't miss a game for anything. Besides, everybody would be there and the town of Whitmire would be almost completely vacated.

He was a hundred yards or so from the old barn and daydreaming when he spotted something round and white on the ground. "A melon!" he said aloud. "That looks like a wild melon. I'll finish up here tonight, and plan to gather that baby Monday around noon. It will go great with lunch."

He parked the tractor in the accustomed place under the dense pecan trees, not too close in case a thunderstorm blew through in the night and attracted lightning, but up under the shade. He made sure to raise the mower off the ground so it wouldn't be grounded. A man learns these tricks after a lifetime of living more or less in the open weather—you don't want your brush hog grounded so it attracts lightning. That's a good way to fry a tractor.

He pulled the aluminum-panel gate closed behind himself when he got to the highway, not bothering with the broken lock. If the man in Houston wanted to secure his pasture, he could put a decent lock on it. But he had nothing of value in that pasture, so why bother.

Whitmire squeaked out another win around 10 p.m., and Darryl almost dozed off on the way home. Just as he topped the hill where BoMac had helped John Quick look for that eyeball the previous summer, he jerked awake and stayed awake all the way home. But he was tired. Mary had been snoring for almost an hour in the front seat of the pickup by the time he skirted the lake in his front yard and pulled up in the driveway.

CHAPTER

FIFTY-FOUR

Charles Henniker would have liked to go to the football game, but he thought maybe he shouldn't. Then he thought maybe he should. Then he thought maybe he shouldn't. He realized that Annie Putnam would be performing her cheerleading stunts all along the sidelines, and he wanted to keep as much space between the two of them as he could without being obvious about it. The last thing he wanted was the whole town watching to see if he glanced at Annie Putnam. He had enough of a struggle without the town being reminded of Miranda Putnam's hysterical accusations. In the course of American history, many people had been killed for less.

Instead, he drove over to Piney Creek to see Lizzie, driving like a moth into a hazy skyline aglow with football stadium lights. The Piney Creek Buccaneers, a 5-A school, were hosting their regional opener against the Conroe Tigers. The glow of the lights through the heavy humidity of the pine forest reminded him of shorelines in the South Indian Sea, along Sri Lanka and Myanmar, but without the sea breezes and unremitting wail of humanity. With few exceptions, East Texas was more like an unpopulated frontier than civilization.

Chillers Banks took one look at Henniker and gave him a Budweiser on the house. Clarence Thomas took one look at Henniker, then at Lizzie as if to say, "You traitorous bitch," and turned his back.

These were behaviors that Henniker noticed and wondered about.

"Never seen Chillers give away a beer before," whispered Lizzie. "And old Clarence over there is acting strange, too."

"Maybe we should leave this nightclub," whispered Henniker back.

"Maybe," she nodded. "Let me think about the room for a minute. Then, sure."

Henniker opened his beer and took a sip, also scanning the room. He noted the video cameras behind the bar covering the entire room. He saw the quiet couples huddled together. It was Friday night, but nearly everybody was at the game, so it was a sparse crowd.

"Okay," said Lizzie taking another sip of her own beer. "Something is going to happen, so I think we should get out. I really don't like it."

Henniker nodded, reached in his wallet for a ten-dollar bill, and helped her to her feet. He left his beer on the table. On their way by the bar, Henniker dropped the ten on the bar counter, waving it at Chillers Banks first so he'd see it, and so would the cameras.

On the street, one of the Piney Creek policemen rolled down his window as Lizzie and Henniker walked by.

"Evening, Lizzie," he said pleasantly, "who's your friend?"

"Hi George. Charles, this is my friend George Patton."

Henniker said anybody named George Patton was worth knowing.

"I never heard of a Henniker before," replied patrolman Patton, sticking his right hand out the window. "Pleased to meet you. Be good to Miss Lizzie."

"Man can only do what he's allowed to do," smiled Henniker, glancing at Lizzie.

"You okay to get home, Lizzie?" asked Patton.

"I'm good," she replied, "thanks for asking. Say hi to Charlene for me."

They were off down the sidewalk, her arm through Henniker's like they were an old married couple. Patton chuckled at them in his patrol car. "They look just like White people," he snickered, "from behind."

"Do you need a piece of my pecan pie?" Lizzie asked as they neared her door. "I have exactly two pieces left."

"Who made it?" asked Henniker. It didn't matter to him, because he'd eat a piece if offered. He just wanted to get her to talk about it a bit.

"I did, of course," she said, slapping his arm. "Who you think? Do you think I am the kind of girl would offer somebody a piece of store-bought pecan pie from a tinfoil plate?"

"Well, no," he said. "Just checking."

"I figure the ballgame will let out around ten," she said, opening the door. "You need to be out of town by eleven. That gives us a few hours to talk."

"Why do I need to be out of here by eleven?" he asked.

"Because if they see a Black man driving around the street after eleven, they are going to pull him over."

"So, if I can drag out eating this piece of pie until after eleven, you'll be morally obligated to put me up for the night," he said.

"You're a clever one," she said. "But no, I'm not morally obligated.

You've been warned." She winked at him.

"That I have," he grinned, closing the door.

One of the most difficult things to describe about East Texas is the smell of early fall. During the day it is unremitting summer, with broiling sun overhead and humidity so close you sweat through your clothes in minutes. And the nights are not much better—maybe only five or ten degrees cooler, which is not much. Then suddenly, one morning the world sidesteps a little, jinks somehow, like one of those basketball players faking out an opponent, and it's fall. You get up to go to school, and the black gum trees that were green yesterday have turned deep purple. The pecans begin dropping their plentiful nuts and the edges of their leaves tinge with yellow, but only the edges. All of those descriptions are full of tactile and visual sensations.

But the most telling change in East Texas is in the smell. The woods just smell different, tangy somehow, an undercurrent of coolness threading invisibly through shoals of warm humidity. You can't tell it from the angle of the sun, because the sun has been declining for almost three months, the days getting shorter, with every day almost indistinguishably shorter than the previous one. No, it is a subtle smell, like distant hickory smoke and the sweet odor of cane syrup cooking just over the next hill. One day is smothering in heat, the next you smell a change and a promise in the air. It might still be hot out under the pines, but the heat lacks permanence. It's like an oven that's been turned off. It retains heat, but it's not adding any. Cooler days are coming, longer nights, the welcome arms of a lover. The mornings smell like cold biscuits. That pretty much sums it up. Cold biscuits. Not biscuits fresh from the oven, all hot and ready for butter, but cold ones waiting for lunch. That's how the change in the weather smells.

Henniker detected that smell in Piney Creek early on Saturday. He had not brought his running shoes with him, so he would skip his morning jog this day. Instead, he just went through Lizzie's kitchen, found her kettle and started heating up water, then stepped out the back door into her yard. He admired her little kitchen garden and went out to check on it. A nice row of herbs, five or six tomato plants in their inverted wire-cone cages covered with bird netting, tomatoes growing red and plump underneath, some sweet potato vines in clumps, carrots, a row of lettuces, a row of beans. Not a large garden, but enough to put up some for the winter if you were living alone, or to share with friends. He had not expected Lizzie King to have that kind of green thumb and was surprised.

Looking beyond the garden, he spotted several rows of fruit trees, mostly pears and peaches, as far as he could tell. The peaches were gone, but the pears looked ripe. And behind those were some young pecan trees, their nuts ready to burst out of the almond-shaped quatrefoil of their woody husks. It was a lot of garden in a small space, but it proved one thing. Lizzie King must own this place. When she said "her house," she meant "the house I own." No one would go to this kind of long-term planning and effort on property they didn't own.

"Good morning, Charles," she called from the kitchen door, her voice a kind of song in the morning air.

"I'm admiring your garden. This is quite something."

"It takes a lot of work in the evenings and weekends, but I enjoy it," she said, coming down the three steps from her back door in her robe, holding out a hand to him. "Thanks for staying," she said, drawing close to him and dropping her eyes. "Will you stay for breakfast?"

An hour or so later, they were sitting in her backyard again surveying the garden. "You could add some chickens," he said. "They'd eat the bugs off of your lettuce and tomatoes."

"If they could get at the bugs, they'd also eat the tomatoes," she said. "I thought about that. Also, I'd rather be able to get up and go off somewhere like San Augustine without worrying about taking care of any animals."

They chatted for a while longer, and then Lizzie said, "By the way, I heard something yesterday that maybe that newspaper guy would like to know."

Henniker looked at her quizzically.

"Yeah, I heard from my friend in the police department. We were having a quick cup of coffee on break. She said that Shorty guy, the one whose wife and daughter went missing, you remember?"

Henniker nodded. "Shorty Fike, I think," he said.

"She said he'd come up with new evidence. She said he finally remembered what had been bugging him. It was a jar of pennies his wife kept on the window ledge over the kitchen sink."

"A jar of pennies?" Henniker exclaimed.

"That's what she said. A jar of pennies. Also, she said he'd tracked down all his wife's expenses. He found a receipt in the trash for her last trip to the grocery store and it listed a two-pound package of ground meat. When he checked the refrigerator, no ground meat. Not in the fridge, not in the freezer. He said he doubted his wife had bought it for her and the little girl, because they preferred chicken and fish. He thinks she bought it to make dinner for him."

Henniker was staring at the garden, his mind turning things over and over.

"So, he sorted through all the trash and couldn't find the package for that ground meat. Now he thinks two things are missing from the trailer: the jar of pennies where they were saving up for a down payment on a house of their own, and that package of meat. Lois, that's the friend, says that puts a whole new light on it for the sheriff's office. With everything else, they are now convinced it was a burglary and probably a kidnapping."

"They need a body or something to make a case for anything other than burglary, though," said Henniker. "Or a ransom request, or something for a kidnapping. Right now, that's all they have."

"They've got those fingerprints from that old woman's house, the one where they found the wallet," said Lizzie.

"I thought they'd identified all those."

"I thought so too, but Lois says they're still looking for a match for one set. Lord, I hope it's not a Black person."

"Me, too," said Henniker, rising. "I need to call BoMac. He's going to want to know about this. I might go out there to meet him."

"Phone's in the hallway," she said, "I'm going to sit out here a minute longer, stare at my tomatoes coming in and listen to that mockingbird over there singing his fool head off."

"Yeah, he's got a nice voice," said Henniker, catching the screen door to stop it from banging.

BoMac said he'd head right over, be there in about forty-five minutes. He'd meet Henniker at the trailer park and the two of them would go talk to Shorty Fike. BoMac could tell a story development when he heard one.

Shorty was more than excited when they arrived. He was literally bouncing. "I told them she didn't run off," he said. "I told them. See, look!" He thrust the receipt at them. "Deputies came out yesterday, took copies of everything. I told them about the jar of pennies being gone. I told them!" He bounced around a minute or two more, then came back to BoMac. "They're gonna find my girls, I'm sure of it. I'm sure of it!" Then he turned and shouted, "Hear that, motherfucker?" in the direction of Jesse Grinder's trailer. "Hear that? They're gonna find 'em!"

Henniker caught BoMac's eye.

"Mr. Fike," he said, "you've shown my friend BoMac here, but do you mind showing me where you found that stepladder and those boot prints?"

"Sure!" shouted Fike. He really could not contain himself.

They went around the back of the trailer, being careful to approach the area without disturbing any more than the Rangers had already done. Near the slope of the dry branch, which only ran water after a rain, Fike pointed out the boot print, still there and intact despite the plaster cast taken by investigators. It was deep, the sole obviously worn down.

"Looks like it's going off that way," pointed Henniker.

"That's what I keep telling them," said Fike. "He took my girls and went that way!"

"What lies that way?" asked Henniker.

"Lots of woods, some trails, but it comes out not far from the end of this trailer home park."

"Anybody live down there?" asked Henniker.

"That motherfucker Jesse Grinder lives down there," spat Fike.

"Anybody talked to Grinder?" asked Henniker.

"The deputies said they talked to him. That's what they said. They wouldn't tell me anything about it."

"Yeah, that's the way they are," Henniker said, nodding. "They won't tell you anything, and then suddenly they have a man on trial for first-degree felony. Cops like to play their cards close to the chest."

"Sons of bitches," spat Fike. "Don't they see, every day goes by is another day my girls maybe are captive somewhere. And that Jesse Grinder knows where they are. I'm sure of it."

"You might be right," said Henniker. "But you might not. It might be somebody else entirely. We need to let the cops do what they can do. If I can think of a way to help you without getting in their way, though, I will." He reached his right hand out to shake Shorty Fike's. "BoMac and I, we've got your back on this. Call one of us if you remember anything else, or just need to talk. Here's my number." He scribbled it down on a scrap of paper he pulled from his pocket. "Anytime, day or night."

Fike's eyes brimmed with tears. "Ain't nobody believed me this whole time," he mumbled, "except this man right here." He pointed at BoMac. "Maybe now we can get somewhere."

CHAPTER
FIFTY-FIVE

Darryl had decided not to work on the weekends. He said he was still recovering from the fright he got at finding Trey Green's body, and he needed to relax. One consequence of his decision to sleep in was to become reacquainted with Mary's strong artist's hands. Since the Lions Club cleaned out his freezer, there had been a distinct lack of Roadrunner cartoons in his life, and Mary planned to make up for that hiatus all in one day. Darryl got worked over and slept until mid-afternoon, when she came back in the bedroom with a sandwich and a cool cloth for his forehead.

Besides the hands, an artist is nearly always adept at other things, too. Darryl enjoyed his sandwich.

On the first Monday after Labor Day, Darryl awoke from his lazy stupor. The air had changed. He could smell autumn, and he was ready to go to work. He needed to finish up that pasture and move on. He had lots to do, and this was the time of year to do it. He whistled on the way out his back door at dawn with a steaming mug of Cajun coffee, trying not to spill any on the grass, carrying a sandwich and a milk jug of frozen water. By noon, the water would have mostly melted. He paused to look at his sparkly red not-bass boat, took a sip of coffee, and then hopped up into the truck. The keys were in the ignition, where they always were. It was Whitmire. Nobody worried about leaving keys in the ignition.

Thirty minutes later he dropped the chain of the gate and pushed it open, gazing for a moment across the unmowed pasture, possibly another hundred acres still to be done. His eyes scanned the work that lay ahead of him, now with just a handful of brilliant white egrets poking around at the far end of the fence line, and then he remembered the melon he'd spotted the previous Friday. He would spot it again and planned his mowing so he'd be passing it about the time lunch rolled around. That would be a welcome addition to the ham sandwich and handful of chips he had with him.

As always, Darryl had left the seat on the tractor propped up so the dew and rain would drain off. Otherwise, it tended to collect, and nothing was more unpleasant than sitting in a puddle of water at the start of a workday. He would be wet through from sweat by day's end anyway, but that was different. Honest sweat in a man's eyes was a kind of blessing, the holy water of labor, redeeming and cleansing. Cold dew on the seat of one's pants, on the other hand, was just damning and thoughtless, and you deserved the discomfort.

The tractor cranked instantly, as though glad to be going to work again, and they were off at a leisurely pace, trundling and swaying back and forth as they traversed the lumpy new-mown pasture. He lined up with the beginning of the next cut without needing to stop, and then set off, buzzing and banging, through the tall weeds and short saplings. Sure enough, he spied the grayish-white sphere of the melon just where he remembered it being and went on down the line to complete that swath across the pasture. Rather than return to the spot where the melon was, he turned left and headed south, going uphill along the far fence. He would mow up and down that line for a while, until lunchtime, then return to retrieve the melon and head back to the shade. His mouth watered with the anticipation of that wild melon, probably a honeydew melon that grew from seeds dropped by some bird. It looked like a honeydew, or maybe it had the netted skin of a cantaloupe, but this long, hot summer and the dry, well-drained soil would make it as sweet as a sugar cube. He could almost taste it already.

He mowed for three hours up and down the west line of the pasture, nearly dropping the tractor once or twice in deep holes that the rains had cut and tangling up in a thicket of blackberry brambles at one point, killing the tractor. He had to disengage the mower, lift it, and back out to get clear, then he restarted the mower. It clanged and protested for a bit as it started, as it always did, with a jerk, then the mower spooled up to its full 650 rpm and he cautiously lowered it back to the ground. It gave a shudder as it settled down, then he raised the cutting height another four or five inches and moved slowly ahead into the thicket. The mower had no trouble at the new height, and he made a clean swath. Then he lowered the mower back to its original height using the little lever next to his right thigh, and mowed back across that patch. He repeated that process for an hour as he leveled the bramble thicket, just glad it had not gone another year. By next June those brambles would have been a pile seven or eight feet tall, high enough to tear his shirt off and leave him bloody with thousands of scratches and snags, like some ancient Chinese torture.

"Man needs to take better care of his land if he wants to keep it," muttered Darryl to himself. "Fucking rich-ass lawyer thinks he's God's gift to poor people because once a year he hires somebody to do his manual labor. Too lazy to care about this place. If he wants to build a house up here, he needs to spend some time getting to know folks. He won't find anybody who will work for him otherwise. And even if he brings in a crew of Mexicans to do the building, sooner or later he's going to need a plumber or somebody local. Foolish man, what I call it."

Darryl went on with this internal monologue for another hour or two, until he had forgotten about the bramble thicket, and then he set his tractor heading north along the west line to return to mowing toward that luscious melon and lunch. It was time. Straight-up high noon.

CHAPTER

FIFTY-SIX

BoMac had completed his first quest for advertising around 11 a.m. on Monday morning. He returned to the office to finish off the Shorty Fike story and get started on the rest of the week's copy, mentally organizing the news stories as he parked and went into the office. Whitmire lost its regional football opener, but not by much. He had quotes from quarterback Willie Dickerson and coach, Al McDonald, for the sports lead. He needed to be sure that lazy waste of time, Sarah Bibber, his so-called assistant, was keeping up with typing the classified ads and getting the club news in (the Boggy Creek Quilting Society, the Good Shepherd Baptist Church Ladies Auxiliary, the Little Cypress Garden Club, and others). He had a new proposed budget the commissioner's court would consider at their meeting next week, and he had the minutes from last week's city council story to write up. And of course, he had the next story on Shorty Fike's missing girls. That would lead off the week and should generate additional interest in the tragedy. He'd work the phrase "Jar of Pennies" into the headline somehow. Maybe all by itself. That would intrigue his readers.

He finished the sports section and his sixth cup of coffee by noon—honestly, sports didn't take much skill since it was mostly scores and statistics. He was just proofing the classified ad copy when all hell broke loose on the Radio Shack police scanner he kept in the office.

"What's it saying, Sarah?" he shouted, rushing from his office with his camera. "Where is it?"

"North," she said, "up the highway then right at, wait a minute, can't say. Get started. You've got a scanner in the truck. Follow the sirens."

Sure enough, every siren in Whitmire was going off. Even the volunteer fire department had put out a general call. He slammed the door on his pickup just as a state trooper roared by, siren and all lights going, squealing into a wide turn north at the highway light. BoMac followed.

He became one in a long procession of speeding vehicles, many with emergency lights. He debated moving over when he saw Whitmire's prized fire truck a quarter-mile behind him, then decided he was going faster than it was, so he just plowed on. The string of flashing red lights ahead of him stretched a mile, and in his rearview mirror he could see another string at least a mile long. Every volunteer fireman, every fire truck, every ambulance and police car in Sweetgum County was speeding north, but where they were going, he didn't know. Nor did he know why.

Over the patchy radio sitting on the seat next to him, BoMac pieced together what happened. Somebody had discovered a skull. That's all. No, wait, also a skeleton.

"So much for the Shorty Fike lead," he muttered to himself, trying to make sure his pickup kept up with the pace of the vehicles in front. They were doing 85 to 90 mph, but his Dodge was up to it. That faithful eight-cylinder hemi never complained at all, even though it would top out at around 105 mph and refuse to go any faster. Still, for a fifteen-year-old truck, she was doing her part, not a shudder or a shimmy at all. He reached up and patted the hard metal dashboard, promising to change the oil and examine the tires when they got back.

The sorry quality of his police scanner meant that BoMac could only interpret snatches of the chatter going back and forth, but it sounded like murder. A murder would trump the Fike story for sure, maybe even butting it off the front page to page three. BoMac tried to keep a mix of news on the front page, some serious and some more heartening or humorous. Trying to hit that balance each week sometimes got him in trouble. For example, some elected officials did not know that the jump line at the bottom of a story, like "continued on page 4A," meant the rest of the story was continued on that page. They thought the story just ended in the middle, sometimes mid-sentence. It took BoMac a long time to realize the level of ignorance of his readers—they weren't stupid, they were just dealing with an unfamiliar technology, if you could still call printed words a technology. And then he remembered Brother Lyncefield telling him to get the whole Trey Green memorial service story on the front page. Maybe Brother Lyncefield knew his flock better than he had thought. Maybe he knew they wouldn't know to turn the page to continue the story. Unfamiliar technology.

"You can't take anything for granted," BoMac reminded himself. "Just be ready."

All of the vehicles in front of him were slowing to turn right, heading off the back way to Piney Creek. He'd been on that road just a few weeks ago with Deputy Jack Lewis, a quiet, scenic road of rolling hills and dark pines. Moments later the emergency vehicles were turning through a gate into a partially mown pasture, and he spotted Lewis talking earnestly to Darryl Stewart, who was pointing at the barn.

"What happened?" BoMac asked.

"Darryl here found a skull," said Lewis. "Said he thought it was a melon and he was saving it for lunch. But when he went to pick it up, he realized it was the skull."

"No shit."

"Pretty much," nodded Lewis, pushing his cowboy hat back with a forefinger.

"Anybody know who it is?"

"Not yet, but we will," he said. "Found more bones in the barn, some shreds of clothes, shoes, that kind of thing."

"Oh wow. More than one skeleton?"

"We've got two skulls, so far," said Lewis. We're roping off the area to keep from disturbing the scene. Looks like some animals got in there."

"Do you think that's how the skull got out in the field? Like it got dragged out there?"

Darryl nodded. "That's what I think," he said. "I found that skull, probably a child's skull, it's so small, and looked up and the door to that barn was standing part open. I ran up there and looked inside, saw a pile of stuff scattered on some old moldy hay bales, and a loop of baling wire hanging down from one of the rafters. Don't know who it was, but it must have been rough."

"Darryl, I gotta quote you on some of this. You don't mind, do you?"

"Hell yes, I mind, but what can I do about it? I'd rather have done anything—even bass fishing—than come on this. Damn it all, BoMac. Damn it all." He took his big red bandana out of the hip pocket of his overalls and wiped his eyes. "Damn it all."

Lewis beckoned BoMac aside.

"No pictures inside the barn, you hear?"

"Yessir," said BoMac. "Unless you need evidence photos."

"We already called the Rangers and the forensics guys in Houston. They have cameras and stuff. Looks like there are tire marks in the dirt of the barn, so we should be able to match that up with some vehicle or other. Might come back to a yellow sedan."

"Oh wow. You thinking what I'm thinking? asked BoMac. "I only know of two missing people, and one of them was a three-year-old girl."

"Gotta think positive," said Lewis, unconsciously moving his right hand to the butt of his revolver, just resting it there. "Gotta hope. Gotta have faith. It's all we can do besides pick up the pieces."

"I'll wait for the state forensics guys to get here from Houston before I head back," said BoMac. "A picture of them going into the barn would make a good front page photo."

They walked off a little to get up under the deep shade of the pecan trees and out of the burning sun, going no closer to the barn. Darryl walked with them, muttering, his hands thrust deep in his pockets and his shoulders shaking.

Then Lewis turned to Darryl and clapped him on the shoulder, a firm but friendly hold. He kept his hand there until Darryl looked up.

"I know it's tough, Darryl," he said. "But you're a good man, and these people were missed by somebody. This might not be the best news in the world to them, but you've done them a big favor finding these bodies. You just remember that."

Darryl looked up at him with bloodshot eyes, just staring, unable to speak. Finally, he nodded. "K," he managed before he turned away.

CHAPTER
FIFTY-SEVEN

"I think they're gonna say it's a woman and a little two- or three-year-old child," reported Deputy Jack Lewis to BoMac about thirty minutes later, who was still waiting under the pecan trees for developments from the discovery of skeletons. "We'll know for sure when the forensics guy says, but I heard him tell some of the others that's what it looked like. He said something about looking for pink tooth in the mature female's skull when he gets it back to the lab. So it's looking like the Fikes."

"What's pink tooth?" asked BoMac.

"Something that happens to the teeth of people who are strangled, so maybe that's a cause of death. The bones are pretty well scattered. All the clothing was in a pile though, so we've got a little to go on."

"Any blood typing, other physical evidence?" asked BoMac, his heart sinking as he remembered the photos of Shorty Fike's missing girls.

"Might be them," said Lewis, nodding in the direction of Shorty Fike's trailer about thirty miles east. "We'll know sometime in the next day or so."

They stood around a bit, watching the activity in the barn, seeing evidence bags coming out. It looked like the state guys were doing an extremely thorough job.

"Does Shorty know yet?" BoMac asked.

"Too soon to tell him," said Lewis. "I expect they'll go out there and tell him face to face, about the same time they go looking for that big guy lives up there, what's his name."

"Jesse Grinder?"

"Yeah, him. Not much to tie him to it yet, but he lives close to Fike and he's mean. Could be him. They'll talk to him, might put him on a polygraph."

275

"Lie detectors are not very reliable," said BoMac.

"Most people don't know that," said Lewis. "Amazing how much they'll confess once you get 'em hooked up and they go to watching those squiggly lines."

They lounged around in the shade for a bit longer, waiting for the forensics team to arrive from Houston. They were only coming because somebody at the Texas Department of Public Safety had ordered it done, because Annabeth Fike was somebody's daughter and little Maria Fike was somebody's granddaughter. Otherwise, the whole investigation would have fallen in the exceptionally narrow lap of John Quick, the undertaker, who might have needed to call for help from Lufkin or Beaumont or Tyler. Reassembling all those bones and looking for injuries could take some time.

"Two sets of clothes," said Lewis, returning from the barn. The forensics team had pulled into the pasture about thirty minutes earlier. "They've got good photos of the tire tracks, good photos of boot prints. Won't take them long to get a match to type of tires or make of boots, so I think they'll have something to go on pretty quick. Might take a little longer to get the plaster casts of them, though. At least they'll have wear patterns to match."

"How are they going to get their film processed so fast?"

"Some of it's Polaroid. But they have film processing in their van, and books of things like tire treads and boot soles. They probably won't find any fingerprints. Might find some blood spots, which might not belong to the perpetrator. Gonna be an interesting investigation, but it's going to go fast."

"They getting prodded, you think?"

"Oh, hell yeah. You ought to hear them talk. Somebody is really putting the blowtorch on their behinds over this."

"I'm worried for Shorty Fike," said BoMac.

"Yeah," said Lewis.

Darryl had unfolded his cot and was lying in the bed of his pickup, his forearm across his eyes, just waiting for someone to tell him he could go home.

BoMac nodded at Darryl and Lewis looked over. Then Lewis shook his head. "Nah," he said, "he's done enough. He doesn't need to know more than he does. He found them. That's the most anybody could do. He's a good man, and he needs some space."

"Yeah," said BoMac. "I agree. I'm standing around out here thinking how to write the story without giving anything away."

"All you need to say is that two skeletons were discovered in a pasture by a man mowing on a tractor," said Lewis. "Maybe fill in a few details but keep it low. I don't think news of this coming out on Wednesday is going to cause any trouble, but maybe."

"It's a two-week story anyway," said BoMac. "Whitmire's not winning state this year either, and just about the only other news we've got in this town is high school football."

"There's lots happening," said Lewis, "but most of it's not big news. No burglaries to speak of, maybe a bicycle or lawnmower. Handful of drunk drivers. Nothing else. So other than this, it's going to be a slow week for you."

"Got some county commissioner news, city council news, that kind of thing," said BoMac. "Certainly, got my front page stories. We've got what, about a hundred locals milling around out here? They will all go back to town with a version of this story, so maybe ads will pick up. Maybe not. I guess I've got enough to go on. If they find a third body or anything, let me know, okay?"

"Sure thing," said Lewis. "First call."

CHAPTER
FIFTY-EIGHT

The tire treads from the barn matched the tires of Annabeth's Chevy Nova. The boot marks matched the boot prints found in the mud behind Fike's trailer. That afternoon, a Texas Ranger, riding with a state trooper, and a Cypress County deputy—not Jasper Rhodes—pulled into the mobile home park where Jesse Grinder lived to ask him some questions.

He wasn't home. His pickup truck was there, but Grinder was gone.

With a search warrant in one paw, the deputy knocked politely at the door a few times, then called the office. Half an hour later, another ten or fifteen deputies, constables, and off-duty Piney Creek policemen arrived, followed by the forensics team from Houston, just in case. BoMac had driven over after he got a call from Ed Nichols, the *Piney Creek Crier* editor. Charles Henniker was supervising school buses at the Whitmire High School after school, or BoMac would have brought him along. Henniker was the kind of cool-headed, reasonable man he liked to talk to, to discuss things.

Grinder's trailer was surrounded by law enforcement officers of various ranks and services, but no one responded to repeated knocks on the door, or blasts from sirens and loudspeakers. So, the deputy kicked at the door, trying to break in.

He hurt his foot. Grinder had reinforced the door.

BoMac loved it. What great photos. Deputy kicking a door and breaking his foot. He felt sorry for the deputy but thought the *Crier* might like the photo even more than he did.

"I bet we could use that old boy's head for a battering ram," muttered one of the state troopers in hearing of BoMac, nodding at the deputy with the hurt foot. His fellow trooper, standing with a shotgun to his shoulder, chuckled.

"Nah," he said, "his face don't ring a bell, so it sure in hell won't break down a door."

"That might be the worst joke I ever heard," said the first trooper, propping his .357 magnum revolver on the roof of their car with both hands, aimed at the trailer.

"It's a fucking mobile home. You could push through a sidewall with almost no effort," muttered the second. "Hasn't anyone ever taught these peckerwoods to enter a mobile home? I mean, look at them. If this guy is armed, they're all dead."

"I've got a can opener in the glove box they can use if this keeps up much longer," added the second trooper.

"I bet he's not home. I bet he heard we were coming and took off into the woods."

"Maybe. I'm going to watch this comedy at the front door for a few minutes, then go around to see if the back door is standing open."

"Got some trigger-happy folks back there," said the first. "Holler when you go."

"There's nobody in that trailer. I can tell."

"Yeah. You're right. It feels empty, don't it."

"It feels empty because it is empty. Ain't nobody in there."

Various deputies and constables took turns bouncing off the door, shaking the whole structure, but failing to open it. Finally, the trooper with the shotgun stepped up, fired almost point blank with his 00 buckshot, and blasted the lock clean through the door. It swung open on a scene of remarkable squalor. The first officers rushing through the door almost gagged at the smell, but Grinder was not there.

They began the tedious process of cataloguing almost two years of food wrappers and empty bean cans and going through everything else in the place. It hardly mattered if they pulled out drawers and dumped the contents on the floor, which at least scared the cockroaches enough that they didn't swarm over their hands. The worst part was the fleas, however. The troopers withdrew to the safety of their cars, spraying their clothes with insect repellent, but the deputies had not had the forethought to bring repellent with them. Usually, they rarely left their cars except when they were first on the scene at a car wreck or a fire, and that almost never happened. Or when they pulled into the donut shop for, quote, "a cup of coffee," so they were not well prepared. They were fresh meat on the hoof to the tiny predators.

The deputies were looking for evidence that tied Grinder to Annabeth Fike and found it in a discarded meat wrapper. It matched a two-pound package of frozen ground beef she had purchased the Saturday before she went missing, something that Shorty Fike had finally come up with. But they kept searching until they had turned the whole place upside down. They found no weapons, no pornography, no drugs. Nothing but trash, and plenty of that.

BoMac went to the door of Grinder's trailer with his camera, looked inside, and immediately spotted a large mason jar of pennies sitting in the kitchen, above the refrigerator. He fixed a telephoto lens to his camera and captured several good shots of it without entering, then wandered around outside, taking pictures of the law in action. Although his presence could have been thought an intrusion by some, especially the state troopers and the Rangers, the local law enforcement officers were happy to get their picture in the paper—any paper—and to receive the notice of their friends and neighbors. BoMac, however, had seen the black specks jumping on their trouser legs and decided he would not enter the trailer even if invited. Not until it had been fumigated.

Finally, one of the cops spotted the jar of pennies on top of the refrigerator and beckoned the forensics guys over.

"Mr. Fike told us to look for a jar of pennies," he said. "This matches his description. Can you get prints from it?"

They wrapped it up to move it without smudging any latent fingerprints and carried it outside to the forensics van. Fifteen minutes later, word filtered around the group that prints both on the outside of the jar and on the inside matched prints from Shorty Fike's trailer and weren't Shorty's. They were undoubtedly Annabeth Fike's.

An arrest warrant for capital murder was issued for Jesse Grinder, and the hunt was on.

At the rear of the trailer park was an eight-thousand-acre tree farm, where a man could hide for years without being seen, if he had a way to get anything to eat. A quick phone call to Huntsville got the prison tracking dogs loaded into cattle trailers and on their way. It would take about two hours, but enough daylight lingered in this early September day that they thought they could run him to ground before dark. If not, they'd continue the next day.

If Jesse Grinder was on foot, he would be in custody by nightfall. He might even live long enough to find safety in a secluded jail cell.
But he might not.

The dogs had been known to bring down more than one running felon. Those dogs were always hungry, and it might be dark-thirty before their handlers called them in for the night. Suppertime.

CHAPTER
FIFTY-NINE

Two hours before the raid on Jesse Grinder's trailer, Abbie Morton and Ben Pickett Jr., the Houston gangsters, walked into Bob McKinney's office at the used car lot. In all his life, McKinney had never sold a car on a Monday. Nobody bought cars on Monday. Mondays were to car dealerships what Tuesday evenings were to restaurants. You stayed open because you had to, but it was all busywork. You couldn't make enough money to pay your workers to show up.

"I bought a yellow car from you," said Morton. Ben Pickett Jr. cracked his knuckles and looked around, guessing if McKinney had a gun someplace it would be under his desk. He sized McKinney up and figured McKinney would sure in hell let them know if he was going to go for his gun, and by the time he got his fist on it, Pickett would already have shot him three times. Pickett liked imagining that scene.

"So?" asked McKinney.

"A yellow Oldsmobile four-door sedan, something wrong with it. Trunk stank like an old lady's dead cat died in it."

"I don't recall," said McKinney. "Why?"

"Me and my friend have a hunch," said Morton. "We have a hunch that somebody is running drugs in this town. We want a piece of that action."

"What's that got to do with a car?" asked McKinney.

"Somebody used that car to deliver drugs," said Morton. "Speed. Meth. Crack. Stuff like that. Some kind of veterinary stuff make a woman forget she hates the man who's fucking her. Military drugs, some of it. Those kinds of recreational drugs."

"I don't know what you're talking about," said McKinney, getting an involuntary clench in his stomach.

"We've been watching this town for four months," said Morton. "I'm not going to tell you how much we know, or how we know it, but I am going to tell you that it is time for you to get out of the business."

"Also," said Ben Pickett Jr. in his gravelly voice, "we want to talk to this person Jesse Grinder, who works for you. He drove that yellow car before you sold it."

"He's not here today," said McKinney. "I can't afford for him to come in every day."

Morton looked around the shabby office, at window blinds that had not been raised in ten years and had spiderwebs between the slats, at the ash tray on the corner of the desk with at least a year's worth of cigarette butts in it. "That's right," said Morton. "You can't afford it. My partner here will explain to you why you don't want to keep moving drugs. You won't like what he has to say, or how he says it, though."

"Are you threatening me?" asked McKinney.

"You are kinda slow for a Monday morning, aren't you," Morton said.

McKinney stood up and pointed at the door. "Get the fuck out of my office," he said, raising his voice. "Get out now!"

McKinney standing suited Ben Pickett Jr. just fine. It was an easier takedown when they were standing, and their guns were out of reach.

"Yellow car," said Morton, unperturbed. He knew that whatever personnel McKinney had at the dealership would be back in the shop as far from the front lot as McKinney could get them. They might hear gunshots, but they wouldn't hear words.

"What about the fucking yellow car?" asked McKinney.

"Where's the guy who drove that car on the day the policeman died?" asked Morton.

"He's not here," said McKinney, red in the face and breathless. McKinney had run track in high school and had not run a step since. This, too, was obvious to Ben Pickett Jr. It would be disappointing, Pickett thought, if this fool dropped dead from a heart attack.

"You'd probably say that even if he was," said Morton. "You have been telling lies for a long time. Hell, your whole business is one big lie, selling these piece-of-shit cars to folks for tons more than they're worth. Does the congressman know you been lying to him, too? Does he know how much you've been taking off the top?"

"You don't know what you're talking about," McKinney said through gritted teeth. "Just get out of here."

"Here's the thing, Bob McKinney," said Morton, walking around the desk and herding McKinney to the front of it, next to Ben Pickett Jr. "Here's the thing." He sat down in McKinney's office chair and located the gun strapped to the underside of the desk, pulling it out while McKinney stared at him wide-eyed. "You've been using Black folks to do all the dirty work. You've been stealing from Black folks; you've been using my esteemed colleague Mr. Chillers Banks and my distinguished friend Mr. Clarence Thomas to run your fucking illegal alcohol and drugs business for years. But my distinguished friends are part of the Black folks' community, and that's like a web. Goes all the way to Chicago and to Baltimore and to San Francisco and to Los Angeles and to Miami and lots of other places. Houston. Are you following me?"

McKinney just stared at him, and Morton leaned back in the chair, putting his feet on McKinney's desk, shoving the ashtray off on the floor where it disappeared in a cloud of ashes and broken glass. "Empty your fucking ashtray," said Morton. "You fool. Just sloppy, that's what you are. Sloppy in everything. I can't believe you let that Jesse Grinder drive your car to deliver drugs, and then he killed that policeman and fucked that White woman to death."

Ben Pickett Jr. had edged in closer to McKinney and leaned forward sniffing him.

"But what you don't know," Morton continued, looking at the dusty revolver, opening and closing the cylinder to make sure it was loaded, staring down the barrel to see if there was any obstruction in it, popping out a few cartridges to check their condition, "is that the network is tired of being robbed by White people and wants a piece of this action. That's where we come in. We are going to move some people out and replace them with our own network."

"I really don't know what you're talking about," said McKinney, sweat stains showing visibly in his armpits. "And get away from me," he said to Ben Pickett Jr. "Just back away."

"You aren't listening, McKinney," said Morton. "You need to be careful about my valued companion. His grin could be the last thing you see."

"Now that's a threat for sure," said McKinney. "I'm going to report you to the police. I'm going to file charges against you."

Morton took his feet off the desk, swept it clear of papers and pens and all the other trash, and leaned forward. He put the gun in the center of the desk and gave it a little twirl.

"Well, look here," he said, "it kinda spins, don't it? Be kinda funny if a man's gun went off accidentally and blew his private parts off. Might happen with a gun not any better taken care of than this one. Big old slugs in it, too. It's a what, a .44? No, it's a .45 revolver with a big, heavy, slow-moving slug must weigh 'bout 250 grains, damn near half an ounce, moves at about 870 feet per second. Rip your privates completely off quicker than a blade. A blade is more fun, though," he said, leaning back again and staring at McKinney. "Where are your personnel records?"

"My what?"

"Your personnel records, where you keep the names and addresses and social security numbers of your employees. I want Jesse Grinder's address."

"Why?"

"None of your business," said Morton, "but it might have something to do with identifying your current customers."

"Right desk drawer, filing drawer," said McKinney.

"Ah, the truth at last," said Morton, pulling up the stack of unfiled papers, sorting through them, finding Grinder's address. "Got that," he said to Ben Pickett Jr. He looked some more. "Where are your tax documents? Your W-2 copies, your W-4 copies, your 1099s, all that?"

"None of your business."

"Perhaps I was not clear in my question," said Morton. "Where are your tax documents, motherfucker?"

"Might be at my accountant's, might not."

"And where is your accountant?" asked Morton.

"Really none of your business. But now I have a question. Why Piney Creek?" asked McKinney. "This shithole doesn't have money. You want money, go to River Oaks in Houston."

"Half the congressman's contributions come from wealthy White fuckers in Houston," replied Morton, unblinking, "and we are talking about millions of dollars every year. We think maybe his little business includes River Oaks. Diet pills, all that."

"What is this? Are you trying to start some kind of race war?" asked McKinney.

"Now you're just trying to buy yourself a little time by raising up irrelevant shit like that," said Morton, picking up McKinney's gun again. "It's too late for you to learn history, though. So instead, tell me how you are getting the smack from Annapolis."

"The heroin?"

"I can't believe you. What have you taken this morning, Monday morning like this, no customers, two guys in the shop a hundred yards away? What are you on?" Morton's dialect began to slip into Third Ward, with its melodious tones and slurring. "Yes, damnit, the heroin, you muthafucker."

"Don't know what you're talking about," said McKinney.

"Maybe it's time for all three of us to go visit the congressman," said Morton.

"Sure," said McKinney. "I was gonna run out there after lunch anyway."

"You sound ready to go," said Morton.

"Best thing that could happen all day," replied McKinney. "You'd be feeding the catfish by sundown."

"You reckon?" grinned Morton. "And who would I be feeding to them?"

"You and this goon," said McKinney, trying to act brave.

"Oh, you mean the Black men he's got as guards, and the Black women he hires to keep his wife dressed. You mean he's got all this protection from all these Black people he's been robbing for decades, so we," he paused for emphasis, "WE would be the ones getting in trouble. Oh, I see now. You think there's not a race war yet, but you are trusting your life and your connections to a handful of armed Black men employed by a crooked White congressman who stole all their inherited property and kept them in poverty for decades. You have a lot of smarts, McKinney. I swear. You want me to name the guards to you? You want me to tell you how many guns they have? You want to talk about the emergency radio communication he has in his office so he can call the sheriff's office and the national guard and all that? What about his telephone lines? Want to know where they run? How about I tell you what radio frequencies he uses? Want to know that? Or how about I tell you the names of all those Black people's children going to school next door to that fucking nightclub you are running for the motherfucker? Little Sally Perkins, Juliet Morrison, Jimmy Hadnot, all those little kids? You don't even know who I'm talking about, but I know them all. So yeah, let's go out there. That might bring all this to a quick resolution."

"It'd get a lot of attention," said McKinney.

"From who?" asked Morton. "Depends on who talks and who doesn't, and even then, nobody would know he's gone until he doesn't show up for the next election and we elect a Black man instead."

"He's been in office for forty years," said McKinney.

"Time he moved aside," said Morton. "The world has changed. Tell me how you get your Annapolis heroin out from under the noses of our brothers in Baltimore."

"No," said McKinney.

"When was the last time you had a glass of whisky with Dennis Nelson? Captain Dennis Nelson, United States Navy. Teaches matrix mathematics and nuclear physics at the Academy. Wants to be an admiral. Kind of ironic he teaches matrix math. Matrix. Get it? Matrix like the network of Black people in this country."

"What the fuck," said McKinney.

"Cut the bullshit. Captain Nelson flies to Houston once a month with two bags. Rents a car. Drives up here to pay the congressman a visit. Goes home with one bag. He will be promoted to admiral this year. When did you see him last?"

McKinney clenched his jaw.

"Okay," said Morton. "He arrived in Houston this morning about an hour ago. He's on his way up here now. He doesn't know some of the brothers are following him. Let's us go have a little talk with everybody up at the congressman's house. What say?"

"You're out of your fucking mind," said McKinney.

"Mr. Ben Pickett Jr.," said Morton, standing and putting the revolver in his front pocket and sealing McKinney's fate by mentioning Pickett's name, "please gag our friend Bob McKinney and escort him to his car. Put the cuffs on his hands and leash him up with the wire 'round his neck, to help him stay calm. Let's go round up this Grinder fool, and if everything turns out, then we'll all go pay our respects to the congressman."

CHAPTER

SIXTY

Thirty or forty trailing hounds can set up quite a commotion when they think they will be set loose for a run in the country. They know their business. As working dogs employed by the State of Texas to track down escaped convicts, these dogs are not living room decorations for gentlemen sipping bourbon in manorial estates. Black-and-tan coonhounds crossbred with Catahoulas and foxhounds, they stay lean and hungry, and they ride in cattle trailers with the horses. They are yoked together in pairs, and once on a scent they will not stop. When they find their quarry, that man better stand perfectly still and upright. If he falls over or tries to fight them off, they will tear him to pieces. These are not pets. They are as rough as any Texas prison inmate. These are the kind of animals about whom the idiomatic expression "dogged" was forged.

The three trailers with horses and dogs pulled into the mobile home park about 3 p.m. with the dogs setting up an excited yelping and howling even before they were released.

"Gotta get a scent pad," said one of the handlers. "Let them get a good sniff of him. Then we'll see if they can find him."

"You bet," said Sheriff Bishop Adams. When he saw the photographer and editor of the *Piney Creek Crier* heading out of town in the direction of the mobile home park, he had followed. Unlike them, he was waved through the cordon of police officers who had marked off the area around Grinder's trailer. He signaled to several of his deputies to get after it, and they disappeared into the trailer. Other officers had gone door-to-door through the park warning people to keep their pets, children, and themselves inside while the dogs were working. "Dangerous dogs," they said. "Don't want them dogs confused. They don't think so good. Used to taking down fleeing prisoners, so we don't want them taking you down by mistake. Whatever you do, don't take off running or they will take you down even if you're not the one they're hunting. We will let you know when it's safe to come out. If the dogs don't come to your door, though, you got nothing to worry about. If they do, then we are coming inside. Just stay put and safe for the time being."

The type of people who lived in the park were not inclined to be visible to law enforcement officers anyway, so their only inconvenience was keeping their kids inside while they fought with one another. They didn't really need anyone warning them to stay inside when there were that many policemen around, and most of them recognized the dogs for what they were. The few who owned dogs of their own brought those inside, where they locked them in the bathroom and turned up the volume on the television to drown out the barking.

Some of the deputies opened Grinder's truck, rummaging through for evidence of any kind, but found nothing except more of his fingerprints and a wallet of lock picks. They tagged it and put it in the evidence box. Others dragged Grinder's naked mattress outside where the dogs could sniff it well, which they did, padding all over it, biting at the mattress cover, pawing it. Then the dog trainers told the dogs to hunt, and they were off baying and yelping, followed by the prison guards on horseback. State troopers were already in their cars and keeping contact with the guards by radio, positioned to stop traffic if the dogs appeared to be heading toward a highway. Others fanned out along pipelines and high lines with binoculars to watch for anyone on foot. Until they had an actual quarry, the state's law enforcement helicopters would not deploy, but once they knew they had someone running, then air cover would come in.

Grinder was assumed to be armed and dangerous, although nobody had heard anything about him having a gun, and neither guns nor ammo were found in his trailer. Still, a possible murderer was always treated like he was about to kill you. You can never tell, with some people.

BoMac had tried calling Henniker from the *Crier* office, but it was still during school, so he called the high school and left a message for him with the secretary. He wanted Henniker to know what had developed during the day, but Henniker called Lizzie as soon as he got home from school and missed BoMac's message. With a constant stream of rumors from her friends in the police department all during the day, Lizzie was able to fill him in about the skeletons and the massive manhunt. She even had a name. "Jesse Grinder," she said.

"I don't recall that name," said Henniker. "I wonder if BoMac knows all this."

"I saw him going in the *Crier* office with Ed Nichols," she said. "The two papers look like they're collaborating on the story."

"It's certainly the most exciting thing to happen since they pulled Trey Green out of the water," said Henniker.

"Since YOU pulled him out," she corrected. "You were the one who pulled him away from that alligator."

"How'd you know about the alligator?" Henniker asked.

"BoMac told me. He saw you do it. I don't think I could have gone in that water knowing there was an alligator there."

"Just a little 'gator," chuckled Henniker. "Probably more scared of me than I was of him. But yes, I kept my eyes open."

"Where'd you learn to be all brave and stuff?" she asked.

"From my wife," he said. "She's the reason I'm teaching school. Facing down an alligator in its home swamp is not nearly as scary as walking into a classroom of teenagers. Frankly, I prefer the 'gator. If things go wrong, you can eat the 'gator. Harder to do with people's children."

They chuckled for a while, exchanging pleasantries, and then Henniker offered to come over and take her for a hamburger.

"Come on, honey," she said. "I'll be looking for you."

"Back when I was in Vietnam, I was a Marine and in the SEALS," said C. L. "Cock-lover" Turner, District Attorney. "I had to kill one of those K9 dogs to rescue his handler."

"I thought you were a bouncer," said BoMac. "Didn't know you were in the SEALS."

"Hell yeah," said C. L., puffing out his chest. "Haven't you seen the bullet holes in my truck?"

"I heard you shot your truck yourself," said BoMac, writing it all down and wishing he was recording this.

"That dog was hard to kill. Had to grab him and slit his throat."

Ten miles north of Grinder's mobile home, Abbie Morton had pulled into Congressman Rip Johnson's estate, waved on by an armed Black man patrolling the property. Grinder was trying to pick the lock of the handcuffs behind his back without letting the goon sitting next to him on the back seat know. Handcuff locks are pretty easy to open. You just need a piece of wire, and Grinder had some picks in his hip pocket. He'd get it in a minute, if he had time. Meanwhile, he tried desperately to think how to get out of the car and make a run for it. Ben Pickett Jr. had a gun on him with one hand while he held a loop of strong wire around Bob McKinney's neck with his other hand. Abbie Morton had McKinney's .45 revolver in his lap, easily accessible, but Grinder's claustrophobia was panicking him. He would risk getting shot if he could just get his hands free. And if he got his hands free, he'd roll out of the car, no matter how fast it was going. Morton was pleased with how the afternoon had gone. They had taken Grinder from his nasty trailer, then driven through most of the residential streets of Piney Creek, noting addresses of some very fancy homes with big green lawns and Cadillacs in front. He was surprised that they were not followed by any police cars, but it looked like all the law enforcement in the county were out of town. The tour had been unnecessary, of course, because Grinder and McKinney had been followed for months by Morton's network. The Black working mothers and unemployed Black fathers of Piney Creek had been happy to earn five dollars watching the two White men, and none of the White people knew it. None of the White people cared what the Black people were doing, or how they were doing it, as long as they stayed quiet and out of sight, so it was easy for Morton to exploit this inattention to his benefit. Armed with that information, he was able to correctly judge whether McKinney and Grinder were answering his questions truthfully, especially when it came to specific types and amounts of drugs being delivered.

Morton was certain that his Third Ward boss, Melton Carr, would be pleased. He might even be pleased enough to increase Morton's percentage of the take from Piney Creek, or maybe let him have the whole Piney Creek operation. And that might include those girls at Fort Polk. Morton found prostitution distasteful, but you had to admit running whorehouses just outside the gates of a military base was historically profitable.
But the big play was coming up. It was time for the congressman and his houseguest, Captain Dennis Nelson, USN, to be informed of business developments that excluded their participation.

He liked the sound of that. "Excluded their participation." That had a nice ring to it.

"What are we doing here?" pleaded McKinney.

"You'll see," said Morton. "Sometimes the flies kill the spider."

CHAPTER

SIXTY-ONE

"Admiral, let me show you my matched ivory-handled pistols. As an experienced military man, you might appreciate them. A supporter gave them to me years ago, quite a treasure. At .32 caliber, they are easy to handle, exceptionally well-balanced, and accurate as hell. I believe I could shoot a sweet gum ball out of that tree over there from here on the porch," said Congressman Rip Johnson to his guest.

The Congressman's wife, a well-tanned, skinny blonde with large breasts far too perky for her obvious age, came out onto the expansive back porch where Rip Johnson was sharing cigars and bourbon with Capt. Nelson, celebrating his pending promotion by addressing him as "admiral."

"Rip," she said, "some men are here to see you. One of them is Bob McKinney. I don't know the others but two of them are Black."

"I'm such a friend of the Black people," boasted Johnson, "I'm sure they're here to pay their respects with money. Ha ha. And you know McKinney." He raised his crystal glass and winked at Nelson, who had stood when Angie Johnson came through the screen door. "You can show 'em in, you hot piece of ass," he said, grinning his tobacco-stained teeth at her.

"If you say so," she said, "but I'm going up to my room. I don't like the looks of them."

"Just Black people, and McKinney," said the Congressman. "Did they have an appointment?"

"No," she said, pausing at the door and looking back appreciatively at Nelson, "I don't think so. I can't find Gwendolyn to check. I think she went home early. I know Charles did. He said he wasn't feeling well."

"Well, damn, who's left? Twenty hired hands out here on this hill, Ad-

293

miral, but you know what they say about good help. Hard to find. Okay, I'll talk to them."

She disappeared inside while the two men admired the pistols. A few moments passed, then there was a commotion from inside and a gunshot in the main hallway echoed onto the porch. The captain checked to make sure his pistol was loaded, working the slide on the semi-automatic, but the congressman ran for the wall next to the screen door, holding his pistol up.

"I hope that wasn't Angie," he whispered hoarsely to Nelson. "It's such a mess when a wife gets killed."

Nelson also came to the wall, avoiding the windows. He leaned against the warm red brick of the house, and then spotted a large man running across the paved courtyard toward the garage.

It was Jesse Grinder. He'd gotten the cuffs off and surprised Abbie Morton with a hard fist to the right temple. Ben Pickett Jr. fired at him, hitting him in the leg as he rushed to the front door, and he was bleeding heavily and limping. Grinder spotted the congressman's dark green Land Rover with the brush guards and gun racks, and hopped in, finding the keys in the ignition. The vehicle cranked and was rolling by the time the two men on the porch realized what was happening.

"He's stealing my damned car!" shouted the congressman, running to the end of the porch and firing at the Land Rover as Grinder roared past.

Captain Nelson was not concerned. The gunshot had come from inside the house, and he was happy to see someone running away. He was more worried about what was happening inside.

Then there were a series of shotgun blasts in the hall, some screaming of wounded men, and more shotgun blasts. A pump shotgun makes a distinctive sound when a shell is jacked into the chamber, and between shots both men heard the gun's action being worked.

"Hope that's somebody on our side," whispered the Captain.

The congressman had returned to the screen door. "We got to go in there," he said. "All the communication stuff is in there."

"What about the suitcase?" asked Nelson. "We don't want a lot of cops messing around out here."

"Yeah, you're right," said the congressman. "I'll go first, head to the right behind the staircase. You come after me, go left into the den. We'll be able to tell more when we get in, maybe get 'em in a cross fire."

"Got it," said the Navy vet. "Say when."

"Now!" whispered Congressman Johnson, rushing the door and catching a load of buckshot in his stomach. His wife had heard the gunshot and come down the stairs with her shotgun and almost forty years of upland game-hunting experience. Three corpses lay at the foot of the stairs, and the congressman was doubled over, slammed against the wall and bleeding out.

When she knelt over him, he was barely conscious, grasping both hands over the pulsing mash of flesh that used to be his stomach.

"You gonna die, honey?" she asked.

He stared at her.

"At last?" she added. "Or do I need to shoot you again?"

"You . . . you . . . ," muttered the congressman.

Rip Johnson's dying vision was of Captain Nelson reaching a hand down to the woman to help her to her feet. "Not how we'd planned it," Johnson heard him say before he passed out, "but pretty damned effective. Let's plant that shotgun on one of those guys."

"I heard a pistol shot first," she said, "then just put two and two together. This seemed like as good a time as any. All the help is gone, so it's just us here in the house. There's a man outside near the highway, but he should stay away until I call him, and the gate's half a mile away through all those trees. They probably didn't hear anything."

"Gonna be hard to leave all this," said Nelson. "Big old estate like this, beautiful house, rolling hills, quarter horses and cattle. And we'll need to make sure it all looks like a crime. Shouldn't be hard. It was a crime."

"You have no idea how I have longed for this moment. You retire on your admiral's pay, we'll move to the mountains where it's cool, and let this piece of shit rot down into the dirt bag he always was."

They did not really need to do much to the scene. Abbie Morton was dead from a blow to his right temple and had fallen to the floor still clutching McKinney's .45, while both McKinney and Ben Pickett Jr. were dead from shotgun blasts. It would be easy to pull his hand to his temple to fire the gun. Angie put the shotgun down on Morton, but Nelson stopped her.

"I saw that big guy running for the garage," he said. "He took the Land Rover and Rip shot at him, but he got away. Let's take the shotgun and chuck it in the river. That way maybe all of this will be blamed on him, and we don't need to mess with shooting this guy in the head."

"You're a genius," said Angie Johnson, her eyes sparkling with excitement.

"Simple matrix math," said Nelson. "Look at the variables, match them up. Not even complex. Get the suitcase, I'll go get the car."

He had her sporty twelve-cylinder Jaguar XKE convertible cranked and rumbling by the time she got back down the stairs with the suitcase. They squeezed it and the shotgun into the tiny trunk and headed down to the smashed gates.

The guard who had been watching the gates when Morton and the others arrived was nowhere to be seen.

They turned right at the highway and headed toward Lufkin. After dinner at the Camelot Country Club, where all the would-be East Texas royalty went, they would return to the house and call the police to report the deaths. Until then, both of them were sighing with happiness. She rested her hand on his, stroking it, leaning back into the passenger seat as though just released from prison.

CHAPTER SIXTY-TWO

"That son of a bitch," Jesse Grinder groaned to himself as the pain in his leg set in. He was a little dizzy and his driving boot was filled with blood. He could feel it squishing when he pressed on the floor pedals to accelerate or stop. He looked around the interior of the vehicle for something to put over the wound but saw nothing. The bullet had missed muscle but cut a large chunk out of the side of his leg, and it stung. His knuckles were a little sore, too, where he'd cracked Abbie Morton's head. He was sitting up tall so he could peer over the spare tire mounted on the hood, and for the moment he was free.

He needed to get back to his trailer to tend to his leg, but when he turned in that direction, he saw a roadblock up ahead, so he turned around. Maybe it would stop bleeding in a minute, he figured. He wasn't about to drive past a couple of state troopers. So instead, he headed back toward Piney Creek, driving carefully.

All the gearshift levers on the floor of the Land Rover confused him. It looked like manual four-wheel drive levers for different terrain, maybe a high range and a low range, he figured. He'd driven standard shift vehicles his whole life but had never been in a four-wheel vehicle before. As he studied the different gearshifts, his attention wandered and he swerved off the road, braking to rest in a ditch. He was shaken but not hurt. However, the vehicle had stuck in soft mud in the bottom of the ditch, half into a tall stand of brush and East Texas weeds.

He struggled to engage the four-wheel-drive transmission, only succeeding in sinking the vehicle to the frame. He was really stuck, and that Land Rover would not be leaving the muddy ditch until it got towed.

Down the highway, the state troopers had watched the Land Rover almost a mile away turn around and head back over a long hill. The hill dipped, though, and they lost sight of it. When they didn't see it top the next hill, one of them called to the other.

"You see that Land Rover turn around?" he shouted.

"Yeah. Didn't see him going up the other side, though. You reckon he stopped to piss?"

"No doubt," said the first trooper. He pushed his uniform cover, a stiff, gray, cowboy-style hat, back on his forehead. "Looked kind of suspicious to me," he added.

"Never can tell," said the other trooper. "I'd go check on him if we didn't need to wait here on the dogs."

"All those dogs do is run two hundred yards from this guy's trailer to another trailer and back again," said the first trooper. "Back and forth, like a hundred times."

"That other trailer, though, is the one where the woman and her daughter went missing."

"Yeah. That's the guy they're looking for."

"Jesse Grinder, right?"

"That's what the APB said. About six-two on his driver's license. Rough-looking, lopsided jawline, White, maybe two-fifty."

"Big guy," said the second trooper. "How big was that woman?"

"She was tiny," said the first trooper. "Not even five feet. And her daughter was also tiny. Sumbitch is an animal."

"You got that right," said the second trooper. He yawned. "That Land Rover still ain't topped the next hill. I been up and down this road a thousand times, and there's no driveway or anything between here and the top of that hill. Just fence-line and ditch. No place to turn off. Not even a good place to pull over for a piss."

"He's had time to pee by now," said the first trooper.

"Where the dogs at?" asked the other. "I'm thinking I'll go up there and check on that vehicle.

"Suspicious type, aren't you," stated the first trooper. "I'll call."

He leaned in through his car window and fingered the mic. A moment later he stood up.

"No traffic coming on this road, and the dogs aren't trailing anything. I've got it covered here if you need to go."

When the second trooper topped the hill, he saw the Land Rover stuck in the ditch. Skid marks from the pavement into the ditch clearly showed what had happened. He got out and walked over to the vehicle, but it was empty. When he looked inside, however, he saw drying blood all over the bare metal floorboard and on the driver's seat, and then he spotted a set of bloody footprints leading off into the woods on the opposite side of the road. Looking again at the Land Rover he spotted two bullet holes in the body of the car.

"Hey, Unit 2471," he radioed to trooper one. "Come in. Over."

A moment later, trooper one answered. "This is 2471. Whatcha got, 2475?" he radioed back.

"Looks like a ten-fifty," said trooper two, using the code for a car wreck. "Bashed up grille on the front, blood all over the seat and floorboard, but no driver. Footprints going off into the woods. Got some bullet holes here. Over."

"Ten-four," said trooper one. "I'm stuck here. I'll call over to the sheriff's office for backup. Over."

"That's a ten-four," said trooper two. "I'm running the plates on this vehicle now. Looks like a '75 Land Rover. Not many of them in this neck of the woods. Over."

Three minutes later, the dispatcher in Piney Creek radioed back.

"Unit 2475," she said, "those plates are registered to Rip Johnson at 1357 FM 362. Vehicle shows to be insured. Over."

"Ten-four," replied trooper 2475. "We better send somebody up to the congressman's house to check on him. This here is his vehicle, but he's not in it. Looks like he might have gotten hurt and wandered off in the woods."

"Ten-four, Unit 2475. Nearly everybody is already out where you are. I'll call them."

"Unnecessary," replied a voice over the radio. "This is Unit One. I'll head up there myself. Where are you, Unit 2475?"

The trooper gave his location and thanked the sheriff for coming to help.

"Might as well," said Sheriff Adams. "Nothing happening out here. The dogs didn't pick up anything, and the prison guys are packing them up now."

"Unit One, this is unit 2471."

"Yo, 2471."

"Should somebody go out to the congressman's house to check on him? Welfare check or something? We've got blood all over the seat of this vehicle."

"Good idea, 2471. S.O., did you hear that?"

"Only person we got in town is Deputy Rhodes," replied the dispatcher. "Should I send him?"

The radio was silent while dozens of law enforcement officials collectively rolled their eyes. The mouth-breathing deputy had a reputation for screwing up everything he was told to do. Sheriff Adams had a flash vision of Rhodes drawing his pistol on the congressman after waiting at the front door. Maybe he could ask the fire chief to go out there instead.

Or the justice of the peace, or just anybody else.

"This is Unit One. I think we need to keep Deputy Rhodes there in town for emergencies," Sheriff Adams replied. "Maybe the mayor would go out, or the fire chief. It's just a welfare check."

"Ten-four, Unit One," replied the dispatcher. "I'll make some calls. One of the commissioners lives out that way."

CHAPTER
SIXTY-THREE

Grinder had only one idea as he struggled through the darkening forest. Get home. Lock the door. Bandage his leg. When he could, he'd get in his truck and take off. He couldn't go home, because his mother would kill him first and then his father would kill him. Besides, he'd have to explain what happened, and he couldn't do that. But he knew instinctively that he could not stay where he was. Maybe he could drive down to the county line, find one of those old girls down there and spend the night. She might doctor him until he could get around. Then he'd head out for somewhere. Nothing in his trailer that he needed, really. He bought what clothes he wore from Walmart, and he was out of food anyway. He'd take that jar of pennies. It'd give him enough cash for a little gas and a loaf of bread. Then he would just drop a match in the place and be gone, and no one would know where he went.

That was as far as his planning ability went.

Going through the woods on that wounded leg was not easy. He kept bleeding and getting dizzy. He stopped once and went to sleep against the trunk of a tree, waking as the woods were growing dark and not knowing where he was. He could hear traffic out on the highway, and every once in a while, he'd hear some kind of radio noise, like cops talking to one another. Gradually getting more and more conscious, he realized he was probably a quarter or half mile from the pavement, and judging by the tire noise, he could tell which way the highway ran. But what highway was it? He couldn't remember. Should he risk going out to the road to take a look?

Standing was painful. His leg had gotten stiff and some kind of stinging insects had swarmed around his bloody trousers. Maybe fire ants, maybe something else. It was hard to see in the twilight.

He parted low-hanging branches, trying to avoid the trailing briars that seemed to be hanging from every shrub. Generations of pine needles had fallen into the thickets of American bay and yaupon, matting into a canopy of decaying microscopic pollen and ticks. If he could crawl, he could pass through without a lot of trouble, but he couldn't crawl on that leg. He needed to stagger along, from trunk to trunk.

Through a slightly less dense area of trees and shrubs he saw the dull gray of the pavement only a hundred or so yards away and made toward it. But before he cleared out of the dense undergrowth at the edge of the right of way, he saw a police cruiser pass by going slowly and shining its spotlight up and down the road.

He did not know if they were after him, but he had stolen the congressman's Land Rover, after all, and then bogged it down in mud. He remembered gunshots, but in his panic to get away from Abbie Morton and that other goon, he had no idea where the shots had come from. Maybe they were aiming at him. He had just run. And as he thought about what had happened, his instinct was to keep running. Even if they were not after him, it was safe to assume they were. They'd find that Land Rover, and then they'd know it was him.

If only he could get back to his trailer and his truck, then he could get away. That's all that was on his mind. To get away.

When he saw the cruiser, he turned away from the road and headed off into the deep woods. Eventually he figured he would come across a branch or a creek he'd recognize, even in the dark, and then get back to his truck.

By 9 p.m., after five hours on foot, Grinder found a familiar landmark. Then he found another. The faint afterglow of sunset was just enough to see by, and a few minutes later he found the spring seep below his trailer. He knew he was almost back, and he felt bolder.

But he also saw that the lights were on in his trailer and strange shadows were moving around inside. Grinder rarely turned on lights—he didn't need them in his own place, and he had no use for them. He knew where the beans were. He knew where the refrigerator was. He knew where the bathroom was. He didn't have a television worth a crap and he didn't read. He didn't need lights after dark. It actually surprised him that lights could be turned on in there. He preferred it dark, like a cave. Man needed to sleep in the dark. Sunlight was for being awake and work.

Getting closer to the back side of the trailer, he spotted several police cars and a large van, with people coming and going from inside. He paused to study what was happening, feeling exhausted and hot and sweaty. He was terribly thirsty, but he dared not drink from any water downhill from his trailer. Maybe he could go over to the manager's office and sleep there, but then what if the man came back and found him? What then? Still, the manager's office was a good solution. He could go open the door, slip a piece of paperclip into the lock so a key couldn't open from outside, and then lock himself in. He'd sleep on the man's couch, drink from his bathroom sink, clean the wound, rinse the blood off his foot and out of his boot. It was damned uncomfortable to walk around in a blood-soaked boot all day. Probably no food in there, but he could make it if he could get some water. And some sleep.

The girls in middle school were merciless when they found out thirteen-year-old Paula Angel was pregnant by her single mother's forty-two-year-old boyfriend. They teased her and called her names until she flew into a rage in the lunch line. In the fight that followed, she bit the nose of one of the girls completely off. BoMac saw her at the county jail when the boyfriend came to bond her out. He stank of gin. Her defiant look matched only one other in his experience: that of a juvenile bald eagle with a broken wing found by the local state game warden.

Grinder awoke the next morning sprawled on the black plastic sofa in the manager's office. It was not quite 6 a.m., according to the red numbers on the manager's desk clock, and the sky was still dark, but he'd slept soundly. He slowly eased himself up, his leg throbbing, and looked out the window. At the end of the lane, he could see the turn going downhill to his trailer, and beyond that a hundred yards was his truck. Maybe the policemen had gone by now.

He rummaged in the manager's desk, looking for anything that might be useful. He found a stale candy bar and a bottle of aspirin, and he washed both down with water cupped in his hand at the sink. Then he let himself out of the door, turning the thumb latch so it would lock behind him. Once he closed the door, he wouldn't be able to get back in either, so he needed to be sure it was the right thing to do. Hell, maybe he'd just leave it standing a little open. That way if he needed to come back in a hurry, he could.

As it turned out, the door to his trailer was open and his mattress was pulled outside in the morning dew, but his truck was in one piece and no one was around. He went inside briefly to see if anything was left that he might need. His old boots were gone, the jar of pennies was gone, but he found a dried bit of bread in the refrigerator and half the cantaloupe he'd started the previous morning. He took these, fished his keys out of his pocket, and cranked the truck, setting off for the county line. The bars were closed at this time of day, but he thought he could find Sue's house again. Maybe she'd put him up for a bit, and then he'd head for Houston, get lost down there. Lots of floors to sweep in Houston.

CHAPTER
SIXTY-FOUR

BoMac was up most of Monday night developing film and putting together the front page. He would finalize the front page on Tuesday afternoon, but he had most of the ads already in place. He might pick up a few more ads, so he stayed as flexible as he could with the layout. Ellen stayed at the paper until around midnight, helping edit and write copy when she wasn't chatting with him in the darkroom. Since most of the darkroom process was done in complete darkness, Ellen stood close to him, touching him, her unseen face close to his and her hands on his body. Then, with the film loaded into its light-tight canisters, BoMac would turn on the dim red light of the darkroom and see her blushing, and his heart just burst with love for her. And of course, her heart for him. Such tenderness contrasted with the carnage emerging in the dim red darkroom light: dead bodies, wrecked cars with fluids spilling across dry pavement—some of it blood—people's homes shrouded in smoke, and finally, for this week, the chilling photo of a jar of pennies sitting on top of Jesse Grinder's refrigerator.

Still, for a few minutes anyway, they had each other and the random lethality of the quiet Texas forests was outside and away.

Ellen always went home before midnight, because she needed to be at school before 7:30 in the morning, but BoMac would stay at the paper working until much later. Then, three hours of sleep in his falling-down garage apartment, and he was up again. He was always too tired on Tuesday mornings to exercise, but he went to meet Henniker at the County Court Cafe for breakfast as he did every morning, and to keep one ear open for gossip circulating with the coffee pot and cigarette smoke among the morning regulars. He found Henniker huddled with Isaac, as always, the two studying a small chessboard on which they had laid out a chess problem.

305

Every person in the cafe asked him about the news. Many of them had seen the skeletons the day before, but late last night they learned that Congressman Rip Johnson had been murdered. They wondered if the two were connected. They wanted the news without waiting until Wednesday morning when the paper came out. And they all had theories. Most had daughters and wives they worried about, so a loose murderer of women and children was of utmost concern to them. A man who murdered a congressman might not be so dangerous, after all. Still, they were worried. They might not be able to get rid of all the timber rattlers or copperheads in the woods the way they had gotten rid of the black bears by 1910, but they could sure hunt down a murderer living among them. The anger and anxiety in the cafe were intense, as thick as the nervous cigarette smoke, tainting everything.

BoMac had not heard about the congressman, so he excused himself to place a call to the *Piney Creek Crier* offices. He figured Ed Nichols or someone else would be in, and since they were collaborating on the Shorty Fike story, he thought maybe the *Crier* would be willing to help him out with the Rip Johnson story. Nichols answered the phone brusquely.

"What do you want?" he asked, not knowing who was calling.

"Ed, it's BoMac. Do you have anything on the congressman?"

"Blown damned near in two by a shotgun," said Nichols. "Three other males—two Blacks from Houston and that used car dealer Bob McKinney—also dead. One of the Black men was killed by what they're calling blunt force trauma to the head, the other two by shotgun. Both the Blacks were armed and wanted for drugs and racketeering. The congressman's Land Rover was stolen but found out on the highway near where Jesse Grinder lived. Had bullet holes in one side and blood all over the driver's seat and floor. Right now, they think it might be Grinder's blood, but what the hell he was doing out at the congressman's is a big mystery. He worked for McKinney sweeping floors and stuff. McKinney was in handcuffs and had a piano wire around his neck."

"Wow. What a story! Thanks, man. I'll drive over photos from Grinder's trailer search about noon, maybe we can swap off."

"They wouldn't let me into the congressman's house with the bodies still inside," said Nichols. "The front gate was smashed outward, like somebody drove through it, and paint scrapes on the metal match the paint of the Land Rover. I did get some good pictures of the Land Rover in a ditch just before they pulled it out, and three or four long shots of the congressman's house. He also represented Sweetgum County, didn't he?"

"Yeah, we're in his district," said BoMac. "Guess this will lead to an election in November."

"I heard that a Black fellow from over here is going to run for the office," said Nichols. "Chillers Banks. Ever heard of him?"

"No. Might be a good story. I'm not sure the powers behind Johnson would like that, but you never know. It all comes down to the ballot box."

"If the ballots can get into the box, and stay there," said Nichols. "See you at noon. Don't be late. We're on deadline over here. Our printer wants the paper no later than 8 p.m."

"Wow, that's close. I'll be there."

BoMac was returning from his call to the *Crier* and standing with his hand on the cafe door when Jesse Grinder slowed for the red light in front of the courthouse.

"Holy shit," he said and stuck his head into the cafe. "That's Grinder! Call the sheriff's office! He's in his pickup right here!" Darryl Stewart was sitting at the counter pretending he liked weak coffee but bounded for the door at BoMac's words. "Where is he?" shouted Stewart. "Where is that motherfucker?"

BoMac, already several yards up the street toward the *Standard* office, pointed at Grinder's dirty blue pickup. "Right there," he shouted. "That's him!"

With Henniker following, BoMac got to his pickup just as the light turned green and Grinder began to pull away. But Darryl Stewart was already behind him, right on his tail. He'd be damned if he'd let that murderer get away. The last time he felt this pumped was while chasing a Viet Cong sniper along the river at Khe Sanh. He was going to get Grinder.

"He's heading down US 385," shouted BoMac to the growing crowd of locals on the sidewalk as they passed the cafe. "Get the highway patrol! We'll try to stay up with him."

Grinder was not aware that he was being followed. In fact, with the pain in his leg and the weakness from more than thirty-six hours with hardly any food, he was barely aware of anything. He drove erratically, but not dangerously, slowing and then speeding up, easing off the gas pedal as the throbbing in his leg grew, then pushing down again when it lessened. By the time he got to the edge of town, passing the feed store, he was in the 55-mph zone, but going 30. It would be easy for the highway patrol to catch up to him, if they were anywhere nearby.

BoMac looked in his rearview mirror to see a string of vehicles pulling up behind him.

"Some of these people will be driving to work in the city," he said. "They're not going to put up with this thirty-mile-an-hour bullshit. I hope we don't cause a wreck. I'd usually pull off on the shoulder to let them go by, but then they'd be behind Grinder."

"Best to stay behind him and Darryl," said Henniker. "You got a weapon or anything in this truck?"

"Just my camera," said BoMac.

"How stout is it?" asked Henniker.

"Got a good strap on it, weighs about three pounds. I think it's pretty tough."

"Anything else? Tire tool, loose cannon, pocketknife, any of that?" Henniker grinned at him.

"Just me. I'm enough of a loose cannon without any help."

"If the cops don't find us, we might need to take him down until they arrive," said Henniker. "That could be a problem."

"That could be a problem," agreed BoMac.

"If he's done all they think he's done, he's not going to give up easily," said Henniker. "How much gas do you have?"

"I've got a full tank. Filled up last night after getting back from his trailer. I'm good for somewhere between three hundred fifty and four hundred miles."

"He's not going that far," said Henniker. "Look at the smoke coming out of that truck."

"Yeah. He's burning plenty of oil."

They were on a straight stretch of highway, and three cars following them pulled out to pass. The third car leaned on his horn, flashing his lights as he went by, going possibly 100 mph. Other cars closed up the gap. Four cars and pickups roared by on the next long straightaway, but still more cars were behind them by then.

It didn't matter, though, as Grinder's truck started slowing down and wandered over on the shoulder, no brake lights. "Damn, Charles," yelled BoMac, "he's coming to a stop."

"Yeah, it's like his engine just quit. Maybe it did," Henniker replied. When Grinder's truck slowed enough, he seemed to ease it down the right of way toward a dark stand of pines, part of a huge pine plantation of fifty- or sixty-year-old timber. The trees loomed toward the sky, completely dark underneath.

"What do you think he's doing?" asked BoMac.

"Maybe his truck died and he's going to make a run for it," said Henniker.

"Shit, he's not even steering," said BoMac. "Maybe he died."

The truck was going less than five miles per hour when it entered the dry ditch and came to a complete stop as it nosed up against a large pine well off the highway. Darryl Stewart pulled his truck up, angled more or less at the driver's side, preventing Grinder from backing up. BoMac put on his emergency flashers and bright lights and pulled up on the rear passenger side. He and Henniker piled out, acknowledging Stewart.

"Think he's armed?" called BoMac, approaching the truck.

"You gotta assume he is," said Henniker, reaching the rear fender of Grinder's pickup. "You and Darryl ease up to the driver's window, tell me what you see. I'll take the passenger side." He was carrying the strap off of BoMac's camera.

BoMac could see Grinder in the side mirror. He seemed to be frozen, his mouth open, his eyes staring straight ahead, unblinking.

"He looks like he's in a trance," said BoMac quietly to Stewart.

"Right. Ease up to the door. We need him on the ground. I might kill him." Stewart grinned, white spittle at the corners of his mouth.

In the distance, they could hear sirens heading their way, but a long line of traffic was driving slowly past, gawking at the scene, wondering if there had been a wreck and hoping for carnage.

BoMac dropped low to the ground, out of sight of the mirror, and eased forward, finally reaching a hand to the driver's side door.

Suddenly Grinder came back from wherever he had gone, and his hand reached out of the window as fast as a rattlesnake, grabbing BoMac. The truck sprang to life, and Grinder threw the truck in reverse, backing away from the tree and ramming Stewart's truck. Stewart reached through the window and grabbed Grinder's head with both hands, but BoMac couldn't get away and was terrified that the wheels would run over his legs, crippling him.

Henniker was instantly through the passenger door and hit Grinder three times, hard, in the face, popping his jaw sideways. He slammed the shift lever into park and hit Grinder again. Stewart now had both his arms around Grinder's head and was dragging him out through the window while Henniker pounded his torso on the other side. BoMac broke free and rolled away, catching his breath. Henniker hit Grinder once more, and then Stewart had the big man lying backwards over the window frame of the truck, while he twisted and pulled his head sideways, trying to tear his head off.

Grinder slumped through the open window and slowly, like an avalanche gathering motion, toppled from the cab onto the ground. Stewart knelt on his neck, daring him to move, while Henniker crawled through the cab and fell on both of them. Within seconds, Grinder was tied up with BoMac's camera strap.

"Everybody okay?" asked Henniker, breathing hard.

"Terrified," said BoMac, "but not hurt. Not too bad. Got my legs out of the way."

"Good. This man is out. I hope it's our guy," said Stewart. "I'd hate to waste this much effort on a mistake."

"Me too," said BoMac, "but until you rearranged his face, it looked like Jesse Grinder. And this is the truck that was parked at his trailer yesterday."

Charles Henniker straightened up, stepped away.

"Now look, BoMac, Darryl," he said, the first state trooper only half a mile away, "I'm not involved here. Understand? I was getting a ride to school with BoMac from the cafe when he took after this guy, and I stayed in the truck the whole time. Understand? It's important."

"But you hammered him. I could never have done that."

"What gives?" asked Stewart.

"I don't care. You two take all the credit. I'm going back to sit in the cab of your truck. You get your camera and start taking pictures, but look, you gotta leave me out of this. For the sake of our friendship and for my own safety, you must leave me out."

"I don't understand," began BoMac, but then the state trooper was cutting through traffic and heading their way.

"I'm in the truck," said Henniker. "I've been there the whole time. You gotta protect me on this."

"Okay, friend. Okay. I got you. But hey," he said as Henniker turned away, "just the same, thank you."

CHAPTER

SIXTY-FIVE

At 5:30 p.m. on a freezing Thursday before Christmas eleven years later, Jesse Grinder walked into the execution chamber at the famous Walls Unit of the Texas state prison in Huntsville. His mother, his father, and his brother were in the audience, weeping. His brother carried a "Bon Voyage" wreath from a local florist. Shorty Fike was also in there, shaking his fist at Grinder and flipping him the bird with both hands, which was expressly forbidden by rules the warden had carefully explained to him. At least he kept his mouth shut, and that cost him a great deal of effort. If he had started shouting curses at Grinder, the warden warned, he would be evicted from the witness room. "This is a solemn occasion," Shorty was told, "and you need to act respectful."

Rip Johnson's wife, Angie, who had remarried, declined the warden's invitation to attend. Abbie Morton, Ben Pickett Jr., and Bob McKinney likewise did not have relatives or acquaintances who cared to attend. Trey Green's widow could not be located, and Belle Guinness's now twice-more-divorced husband also declined. For a man convicted of eight murders—some of which he committed—Jesse Grinder's send-off was sparsely attended.

A reporter from the *Huntsville Item* newspaper was also there, an official witness to more executions than anyone else ever, stretching back into the early fifties and the days of the electric chair. He had been assigned high school sports during the ten-year period when Texas did not execute criminals because of a Supreme Court decision, but now executions had resumed and no one else wanted to attend. He liked the antiseptic nature of death by lethal injection. At least he didn't need to smell the singeing flesh or the often botched and cruel application of high doses of electricity to the soft flesh of a human body. Grinder would be his one-hundredth execution. He decided he'd retire the next day after he filed his story on the execution, a decision he had kept from his editor just because.

Grinder walked into the death chamber led by two guards and followed by a Jehovah's Witness elder and two more guards. The elder had spent the previous night with Grinder, at his request, praying in his cell. Agitated in the days leading up to the execution, Jesse had calmed significantly from the drugs slipped into his last meal by the prison chef, a kindness that always eluded the warden and definitely eluded the governor of the state. The guards instructed him where to lie on the gurney, then strapped his arms and legs to the table. The warden asked him if he had any last words.

"Yes, sir," he said, raising his head to look at his mother. "I just want you all to know that I love you and I'll see you again on the other side."

Then he lay back.

The anticlimax of his death was a huge disappointment to Shorty Fike, who had hoped he would writhe and scream in agony, but the execution was flawless. Grinder had good veins, it was easy for the prison phlebotomist to insert the needles, one in each arm, and all went smoothly. Grinder did not even know when the deadly cocktail began flowing, because the warden and the state executioner were standing in a separate room out of sight waiting for the final moment. When the clock struck the fatal hour of 6 p.m., the warden nodded to the executioner, who reached forward and opened the flow of drugs from the three graduated cylinders mounted to the wall. The first, sodium thiopental, anesthetized Grinder's arms and put his brain into a coma. The next two stopped his heart. Within eight minutes, he was pronounced dead by the state's medical supervisor, and his body was wheeled out of the execution chamber to a cheap pine box and a grave marked only by his inmate number, not his name. The warden went home to a dinner of chicken-fried steak and mashed potatoes with cream gravy.

Jesse Grinder's mother never spoke again. She watched her oldest son die, and then stood up and walked out of the witness box, followed by her husband and her other son. She said nothing that night, not on the long drive back home, not the next day, nor ever again. She stopped eating, then she stopped moving, and then in a few months she was dead. The other Grinders carried on, because that was what Grinders did. The father had a heart attack several years later but recovered. The brother had a heart attack while returning from work one night and died on the side of the road.

Shorty Fike eventually moved to Louisiana to be closer to his work offshore on drilling rigs, and found a divorced mother working in a coffee shop, whom he married about three years later. But he never forgot compact, gutsy Annabeth. Sometimes at night he still woke screaming her name, flailing about, seeing her corpse falling from the baling wire in the barn, seeing some nasty coyote dragging his daughter's skull out into the pasture to gnaw. Shorty died at forty-one, before another decade passed, trying to work himself hard enough to escape the memories and the visions.

Jane Elkins developed Alzheimer's disease and began a steady decline. When Betty Lou and Henry realized what was happening to her, they both "retired" and sued her for unpaid social security and other taxes. Mrs. Elkins was moved to a private room in the hospital, where she was strapped into a hospital bed and kept alive into her one-hundredth year by intravenous infusions. Both Betty Lou and Henry were awarded over $500,000 to settle their lawsuit, but others of her employees were not so fortunate.

BoMac was asked by the bank to continue running the *Whitmire Standard*, but he struck a hard deal with them. He demanded complete autonomy and zero debt. They compromised on complete autonomy and some of the debt, but he still had a substantial sum to repay for his sole ownership of the property. Nevertheless, it was less than his college loans would have been to the University of Virginia, and besides, he was a kind of local hero now, having captured Grinder.

C. L. "Cock-lover" Turner, the former district attorney, still hated him, and BoMac was fine with that. Turner had been an elected official too proud to hug votes the way Commissioner George Brown did and was voted out of office as soon as another lawyer could be recruited to the county. Incompetence was common among elected officials; priding yourself on being better than everybody else was rare among those who stayed in office. Meanwhile, BoMac kept urging graduating high school students to study law and come back to take the job. Regardless of who took the position, sooner or later the power of the job would corrupt them. Some students thought about it; most didn't, because they knew their futures were at the handle end of saws in the woods. People kept urging BoMac to run for office, or even for US Congress, but he demurred. All he wanted to do was keep his finger on the pulse of the community and record its daily life, in all its boring sameness and in all its occasional sniffs of glory. And he had married Ellen Etheridge, who might get pregnant someday. He had a wife and a mortgage, in the good old American tradition. He'd moved from the Virginia piedmont to the dark forests of East Texas, and he had put down roots like so many others from the East Coast.

Charles and Lizzie Henniker moved to San Augustine to be closer to family. Their son, King, became a world-famous tennis player in his late teens, a few years after Grinder's execution.

Willis Macklin was eighty-two and worth millions when he married eighteen-year-old Lydia Adler. Willis lived in the house in Whitmire where he'd been born. It had one lightbulb and an outhouse. But Lydia's parents kept a mobile home rent-free on Willis's property in return for cleaning for him. Willis, never previously married, considered marriage a simple contractual agreement. He sent Lydia to beauty school, where she fell in love with an older woman and divorced him. He paid alimony only if she spent one night a month with him. After four years, she sued and won half of his millions.

It was Friday, Christmas Eve before the beginning of a new millennium. The churchgoers had all gone home with their candles, humming carols and linking arms. Their warm houses glowed with joy and love, spilling out across their brown lawns. A cold front had moved through Sweetgum County a few days prior, dropping the temperature from a balmy seventy-five degrees to a frigid twenty-seven, and leaving a sheathing of ice on trees and steeples.

BoMac was strolling home after checking one last time in the office of the *Standard*, and it was late. It was almost late enough for the annual toy parade of pickups to depart for hunting camps to collect the Christmas goodies. There might also be a bit of wassail to share with hunting buddies over a low campfire, listening to the dark, primitive forest. BoMac hunched his shoulders against the cold, pulling his knitted fleece tighter, enjoying the nip of cold on the tip of his nose and the unusual fog of his breath. A puff of wind shook down a glitter of ice from the old trees on the courthouse lawn, and beyond them the quiet crucifix atop the steeple of First Fundamentalist Church gleamed like a beacon.

"Nothing changes," muttered BoMac, "and maybe that's good."

The echo of his feet in the quiet street faded away as he descended Hill Street toward Ellen.

In the basement of the courthouse, old Davey Jones settled once more into his wooden chair across from the electric furnace and leaned back against the wall. He had held the job of furnace tender since 1940, when the furnace was coal. He had continued to report for work every night for sixty years, the last thirty-five of them to watch an electric furnace that needed no tending. In those six decades he had worn out dozens of wooden chairs he'd taken from various offices in the courthouse at night when no one was watching. He took a number of chairs from the jury box in the district courtroom, until a judge realized they were disappearing and had them screwed to the floor. When a chair wore out, usually because the back legs had been ground down to nubs, he discarded it in dark places underneath the courthouse floor. He was four years into sitting in a chair he'd taken out of the county treasurer's office. No one in the treasurer's office had noticed it missing.

It was warm in the basement room, and Davey closed his eyes with his head against the concrete wall. Recently he'd been having visions of people dressed in radiant white gowns, walking slowly on dirt roads and singing. He was certain that it was heaven, both White people and Black people singing together. He knew this was the heaven the preacher told them about, the place where love began and back to which love led. Davey longed for that with all his heart, and with his eyes closed to hold the vision, he hummed quietly to himself some old gospel spiritual. Until he didn't hum anymore. And then he didn't breathe anymore, either.

From the deep shadows under the courthouse, the unwinking head of Old Coil, ancient rattlesnake, quietly eased out of a hole above Davey Jones's head and slithered his fourteen-foot-long body down the wall and across Jones's lap, heading for the warmth of the furnace. His rattles, more than a hundred of them, made a slight scratching sound on the clean-swept concrete floor as he eased behind the warm machine, only the tip of his tail remaining visible. He settled down to sleep the rest of the century away, biding his time for rats and the mating imperative of spring.

THE END

Made in United States
North Haven, CT
16 January 2024

47563311R00190